# WILD CARD

# WILD CARD

Written by

MARTY DELMON

TATE PUBLISHING & *Enterprises*

*Wild Card*
Copyright © 2008 by Marty Delmon. All rights reserved.

This title is also available as a Tate Out Loud product. Visit www.tatepublishing.com for more information.

No part of this publication may be reproduced, stored in a retrieval system or transmitted in any way by any means, electronic, mechanical, photocopy, recording or otherwise without the prior permission of the author except as provided by USA copyright law.

The opinions expressed by the author are not necessarily those of Tate Publishing, LLC.

Published by Tate Publishing & Enterprises, LLC
127 E. Trade Center Terrace | Mustang, Oklahoma 73064 USA
1.888.361.9473 | www.tatepublishing.com

Tate Publishing is committed to excellence in the publishing industry. The company reflects the philosophy established by the founders, based on Psalm 68:11,
*"The Lord gave the word and great was the company of those who published it."*

Book design copyright © 2008 by Tate Publishing, LLC. All rights reserved.
*Cover design by Isaiah R. McKee*
*Interior design by Summer Floyd Harvey*

Published in the United States of America

ISBN: 978-1-60604-486-5
1. Fiction: Religious: Romance/Contemporary
08.07.21

# TABLE OF CONTENTS

**THE DINNER PARTY**
7

**THE PICNIC**
17

**THE DATING GAME**
27

**KIRK'S PLOT**
35

**GETTING TO KNOW YOU**
47

**GOING TO SEA**
61

**LITTLE BROWN CHURCH IN THE HAIGHT ASHBURY**
79

**MOVING ON**
91

**THE CENTER OF DIVINE PEACE**
103

**THE PLAN UNFOLDS**
111

**THE TRANSFORMATION**
127

**VANGUARD INTERPRETIVE VISUAL ARTS**
147

**THE MOVIE**
169

**FEVERED FILM MAKING**
185

**THE MOUNTAINS**
201

**THE MOUNTAIN MAN**
211

**THE EVIDENCE**
225

**RON RUNS HOME**
241

**THE GLORY TRAIN**
273

**LAYING THE PLAN ON THE TABLE**
293

**THE CHRISTIAN SCREENWRITER**
305

Chapter One
# THE DINNER PARTY

Panting after racing up three flights of stairs two at a time to his Russian Hill apartment, Kirk doubled over attempting to gain his breath before crashing through the door. Holding his ribs with one hand, calming them from compacting and crushing his internal organs, he thrust his fistful of flowers at his wife. Standing by the archaic sink in the kitchen alcove, shaking water from large lettuce leaves, Darce smiled and took the bouquet.

"To be gasping like that you must have parked at the bottom of the hill and run up the hill and the stairs. Breathe, sweetheart, breathe." She turned her attention to the flowers, "Perfect. Good choice, Kirky." Finding the right vase she filled it with water and centered the arrangement on the circular table positioned just inside the front door. The gladiolas spiked toward the ceiling, erupting into violent color bursting from the end of the stalks.

"You sure you got everything!" Kirk sucked in air.

"Everything. I've never worked so hard on a dinner in my life." Darce returned to the turgid lettuce leaves in the sink, absorbing herself in the removal of water spots. "Remember, it's gotta be timed, Kirky. If everything doesn't happen exactly on time, I'm cooked."

Nervously inspecting the room, dashing to the bookshelves to pull an indented book forward, Kirk said, "And if we offend this guy in any way, I'm cooked. Clients can be so touchy. One little spark and, poof, they're gone."

"That's why I didn't think it to be wisdom on your part to invite him to dinner. It's not like I'm a gourmet cook or anything." She wiped the water from the sink and peeked into the stove, very delicately opening the door a tiny crack, then closing it like a whisper.

Kirk spun around impersonating Fred Astaire. "This is the one, baby, I can feel it in my bones; we've got a fortune maker in our grip. He's gonna take us to the top. I've always known there would be one shining investor, one bighearted deep pocket, one openhanded high roller. He's the one! Hang onto this guy, Darce! Hang on tight to this guy!" He snapped his fingers and did a little tap dance, though not exactly a step, shuffle, ball, change.

"Remember, Kirk, tonight–timing–get that in your brain - timing!"

"Yeah, yeah, yeah sure, let's take a look here." He circled the table set with Cost Plus finery. "He's due any minute. The place looks great, everything's immaculate, the table's set, knives, forks, spoons, gla ... Why do you have four place settings? Do you think he's bringing a date?"

Darce looked up in alarm, "I never thought of that! Is he?"

"He didn't say anything to me. But you're set up for four people!"

She eyed him warily, "Are you sure he didn't mention a date?"

"Positive!" Kirk sputtered. "Who's the fourth person?"

Darce turned back to wiping down the counter, "I invited Summer."

"What?" his face contorted.

She said it slowly, "I invited Summer."

"What the H E double hockey sticks for?" he exploded.

She turned to him matter of factly, "You invited a friend; I invited a friend."

"She's not a friend; she's a disaster!"

Someone knocked. He glared at her as she raised her eyebrows and opened the door. "Summer. Right on time. I'm so glad you could come."

A lithe blond presenting an ever wistful expression, smiled tenderly and flowed into the apartment on ballerina feet. "Me, too. Thanks for inviting me." The tiny amber flowers floating on her dark brown dress matched the amber darts punctuating her equally dark brown eyes.

She handed Darce the exact same bouquet Kirk had brought. "Oh, thanks. How thoughtful of you!" Darce glared at Kirk behind Summer's back with a 'don't you dare say anything' look, then whisked the flowers off the table and arranged both bunches in a larger vase which she again placed as the centerpiece.

Kirk sighed deeply and tried to salvage the situation. "Look, Summer, the guy I invited tonight, I mean, oh man, he is, without a doubt, the most important client I have. Don't mess it up for me."

"Kirk, when have I ever messed anything up for you? If you're honest, you'll admit that I've been the second best thing that has happened to you since kindergarten. Of course Darce stands in the winner's circle for being the best thing that ever happened to either one of us."

Darce came out of the alcove to acknowledge this compliment with a smile when someone else knocked. Suddenly turning wooden, Darce and Kirk stared at each other in terror; Summer took action and headed for the door, but Kirk grabbed her shoulder as she strode by and pulled her back. "I'll answer it, thank you!"

Kirk swung the door wide and both Darce and Summer stood riveted at the sight of the man waiting on the threshold. One would not have called him handsome, attractive yes, but he possessed an alluring power that radiated from him. He emanated self-confidence. Measuring an inch shorter than Kirk, who looked meager in comparison, Ron seemed the bigger man. Perhaps Kirk's blanched blond hair, darting blue eyes and pallid skin, tightened on the lanky frame paled against the dark brown hair, penetrating brown eyes and the olive skin on Ron's fuller body. Whatever composed the ingredients, both women felt they must avert their eyes before they betrayed too much admiration.

"Hey, buddy boy, come on in here." Kirk grabbed Ron's arm and pulled him inside.

Ron extended his arm to present a bunch of flowers to Summer, an exact duplicate of the bouquet she had brought, "For the lady of the house," he smiled.

"That would not be her," Kirk said through a stiff smile. "Meet my lovely wife." He indicated Darce and Ron's head swiveled to take in the petite brown-haired woman in the archway of the kitchen alcove. He presented the flowers to her. She caught herself before a look of dismay could settle on her face. What would she do with these?

"Well, I'm glad to finally meet the stabilizing half of this guy! You've got a go getter for a husband. You must have to tie him down with a string at night like a hot air balloon." She chuckled in agreement, thanked him for the flowers and when he turned to meet Summer, Darce took the vase as if to arrange them, but actually stuck his bunch into a Mason jar she filled with water and shoved into the broom closet.

As she came to stand by Kirk and nervously take his hand, Ron went to the window to look down at the backyard, a four story drop, the first floor opening below street level. He turned to his hosts, "Can we stand on your balcony without threat of catapulting to our deaths?'"

"Sure." Kirk said a little too loudly.

"There's one of our Destroyers on the bay. It's moving out to display a little brawn. I think we can see it from here."

Ron escorted them out the French doors to gingerly step onto the three foot balcony extending the length of the aged apartment. He, however, hung back to look Summer up and down. A huge artillery ship slipped through the water, its lights dimmed.

Standing behind the three Ron said, "There's a Russian sub sitting just out in international waters. It wants to make its presence known because the Official Representative of China meets our Secretary of State here this weekend."

"Really?" Summer's eyes widened. "What're they doing here?"

"The Russians encroached on a section of China's border. The Chinese want our help, but their Chairman refuses to visit Washington D.C. and fly across our country. And since our President won't lower himself to come all the way here to meet with a lesser official, Treasure Island got the job of putting on an inspiring show for the Representative. The President sent the white house china for the dinner tonight. I wonder how much of that will get returned.

"Why don't they ever tell us what's going on in our city?" Summer pouted.

"I knew that." Kirk boasted. "I think I read it in the paper."

"And if you didn't," Ron grinned, knowing he had effectively kept it from the media, "I just let you in on a little Navy secret."

"You're in the Navy?" Summer breathed in admiration.

"Lieutenant, jg."

"Jg?"

"Junior Grade."

"Oh, I thought you were a professional investor. I thought Kirk handled your stocks," she looked at Kirk hesitatingly, "being your stockbroker and all, and that all you ever did was buy and sell."

Ron gave her a conspiratorial look. "Have you ever heard of a cover? That's the Navy for me. I am a professional investor. It's my passion. I call Kirk to talk stock market about six times a day."

Kirk clapped Ron on the back.

When the Destroyer disappeared they drifted back into the apartment, Summer settling on the couch while the two men stood. Darce appeared with a tray of Kir. They each took a glass; she put the tray down and perched on the couch with Summer. Kirk took Ron's arm and pulled him toward the bookcase. "Listen, buddy boy, I surfed the net today looking for Webster's Design, like you wanted, and when I patch all the pieces together it sure seems to me like they're trying to buy ... "

"Don't you ever take a break?" Ron asked affably, pulling away and heading toward Summer. "We're not going to lose anything if we don't talk stock tonight."

Chagrinned, Kirk ambled over to Darce. He hovered on the arm of the couch, feigning interest, nodding as if listening. Then suddenly he popped up and rushed around the coffee table to bend down on one knee beside Ron who, settled comfortably beside her, had engaged Summer in conversation.

Kirk broke in, "But get this, while I rummaged around Webster's Design, I stumbled onto a group called Theatre Lights that has come out with a penny stock."

Ron put up his hand. "Kirk. Stop. You're going to make me a millionaire. And I'm going to make you one, too. But not tonight. Tonight we relax. I can't stay out late; I've got a 7 a.m. inspection for the visiting brass. Let me get to know your friend here." He turned to smile at Summer.

But Summer looked at Kirk. Steel left his eyes ramming straight into hers. Darce excused herself to the kitchen and Summer, breaking the eyebeam that bound her to Kirk, jumped to follow, "I'll help."

Darce glanced at Kirk, rolled her eyes at his revolt against Summer and said, "Okay."

Ron sat up, put his forearms on his knees and gave Kirk his full attention to digest the information about Theatre Lights. But when Summer brought the chilled salad plates out, lined with crisp lettuce leaves, a half avocado filled with crab salad in the middle, surrounded with dollops of red herring eggs, Ron quickly stood to his feet. Kirk followed suit, thinking something to be wrong.

Summer swiftly returned to the kitchen and Ron, to cover his eagerness, said, "Let's have some music. What do you have, Kirk?"

They went to the bookcase to select a CD. As if in a sprint, the two women returned from the alcove and stood by the table as the soft music began to play. "Dinner is served." Darce smiled frantically.

The two men strode to the table, Ron to pull out the chair for Summer, and Kirk, remembering the warning issued about timing, rushed as if to a fire. He pulled out Darce's chair and sat beside her.

Ron waved his hand over the table resembling a manner of blessing. "Such a beautiful setting. Look at what you did with my flowers! What's your background, Darce? I bet you're Italian. Italians have a way with hospitality."

Darce nearly choked and put her napkin to her mouth. But before she could reply, Ron shoved his chair back, stood, leaned over Summer, took her hand and said, "My favorite song," referring to 'It Had To Be You' filling the room. "You wouldn't mind dancing with me, would you?" He pulled her to her feet.

With arched eyebrows that asked Darce what to do, before she could detect an answer Summer found herself in his arms, swirling in front of the French windows. Ron, a good dancer, and Summer, floating on her feet, danced as if she and Ron rehearsed for hours. Darce started eating her salad with a vengeance.

"What do you think you're doing?" Kirk hissed.

"We have four minutes to finish this salad and clear these dishes." Darce hissed back.

"You've got to wait for them!" he whispered in return.

"No! My Boeuf Flambé will be ruined!"

"It will all work out! Calm down!"

"That song takes five minutes. I'm going to clear the plates and bring in the main dish."

Kirk grabbed her arm, but realized that Ron and Summer were in a dip and had turned their faces to see why their hosts were whispering. He stroked Darce's arm and they both offered cheesy smiles. The dancers returned to their soliloquy.

"Okay!" Darce acquiesced. "I'll put the salad dishes to the side, but if I don't serve that Boeuf thing, my corn soufflé will fall!"

"Alright. That should work. Just don't make him feel uncomfortable!"

"I'm doing my best!" she sputtered. Darce stood, moved the salad plates to the side and took away the floral centerpiece creating space for the Boeuf Flambé. The dancers progressed into the second song, oblivious to the consternation of their hosts. Darce brought a white fluted porcelain casserole to the table, obviously making its virgin voyage, and set it in the middle. She poured a cup of brandy into a tiny chafing dish designed to heat the liqueur for flaming purposes.

"Main course coming up," she called gaily, totally belying her fluttering heart. "I'm setting fire to the brandy right now. This is the floor show. Don't miss it." The dancers paused as the flames leapt toward the ceiling.

"Whoa!" Ron exhorted. "Did you plan the floor show for this level or the upstairs crowd?"

Kirk anxiously half stood, but the flames abated after the first burst. Ron and Summer applauded and he escorted her to her chair. Compelled by a desire to win Summer's approval and perhaps to conquer, he did not sit down. Ron took Darce's arm and pulled her to the postage stamp dance floor. "My turn to dance with the lady of the house."

In wild despair Darce gaped at Kirk for rescue, but he gave her a look that said, "Dance with him!"

Catching the look, Summer whispered, "What's wrong with you two? I've never seen you act like this."

"And what's wrong with you? You know Darce's worried about her dinner and you know I'm worried about keeping my client and you act like you're going to do us both in. Some friend. You wanted to know when you ever did anything against me? Well, how about tonight!"

Summer hissed between her teeth, "Kirk, he's having a good time! Look at him." They both turned to peek discreetly and he and Darce were indeed laughing and dancing, she perhaps a bit too brightly.

At that moment, Darce clapped her head as if remembering her corn soufflé and fled to the kitchen. Ron sat down and Darce entered the dining room carrying at arm's length between mittened hands a white porcelain soufflé dish to match the new fluted casserole. Crumpled on the floor of the dish lay a flat pancake with kernels of corn poking up.

As they gawked at the ruined soufflé, Ron spread his fingers on his chest. "That's my fault, that's very clear." He couldn't seem to tear his eyes away from the debacle of denuded corn and stringy egg. "You made this perfectly timed dinner and I ruined your timing with dancing, didn't I?"

Darce nodded her head yes as she placed the soufflé dish on the table. She looked as if to cry.

"You know what?" Ron asked solicitously. "I've had flattened soufflés before and they taste just as good as puffy ones. You can call this one Ron's Ruination and you watch and see. Every last bite of it will be gone before dinner is over."

Kirk helped himself to the souffle, sniffing a forkful, squinting his eyes and delicately taking it into his mouth. He rolled his head back like a corn connoisseur. "There's no ruination in this dish. I dub it Darce's Delight!" Then he kissed his wife and she laughed.

For the rest of the evening they relaxed, bubbled with good will, and ate. They danced and Ron's prediction turned out to be accurate. Not a kernel of corn or scrap of egg remained of the soufflé. 10:30 crept up on them like a stealthy sentinel, reminding Ron to prepare for his early morning inspection. At the door he asked, "Let me make up for Ron's Ruination tonight. I'll be free by noon tomorrow, how about a picnic on Angel Island? You three up for that?" They agreed, Ron said he would bring the lunch and they made plans to meet.

Chapter Two
# THE PICNIC

Sunday morning presented itself in a gray dress of clouds with contrary winds whipping the water in lighthearted swirls of lace. Summer, coming from the Haight Ashbury, drove to the front of the Dalton's apartment. She double parked and honked the horn, Darce looked out the bathroom window, which she had left open to hear the honk, as prearranged, then threw on her parka and called to Kirk, "She's here."

She drove them to the bottom of the hill and waited while they got into their car. When they pulled out of their parking space, she pulled into it and joined the Dalton's in their car. They sailed through San Francisco, every true San Franciscan being at home reading The Chronicle. However, the guard at Treasure Island Gate would not let them enter. They waited in the anteroom until Ron appeared.

"Sorry. With all the brass we've got running around here the public has been denied entrance."

Ron carried an old fashioned wicker picnic basket. "Ms.

Farnsworth made this for me. She's been around for 50 years and even though she's retired, she still volunteers as if she's on duty."

"I didn't know women were in the Navy 50 years ago." Summer said.

"They weren't; they were in the Waves. And she wasn't in the Waves, either, but her Dad was Captain of the Mess for 35 years. She landed on the payroll under the title of Protocol Agent, or something like that, as she took care of the Officer's Wives. Everybody loved her, so when her Dad died they kept her around. Fortunately, she's taken a liking to me."

"Well, who wouldn't?" said Darce, patting his arm. "Ron, I've been wondering, how are we getting to Angel Island?"

"My dear, I'm in the Navy."

"So then there's a ferry boat or something?"

"Come and see, my fine feathered friends." Ron led the way to a dock where a row of 20 foot sailboats were tied. He checked a slip of paper, found the number on the dock and said, "There's our beauty."

"Who's our beauty?" Kirk demanded a bit breathlessly.

"Your chariot of the winds," said Ron. He looked at his three guests. They were standing like ducks in a row staring at the boat as if it might be the Titanic.

"Have any of you sailed before?" Ron asked. The three shook their heads no in unison. "Don't they have any bodies of water where you come from?"

"We've got the Mighty Mississippi, but nobody sails on that. There's so much junk in that river you can't even water ski anymore." Kirk said, not lifting his eyes.

Ron realized he had embarrassed them, "Then today I'm your teacher. Nothing to it. You'll love it. Kirk, jump in there and help the ladies on board. I'll free the lines and push us off."

Kirk didn't budge. He stared suspiciously into the boat. "Are you going to be on the dock when you push us off?"

Ron laughed, "No. I'll get in first."

Kirk swung his leg gingerly over the gunwale and stepped

into the boat. Ron held it to the dock while Kirk took the hands of Darce and Summer as they stepped down and quickly sat on the bench along the side.

"Could you two move over to the other side?" Ron asked, and the women cautiously shifted to the other bench.

Handing in the picnic basket, Ron climbed aboard and released the sailboat from the dock. He started the motor to get them out into the bay before hoisting the sail. Once into the open water he put them to work getting the sail in position and with a little experience they began to relax and not sit like pegs hammered into the benches. But then slightly at ease can prove to be far more dangerous than being terrified.

Ron planned to go around the westward end of Angel Island so they could see Sausalito and Tiburon. With the wind being feisty, he thought he would tack in short bursts that way he would not pick up too much speed at the beginning, thinking he might scare his passengers. The three of them were like kids in a candy store.

"Look at Alcatraz! Can we go there?"

"Not without permission. Maybe another time."

"What about going underneath the Golden Gate?"

"We'd need a bigger boat."

As they continued to exclaim, Ron said, "Okay, I'm going to come about." Darce, moved by the splendor of being on the bay and seeing the sights, chose that precise moment to stand and move to the other side to sit in the circle of Kirk's arm. As Ron pulled the rudder, the boat shifted, which caused Darce to stagger and remain upright trying to get her balance, instead of quickly sitting. The boom swung faster than Ron anticipated. Summer saw it and ducked. Darce, however, faced away from the sail making her a prime target for the mischievous wind. The boom swung right into her backside and tossed her overboard.

Kirk dodged the boom just in time to miss having it crash into his head and then he reached frantically for his wife. His arms and legs flailed as he shouted, "Darce! Darce!"

Summer pushed Kirk out of the way and grabbed Darce's left arm. Ron let go of the line, allowing the boat to flounder and the boom to find its own rest, while he grabbed her right arm. Tugging, they got Darce against the side of the boat but couldn't pull her in. Her parka, loaded with water, weighed her down. "Kirk!" Ron yelled. "Get her parka off so we can haul her into the boat."

In a classic state of shock regarding the danger to his wife, with behavior that seemed appropriate to him, Kirk stood up, put his hands on his hips and began to lecture Ron and Summer. "I don't know what the two of you think you're going to do with her now … " He cried rhetorically, when the boom, dancing with another mischievous breeze swooped over to pitch Kirk into the water as well. Astonished by the impact of the cold bay, Kirk thrashed to the side of the boat and grabbed the gunwales.

Darce began to laugh hysterically. The two of them dangled from the boat like colorful buoys. Summer just about had the offending parka unzipped when the Coast Guard approached. They threw a lifebuoy to Kirk, another to Darce and lowered a ladder over the sides. Drifting the lifeboat close, the guardsmen pulled the two waterlogged victims on board while Summer and Ron held the boats apart. The crew had blankets and hot liquids at the ready. Over a bullhorn a crisply uniformed young man announced. "Sir, please follow us to port."

As he and Summer furled the sail and he started the motor, she asked, "How did those sailors know you're an officer?"

"It's a Navy issue sailboat that only officers are allowed to take out. That's why they were here within seconds."

"Oh," she said, "How embarrassing for you."

He smiled. "Not really. I told you I joined the Navy to serve my country, but I actually joined it for the fun. See what fun we're having?"

Summer's teeth chattered. "Yeah! It's a riot."

Both of them were sopping wet from reaching into the bay. He pulled her next to him and put his arm around her as they made their way to the dock. "I'm afraid we have to keep each other warm."

Ron released the boat to the Coast Guard who returned it to its slip. The four of them warmed up in the Guard house, lacing hot chocolate down their throats. At first they sat glumly wrapped in thermal blankets while Ron filled out paperwork, not meeting each other's glances. Then one of them grinned, another chuckled and finally the four of them were busting a gut at their absurd sea adventure.

A Guardsman drove them to their car so they wouldn't have to be in the wind. Kirk cranked up the heat while they waited for Ron to change clothes, having decided to picnic in the Dalton's apartment. When Ron returned he opened the back door, "Summer, why don't you ride with me; that way the picnic basket won't crowd you."

She nodded and quickly changed cars, settling into Ron's little 350Z. They drove quietly to Russian Hill. "You certainly respond well under pressure," Ron commented.

"Thank you. I'm not often under pressure. I've lived a very simple life until I got to San Francisco." She paused, "Actually, until I met you."

Ron looked surprised. "You only met me last night."

"Yes, and for the first time I experienced dancing during dinner. I've only seen that in the movies. Come to think of it, another first time happened last night. A ruined dinner did not send the hostess into histrionics because the one causing the ruination took full responsibility for it. That was definitely a first. And consider today. I've never been sailing before, nor have my friends ever fallen overboard; and if we're counting first times, think of it, I've been rescued at sea. See what I mean? Life in Cape Girardeau, Missouri plods along very simply."

Ron grinned. "Are you staying awhile? I'll show you the bright lights and the big city."

She grinned in return. "My teaching contract runs out next June. Does that give you enough time?"

Arriving at the Dalton's apartment, Ron parked directly in front, unduly impressing Summer. "My, you do have the San Francisco touch. Only natives find good parking places."

Upstairs, Darce gave Summer a sweatshirt to put on in place of her wet one, and then Kirk and Darce showered to warm up and put on dry clothes. Still chilled to the bone, Ron and Summer pulled chairs up to the radiator in the living room. They were laughing, their heads practically touching, when Kirk bounded into the room and pulled a chair up right between them. He gave Summer a look to let her know that he would take over now and not to encroach on his property.

Darce came in and unloaded the picnic basket on the table. She spread a blanket on the floor so they could pretend they were picnicking. After loading their plates they sat on the blanket and ate. They played Scattergories and Phase Ten, both of which Summer won.

"Well, no wonder she wins!" Kirk griped. "Her parents teach school, for crying' out loud."

"Her father's a principal." Darce corrected.

"It's the same thing!" Kirk pouted.

"What do they teach?" Ron asked.

"Actually, Dad doesn't teach anymore. As principal he commandeers Mark Twain High School in Cape Girardeau. He'd make a good captain of a boat. My mother keeps a low profile and teaches $12^{th}$ grade history in the same school."

"Same school?" Ron puzzled. "Normally nepotism's against the law."

"Not there." She shook her head. "They've been there 25 years, since they graduated from college in fact. My Dad taught history too, until he went into administration."

"Did you attend Mark Twain High?"

"Yup. Kirk, Darce and I all graduated the same year."

"Didn't you find that awkward having your parents teaching at the same school you attended?"

"Awkward?" Kirk interjected. "The favorite of all the teachers? Little spoiled brat?"

"Are you still jealous of me?" Summer asked with a mocking voice.

"Jealous? Of you? Why should I be jealous of little miss only child who always got everything she wanted in life!"

"Kirk!" Darce warned.

"Well, look at her. Even today. There were three of us on that boat who have never sailed. Who gets dunked in the drink? Not her!"

"That's not being spoiled," Ron exclaimed. "That's showing a little wisdom." He grinned as Darce pushed him.

"Oh, yeah? You'd better watch yourself, Mr. Ron La Fave. You should have seen what you looked like from the water!" They fell into paroxysms of laughter again remembering their little crisis.

When the laughter died Ron asked Summer, "What would your parents think of our adventure at sea?"

"My parents consider themselves to be avant garde. They would think it droll."

"I know what avant garde means, but how does that describe your parents?" Ron asked.

"They try to stay ahead of their time. For example, they've never married. I've never had turkey on Thanksgiving. They … "

"Wait a minute, wait a minute. Your folks aren't married?" Kirk demanded.

"No. They thought it over and considered marriage to be a silly, social convention. They moved in with each other during college and stayed together."

"That's horrible!" Kirk roared. "Why, all those kids that graduated from Mark Twain, what a bad influence on them! It's unbelievable!"

"Did it influence you?" Summer asked sarcastically.

"No, I didn't know they weren't married."

"Neither did the other kids. My mother used her own name

and everyone thought she used her maiden name so as not to confuse people as to which one taught the class."

"I always thought they were married, too." Darce said.

"Technically they are." Ron intervened. "How long have they been together?"

Summer shrugged, "I'm 24 so it has to be 27 years now."

"After seven years the statutes say they have a common law marriage."

"Oh! Don't tell them that. They can't stand to think of themselves as common."

"What about their daughter? Would you call her avant garde as well? It seems to me you said something about living a simple life." Ron teased.

"That's the anomaly, at least for them. They tried their best to get me to do every unconventional thing and I'm the most conventional person I know. But that's why Kirk thinks I'm spoiled. To him I got everything I ever wanted. The real truth being, I got everything Kirk ever wanted."

Ron looked at his stockbroker with renewed interest. "What did Kirk want?"

"He wanted some attention. He didn't realize that too much attention can be stifling. Kirk had too much freedom to do anything he wanted. I think I used to be jealous of him."

"Now you're free and Kirk has lots of attention." Ron surmised.

"Maybe the tables have turned." Summer nodded.

"At least now I know why you're such a ditzy blond," Kirk gave her a mollified sideways look.

As the day drooped into the gloaming, a burst of sunlight blistered the bay from the horizon. They stood on the balcony to marvel in the glory of it. As the light died away, Ron said, "Summer, these two pals of ours are definitely loads of fun, but they're very distracting, and if you and I have any hopes of getting to know each other then maybe we need to spend some time just the two of us."

Over Ron's shoulder, Kirk shook his head no with the most menacing look he could muster.

"Well, why don't you call me, Ron, and we can talk about it".

Kirk bared his teeth at her.

"Okay." Ron agreed with surprise.

Kirk and Darce stood on their landing saying their goodbyes as Ron and Summer slowly descended the staircase. Then they watched out the bay window of the landing as the two talked on the sidewalk.

"She's going to ruin everything, I just know it." Kirk said despondently.

"You don't know that!" Darce put her arm around his waist.

Kirk sighed deeply. "Why did you invite her anyway?"

"She's my best friend. I needed her support, Kirky; that dinner scared me to death. But it turned out okay in the end."

He grinned sheepishly. "That dinner can only be described as awesome! Thank you!" He kissed her. "Now, if your best friend will leave my best client alone, that dinner will have been a great success."

"What can she possibly do, Kirk? She's just a confused girl who never learned to make her own decisions."

"She can get his mind off business and then he'll call her six times a day instead of me. I'm telling you, I need this guy, Darce."

"Kirky. You can have him during the week and she can have him on the weekends. That's all. That way, I can have you on the weekends, too." She put her face up for another kiss to which he complied but suddenly broke away.

"She's getting in his car!"

"Kirk!" Darce pulled his face back to hers. "It's my turn now!"

Chapter Three
# THE DATING GAME

The following Friday night Ron and Summer wandered on Fisherman's Wharf dodging the swooping seagulls. Foghorns sounded like hollow beer barrel belches as the heavy, thick air coated buildings and shadowed boats. They dined late where the locals ate on the pier behind the big name tourist restaurants.

"Why did you become a school teacher?"

"I didn't want to. I wanted to be a journalist. But my parents wanted me to teach school. I really think they thought I would be with them for the rest of my life, all of us teaching together at Mark Twain. My Dad drew up a contract, even though I didn't apply. I went to St. Charles instead and taught at St. Charles High."

"Why French?" he asked. "Why don't you teach history like your parents? Or English, if you wanted to write?"

"I like to write, but teaching it would make me miserable because I wouldn't be doing it, I'd be teaching it. Can you understand that?"

Ron nodded and smiled.

"And, I think teaching French became my first step toward independence. They'd brought a French woman over to be kind of a nanny/housekeeper sometime during first grade. The Spanish woman they'd had since I was born, retired. When I entered kindergarten I had two mother tongues: English and Spanish. Then I learned French as well as English. Why not teach it?"

"You make it sound so simple."

"That's how I see life. Simple. If you don't resist, it rolls along."

"Why aren't you still in St. Charles? What brought you to San Francisco?"

"Depression. I'd never really been out on my own. I missed Darce. She and Kirk married the first weekend after graduation, threw their things in the trunk of their old Pontiac and headed out here. She easily got a job teaching third grade and Kirk got hired right away by Waterston and Meddling. I called her almost every night to whine, and she convinced me to come join them.

"As soon as school closed for the summer, I hightailed it out here and got a job teaching high school French at Galileo. I didn't realize they needed teachers so badly. I thought they hired me for my merits. The first day of school I discovered the truth. Any place where they make the students go through a metal detector in order to enter the building, should give you pause. My very first day at school I had to break up a knife fight.

"I know it sounds crazy because I'm not at all a tough broad, but I like it there. The kids like me, I like them, I'm near my best friend, Darce, and I'm starting to get into the single life of San Francisco."

Ron frowned, "You mean you don't have a plan for your life? Or is that your plan, following Darce around?"

She looked pensive. "I think I watched my parents try to design their lives and fail everywhere except at school. My philosophy seems to be that life is something that happens while you're busy making other plans. It's easier just to go along for the ride. Why did you ask that question? Do you have a life plan?"

"Absolutely. I'll tell you about it someday."

He kept her talking until the wait staff stood nearby flipping towels at specks of dust and they realized they were the only ones left in the restaurant. Ron apologized and tossed an extra twenty on the table for their inconvenience.

On Monday Kirk called Ron. "Hey, buddy boy, can you get into the city for lunch?"

"I'll find some kind of protocol excuse. Meet you at Tad's Grill?"

"Noon. Straight up."

"You got it."

Settled in a high backed dark wood booth, Kirk pushed his Orange Roughy sandwich aside while he animatedly discussed their recent trades. Ron tackled grilled Sand Dabs and listened enthusiastically.

"That's it!" he'd punctuate the air with his fork every so often.

Finished, he pushed his plate aside while Kirk plunged into his sandwich. Intensely leaning forward Ron emphasized, "That's what I want. Buy. Sell. Buy. Sell. Build the equity. But remember, one third of the gain has to go into that blue chip account and even though it's mine, it can never be traced back to me. You understand how much that means to me, don't you Kirk?"

"I do. It's sealed. Don't worry; I'm on your side."

Ron smiled. "I know you back me 100 percent. And you're putting your money in right behind mine, aren't you?"

"I don't have as much to put in, but you bet your boots I am. Like you said not too long ago, we're going to make each other into millionaires."

"That's right. And I'm going to get there before I'm 35. That's seven years from now, my friend, so let's stay on track."

"Ron, it's for that exact reason that I wanted to talk to you. Summer McBride can derail you. Forget her!"

"I took her out Friday night."

"I know. I know. She called Darce all atwitter about what a good time she had."

"She said Darce was her best friend."

"Look, when Darce went to kindergarten she couldn't speak English. Her family came over from Poland. They were sponsored by my church. Summer went up to her on the playground that first day, gave her a tissue to dry her tears and started helping her understand English. They've been inseparable ever since. I admire my wife's loyalty, but that woman brings nothing but friction to my marriage. She's a disaster."

"Like what? What kind of a disaster?"

"Like the time her picture got plastered all over the local newspaper! Twelve years old and she'd been caught shoplifting! Having a principal of the high school for a father didn't hurt her any; nothing ever came of it."

"So you think there's a little larceny in the fair lady?"

"Let's just say I don't trust her and I don't want you to get burned, or distracted."

"Which concerns you more, my getting burned or my getting distracted?"

Kirk narrowed his eyes, "Both."

"Trust me. I never get distracted. My life has been planned since junior high and I have never deviated. As for being burned … I'm a big boy. I don't have much time left on the west coast. I can watch out for myself. But thanks for the warning, Kirk. Let's you and me stick to business."

That Saturday Ron picked Summer up at 11 a.m. for a day to wander around San Francisco. Ducking underneath Union Square, he parked his 350Z, angling it to occupy two spaces. They strolled through clogged streets fronting department stores and ribboned alleys of boutiques. Ron could not seem to stop making comparisons between the grand boulevards and stores of New York City with the small town feel of San Francisco.

"There are only 700,000 people here, Ron. Are you such a big city boy you can't appreciate this?"

"No. It's quaint. But I am a big city boy, as you put it. Come on. I hear there's a great place for lunch at Neiman Marcus."

Using his San Francisco touch Ron arranged to be seated at a table by the expansive windows overlooking Union Square. After a lavish lunch, lingering over coffee he asked, "So what's this about you being a shoplifter?"

Summer looked surprised and then laughed. "That Kirk! He's Machiavellian! Okay, it happened on a Saturday. I went shopping with four of my friends. I was in the dressing room in Rathbone's Department Store looking at myself in the mirror as I tried on a black skirt. I had hung my jeans on the hook. Beth came running into the cubicle, squealing that she saw the captain of the football team coming down the street.

"Now you've got to understand that for us seventh graders who never missed the ball games on Friday nights, this sighting could only be compared to seeing a real live movie star up close. The five of us careened out of the store, screaming, girls can incite each other like that, and when we passed through the metal detector, it went off because of the tag on the skirt. But I didn't think anything about it and ran to the corner with the rest of them.

"The captain that year happened to be a really nice guy. He came over and gave us a little pep talk about not throwing ourselves at guys and waiting for the right one to come along. Anyway, I suddenly looked down and realized I had the store's skirt on. I ran back by myself to change into my jeans. When I got there a policeman was waiting.

"I put my jeans on and he took me to the station where he called my parents. The newspapers heard about it and they got to the station before my dad did. Since being the principal's daughter makes you somebody in Cape Girardeau, the incident got a lot of attention. They printed a full page spread in the local newspaper. The store didn't press charges; they understood. But the kids at school ragged me about it for months." She frowned pensively, "Now why would Kirk tell you that story?"

Ron smiled. "I think he wants me to know what a colorful character you are."

"Me? Hardly."

They took the cable car to the top of Nob Hill. Looking at the imposing architecture of Grace Cathedral, they stalled in admiration until Summer put them in gear by suggesting they go inside. Thinking themselves to be on tiptoe, they whispered to each other, even though only a handful of people ambled through the building, tourists dead-panning at the art and gaping at the sanctuary. Sunlight crashed through the Rose window like a strong-willed rainbow, washing their faces, puddling at their feet.

Ron asked cautiously, "How do you feel in here?"

"Free!" Summer breathed the word out as if setting a bird to flight. "How do you feel?"

"Suffocated." He looked around apprehensively.

Summer indicated the pews. "Would it bother you if we sat down for a couple of minutes?"

"Good idea. Maybe I can figure out why I feel claustrophobic in this vast expanse."

He looked at her and saw a gleam in her eyes. "Does this mean something to you, being in this place?"

"It's beautiful, that's all." They sat in silence absorbing the magnificence of the Cathedral. Then Summer continued whispering, "Darce's the church goer. My folks never went, that's for sure. But they let me go to church camp with Darce one summer. I think I was fourteen. This place reminds me of a certain night in that camp. We stood on top of a little hill. The moon hadn't come up yet. The only light came from the stars and a bonfire, but our backs were turned to it. It's amazing how bright stars can be.

"We each had a little candle and as we lit them we told Jesus we would be lights for Him. I think about that moment every once in a while. It's a very special memory and I don't know why. I'll have to remember to ask Darce about that sometime because she cried all night. I tried to get her to stop, but when I asked her why she cried she said over and over, 'I'm so happy. I'm so happy. I'm so happy."

She turned to look at him. "Have you figured out why you feel suffocated in here?"

"Maybe I'm more atheist than I thought." He said as he stood. "Let's get out of here."

They scurried and jumped onto another cable car starting its slide and hopped off at North Beach. Trying their luck, they stopped by Beach Blanket Babylon and hit the jackpot. There were two tickets left, which they snapped up and then puttered in the shops and snacked on Italian deli till show time.

When Ron took her home he kissed her at the door and asked, "Mind if I come in?"

She looked into his eyes, "Yes, I do mind. Remember? I'm a conventional girl."

"But that is the convention these days. It's part of getting to know each other."

She didn't move. "You're right, but then I warned you some of my conventions can be old fashioned."

He cocked his head, "You won't mind if I keep asking, will you?"

"Only if you don't mind that I withdraw and don't see you anymore."

"You make your point rather forcefully." Ron took a step back.

She stepped forward and kissed him. "I like you, Ron. I hope you like me just as I am," and then she went inside.

Chapter Four
# KIRK'S PLOT

The next afternoon Summer called her best friend to tell her every detail of the day and evening she spent with Ron La Fave. When Darce relayed the information to Kirk, he stewed sullenly until he got to work the next morning. As soon as he could he took a coffee break and sauntered casually down to the accounting office to chat with Melissa, a stunning blond.

"Listen. I've got a client who's in the Navy for awhile, but he's moving back to New York soon. I want to make sure he enjoys himself while he's here because I want to keep him as a client. Can you give me a hand and go out with this guy?"

She frowned so he quickly added, "It would be a double date. My wife and I will be with you. We'll pick you up and he can meet us. If you don't like the looks of him, we'll take you home, too. I thought we might go down to Pier 39 for dinner and play some of the games this Friday night. Would you be willing to help me out with this?" Melissa considered and smiled. "Sure, Kirk. I'll be happy to go."

Kirk strolling back to his office, a gleeful grin on his face, called Ron La Fave. "Hey, Ron. I've got a gal I want you to meet."

"I'm listening."

Kirk described her statuesque beauty and her financial brains. "She said she's free Friday night. I'm up for an evening at Pier 39. What do you say?"

"I'd say I'm interested. Your friend, Summer, kind of gave me the brush-off Saturday night."

"She did?"

"Kind of. We had a great day together. I think I'm still going to ask her out for next Saturday but I wouldn't mind meeting somebody else. Okay, you're on. Friday night. Pier 39. Kids night out."

"That's the spirit! I'm a whiz at the pinball."

"Nobody beats a New Yorker at the pinball, my friend! You're on!"

That night, over dinner, Kirk casually mentioned, "You know, I've been feeling like I'm being hard on Summer. She's your best friend, whether I like it or not. And she's not such a bad kid now that's she's grown up. Why don't we go out Friday night? See if Summer can't get a date and we'll go to Pier 39, play some games, eat dinner, and hang out for an evening."

Darce came around the table and sat on his lap. "Oh, Kirky. What a Romeo you are. Next to you, Summer's the best thing that ever happened to me and I want my Romeo to be her friend, too." She planted a big kiss on him before returning to her chair. "Can she ask Ron? They seem to have a really good time together."

"No. I don't want her to do that. I think my client stockbroker relationship will work best if they see each other on their own time. And I wouldn't want him to know we are doing something without him, either. So don't you dare let her call Ron! I can probably get her a date if she can't get one. There's a new stockbroker, he's not the best looking guy I've ever seen, but he's single. I'd only ask him as a last resort, though. Didn't she mention some teacher on her staff that was interested in her?"

"Yeah, I remember her talking about him, but he didn't rev her motor. I'll give her a call."

Darce did exactly what Kirk thought she would do. She went into the bathroom and called Summer while running a bath so that he couldn't hear the conversation. "Now remember! You can't tell Ron that we're double dating. If he shows up, you know, like you didn't really understand, Kirk will be okay. But if you tell Ron that it's Kirk and me on Friday night, he'll mention it to Kirk and then my goose is cooked! You've got to promise me, Summer."

"Okay. I got it. So you want us all to meet at Pier 39?"

"Yeah, about 7:30."

"Good. I'll call him right now."

Ron, pleased to get a call from Summer, asked her out for Saturday night before she had a chance to speak. Somewhat taken aback, Summer responded, "Actually, Ron, although I'm unaccustomed to doing this, I'm calling to ask you out for Friday night."

"Hmmm. Being the negotiator that I am I will stick to form and insist that my question be answered first."

"Saturday?"

"Yes."

"Sure. I'd love to go out with you on Saturday. Now, to my question."

"Friday?"

"Yes."

"I'm sorry. I really am. I've already made other plans."

"Oh. Okay. Well, I'll look forward to Saturday."

When they finished, Summer called Darce. "He's got other plans. Now what?"

"Hang on." She called to her husband. "Kirk, can Summer come alone on Friday?"

"That's no fun for me. I want another guy there. Tell her I'll get that stockbroker if she wants. He's kind of fat, though."

She called back into the living room. "When you say that

about a guy, it means he's a lardo. When you say that about a girl, it means she's two pounds overweight."

Darce went back to her conversation with Summer and the discussion of the teacher Kirk remembered. But Kirk sat grinning in the living room. Summer had called Ron and he couldn't make it since he had other plans. Now Summer would sit home and maybe he could get Ron diverted with Melissa. This way Kirk satisfied his wife with his inclusion of Summer, even though he knew full well she couldn't make it. She'd never invited a boy out in her life; she wouldn't know how to get a date. He gloated over the perfection of his plan.

On Thursday, when Darce reported that Summer had indeed invited Rusty, the computer teacher at school, Kirk paused. He hadn't figured out a way to tell Darce about picking up Melissa and meeting up with Ron. Now this had been added to the evening. To tell the truth, this placed his plan at the highest level of intrigue, but beyond his ability to control it any longer. Perhaps divine intervention had chosen to play the cards for him. He decided to keep a poker face and not give anything away.

After school on Friday, Darce came home humming to herself looking forward to a very pleasant evening. She took a long bath followed by lengthy preparations for her night out. 'Getting ready is half the fun,' she thought. Kirk sprawled on the couch watching football clips. He put his arm out as Darce passed through the room and she sank down beside him.

He put his face into her hair, "You smell good."

"You feel good," she said. "But don't get any ideas. The good stuff comes later."

"Why don't we forget Pier 39 and stay home?"

"No dice, Romeo. We're going out and we're going to have a good time!" She kissed him and continued her journey to the bedroom to finish getting ready.

When they left their apartment building, Kirk fished his car keys out of his pocket. Darce shook her head. "Let's walk. It's such a mild night for November."

Thinking quickly Kirk remarked, "But these mild nights turn into bitter cold when it's time to come home."

"Oh, you're right."

Darce didn't really watch where Kirk was driving until he stopped in front of an apartment at the bottom of Telegraph Hill. "What are we doing here?"

"Don't you remember?" he asked.

"Remember what?"

"That Melissa decided to play some pinball with us."

"Melissa who?"

"From the office. You remember her, don't you? When you told me Summer couldn't get a date, I asked Melissa to come along and that we'd pick her up and she could meet her date at the pier. I'm positive I told you that."

"I don't remember you saying anything like that. But it doesn't matter. I think I know her, if I remember correctly. A stunning blond, right? What other surprises do you have, anybody else coming? It's turning into a big party."

At that moment, Melissa opened the back door having seen them from her window. They got on their way amid opening pleasantries, "How are you? Glad you could come."

"Fine, thanks. I'm really looking forward to this. Now, Kirk, what's my date's name?"

"Ron. Ron La Fave."

Darce's mouth almost dropped open, but she ground it shut. She gave him a sideways look of indictment and then made forced polite conversation with Melissa. They parked the car in the lot across from Pier 39. Darce jammed her fists into her coat pocket and walked stiffly by Kirk's side. Melissa swung along on Kirk's other side, an air of excitement pulsing in her words.

"I love New Yorkers. They have such a droll sense of humor."

Darce suppressed a snort and instead smiled with her lips only.

As it turned out, Ron had parked on the street. Summer and

Rusty, arriving early, had taken a short walk on the pier; so the members of the triple date met in the middle from triangular points of entry. When Ron saw Summer he looked sharply at Kirk who shrugged his shoulders and cocked his head toward Darce as if it were her fault. When Summer saw Ron she looked sharply at Darce who shrugged her shoulders and cocked her head toward Kirk as if it were his fault.

They paired up and strolled down the pier, four of them making stilted small talk. However, Rusty and Melissa, unaware of any complications, smacked of good will and offered clever comments inviting a hardy discourse. The four did their best to respond, but Rusty and Melissa batted the clever comments back and forth as if they were playing ping pong. At dinner the four uptight ones assessed the situation and decided to make the best of the evening.

Afterwards they headed for the game gallery at the end of the pier. Summer, talking with Rusty about the teacher's meeting that day, went down three steps with the rest of them, but thought there was a fourth. This misstep caused her to fall to the ground and twist her ankle. "Aaawww!" she groaned loudly and grabbed her painful limb.

Ron, dropping all pretense of not noticing her, raced to her side and knelt beside her. "What's the matter, Summer? Where does it hurt?"

"My ankle. I twisted my ankle. I thought there were four steps and there were only three."

"Yeah, that fourth step will get you every time." She smiled at his attempt to cajole her. "We need to get somebody to look at it."

"No, no. I'll be alright. If you'll help me up I'm sure I'll be able to walk."

"If you can't get up on your own, then you shouldn't get up at all." Ron looked around for a solution and saw a guard strolling away from them at the other end of the pier. "Kirk, you can whistle can't you? Whistle for that guy."

Kirk put two fingers in his mouth and blasted a shrill note that caused everyone on the pier to turn around. Then he waved vigorously at the guard who rushed to them.

"I'm sure if I simply walked around a bit the ankle will be alright. Please, somebody help me up." Melissa and Darce came to her sides, but Ron put a restraining hand on her shoulder until the guard arrived.

"Our friend, here, fell on the stairs and has a painful ankle. Can you help us? Is there an emergency room nearby? What can be done for her?"

"We've got a medic on call. Let's get her into the first aid room. I'll go get the wheelchair and then we can call the medic." He hurriedly left them and swiftly returned with a wheelchair. The guard and Ron lifted her with their arms under her shoulders into the chair amid her little cries of "Oooo! Aw! Oh!"

The antiseptic first aid room, crouched around the corner and stuffed under the stairs, had been designed to hold two adults and two children in cherished intimacy. All six concerned adults in this party could not crowd into the room, especially since the painstaking guard lifted the rail on the chair to hold Summer's leg.

Ron took command, "Listen, we all know this will prove to be a lengthy event tonight. Rusty and Melissa, I hate to ask this of you, but would you mind finishing the evening together? Rusty, can you take Melissa home for me?"

Having been eyeing each other all through dinner, they said a bit too eagerly they would certainly continue the evening together. But when Ron suggested Kirk and Darce go with them, since Melissa was Kirk's friend and all, the two adamantly refused, insisting on taking their rightful place with Summer.

Ron, Kirk and Darce walked out to the pier to speed Rusty and Melissa on their way. As they squeezed back into the confining first aid room, the wheelchair demanding most of the floor space, Ron clapped a hand on Kirk's shoulder and the other on Darce's. "You two are uncanny. I don't know how this evening got so cockeyed and I bet you don't either. But I'm going to take care of Summer, so why don't you two just toddle on home."

Darce pulled away. "What do you want, Summer?"

"I'm sure it's not as bad as it feels. I'll be okay. If Ron can run me home, I'll crawl into bed and by tomorrow I'll be fine."

"Okay, but I'll be over first thing in the morning to help. A twisted ankle can be a real nuisance."

"No need, Darce." Ron towered over her. "I've got tomorrow covered. But I can't be there Sunday as I have Duty. Can you show up then?"

"Sure." Darce looked covertly at Summer and raised her eyebrows. "How's that sound to you?"

"Call me in the morning, Darce. I'll be just fine and I won't need any nursemaids."

"Great!" Kirk rubbed his hands together. "Come on, my Juliet, let's go home."

Darce gave him an icy stare. "Romeo? I don't know anybody by that name."

On the way home she railed at him, "You set that whole thing up!"

"Not quite. I just set it in motion."

"Well, it backfired on you! Sounds to me like he's going to be camping out at her place. Why can't you let Ron and Summer have a relationship? I don't get it!"

"You don't have to get it, Darce." His temper flaring. "He's my client. He told me who he's going to marry and I don't want Summer ruining his plans."

"He's got a fiancée?"

"No. I didn't say that. He knows the kind of woman he needs to marry in order to achieve what he wants in life. Summer, bless her sweet heart, will never be that kind of a woman."

"And Melissa is?"

"No, but Ron would figure that out. Now, Darce, stay out of my business!"

They rode the rest of the way in silence and slept on the edges of the bed.

The Port Authority kept a Resident Doctor and a nurse from S. F. General on standing order. They also kept them very busy. It took two hours before the professional pair came to crowd into the tiny first aid room and pronounce Summer to have a sprain. The doctor wrapped it and told her to stay off her feet for a week, if at all possible.

The guard wheeled Summer to the curb and Ron brought his car up to receive her. On Clayton Street he managed to park directly in front of her building. When he pulled her out of the car, he whispered, "Now, don't stagger. The neighbors will think you've been drinking. Put your arm around my neck; that way they'll just think you're horny."

She giggled, "You're incorrigible, Ron!"

Taking one painful step after another, they slowly walked down the sloped wooden walkway that led to the back of the building where her deck cantilevered over a deep gully. He sat her in a chair while he found her keys, went in, turned on some lights, and then helped her to limp inside. "Where's your nightgown?"

"I can get my own self ready for bed!"

"No you can't. Where is it?"

"Ron!"

"I have a sister, Summer. She's twenty years old, a junior in college, and I have helped her do a lot more intimate things than taking her nightgown to the bathroom and helping her get in there to change into it by herself."

Her face reddened. "It's in the second drawer down. And I don't wear a nightgown. I wear a top and some shorts. They're lime green and blue."

He opened the drawer and pulled out the shiny items. "These?"

She nodded.

He took them to the bathroom, then came back to get her.

"I'll make an ice pack for you to sleep with. Do you have a container or do I just use plastic bags?"

"It's under the sink in the bathroom."

She handed him the ice bag and closed the door. When she opened it again, dressed in the top and shorts, he had pulled down the covers, positioned the filled ice bag on a flattened pillow and had turned out all the lights except the one glowing on her bed stand.

Her face reddened as he came to put his arm around her to help her to the bed. As they hobbled across the floor, he said, "I'm willing to take all the blame for this. If I had followed my instincts last Monday when you called, this wouldn't have happened. I wanted to say yes, I'd go with you, and to call Kirk back and cancel out on the blind date. If I'd done that, you and I wouldn't have been working so hard to be good companions to likeable people, but people we didn't want to be with. Then you wouldn't have sprained your ankle."

"How do you know I didn't want to be with Rusty?"

"Because he could have brought you home just as easily as me."

"I don't remember being given that option."

"But you didn't say no to my plan."

She smiled. "No, I didn't. I liked it very much."

He held her hands as she sat on the bed and then he lifted her legs to position them, placing the one on the ice pack. Pulling the covers over her, making sure they weren't too heavily settled on the wounded ankle, he tucked her in and then knelt down by the bed. Taking her hand in his two hands he said, "What I'd like to do, if you don't mind, is to take an extra set of your keys, if you have one … "

"Yes. In the cupboard on the left side of the sink, hanging on a hook."

"Good. I'll lock you in. Tomorrow I'll be here first thing in the morning and I'll bring breakfast. Those pain pills he gave you should make you sleep all night, but if you need anything, call me. I put my card right here by the phone and I can be here in 20 minutes flat. So don't hesitate. Got that?"

"Thank you."

"You didn't answer my question. You got that?"

"Ron, I am not going to need anything in the middle of the night, but yes, I got that!"

"Good." He kissed her tenderly, stood, retrieved the keys, stooped to kiss her forehead, turned out the light and left.

Chapter Five
# GETTING TO KNOW YOU

At 9 a.m. when he opened her front door, he stopped and stared. Her bed, separated from the living area by one step up and a wrought iron hip high railing, lay swathed in sunlight streaking in from the plate glass window overlooking the deck. Summer, on her side, the ice pack conveniently kicked to the floor, slept with her head back, her arm tossed overhead and her golden hair splayed across the pillow.

Tiptoeing, he arranged the lox and bagels he brought on the coffee table in front of the couch which backed up to the railing. Quietly observing her sleeping posture, he bent over and planted a lingering kiss on her lips, then straightened as she awoke. Responding fully, Summer inhaled sharply, her chest heaving. "Oh! What a way to wake up!"

Ron grinned. "I'm sorry. I just couldn't resist. I don't think I've ever seen anything so beautiful in my life."

She tried to sit up and winced. "Ron, did he give me any pain pills for today?"

"Yeah. I put them on the counter. I'll get you a glass of water."

Once again he helped her to the bathroom, retrieved the clothes she wanted to wear from her closet and bureau and brought them to her. When she deemed herself to be ready he helped her to the couch where they sat and ate the breakfast so amply spread before them. Lingering over coffee, Ron prodded for information as usual.

"Why do you get to ask so many questions?" Summer accused. "Now it's my turn."

"Are you a lawyer?" he asked.

"No. But you're not either."

"Yes, I am." He replied gravely. "That's exactly what I am."

Confused, she asked, "A lawyer for the Navy?"

"They only have me for two years so they assigned me to the Office of Protocol on the Island, not much to do with legal work."

"Then what do you mean you're a lawyer?"

"I mean that I graduated from Columbia with a law degree before I reported for duty with the Navy. When I'm through here I'll go back to New York and work for FCA. They hired me two months before I received my diploma."

She looked at him a long time and saw what could have been pain mixed with resolve, but she couldn't be sure. "Well, you are a man filled with surprises. Tell me about FCA."

"Footlights Corporation of America. They're the parent company for the GUS Theatre in New York City. You've heard of that, haven't you? Gateway to the United States, or GUS."

"Absolutely. It's gorgeous. My parents and I traveled every summer. We stayed in New York for a couple of exciting weeks when I was twelve; we attended a different theatre every night. We went to the GUS twice, once to attend the big theatre and once to experience a smaller salon. Then we spent Christmas vacation in New York because I had to ice skate around that fabulous tree!"

"I know what you mean. That tree, in my mind, represents magic. I fell in love with the GUS as a kid," Ron reflected. "My parents sent me to private schools and in sixth grade the school rented buses and took us to the GUS. I couldn't believe the beauty of those ceilings and the gold flowing curtain; I had to be a part of the GUS, somehow. Every weekend I nagged and begged my father to take me there, and he usually complied. In high school I joined the Friends of GUS organization and volunteered whenever I could.

"In college I interned at the GUS in their public relations office. I majored in Communications but I knew if I continued and got my law degree right away, I would be nothing more than another kid with a diploma. So I took two years off and went full time for the P.R.

"I made friends in the legal department and secured a part time job for while I studied law. In other words, I made myself indispensable. By the time I graduated, FCA wanted me as badly as I wanted them. Right now they are paying me one third of my salary, in order to keep me, while I do my time with the Navy."

"My goodness! I'm impressed. Is this what you mean by a life plan?"

"It's part of it. I'll tell you the rest someday."

"Why did you go in the Navy? It's not wartime; there's no draft."

"My Dad emigrated from France and he became the most dedicated citizen of the United States that I know. He instilled love for this country in me. His parents were Pieds Noirs and not treated very well. I always knew I would give my country two years. I just didn't realize the Navy would be giving more to me than I would be giving to the Navy."

"That's very patriotic. What are they giving you?"

"Time on Treasure Island, for one thing. I'm going to spend six months at sea; these are little boy dreams and I get to live them."

"If its adventure you want, why not join the French Foreign Legion?"

"I'm not that French, nor that adventurous."

Summer looked at him quizzically but chose to change the subject. "What's your dad do?"

"He's a tailor for Stauffer's; that's a fine menswear establishment in Manhattan. When I was in junior high school Stauffer got into costume-making for the theatres as welll. My dad split his time between the two businesses. My father is amazing with a needle and threat. He makes them fly. He taught me about fabrics and introduced me to the trade, but my interest always centered on the intriguing business end of entertainment."

"And your Mom?"

"She's the accountant for the Boys and Girls Center."

"Did you involve yourself in the Center growing up?"

"Not so much. I'd go there after school sometimes and hang out in her office, but I didn't take part in the Center."

"And your sister?"

"Sarah and I love each other like two interested strangers. I know a lot about her, but I don't know her. She's too young. I hope later in life we can be good friends."

Summer smiled. "Thanks. Now I've got a frame to put you in."

"That's a refreshing response. Most people say, 'Now I know you.' But a person's stats don't tell you who they are. You're right. You've put a frame around me."

The two talked through the rest of the morning, hardly noting the passage of time. Later, in the afternoon, Darce called. "Did Ron spend the night?"

"Darce! You know me better than that! He's surprisingly quite the gentleman. He simply packed my ankle in ice and left. This morning he came back before I woke up with lox and bagels for breakfast.

"And now? Did he hang around all day?"

"He went shopping. He didn't think I had enough in my

refrigerator and he's going to make crepes for dinner. I think he's getting a video, too. I really like this guy, Darce. Will Kirk have a fit if I keep seeing him?"

"Yes. But when has that stopped you?"

Summer laughed. "I hear him at the gate now. Shall I ask if I should invite you over?"

"Are you crazy? Enjoy the attention while you've got it!"

Ron came around the corner carrying four bags of groceries. "Hey, by any chance are you talking to Darce?"

Summer nodded.

"Don't hang up. I want to speak to her."

He took the bags to the kitchen and returned, taking the receiver from Summer. Covering the mouthpiece he asked, "Are you free for Thanksgiving? It's this Thursday."

Startled, she said, "Yeah, I know. I guess I am."

"Good." Then he addressed Darce. "Hello, lady of the house. I had a really good idea while I was shuffling around the supermarket. Would you and Kirk join Summer and me for Thanksgiving dinner in the Officer's Dining Room at Treasure Island?"

"Oh! What a great invitation! Even if Kirk says no, I'll make him say yes."

"Good. I'll have to wear my dress uniform and you'll have to wear your best; it'll be fun. Okay. It's a date."

By Thursday Summer could limp, but only in flat shoes. She entered the Officer's Dining Room, clutching Ron's arm, wearing a powder blue suit and one black flat, her wounded ankle being wrapped and secured in a moon boot. When they were seated, Ron reached under the table and pulled her injured ankle onto his lap.

She squirmed and rolled her eyes. "Ron," she whispered. "People will stare."

"That doesn't bother me, and I'm the one who has to live with these guys. Your ankle has to be elevated. "

She leaned back and smiled at him.

Kirk looked under the table and cocked his head at Ron. He

picked up his knife and started a rhythm tapping the edge of the table. Noticing a man whose shoulders were covered with ribbons giving him a raised eyebrow, he put the knife down.

Mrs. Farnsworth stopped by their table. "I've heard all about this ankle, which one of you is the afflicted one?" She looked from Darce to Summer and back again.

Darce puckered her lips, glanced under the table at her friend's foot in Ron's lap and nodded toward her for the elder woman's information. Summer then rolled her eyes at Darce as Ron introduced them.

"This is Mrs. Farnsworth who made lunch for us on that infamous day."

"That was the best picnic basket I've ever opened." Darce smiled, "Thank you."

"You're welcome." Mrs. Farnsworth stood behind Summer and stroked her aged hand down the blond hair and rested it on the young woman's shoulder. "I've heard mighty fine things about you, young lady. I'm sure he's taking good care of you. You be sure and take good care of him, too. He's a wonderful young man, almost like a grandson to me. Happy Thanksgiving to you all." She left before anyone could respond.

Another uniformed man with myriads of ribbons stopped by the table. Ron gently lowered Summer's ankle, then jumped to his feet and saluted.

"As you were, Lieutenant."

"Yes sir." But he did not sit down. "Sir, may I present my friends, Kirk and Darce Dalton and Summer McBride. Kirk is a stockbroker in the city and the ladies teach school, also in the city."

Kirk stood but before he could extend his hand, the officer chuckled and said, "I've seen you before, only you looked like beached seals the last time. You gave me the most amusing Sunday afternoon I've ever spent at the bar. I'm glad you survived." He smiled broadly at all of them and ambled on his way.

Darce buried her face in her hands. "I never thought about

that! We must have made quite a spectacle for the bystanders that day we went sailing."

Kirk had the knife between his fingers again flipping it back and forth trying to control his laughter. "You should have seen your face, man." He said to Ron. Then he couldn't control it anymore and began laughing out loud.

"What did he look like?" Summer caught the contagious laugh.

Darce's body rippled with laughter, too. "Like one of those fish … " her mouth aped a round hole opening and closing and she bugged her eyes open as far as she could.

"Ron, what were you doing?" Summer gasped.

Trying to remember what put his face into such a contortion, Ron started laughing, too. "In my mind, I could see Darce slip out of that parka and disappear under the water. With all my force I shouted No! No! No!"

"That must have been what saved the day!" Summer laughed. "What did I look like?"

Darce erupted into another gale of giggles, "You looked like you were teaching school. Earnest. Sincere. Methodical."

"So I held it together? Ron turned into a fish? Kirk turned into a ballet dancer? And Darce, laughing away in her water logged parka, turned into the fat lady at the fun house?"

Kirk, tears running down his cheeks, threw his napkin at Summer, then blushed and picked it up off the floor. He put his hand on his chest to catch his breath. "Sorry, buddy boy, for making such a scene in your fancy dining room."

Darce looked at the three with tender affection. "You know, our adventure at sea will bind us together for the rest of our lives."

The assistant chef approached the table at that point rolling a cart before him to slice the gleaming roasted turkey for individual requests. "Summer," Ron said, "This is turkey."

On Saturday Ron took Summer on a road trip in his curve-hugging 350Z. They drove out to Stinson Beach where they lunched and then wove their way up the coast to isolated Goat Rock Beach, headed over to Healdsburg for dinner and then wandered home. The bucket seats didn't promote any car cuddling, but Ron did hold her hand from time to time. Summer couldn't help but marvel at how comfortable she felt with Ron. They talked non stop and when they disagreed, they did it congenially.

On Monday Ron and Kirk met for lunch at their revered Tad's Grill. "Thanks again for inviting us for Thanksgiving. Treasure Island's quite a place. I hope we didn't get you into trouble. Everybody else in the dining room acted so dignified and we rolled in the aisles."

"Don't worry about it. Some of the officers said our contagious laughter jumped over on them and they enjoyed it vicariously. I had a good time. I'm glad you came."

"Did you see Summer this weekend?"

"Doesn't Darce give you a blow by blow?"

"We try to avoid Summer conversations. It's the only thing we ever argue about."

"For the life of me, Kirk, I can't see what you have against her."

"Well, try this on for size. In our senior year of high school, Summer was elected both Homecoming Queen and Prom Queen. How did she get those honors?"

"Because she was pretty?" Ron offered.

"No. Because the entire football team had her."

"The entire football team always lies through their teeth. It's fantasy talk. They never think above their belts. Give me a break. You believe locker room talk?"

"Yeah. Yeah. Listen. After the Homecoming Dance, the girls had a slumber party. Summer came in about four in the morning with blood all over her gown. Said it came from some fight in a bowling alley and she was an innocent bystander. Who goes to a bowling alley after the Homecoming Dance? Nobody believed her. The locker room talk, as you call it, said there'd been so many guys with her they couldn't remember who. Now is that the kind of a woman you want to hang around with?"

"Kirk, without even hearing it, I believe Summer's story. You know what I think? I think you liked Summer at some point in your growing up, and she didn't fall for you. Am I right or wrong?"

Kirk threw up his hands, "I give up. I've warned you in every way I know how. I leave you with one last thought. She's not the woman you described to me when we first met. She won't get you where you want to go."

Ron nodded his head. "You're probably right about that. But I'm right about you liking her, aren't I?"

"Okay, okay. So I had a crush on her in seventh grade."

"Ouch. Hard time to have a crush. Too much pride in the seventh grade."

"Believe me. It's no longer a factor."

"I realize that. It just established a tradition in your relationship, that's all. But let's move on. We have important business to handle. I'm leaving on a nuclear sub for six months of maneuvers. Our departure date is January 20$^{th}$. It's time I gave you power of attorney to make my investments for me.

"You know what I want. You've become a whiz at finding investments in the Theatre and Entertainment genre. In the last six months you've done all the research and I've followed every bit of advice you gave and we've doubled our money. I figure if you keep doing that well for us, I'll make millionaire in the next two years!

"I'll have my check from FCA deposited directly into my account with Waterston and Meddling. I'm tempted to have the Navy do the same because I certainly won't be needing money at sea. But something in here," he pointed to his heart, "tells me to stick with my plan. I planned to find a stockbroker I could train and trust, and I have, and I planned to give him my FCA money to make a fortune with, and you will. I'll stick with that."

Kirk took Ron back to his office and had Melissa come in

with all the necessary papers. "Hi, Ron. How's your friend with the twisted ankle?"

"Doing great. Sorry I had to ask someone else to take you home."

"Oh, don't be. We had a wonderful time and we've been seeing each other ever since."

"Funny how life works things out that way isn't it?" They got all the paperwork signed and Kirk walked Ron to the ground floor.

"Don't worry about a thing, Ron. I'll be sure to put the third into the Blue Chips as well. I'll make you a millionaire as fast as I can."

"And you, too. When I'm strolling down the Champs Elysees smoking my big fat cigar and wearing my Italian boots, I want you and Darce by my side."

"It's a date. Will there be anyone else with us?"

"I'll keep you posted."

The following weekend, on the way to pick up Summer, Ron stopped by a pet store and bought the turtle he ordered. He put it in a plastic tub he borrowed from Mrs. Farnsworth, along with a glob of raw hamburger from the Officer's Mess. He wanted his turtle ready to battle.

When he settled Summer in the front seat of his 350Z, he placed the tub in her lap. "You told me to dress casual, but I didn't think we were going turtle hunting," she said in surprise.

"Not hunting, racing."

"Racing? They race turtles? As a kid I hunted turtles, probably something a big city boy like you didn't do, but I never heard of anyone racing turtles. They barely move. Who wins? The one who doesn't move at all?"

"See? The big city boy has something bucolic to show the little country girl."

They crossed the Golden Gate Bridge and dropped into Sausalito. On the way to the racing turtle arena, Ron said, "I think I'll name him Fred. Doesn't that sound like a solid racing name? I came here eight or nine months ago and all the competing turtles had these pompous names, like Green Streak, or Water Winner. The one I really liked, The Tortoise with a Porpoise, sat there like a bump on a log. You have to have a water turtle for speed."

"Speaking of water, shouldn't we get some for this guy?"

"He'll have plenty of water in a minute. We'll fill that tub up with hot water so that when I put him on the race track he'll run like crazy!"

"That's cruel, Ron."

"It's not boiling water. That would kill him. It's really warm water so that he wants to get out of there and when he lands on the pavement he'll run for cover."

"How can you make a turtle run on a track?"

"You don't. It's a big circle with the starting circle in the middle. All the owners stand around the starting circle and at the sound of a horn they place their turtles in the little circle facing outward. Then the owners retreat behind the big circle and hold out food, or shout, or slap the concrete to get their turtles to run. The first turtle across the line of the big circle is the winner."

They raced Fred three times and three times Fred proved to be unbeatable. Luxuriating in their victory they graciously received a plastic trophy that said "Winner" around the rim. Ron gallantly awarded Fred to the runner-up, a discomfited regular who made a Friday night event of the races. Obviously accustomed to winning, his turtles appearing to be his best friends, the contender politely accepted the plastic trophy.

The night hovering over the bay brewed balmy, almost short sleeve weather. Ron and Summer strolled down to sit on the concrete embankment, the darkened Venetian deli behind them, their legs dangling over the tiny waves slapping against the wall. A panorama of San Francisco backed by black velvet and twinkling stars wavered across the water.

"Okay, you want to tell me your version?" Ron asked.

"My version of what?"

"Showing up at the Homecoming slumber party with blood on your gown."

Summer had to laugh out loud. "Kirk. Kirk. Kirk. What am I going to do with that boy? Don't tell me the version he told you, okay?"

"My lips are sealed."

"Ernie Ratcliffe took me to the Prom, captain of the football team and one of the nicest guys in school. You know you're supposed to party all night at those balls, but Ernie and some of his football friends from his youth group at church didn't want to party with the others. They didn't want any drugs or booze or anything like that. So we went to an all night bowling alley.

"We had great fun, bowling in our ball gowns and the fellas in their tuxes. About three o'clock in the morning, on my way back from the ladies room I passed a table loaded with empty beer bottles. From out of nowhere this guy grabbed a bottle, smashed it in half on the edge of the table, showering me with glass shards and he swung it at this other guy who charged at him.

"Through no fault of my own I found myself right in the middle of this fight! The guy with the broken beer bottle swung his arm in a full circle, smashing the other guy's face and ending by ripping through my skirt. The blood from the face soaked right into my shredded gown.

"An ambulance came for the guy whose face had been gouged; they wanted to take me, too, but I hadn't been hurt. Before the police took the guy with the bottle away, he came over to me in tears and apologized. I never did find out what triggered the fight. I had to throw my dress away and I really liked that one, but I probably wouldn't have worn it again, anyway."

Ron chuckled. "I told Kirk I would believe your story without even hearing it. But I'm glad I heard it. It's amazing that so many of us actually make it through those horrible years of high school."

"Especially Kirk. Thank goodness he had his stocks."

"Why especially Kirk? What made his years so difficult?"

"His three younger sisters made it hard on him. They're triplets. Triplets are a lot of work for any mother, but particularly for Kirk's mom. Both his parents have always worked at the auto parts factory outside of town. She couldn't quit when triplets were born; they needed the money. Kirk and his sisters stayed with grandma, but three babies and Kirk were too much for her.

"She put Kirk outside to play and wouldn't allow him back in till his mother got home. He wandered everywhere, all by himself. I remember him as a gaunt little boy with big, sad eyes. And dirty. I never understood why his mother didn't at least make him take a bath; but that just shows how neglected he was.

"In ninth grade a Math teacher that we all loved took pity on Kirk. Mr. Warner formed an investments club, one could join by invitation only and Kirk had the stellar position of being the first one he invited to join. They met at lunch and made trades on paper. Mr. Warner's the one who got Kirk cleaned up and instilled in him a drive for education.

"Kirk got a job as a paper boy in order to earn money to buy the Wall Street Journal. He read it from cover to cover every day. That kid had to get up at four in the morning to do that paper route.

"Some people said Mr. Warner's money started Kirk in the investment business, but I think his grandmother offered to start him. When he showed her his success on paper, she gave him some money, I heard $50, to trade for real. I don't know how much he made. I do know he put himself through college with his investments.

"By senior year at Mark Twain he became a regular fellow, looked like anybody else. He had some money to spend and could buy nice clothes. That's the year he and Darce fell in love."

Ron said, "He told me he had a crush on you in seventh grade."

"Yeah. And I wasn't too kind to him either, not that I intended to be cruel, it just turned out that way. I don't know why, I never asked for it or even wanted it, but I was always popular. I hope that doesn't sound arrogant to you but the truth is I always had people hanging around me. So when Kirk, who had no social grace whatsoever, stopped in the cafeteria by my table and kissed me on the cheek, a crowd of kids hanging around me, watched.

"He stank to high heaven and I thought I would throw up. I pushed him away, he landed on the floor, and I said, without thinking, 'Oooo! What's that smell?' For the rest of the year whenever the boys would pass Kirk in the hall they would mimic me in a falsetto voice, 'Oooo! What's that smell?'

"I tried to approach him to say I was sorry, but every time he saw me coming he turned and ran away." She paused for a moment, "I hope what I'm telling you will not turn you against Kirk. He was just a lonely forgotten little boy who has turned out very well, I think."

"No. It makes me appreciate him even more."

Chapter Six
# GOING TO SEA

Darce invited Ron and Summer for the day on Christmas. Before feasting on Chinatown delicacies, like roasted duck, they exchanged specially selected gifts costing less than $10. Ron found life jackets at the marshaled Army/Navy surplus store which he purchased for Darce and Kirk. For Summer he bought a sailboat in a glass bottle, but he had something else to present later on.

Summer had matching mugs made with their names painted on them, all four names, paired, on all four cups. Darce bought three elegant hand-blown glass Christmas tree ornaments with the date etched into the glass.

Kirk had only one gift, for only one person, Ron. He wrapped it in a shoe box and carried it around under his arm all that day until Darce finally allowed them to open their gifts. He paced back and forth as Ron removed the paper with painstaking care. "Well, well, well, what have we here?" he grinned as he slowly opened the lid.

He pulled out a piece of paper that kept unfolding until it

showed a graph measuring three feet square. "What's this?" Ron puzzled.

"Give it to me!" Unable to manage his manic excitement, Kirk seized the graph from a surprised Ron and spread it on the wall, since what remained of dinner and the gift wrappings afforded no space on the table. "You gave me power of attorney in December, right?"

Ron nodded, "Right."

"Look here. This column indicates what we had on that day. This column shows their value that day. The next columns mark the trades I made on the days I made them with their values and this column wraps it all up in what we have today and the last one fairly shouts what its worth."

Ron's mouth dropped open. He took the graph from Kirk's hands and walked around the room with it, gaping as he absorbed the work of his stockbroker. "You've doubled my money, Kirk. You've doubled my money!"

He looked at Summer incredulously, "He doubled my money." To Darce he said, "In less than a month, he doubled my money!"

Ron crushed the paper to his chest. "You've doubled my money!" Then he reached out with one arm and crushed Kirk to his chest with the graph squashed between them. They both started jumping up and down. "We've doubled our money! We've doubled our money!"

When they finally calmed down, Ron said, still in amazement, "You keep this up and I could be a millionaire by the time I get out of the Navy!"

"I'll do my best!" Kirk said.

There was no getting their minds on anything else. The two men analyzed the graph for the rest of the day, discussing each trade, each company. Kirk's research, being so thorough he could describe what the CEO's ate for breakfast, fueled Ron's dreams. "See what I told you? Stick with the entertainment industry. That's where I'm going to make my mark. I need to be involved everywhere and understand everything."

"I'm going with you Ron. I intend to know the industry better than you do."

Admiration flared in Ron's eyes. "You do that, Kirk. You won't be sorry, I promise you."

As the evening wore on, Ron remembered Summer and his surprise for her. She and Darce had slipped into the bedroom and were watching a video, the traditional Christmas offering of "It's a Wonderful Life."

"Summer? Are you ready to leave? I don't want to pull you away from the movie if you're engrossed."

"Yeah, I'm ready. I've seen this one every year since I was a kid. Not at my house, mind you, but I saw it at some friend's or another's. Usually Darce's." She found her shoes, collected her coat, carefully packed her ship in a bottle, her mug and her glass ornament, snuggling them in a box, kissed Darce's cheek and said thank you for giving her a lovely day and dinner.

In the car Ron asked, "Would you mind going someplace special with me? It won't take too long. I'm not going to tell you where, though. It's a surprise."

"Once again, you're full of surprises. Sure. I'm game."

Ron negotiated the curves through the Presidio to pick up highway 280. They mostly drove in silence, comfortable to be together. Taking the ribbon that rode the tops of the hills, Ron turned down to the Reservoir and parked. He came around, opened the car door and took her hand. "There's a special place I want you to see."

Yards and yards of clipped grass spread before them in the lush park setting as they strolled to and stopped before an open air Greek temple. As they approached Summer heard a sound she could not quite identify rising toward them. In the center of the temple an ornate barrier circled what appeared to be a wide well. "Listen." Ron said. The sounds of what Summer now perceived to be rushing water flooded their ears. He led her under the portico and they looked down at the white froth exposed by the open circle, the sound reverberating in their ears. They had to shout to be heard. The water bounced and crashed into itself off the stone walls of the Grecian well.

"It's from the Hetch Hetchy Reservoir near Yosemite. That's how San Francisco gets its fresh water."

Summer looked up with tears in her eyes. "It's magnificent! The power … It's overwhelming." They gazed down into the turbulent water, absorbed in their own thoughts, engulfed by the roar. Finally, he led her away to a bench in the gardens. They didn't speak. He fumbled in his pocket and took her left hand.

"Summer, you've come to mean a lot to me. I've got a life plan, like I told you, and to be honest, I don't know how this all fits, but I want you to wear what the jeweler called a friendship ring. I've heard it called a promise ring. I don't want to think of my life, my future, without you. I'll be away for six months, which gives us both time to think, and I'd like you to wear this ring so that you'll think about me."

He slipped the ring on her finger. Though sitting in the dark, she could see a circular aquamarine rimmed with diamond chips. She inhaled sharply and held her breath. She shook her head several times trying to form her thoughts and then she looked into his eyes and said, "Yes. I'd love to wear your" she paused, "friendship ring. I'll be thinking about you the whole time you're gone, anyway."

She kissed him. "I'm sorry. I really didn't think our relationship had come to the stage where I should buy you a special gift. I thought my no sex edict had turned you off and we were just meant to be fun friends."

He smiled, "That came as a shock, I'll admit. But I liked you and I decided that maybe getting to know you first could be the better course to take. I'm glad it worked that way. You're a wise woman. But Summer, you've got to know that … " He kissed her with more passion than she had ever experienced in her life.

As his lips then moved down her neck she mustered the strength to say, "But this won't help my thinking process."

He stopped, hugged her to him and breathed into her hair, "I admire you too much, Summer, to dishonor you." Then he put his forehead on hers, nose to nose and grinned, "You're the boss."

On New Year's Eve the foursome chose to dance the night away at the Sir Francis Drake. Ron and Summer, inseparable on the dance floor, fast or slow, hot and sweaty or cooling down, stayed plastered against each other. During a romantic slow song Ron spoke breathlessly into her ear, "Summer, I seem to be doing all my thinking at once and my thoughts are tangled. The one thing I know, of this I'm sure, I need you. The thought of being away from you for six months almost makes me ill."

They swayed to the music and then Summer whispered in his ear. "Ron, since you put that ring on my finger I have only been able to think of you. I can't seem to function in life anymore and think of mundane things, like paying my rent. I don't even know if I paid it. All I know is that–I love you."

"I love you, too." He said huskily and then kissed her with a deep sense of giving himself.

The band swung into a fast beat, but they kept swaying to their own soft, slow music, staring into each other's eyes, their bodies locked together, her arms around his neck, his arms holding her tight. They studied each other's faces.

Several songs later he frowned. "We have 19 days until I leave. And when I leave I can't contact you. I'll be on a nuclear submarine, out doing secret maneuvers. I can't let anybody know where I am or what I'm doing. If there were an emergency the Navy would handle it for me. Even if one of my parents dies, I won't know about it until I get home."

Tears formed in Summer's eyes.

"Please don't cry. I can't bear it."

"What you said makes me sad. What'll I do when I can't hear from you and I can't say, even over a phone, 'I love you, Ron'?"

He tightened his hold and they danced poignantly. They didn't say a word, swaying through many songs until Ron led her to a quiet table distancing them from Kirk and Darce and the pulsating noise of the dance floor. He took her hands between his and brought them to his lips to kiss her fingertips.

"My darling Summer, you said to me once that life is something that happens while you are busy making other plans. I've been following a strict plan since I formed it. Your plan has only one rule, but you've followed it strictly as well. Don't answer right now, but will you consider throwing away our plans and spending my last weekend with me in Carmel? Now don't hate me for asking that. Think of us and our future."

She looked away and frowned, but then looked back with wide eyes. "I made that vow when I was 14. I made it at the camp I told you about that I went to with Darce. The leaders proposed a chastity vow that we would keep until we gave ourselves to our husbands." She looked at him questioningly.

He answered, in halting words, "But if you've found your husband, does it really matter if you wait until you're married? Isn't that where we're headed, Summer? I know everything's happening so fast and I want us to take the six months to be certain, but I need you before I go. I've never been so sure about loving someone as I am about loving you. And if you say no ... " He looked away as if in pain and then looked back to say with a quiet smile, "You're the boss."

She smiled as she stood and led him to the dance floor. In his arms she kissed him, and whispered, "I'll go. But not before."

He exhaled deeply. "No. Not before. I want it to be special. I want our weekend to be something I can carry with me and remember all those months at sea, and you can think of me as the lover I want to be to you."

The next two weeks passed agonizingly slow and amazingly fast. Summer's students speculated she must be in love. No one could be as forgetful or as unorganized as their teacher appeared to be these days unless they were senile or in love. Ron had class after class, inspection after inspection to be completed before his maiden voyage in a nuclear sub.

Finally the fourteenth of January arrived and Ron came to

Summer's door with a dozen long-stemmed red roses and a bow-tied box from Saks Fifth Avenue. The roses she put in water and with trembling fingers opened the present. A stunning, sheer, peach colored negligee lay in the crisp papers. "It's beautiful!" she breathed.

He smiled. "To me we are going on our pre-honeymoon. If this were a post-honeymoon, you would have received one of those as a gift from someone else. I like this way better. I got to choose what I wanted to see you wear."

She blushed heavily, "It's so sheer."

"Like I said. I got to choose."

She opened her small suitcase and placed the nightgown on top. He zipped it closed. He took it outside and set it on the deck. When he returned he found her slipping on her coat. "All set?" he asked. She looked around and nodded.

To her surprise he picked her up and carried her outside. "Since we're doing things in reverse I thought I'd carry you out the door instead of in."

"You nut!" she laughed and kissed him as he put her down.

On Sunday morning around 10 a.m., someone pounded heavily on the door to Ron and Summer's cottage. "What the ... ? Who's there?" Ron called.

"Your favorite matchmaker. Open up!"

"Kirk?" Summer questioned.

"I can't believe this!" Ron got up, pulled his robe on and strode to the door. Yanking it open he said, "What are you doing here?"

Kirk and Darce peered into the room. Summer, wrapped in a sheet to hide the sheer peach gown peered back at them from the door to the bedroom. "It's a chivaree!" They cried in unison.

Ron turned to Summer indignantly, "Do you know what they're talking about?"

Summer snorted and buried her face in her free hand. Then lifting a reddened face she laughed. "It's an old Missouri custom.

Close the door, Ron, before they come in. We'll have to feed them if they do."

Trying to rise to the occasion, Ron negotiated a rendezvous in an hour at a restaurant serving brunch. Ron arranged to keep the cottage until eight o'clock that night. Thus mollified, he agreed to let Kirk and Darce chivaree them.

After lunch they walked along the beach, Kirk dawdling with Ron, Darce hovering near Summer.

"How'd you find us?" Summer wanted to know.

"Kirk told Ron about this place and Ron asked him to make the reservations. Duh! Did he really think we'd leave you alone?"

"Darce, tell me something. Do you remember those vows we made at summer camp to wait to have sex till we married?"

"Did we sign vows?"

"We certainly did! Don't you remember?"

"No. What about it?"

"I just wondered if you kept yours."

"Well, if I signed one, I kept it. Actually, Kirk and I ... " her voice trailed off, "What about you? You waited, didn't you? At least until now. I hope this has been a pretty good weekend for you!"

"It was good, Darce. It was good. I did wait, until I couldn't. I am curious, though. How did you and Kirk manage to be boyfriend and girlfriend for five years and not have sex?"

"I think going to church every Sunday of our lives played a big part. And you know me. I'm a third grade teacher and I tend to treat people as if they were third graders. When Kirk and I confessed we loved each other, I sat him down and explained I was madly in love with him and wanted to marry him someday, but I didn't want to have sex until then.

"Frankly, I thought he'd dump me. But he agreed. He said he'd always wanted somebody just for himself and he didn't want to know anybody else beforehand. You have no idea how much more that made me love him."

"But how did you control the desire? Love makes you want somebody, makes you want to give yourself to him."

"We didn't allow ourselves to get into that kind of a situation. We never parked; we never groped; we honored each other."

"Darce! You had to be tempted."

"I didn't say that. Of course we were tempted and we talked each other out of it. We got involved with things. I learned almost as much about stocks as Kirk knows. He took an interest in teaching and kids. Even now he visits my classroom about once a month and encourages the kids to follow their dreams."

She looked at Summer sharply, "Why all these questions? Are you okay with what happened this weekend?"

"Except for that little niggling guilt, or whatever it is, rumbling around in me."

"Relax. You're gonna marry the guy, aren't you? Anyway, it's done. And it was good, right?"

Kirk elbowed Ron in the ribs, "So?"

Ron frowned. "So what?"

"So, was she?"

Ron laughed. "She was, Kirk. She was."

Kirk snorted. "Pull the other one, Ron!"

"She was. Hate to burst your bubble, but Summer was a virgin."

The two chivareers finally left for the city at 5 o'clock. When Ron dropped Summer at her apartment he explained he could not see her until Wednesday night due to drills and exercises they were doing before departure. Wednesday the crew had leave starting at noon in order to finish any personal business.

"Why don't I take the day off on Wednesday? The minute you're free, come to me."

"Can you do that?"

"I still have seven sick days and I'll take one because I'm lovesick."

He smiled. "The leave lasts 24 hours. Can I spend the night?"

"I'm no longer the boss, Ron. You are."

"Then take Thursday off, too. Expect to be my prisoner of love for 24 hours."

"Aye, aye, sir."

"Will you come to see me off on Thursday, we leave about three, and wave from the shore?"

"Oh, I'd love to do that Ron," she sighed. "Just like a real Navy wife."

He gave her a long kiss and left.

On Tuesday Ron called Kirk. "Can you meet me for lunch tomorrow? I can be there at 12:30 and we can go over any final details about the next six months."

"Sure." Kirk said in surprise. "I thought we had all that covered."

"There's just one more thing I need to talk to you about."

They sat in their preferred booth at Tad's Grill. "What's up, buddy boy? You all set for this adventure?"

"Yup. My gear is shipshape as they say."

"What about our business together? You have a new idea or something?"

"No. I trust you, Kirk. You just keep doing what you do best and we'll both be happy with the results."

"Then what'd you need to talk about?"

Ron rubbed his eyes and pinched the bridge of his nose between his thumb and forefinger. "It's Summer." He looked away for a long time and finally back into Kirk's eyes. "I don't know what to say."

"Say about what?"

"I just don't know, Kirk. Except that she's wonderful."

"Well, great! You like her, she likes you. Darce and I are both happy for you; I mean even me. I finally let go and now I think you're a great couple."

"Yeah, but what if you were right? Think about it Kirk. What if you were right and Summer turns out not to be the woman to get me where I want to go? I told you when we first sat down together that I needed to marry the daughter of a producer or an investor or someone high up in the entertainment industry. I know I can do it. I know I can be what I've always dreamed of being: a big player in the business end of theatrics."

He sat back in his chair and rubbed his temples, his eyes shut, "And then I fell in love with Summer."

Kirk shrugged, "Maybe you don't need a wife like you described. Maybe you'll make it through your investments and through your job. Maybe you'll meet the right people and have the right breaks ... "

Ron butted in, "It's who you know Kirk. It's always who you know."

"But you can meet people without coming in the back door like that."

"That back door happens to be my insurance. If I need a leg up, having an influential father-in-law will be my protection. I had it all planned and then Summer came along and threw a wrench in my plans. What am I going to do?"

Kirk looked at the tablecloth and drew circles on it with his knife. He tried to hide the sadness in his face. "Are you thinking of breaking up with Summer?" Kirk couldn't bring himself to raise his eyes.

Ron looked at him a long time before answering. "No. That would break my heart. I'm supposed to be at her place right now. This 24 hour leave should have been all hers. But I know if I go over there, I will put her in the car and drive to Reno and marry her. I'm no different than any other swabbie. I want my woman and I want her to be mine."

"Then why don't you do it? I'll go get Darce out of school; we'll go with you and be your witnesses. It'll be great!"

"The thing of it is, Kirk, listen, hear me out. Summer never had a life plan. She only had a life rule, to be a virgin when she married. She threw her life rule away and as much as I'm glad she chose me to ditch it with, it made me stop and think. Am I willing to throw away my life plan? I'm so crazy about her, I can't think clearly to answer that question."

Kirk drew more designs on the tablecloth. "I'd hate to see you marry Summer and then regret having married her later on. If you're going to hurt her, I guess I'd rather you hurt her now."

Ron answered with passion, "I'd never regret having married Summer. I don't want to hurt her. But would I regret having given up my plan? Could it be there's another plan I just don't see?"

"I don't know what to tell you, buddy boy."

They sat for a long time in silence. Ron spoke in a reedy voice, "I can't see her today, Kirk. I can't do it. I'd break down and throw it all away. I need these six months to figure out what I want the most, Summer or my plan. Will you cover for me?"

"What do you want me to do?"

"Call her and make some excuse why I can't see her before I leave."

"I'll take care of it." Kirk said quietly. "What are you going to do?"

"I don't know. I can't go back to the barracks because she'll call. I think I'll join some of the guys down in the Tenderloin and get roaring drunk."

"Don't do that. Come over to the apartment or something."

"No. Darce will never forgive me as it is. I may never forgive myself." He grabbed his head. "She's got to be here when I get back." He exhaled sharply and dropped his hands. "You're right. I don't need to get drunk. I've never been drunk in my life. I'll go to one of those cinema complexes that have 25 movies in it. I'll go from movie to movie till it's time for the sub to leave."

Kirk reached across the table and took his friend's arm. "Ron, you're overwrought. Go to the movies; that's a good idea. You can even sleep through a few. I'll take care of business. I'll work this out with Summer, somehow, and you go take your six months to think this through."

Ron's eyes misted. "Thank you."

"Come on," Kirk slid out of the booth. "Let's get out of here."

He peeled off some bills to pay the check. Ron feebly raised his hand in protest. "You know better than that, Ron. The client always pays. I'll take it out of your account." The client dully smiled at his broker's wit.

"I'm so tired all of a sudden."

Kirk helped him on with his pea coat, put his arm around him and led him outside. "You sure you want to do this? Reno's only four hours away."

Ron mutely nodded, his internal pain weighing down his shoulders.

"Well then, lay low till your ship sails, or your sub floats, or whatever they say. Don't worry about this mess. You're the closest thing I've ever had to a brother. I'll take care of you." Kirk walked him to his car and watched him slowly drive away.

'Holy Cannoli!' Kirk muttered to himself. 'What do I do now?' He walked the streets thinking of schemes to keep Summer's heart from being broken and to save Ron's interest in her, if an interest really existed. 'What happened here? Has Ron used Summer and now he's discarding her? No!' Kirk respected Ron too much to think that. 'Sheesh! That guy is focused.'

Settling it in his mind that Ron was more self-contained than he thought, and that was exactly the kind of guy Kirk needed to ride with to the top, he suddenly thought of a plan. Ducking into a liquor store he asked the clerk for a pint of the stinkiest alcohol he had. He stuffed the bottle of rum the clerk called 'rotgut' into his pocket and headed for his apartment.

Without changing clothes he turned the TV on but muted the sound. The phone rang several times. Caller ID identified the first call as being from Summer; the second from his office; the third: Summer again. About a quarter to four he went down to the dumpster at the back of his building, taking the pint of rotgut with him. Making sure no one could watch, he poured the entire bottle all over himself, suit jacket, trousers, Florsheims, shirt, tie and everything. Then he threw the bottle in the trash.

He walked around outside until the sticky liquid dried, then went back upstairs and sprawled out on the bed as if he had passed out. Darce would be home at 4:30 and he half expected Summer to be with her. And she was.

He heard the keys in the door. Their muffled voices filtered down the hall as Darce dumped her books and shed her coat. Suddenly they were quiet. He almost laughed when he heard Summer say, "Oooo! What's that smell?" It took every ounce of courage that he had to hold it together when they burst through the bedroom door, but he bravely snored.

"Kirk!" Darce shouted. He allowed his eyes to roll open, but only stared at the ceiling. The women didn't have any more experience with drunks than he did so he knew whatever his performance was, they would accept it. He closed his eyes again.

Darce came to stand over him. "Kirk!" she shouted. He rolled his eyes open again.

"You don't have to shout." He slurred.

"Are you drunk?"

"Naw, jus' takin' a lil nap."

"You stink to high heaven! Where have you been?"

"I been sayin' goobye t' Ronnie boy." He rolled his head and saw Summer. "Oh, ther you ar. He sez t' say goobye t' you toooo."

"Kirk! I've never known you to drink! Get off that bed, get out of those clothes, and go take a shower! I'm going to make some coffee. We've got to make some sense out of this."

"Gooidea." He lurched to his feet and immediately began to strip.

"At least wait till Summer gets out of the room!"

"Oh. Sorry 'bout tha'." But he continued to strip. The two women hustled from the room closing the door behind them. He kept the act up in case Darce came back in. After his shower when he opened the drawer to pull out his grey sweat suit he allowed it to slip off its track and land on the floor.

Barefoot, he staggered down the hall. He languidly wrapped himself around Darce and gave her a sloppy, wet kiss. 'This is kind of fun,' he thought. 'If I'm drunk I'm not responsible for my actions,'

"Get away from me!" she pushed him and he staggered back. But then she cocked her head with a frown. "There's no alcohol on your breath, Kirk Dalton."

"I brusht my teef." He said, noting to himself that if he ever had to do this again he must remember to swill some of the rotgut around in his mouth.

"Sit down and drink that coffee!"

He saw the cup across the table and the chair pulled out for him, but he fell into the closest chair, the one by Summer. She wiped away a tear. 'I better make this good.' He thought.

He leaned toward her, "Lil Summer baby. Tha's what he kep callin' you. Lil Summer baby. When I lef to cum hom 'n tak mynap, ol' Ronnie boy was pass out on th'floor."

Now tears streamed down her cheeks. "Where, Kirk? I can go get him. I can go help him."

He screwed his face up as if trying to remember. "I dunno."

"Try to remember!" his wife callously scorned. "Summer called your office and the receptionist said you went to lunch with Mr. La Fave and never returned. Where did you meet Ron for lunch?"

He rolled his head around as if trying to remember, but couldn't come up with anything.

"Drink this!"

He drank the coffee, but grimaced. "I wanna Irsh coffee. Les go downahill."

"You can't even go down the hall, much less down the hill. Drink that coffee."

He took another gulp. "Toohot."

Darce pulled his head back by his hair. "Kirk, this maybe the most important day of Summer's life. Where is Ron?"

"His goin' on a sumarine."

"Where is he right now? Sober up and tell us!"

In response Kirk rolled his head around and crashed it to the table, pretending to pass out. He listened while Summer poured her heart out to his wife. His heart went out to her; she was his wife's best friend, but she was his friend, too. Somehow he had to protect her as well as protecting Ron and his own future with Ron.

Finally, after hours of 'sobering up', he established the fact that someone from the crew rented a room at the Hyatt, but he couldn't remember if it was the Regency or the one on Union Square. Ron invited him down to have a bon voyage drink with his buddies. The women concluded the drink must have been spiked to have such an instantaneous and debilitating affect on Ron and Kirk, both non-drinkers.

Summer suddenly stood up. "I better go home. He might sober up and call. He might even be passed out on my deck." She grabbed her things and rushed out the door.

Darce put Kirk to bed about eight o'clock. He lay in the dark, grinning at his performance, and then frowning at Summer's disappointment. On awaking in the morning he instantly remembered his role and feigned the famed hang over.

When he arrived home at 4 o'clock, he found Summer sitting on the steps to his apartment. She'd been crying.

"Want to come up?" he asked. She shook her head no. He sat beside her. He didn't know what to say so Kirk waited for her to speak.

"He didn't call. He didn't come see me. He didn't call this morning and ask me to come down and see him off." She paused, gathering her forces to speak again. "I did see him off, though. I waved goodbye like a real Navy wife. I went down to Fort Point and watched the submarine float by about three o'clock. I watched it go under the Golden Gate Bridge with all the sailors on top, standing in formation. If he was facing south he had to have seen me. I waved goodbye the whole time the submarine passed."

"Summer, I know he's crazy about you. Just wait for him, will you? You're supposed to spend this six months being certain, will you please wait the six months?"

"He's already made up his mind, Kirk."

"Listen. At that party, I remember him saying how he wanted to go get you and drive to Reno, get married and then you'd be his."

"But he didn't do it, did he? He didn't even call."

They sat silently for awhile, and then Summer spoke. "I didn't sleep all last night. I laid awake thinking over every detail that happened or had been said during these last three months. And here's what I concluded.

"You weren't drunk last night; you put on a pretty good act. I know you too well. You were covering for your friend, your client, the man you believe to be the most important ingredient in your career. You did a good job of it, too. A very convincing performance. Your wife probably doesn't even know it was an act. But I had too much at stake; I had to analyze it.

"I may be wrong, but I truly believe that Ron loves me. I couldn't come to any other conclusion than that. But I also concluded I don't fit into his life's plan, whatever that is. Until he wakes up to the fact that life really is something that happens while you're busy making other plans, there won't be any room in his life for me.

"There was something else I saw. In your own way, you've been trying to protect me as much as you were trying to protect him. Thank you for that, Kirk. I tease you about my being the second best thing that ever happened to you, but maybe you're the third best thing that ever happened to me. Darce's second of course."

"What was the first best thing?" Kirk asked through a constricted throat.

Beginning to weep Summer said, "I thought Ron was." She stood. "Tell Darce I'm going home to get some sleep."

"Shall we do something this weekend?"

"I'd be very poor company. I'm just going to stay home."

Chapter Seven
# THE LITTLE BROWN CHURCH IN THE HAIGHT ASHBURY

Before crawling into bed Summer called the Education Office and left a message on the tape saying she would not be in school on Friday. Saturday afternoon, after almost 48 hours of crying herself to sleep, waking, crying herself to sleep and waking again, she finally emerged, dressed and went out on her deck. A thin San Francisco afternoon awaited her, one where the sun comes out for two solid hours wedged between the banks of fog that cascade into her gully, morning and night. Weak rays of warmth tried vainly to penetrate her clothing to chaff her skin to life.

Shivering, she leaned on the railing looking down into the lush greenery clotting the ravine. Wondering what it would be like to land on such a hammock, she straightened, repulsed, and shook her head to clear those thoughts. Going inside for a coat, she also picked up her purse and decided to walk down the hill to the market. At the door she remembered something.

Taking a plastic bag, she opened the refrigerator and scooped all the gourmet treats she had purchased, for her 24 hours of being a captured prisoner of love, into the sack. She swung it by her side as she walked down the hill. There were always street people lingering on The Haight. They'd be delighted to receive her stash.

A toothless gem pushing a shopping cart filled with some man's junk, but obviously this man's treasure, gladly received her goodies. "Thank you, ma'am. I'm going to write this in my book. That way you'll get repaid."

Without an acknowledging smile she turned to head for the market when a brown shingled building caught her eye. It couldn't have been so much the bland building that attracted her, no, spiked up from the roof a white cross glinted in her eye. She idly walked inside and stepped into a heated argument batting about in the narthex.

Six women and two men discussed the merits of having the speaker walk down the aisle after seating everyone else, or having him on the platform before people arrived. Summer didn't even consider backing out the door; she wanted to see the sanctuary. "Excuse me,"

"Can't you see we're busy here?" one of the men snapped.

Summer nodded in reply and edged toward the big double doors. The voices did not vary their decibels as Summer opened one door and slipped into the quiet of the chamber of worship. She walked down the center aisle, ending at a railing with a padded, red velvet two by four running along the bottom. She had never seen a kneeling rail, but quickly surmised the purpose of this rosy board and looking around, finding herself alone, she knelt.

No words came to her mind or her lips. She simply looked at the hushed splendor around her and felt a peace. She wanted to lay down right there on the thick carpet, put her head on the red velvet cushion and take another nap. Maybe she would find some real rest here. But of course she didn't do it. There were those distracting eight quarrelers outside the door.

She wondered what to do next when she felt a hand on her shoulder. "Hello. My name is Alice. I was in the front hall when you came through. Forgive us for being so unfriendly. We're having a special meeting here tonight and everybody's nerves are frayed getting ready for it."

"Oh, that's okay," Summer said in a rather sickroom voice.

Alice bent over, solicitiously, "What's your name?"

"Summer." Before Summer could stand up, Alice joined her on the kneeling rail.

"It's peaceful here, isn't it? The Presence of God hangs around this place no matter how naughty we are." She nodded toward the narthex with a smile.

"Do you live around here Summer?"

"A block and a half up the hill."

"Do you live alone? Are you married?"

"I was." Summer looked at the blue aquamarine.

"And now you wear that ring to hide the indentations from your wedding ring." Alice smiled sweetly and Summer covered Ron's ring with her other hand.

"You are divorced, aren't you my dear?"

She shook her head and started to cry. "No. I'm not. I'm a widow. He's dead."

Alice, a thin, graceful woman dressed in corduroy trousers, a thick hand-knit sweater and clogs, took Summer in her arms and cried with her. They moved back to a pew and talked. Then she took Summer home for dinner and to return for the evening. Her husband, Charles, the snapping gentleman in the entry hall, assured Summer her jeans and sweatshirt were most appropriate for a church service, "After all. It's the 21st century!"

The speaker neither sat on the platform, nor piously entered after every one was seated. He milled around with the people. Alice introduced him to Summer. "My dear, I'd like for you to meet Tommy Tyson. He's a missionary to Switzerland and is doing an awesome work over there. He's opened a retreat center that plays an important role and is having an enormous impact on the nation, but especially in the French sector.

"Poor dear. He has to come home and raise money while his wife stays in Switzerland running things. How I wish missionaries were better cared for! Charles and I have spent the last five summers with the Tysons, helping out, gardening, mundane things, but our summers are the highest spiritual moments of our lives."

Tommy, an enthusiastic hand shaker, spilled his regaling laughter over her while his layers of flesh shook with his gusto. "Welcome. Welcome tonight."

Summer sat through the evening, kind of enshrouded in peace, but she didn't ask herself any questions. She simply allowed herself to be in the "now" of the moment. She even allowed Alice and Charles to drive her up the hill after the last attendee left the premises.

The next morning Summer awoke with just enough time to get to the Church service where Tommy Tyson was speaking. He caught her arm when she entered the door. "I had a dream about you last night. I dreamed you were living in Switzerland and were a tremendous blessing to the conference center."

Someone next to her mumbled, "Better pack your bags. His dreams always come true."

"I think he's confused me with someone else." Summer mumbled back.

Though glad she attended the service, immediately after church, desperate again for her solitude, she puffed her way up the hill. Summer found Darce sitting on her deck. "What are you doing here?"

"Are you kidding? After what you've been through? I called you yesterday afternoon, last night and now this morning. Where have you been?"

Summer unlocked the door, went inside and Darce trailed behind her. "I've been in church."

"Church?"

"I know. I don't go to church. But I went in this one and a woman asked me if I was married, I said I had been. She wanted to know if I was divorced at so young an age. I told her my husband died ... " Summer sat down heavily on the couch. The tears started again.

Darce sat beside her and linked her arm through Summer's. "Why did you say that?"

"Because it's the only way I can look at it."

"He's coming back in six months."

"But he's not coming back for me."

"You don't know that."

Unable to speak, Summer nodded her head up and down. Then she continued. "Anyway, this couple, Alice and Charles, somewhere in their forties, took me home for dinner and then there was a special meeting last night. Some missionary spoke. So I went again this morning. They're great people. They both teach at the University of San Francisco, they've never had kids but they love to help people. They kind of took me under their wing."

Darce spent the rest of the day with Summer; they took a long walk through Golden Gate Park talking about everything but the forbidden subject, Ron. Whenever Darce introduced it, Summer said, "Don't. Not yet."

For months following that Sunday the two women maintained a distance. Darce gave her friend the space to grieve and Summer preferred her solitude. She had not stepped foot in the Dalton's apartment since Christmas. On the Saturday morning before Easter, she called, "Are you going anywhere today? Can I come by and see you this afternoon?"

"Summer, come with us! I'm making a picnic because Kirky bought two spectacular kites and we're going to the Marina Greens to fly them."

"How fun. I'll go down the hill and buy one for myself."

"Come about twelve. Honk the horn and we'll come down."

"No. I'm coming up. I have something for you."

Summer swung two brightly colored Easter baskets in the door when Kirk answered her knock. A little stuffed bunny stood at the helm overseeing mounds of candy squashing the green shreds of plastic straw. Nestled beside each bunny lay an Easter card, one for Kirk, one for Darce.

"Hey! Great! You're taking up where your mother left off! Look Darce, the baskets are back!"

His wife came out of the bathroom brushing her hair. "Oh, thank you, Summer."

"Don't thank me. A florist arrived this morning with three baskets. One addressed to me and these two came for you. My mother sent them."

"Your mother? I thought when you left Cape Girardeau the two of you stopped talking."

"We never completely stopped talking. I mean we are family. But she's been very friendly lately."

"Why is that?"

"She called one time when I was on my way out the door to attend church and she panicked. She warned me about everything down to torture chambers hiding in the basements of every church. I've gotten a couple of nice gifts from her lately. I think she's trying to woo me away from the impending danger."

On the Greens Darce spread out an inviting bedspread on which she unveiled her country cooking and they dug into the fried chicken she'd brought, still warm from her skillet. They devoured the store bought potato salad, as they did the fruit salad. But the mouth-watering chocolate cake, straight Betty Crocker, an unbeatable recipe, added the piece de resistance.

Afterwards the three sprawled out on the bedspread, laying on their backs, looking at he sky, their heads almost touching, reminiscing. They realized they had been together for six Easters, and it would have been seven if Summer had not been in St. Charles last year.

"All those Easters and not once did we go to church together." Summer said.

"Shall we go tomorrow?" Darce asked mildly. "I'd kind of like to go to that Grace Cathedral. Kirk and I have talked about going to see it but we never have."

"I'd rather not." Summer whispered.

"Why not?" Darce turned her head to look at her friend in time to see a single tear run down toward her ear.

She took Summer's hand, "Did you and Ron go there?"

Summer nodded her head.

Kirk had turned to look but he missed the tear. He rolled over. "Ron La Fave went to Grace Cathedral? I'd like to know how … " Then he saw the second tear take the same journey. "No. I don't want to know at all." He rolled over to his stomach.

Remaining still for a moment, Kirk jumped to his feet. "Okay, ladies. Time to fly those kites!" He removed his from the package and shook it free. The two women did the same with theirs. Soon they all three had them sky born and through hours of trial and error learned to manipulate their strings to make their kites do admirable things.

Darce and Summer tired first, their shoulders and upper arms aching. By now Kirk had a following of little boys, running with him and shrieking as the kite dove and looped. "He'll be at this till dark! I'll have to drag him home."

She and Summer lay down on the bedspread again, watching dozens of kites fly overhead. "I see you are still wearing Ron's ring." Darce said softly.

"I'll probably never take it off."

"Then you're expecting him to come back to you?"

"I didn't say that. I don't know if he will or if he won't. I don't allow myself to think about that."

"What do you think about?"

"Oddly enough, I think about my life plan. I think I have a purpose here on this earth and I want to know what it is."

"Isn't the purpose of life to find someone to love, get married, love him, have his children, love them and do your best to be and do good?"

Summer smiled at Darce's simplistic response. "No, those are like the perks."

Darce rolled over to lean on her elbows. "How do you find your purpose?"

"You follow your heart."

"Well, see? Your heart leads you to find someone to love and so on!"

Summer rolled over to lean on her elbows. "Your heart has so much more depth than that. Way down in your heart there's a plan, planted there by a divine hand, and only when you follow that plan will you be truly happy." She frowned. "Ron said he had a life plan, but it was the wrong one because he's the one who devised it. The plan you follow has to come from the One who created you, from God Himself."

"Ooo. You're giving me the creeps. This is too deep for me. Where have you been getting this stuff? From that church?"

Summer nodded and plucked some grass, putting one long blade between her teeth.

"What else have they told you?"

Summer gave her friend a slow smile. "They've been more than kind, Darce. I finally confessed to that couple, you know, Alice and Charles, the whole story, the truth, that Ron is not dead and that we slept together like husband and wife.

"They said that sex before marriage is certainly a sin, but it's not an unforgiveable sin. If I confess to God, He will be faithful to forgive me. I told them I didn't want to be forgiven. I said I wouldn't take that weekend back for anything. I consider myself married to him, even though he dumped me. They're really concerned about me now. They told me I had to ask for forgiveness."

Darce sat up, "Summer, you are involved in a cult!"

Summer sat up laughing. "Darce, how would you know what a cult is?"

"I read. I listen to the news. A cult is any group that tries to control you."

"They're not controlling me. I fell in love with Ron La Fave when he asked me to dance at your dinner party. I'll never stop loving him. In that sense I am married to him. I'll never marry anybody else."

Great concern flashed from Darce's eyes. "But what if he doesn't come back to you?"

Summer smiled sadly, "I don't expect him to."

"But you didn't know him long enough to make such a commitment!"

"It's not a commitment. It's not a promise. I gave him my chastity."

"But ... !" Darce sputtered.

"Don't. Don't talk about it; that will stir me up and I don't need that."

Stifled, Darce stuffed her friend's pain into her own heart, knowing it would be safe there as Summer had no one else with whom she could confide. She and Kirk maintained an unspoken truce never to speak about Summer McBride. Kirk did not divulge his drunk act, or his talk with Summer on the stairs. Darce did not divulge her conversation on the bedspread. Both managed to protect Summer with ferocity of intention.

Mid-May Summer called Darce. "I've made a major decision and since you're all I've got I need to sit down with you face to face to tell you my plan."

"Sounds pretty serious, Summer. Have you told your folks whatever it is?"

"Yes. And my mother said they disowned me."

There was an astonished pause, "Get over here right now and tell me what it is."

"I'd rather not talk about it in front of Kirk. Can you come over here?"

"I can't. Kirky doesn't want me in your neighborhood at night."

"He's turning into a cantankerous old man."

"I know. I know."

"Okay, your neighborhood. Shall we meet at the B.V.?"

"Too noisy. How about the outside tables of the Cannery?"

"Perfect. In an hour?"

"You got it."

Settled with their cappuccinos at a quiet table in the far corner, Darce said, "Okay. No small talk. Just straight to it."

"Let me give you some background. Remember when we flew our kites?"

Darce nodded.

"That night I went to bed early. Since Ron left I sleep a lot. I lay in bed, staring at the ceiling and I decided to pray about my purpose. I told God I would do anything He wanted me to do. I preferred not being a school teacher, but if that's what He wanted, then that's what I'd do. However, if He had something better for me, I told Him I wished it would show up tomorrow. I was getting sick of being depressed all the time and I wanted to be happy again.

"The next morning when I went to church the Pastor took me aside and gave me a letter. It had been sent by the missionary who had spoken the very first weekend I went to that church, Tommy Tyson. In the letter he asked the Pastor to find someone who could be an administrative assistant to his wife.

"The Pastor said he thought of me when he read the letter. The Tysons are in their 50s, he wants his wife to be able to travel with him some and the work grows faster and faster and frankly, they can't handle it anymore." She shook her head, "Isn't that uncanny? I pray Saturday night and that letter ends up in my hand Sunday morning. I still can't believe it.

"Anyway, I applied for the job through a Mission Agency, and after running me through all kinds of tests and applications, they accepted me. The Retreat Center, its called Le Centre de la Paix Divine, will pay me a pittance. They certainly won't pay as much as I'm making as a teacher, but they will give me room and board."

"Where is this place, Summer?"

"Switzerland."

"Switzerland!" Darce shouted.

"Isn't that perfect?"

"Why is that perfect? It's halfway around the world?"

"Because I speak French."

"But Summer, it took all my courage to come to San Francisco! How will I ever get to Switzerland to see you?"

"Don't be silly. You'll be there within a year. We'll hike in the Alps and learn to yodel. Besides, you have to visit Poland, and Switzerland is nothing more than a stop along the way."

Darce grimaced, "Spare me."

"I'm very excited about going, Darce, so please don't rain on my parade."

"Why didn't you want to tell Kirk? You don't mind if I tell him, do you? I mean, he has to know."

"You can tell him. I just couldn't. Kirk is very strong about what he thinks is right and I don't think he would think this is right. He would think I am running away."

"Are you?"

"No. There's no place to run to or from. If Ron ever wants me, he'll find me."

"Is this why your parents said they would disown you?"

"Not because I'm going to Switzerland. For me to live in another country is an exotic thing, a most unconventional thing for me to do. No, it was when I told my mother that I loved Jesus. She went berserk. Called me a Jesus Freak, whatever that is. I haven't heard from her since, but I've heard from her lawyer. He wrote an official letter to officially tell me that I had been officially taken out of the official will. Can you believe that? Just for loving Jesus."

"You must have laid it on pretty thick."

"I told her what was in my heart. From December 25th to January 20th, I lived the greatest passion I have ever known. I loved with abandon. I feel that same way about Jesus. My body may never know that passion again, but my heart will always have that passion with Jesus."

Darce's eyes misted. "I think I knew Jesus like that once."

"I know you did. I remember you at camp, a sophisticated fourteen year old who cried all night and when I asked you what was wrong, you said you were happy."

"I remember that! There was some kind of candlelight service, wasn't there?"

"Up on a hill."

"Yes, I remember! My heart was so full. I guess full of Jesus. I wanted to give Him my heart and ask Him to live in it. I wanted to surrender to Him. Strange. I can remember wanting that, like I was captured in battle, or something. But I don't remember actually doing it. I just remember feeling really happy with the thought of doing that." Darce rubbed her friend's arm. "We've been through a lot together, haven't we?"

Summer nodded.

"We're going to be together forever, Summer. The fact that you are moving to Switzerland will not separate us. I don't know how, but it won't."

Chapter Eight
# MOVING ON

Summer thought it rather symbolic that she left San Francisco on June 20$^{th}$, exactly five months after Ron left. Landing in Geneva she called Darce from a pay phone in the airport, "I made it! Tommy Tyson and his wife, Ruth, have met me and told me to call anyone who needs to know I'm safe because the phone system is difficult at the retreat center. I'll write a long letter tomorrow describing everything."

The letter arrived two weeks later.

> Dear Darce and Kirk,
>
> Remember the scenery in The Sound Of Music? This place is a hundred times more beautiful! The retreat center is an old chateau nestled in the hills, or I should say tucked in a crevasse of the mountain. All walking is done on the vertical. The building is made of dark native wood, but the interior is stone and marble, huge spiral staircases, windows with little diamond shaped glass–impossible to clean!

There are forty guest rooms, big rooms, too. Forty guests aren't many to take care of except that each one requires sooooo much attention; they're here for psychological rest. I have a staff of five: a cook, a waiter/kitchen helper, a housekeeper, a grounds man and an office worker. I could use five more. A psychologist comes once a week and holds group therapy sessions. The local doctor is on call, and he's been here twice today. Europeans have a different point of view about medical personnel than Americans. Doctors still make house calls here.

I live in one of the guest rooms; it's big and roomy and has the most incredible view. There are actually 45 guest rooms, but five of them are reserved for the workers. The Tysons have a little cottage on the property and the grounds man lives in town. The town is adorable. I can hardly wait for you to see it, Darce.

Ruth and I will organize the guest's time: recreation, etc. But she intends to turn the running of the place over to me at the end of the month. Yikes! All Tommy does is fund raise, whether he's in the States or here in Switzerland. But he also preaches at the retreat center.

My address is:
Summer McBride
Centre De La Paix Divine
14 rue du Chien de Berger
1740 Stade des Etoiles
Suisse

Ron will be back in San Francisco soon. Please don't give him my address. I would like to know if he asks about me, though. Please write. I love you two!

*Summer*

Ron's nuclear submarine ended maneuvers and floated into San Francisco Bay, berthing on July 20th, six months after its heartbreaking departure. As soon as he could get his gear dumped into his barracks and pull his 350Z out of storage, he headed for Clayton Street in the Haight Ashbury, stopping only to buy a dozen red roses.

He tried the gate to the wooden walkway. Locked. Odd. He rang the bell. A demure young Oriental woman peeked around the corner. "Yes, may I help you?"

"I'm looking for Summer McBride. She lives here."

"You are mistaken. She does not live here. My husband and I moved into this apartment on July 1. I think you must be referring to the lady who lived here before us. She moved away. We never met her so we don't know where she is. I'm sorry." She disappeared around the corner of the building.

Ron pulled out his cell phone and called Kirk at the office. It was closed; there was no one at the switch board. He looked at his watch, 5:30. He called Kirk's apartment. No answer. He called Kirk's cell phone.

"Hello?"

"Kirk, I'm frantic here!"

"Ron! You're back!"

"Yeah, and I'm at Summer's place and she's not here."

"Well, that's a long story best told in person. Darce and I are about to sit down to dinner at The Waters. Want to come join us?"

"I'll be right down."

While they waited for Ron, Kirk tersely reminded Darce, "Remember. We're not playing God. Whatever happens between Ron and Summer is between them."

"Don't worry about me, Kirk. I still haven't forgiven him for what he did to my best friend."

When Ron arrived, Kirk and Darce, already seated, were all smiles. But Ron charged into the restaurant with one thing on his mind. "Where's Summer?"

"Hey, Ron," Kirk chuckled. "We're glad to see you too."

"How were your months at sea?" Darce smiled encouragingly.

Ron looked at them incredulously. Then he breathed out, relaxing his body and smiled at them affectionately. "Of course. You guys don't know what I've been going through."

"No." said Darce enthusiastically, 'Tell us all about it."

"My voyage started and ended as we left San Francisco Bay. The whole crew mustered on deck, standing in formation and I stood on the port side, facing south. As we passed the city I thought how fortunate I had been to have escaped a marriage that wouldn't have worked for me.

"Then as we passed Fort Point, I saw her. All alone, the only one down there waving goodbye. As I watched that beautiful figure languidly waving, her arm overhead moving back and forth, her skirt rippling in the breeze, I realized I had missed the most wonderful marriage I could ever make. I couldn't break formation, I couldn't move, I couldn't wave back, but my heart leaped out of my body to rush to her and beg her to please wait for me.

"My voyage ended then because no matter what I did for the rest of the time at sea I thought about Summer. I dreamt of Summer. I despaired for Summer. I'd try to focus on what I had been ordered to do and within minutes she would be back in my arms. Now where do I find her?"

Darce stifled an icy look. "You thought you saw Summer at Fort Point? That couldn't have been her. She would have told me if she had done something like that. See, you saw some other woman waving goodbye. Probably in the haze of your hangover you imagined it to be Summer. Actually," Darce rolled her eyes up as if in reflection, "if I remember correctly, when you didn't show up on Wednesday, Summer went back to school on Thursday. She got out at 3:30, as always, and went home for a nap because she had waited up quite late for you. "

"You're not very convincing. Summer stood and waved from Fort Point, Darce. I know Summer. Please tell me where I can find her."

"Well, we're very excited for her, aren't we Kirk? She's moved to Switzerland."

Kirk kicked her under the table, "Well, at least that's where she said she would probably be heading." Darce added lamely.

"Did she find a teaching job over there?"

Darce laughed a falsetto laugh, "I don't think French speaking people need Americans to teach them their own language. Summer wanted to stop teaching, so I imagine she'll find something else."

"How long will she be gone?" Ron asked crestfallen.

"As I understand it, Summer has made a permanent move, Ron. She told me that if I wanted to see her I would have to visit her there."

"In Switzerland." He clarified.

"Wherever. I'm sure she'll let me know where to find her. Sometime."

Ron looked at Kirk, "So she's not in San Francisco?"

Kirk, flipping a pen between his fingers shook his head no.

Then Ron addressed Darce. "I can see you are angry with me, Darce."

"Why no, not at all. Did you visit any exciting ports of call that you can tell us about? We don't want to know the government's secrets of course."

He turned to Kirk, "I don't think I'm up for this tonight. Can you and I have lunch at Tad's tomorrow?"

"I've already got you penciled in, buddy boy. I'll bring the paperwork. We're this close." Kirk pinched his thumb and forefinger almost together. "You get some rest tonight. We can talk about how to top off that million tomorrow. Anything I can do for you? Anything at all?"

Ron put his hand on Kirk's shoulder, "No. If you can't provide Summer, you can't do anything for me. But I sure am glad to see you. You're right. I'm tired. I'm going back to the barracks now, but tomorrow I'll be cool."

"Like I said, you get some rest. I can give you the whole day. You let me know what you want. I'm glad you're back!"

As he stood to leave, Ron leaned over Darce and kissed her cheek. "I'm still a good guy." He whispered.

When Ron left Darce hissed between her teeth, "I wanted to gouge his eyes out!"

Kirk chuckled, "Funny, I thought you did."

"Listen, sweetie, I don't want to socialize with that man one bit while he's here. You said he officially leaves the Navy July 31 and then he's off to New York. I'll do whatever it takes to keep him as your client and get him out of town, but please keep it at a minimum."

The next day, commandeering their preferred booth at Tad's Grill, Kirk pulled out another squared graph, but Ron stopped him, "After lunch will be soon enough."

"You've got to be kidding me! I'm holding the greatest news on the earth in my fist and you want to wait until we eat?"

"I want to wait until you fill me in about Summer."

Kirk folded the paper, replaced it in his inner coat pocket, folded his arms on the table and said, "Okay. Ask me what you want to know. I probably won't have very many answers for you, though."

"Darce has the answers, doesn't she? And you and Darce still don't talk about Summer?"

"You got it. So ask away."

"Where is she?"

"Switzerland."

"Can you be more specific?"

"No."

"Is that because you won't be, or you don't know?"

"I don't know." Kirk lied.

"Can I get in touch with her?"

Kirk's knee, which had been popping up and down, now stopped in trepidation over his answer. "She doesn't want to hear from you, Ron. She's moved on with her life. You will too."

Tears came to Ron's eyes; he looked at the table as he swallowed, trying to make himself capable of talking. "What happened the night I left? How did you handle it with Summer?"

Kirk's knee started popping up and down again as he swung into the description of his class A performance as a drunk. Ron even smiled a few times during the telling. "You chose a good way to handle it. Did it work? Did she believe you?"

"At first. She and Darce gave me what-for about getting drunk! But Summer's a smart cookie. I've never told Darce this but Summer came to see me the next day. She'd been up all night putting the pieces together and she'd figured out my drunk had been an act. You were right. That was her down on Fort Point, Darce just doesn't know that. Please don't tell her.

"Summer also had you pretty well figured out, ol' buddy boy. She knew you hadn't been drunk either and she guessed she didn't fit your future lifestyle. She didn't ask me to confirm her conclusions and I didn't.

"I've come to admire Summer. She really has moved on. By the time she left, she'd lost interest in you. Now you've gotta do the same. You've gotta move on. I hate to be so harsh, but that's how it is."

"Why did she come to you instead of telling Darce all this?"

"I think she wanted to thank me for trying to protect her."

"Protect her?"

"With my drunk act. I've never seen a woman so broken up and though she didn't express it, I could sense she gushed with gratitude that I tried to soften the blow."

"See? If I could just go to her! Get the address from Darce for me! Will you Kirk? Please?"

"I've asked her for it already and she says over her dead body. But there's no point, Ron. Summer's gone and I think she's happy now. Leave her alone. Let me show you the good news. You're so much closer to your goals. You'll be out of here in a week, a week and a half, back to New York where you'll begin your finesse and your finagling into the Entertainment world. All those dreams are about to come to pass."

Grinning, Kirk pulled the paper out of his pocket and spread it on the table. Ron gave him lackluster attention at first, but then got caught up in the fervor of his dreams materializing on paper.

Kirk said, "You've been giving me $3000 a month to invest for 18 months. Here's the progression from where we started. The first eleven months were slower because I had to wait for your decision to buy or sell."

"And in the seven months you've had power of attorney?" Ron asked with wide eyes putting his hand on his heart. "Am I ready to see where we are today?"

Kirk turned the paper over to reveal the last seven months and sat back waiting to bask in Ron's appreciation.

"Kirk, this can't be true. The paper you showed me at Christmas was $106,111. It was an easy number to remember. Surely there's an error in this. How could you make $106,111 multiply to $836,797?"

"Hey, I made 12, 15 trades a day. I've had an awesome time! And that's not all, buddy boy, that's just your risk stock. There's another third in Blue Chips." Kirk pulled out another graph showing the moderate third. "See, I didn't take a third out of the $3000, which is maybe what you wanted me to do, but I took it out of the earnings at the end of each month. Therefore, I had a lot more to put into Blue Chips."

"Then I'm a millionaire! There's $218,403 in these!"

"No you're not a millionaire yet. Don't even allow yourself to think that way. The Blue Chips are unnamed, unknown and unidentifiable because they are sitting on the back burner in case of emergency, remember? Don't even think about them. You and I picked the stocks we thought were the safest and every month I'll keep slugging money into them just like I've been doing. Maybe next year we'll analyze the lot and see if we want to change any.

But otherwise, they are off-limits, so don't include them in your plans."

The two men had stood to lean over the graphs like architects over a drawing board. Ron poked Kirk's chest with his finger. "What I want, now that I see what you can do when you're given the freedom, is to be able to invest in a movie. I want you to earn me enough money to bankroll a low budget movie. My name will be on it. I'll start making my mark."

"What'll that take?"

"Maybe four million?"

"That's not very much for a movie."

"There's a ton of them being made for less than that every year. Everybody's looking for an 'Easy Rider.'"

"What's that?"

"A low budget movie produced for less than $400,000 and which brought home over $50,000,000."

"Wow! Then what we have to do is build you up to 12 million so that you only take out one third of what you've got. We've got to keep building your profits."

"In the time it takes you to build the financial base, I'll be able to find a winning script!"

"Remember, I'm in this with you. Two thirds of my earnings go into this project."

"And how are you doing?" Ron asked solicitously.

"Darce and I agreed we would live on her teacher's salary so I could pour my money into a parallel position with you. I've averaged $1500 every month to put in there. I've got half, buddy boy, half of what I've earned for you. And you know where it comes from? My commissions off of your trades. You're my only client now."

"What does Waterston and Meddling say about that?"

"They're happy. They get a chunk out of you as well and they see a bright future with you."

"Don't you mean with you? You're the one making money for all of us."

Kirk shrugged. "I stay focused, Ron. Focused. You stay focused and we'll hit the big time."

Summer's letters came every week, but Kirk didn't read them. He didn't want to know any information in case Ron should ask. And Ron asked every week, "Have you heard from Summer?" Even when he moved back to New York and started working at FCA, it remained a weekly question.

And Kirk could say, "Don't know a thing."

Sometime in mid-October they received a letter from Summer that greatly upset Darce. "She's in a cult, Kirk, I know it!"

"How do you know?"

"She never has any time off, she has to do whatever they say, she's like a prisoner there!"

"Did she say that in so many words?"

"Kirk! I know my friend. She wouldn't say that. I can read between the lines."

"Even if that's the truth, there's nothing you can do about it. Until Summer gets fed up and gets out of there, she'll have to suffer."

"I've been reading about people who kidnap their loved ones who are caught up in a cult. Maybe we should go over there and take a look-see, you know, check it out for ourselves."

Kirk, standing in his underwear and slippers before the television, flipping through the channels, turned to her incredulously. "Do I look like the kind of guy who goes to Switzerland and kidnaps people?"

"We could at least take a spy trip and uncover what's wrong!" she huffed.

"I've never been out of the United States and you want me to play James Bond in a country where I can't speak the language? At least everywhere he went they spoke English!"

"Well my mind's made up! We're going over Christmas!"

"Christmas! They'll be up to the gazoo in snow! I can just see me now, floundering around in snowdrifts over my head, sliding all over the place and not being able to say an intelligible word.

I'll be yelling 'Help!' and they'll be smiling and waving at me! Darce, can't we talk this over?"

He didn't break the news to Ron until the second week of December. "My wife seems to think we need to spend Christmas with Summer so we're headed to Switzerland for Darce's two weeks vacation from school."

"Kirk! Take me with you!"

"Agh! You don't want to go on this trip. I hardly want to go. Those two women will be yapping day and night, catching up on six months. I remember what it was like when Summer came to San Francisco. I thought I'd never get my wife to myself."

"Kirk. Kirk. Can't you hear my heart? I want another chance with Summer. I'm miserable here in New York! I bum around the streets acting like an old wino."

"Get yourself a date, Ron. Socialize. Force yourself. You'll like it after awhile."

A long silence ensued and then Ron said, "I don't want anybody but Summer."

Chapter Nine
# THE CENTER OF DIVINE PEACE

Summer met Kirk and Darce in Geneva and drove them directly to Stade des Etoiles. Flashing by the stunning architecture of the city Darce complained, "Can't we see Geneva?"

"Maybe later. Right now I have to rush to get us back in time for Sunday morning services."

Darce raised her eyebrows and gave an over the shoulder look to Kirk. He shook his head as if to caution her from jumping to conclusions. Then she replied to Summer, "Oh, good. I'd love to hear this Tommy Tyson preach, you've raved about him so."

As they drove, Kirk commented from the back. "Do you get a lot of nose bleeds?"

"You mean from the altitude?"

"Exactly."

"Relax, Kirk."

"How about motion sickness?"

She swung around a work horse pulling a hay wagon and darted back in her lane as an approaching car thundered past them. Kirk jerked his head to see if the car would clip Summer's car. "That was only inches to spare!"

"You have to learn to drive like they do! Kirk, please relax."

He tapped Darce on the shoulder, "Remember how I told you I would be floundering in the snow and yelling help while they smiled and waved?"

She nodded.

"Change that. They won't smile and wave. They'll flatten me like a pancake and never even notice the bump in the road."

"What's that?" Summer asked Darce.

"Don't pay any attention to him."

Tommy Tyson gave a stirring and poignant sermon on love that moved Kirk to whisper to Darce after it was over, "That was great! Almost makes me want to become a Christian."

"I thought you were one."

"I thought so, too. But this guy makes me wonder if I live like one. After that sermon don't you think this guy is on the up and up?"

"Kirky, trust me. This is one subject in which you are really ignorant. All cults preach love! That's how they draw in their followers. Everyone's hungry for love."

They ate lunch in the dining hall with Tommy and Ruth Tyson. Tommy, bear-sized, belted a laugh from his upturned lips at every bend of the streaming conversation. Ruth, a small bedraggled woman, obviously bearing the burden of the Center of Divine Peace on her sloping shoulders, spoke softly, attending to Summer. Tommy, however, cornered Kirk.

"A stockbroker, huh? I bet you think you can buy your way into heaven!" This caused him no undue sense of glee. "But tell me, honestly, how can you break a stock in order to earn the title of stockbroker? Is it kind of like breaking a horse?" His flesh rippled as he privately enjoyed his little joke.

"Tommy, please." Ruth quieted him.

"Kirk, here, he thinks I'm funny. I mean what's the point of living if you can't have joy? Jesus was the most glad of all his fellows! I'm glad! I'm just plain glad and I like to laugh. My dear sweet wife takes things too seriously. That's why I'm glad Summer's come to be part of us. It makes things much easier for my Ruthie. Now how about you, Kirk, aren't you glad about Jesus?"

His mouth hanging open, Kirk looked at Darce, "I think it might be time for me to go flounder in a snowdrift."

"You? Floundering?" Tommy put down his fork and pulled Kirk to his feet. "Come with me, boy. Lunch can wait when eternity calls."

Kirk walked backward as he said to his wife, "What'd I tell you! Flat as a pancake."

Tommy sat Kirk down on the far side of the dining room and huddled in conversation with him. "He'll have Kirk born again before they return to the table." Summer smiled.

"Born again?" Darce questioned.

"Darce, that's what happened to you when you were 14 and you cried all night. You just haven't been living for Him, that's all."

"What do you mean? I'm a good person!"

"Of course you are, but living for Him means to know Him and to love Him and to obey Him."

"You mean, Jesus?"

"Of course. There's no other living God. All the other gods, like Buddha and Mohammed, left rules and traditions and then they died. Jesus lives, today; He's God, the Lord of our lives. To know Him is to love Him; to love Him is to obey Him."

"That sounds like a circular mantra, Summer. Listen to it. 'To know him is to love him; to love him is to obey him, to obey him is to know him; to know him is to love him; to love him is to obey him; to obey him is to know him.'"

"It's not a mantra to me. It's how I live. It's how we all live."

Darce turned to Ruth. "How about you? You look like you're the pragmatic one of the bunch. Do you think the things that go on here are a little strange?"

A smile wreathed Ruth's face that made it seem like sunshine broke out in the room. "No. I wish the whole world could live like we do. We live in harmony, peace and joy. I know my face looks dour, but that's because I've always taken on too much responsibility. The Lord doesn't put that on my shoulders, I do. It's a terrible guilt left over from my childhood, added to a bit of perfectionism in me, but I'm getting better. I can't help but get better with Summer here." Ruth looked around her. "The Presence of God fills this place. Can't you feel it?"

Summer looked at Darce hopefully.

Darce looked down and frowned, "No. I can't."

Tommy returned to the table and Darce saw Kirk go down the stairs toward the chapel. "Your husband needs a little time alone. When you meet Jesus face to face you need some quiet time. Now, how about you, Darce?"

She straightened her shoulders, "To tell the truth, I think my friend Summer has been caught up by a cult. I came over here to help her escape, if possible."

Summer snorted and covered her grin with her hand. Tommy stood again, "Darce, could you and I talk over in that same corner where I sat with your husband?"

"Don't you want to eat your lunch?" she asked, hoping to divert him.

He laughed a belly laugh, "Do I look like I've missed any meals? Come on, now. I won't bite and the whole world is watching. I promise I won't hypnotize you or do anything scary."

Darce, not to be cowed by the man, went to the corner. They talked for two hours. Summer and Ruth cleared the dining room and helped the few remaining guests back to their rooms.

Most guests gleefully hobbled home for the two weeks vacation to be with family. Cook took the first week off and the kitchen helper, deferring to the boss, took the second. The office manager managed to swing both weeks. The housekeeper arranged to take three days each week and the groundskeeper only dropped by to clear away freshly fallen snow.

Summer dutifully stayed on the job permitting Tommy and

Ruth to join their children in Florida to take a family vacation at Disney World. With only eight guests in residence and a reduced staff, Summer planned to take daily outings with Kirk and Darce.

They laughed and played in the snow like the three little kids they used to be. Christmas day they exchanged gifts and gave the guests a little something Summer prepared and wrapped for each one. On various nights they visited the numerous café-bars in the village or they sat around the enormous fire they made in the living room fireplace and reminisced. Inevitably the conversation turned to Ron and Summer would say, "I don't know why I brought that up. I don't want to hear about him."

In bed one night, the duvet pulled to their chins in the chilly room, Kirk whispered, "Do you think I should try to get Ron and Summer back together? Ron says he only wants her, nobody else."

Darce snuggled up to him, "Kirk, if I was in Switzerland and you were in New York and you thought you wanted only me, what would you do?"

Kirk half smiled, "I'd swim to Switzerland, if I had to. I'd go crying through every village, I'd climb every mountain, I'd cover every inch of this country and I'd constantly yell, "Darce, your lover boy needs you!" until I found you."

She giggled, "I hope you would find something a little more romantic to yell, but the point is you wouldn't be sitting in New York, would you?"

"No." He rolled over and pulled her to him to whisper hoarsely in her ear. "I'd yell, 'Darce, I love you. I can't live without you. You're everything to me. Please don't ever leave me again or I'll die.'" Their kisses blotted out the rest of his words.

The first morning back in San Francisco, Kirk's office phone rang at nine a.m. Normally, Ron called at eight, saving the longer conversations for later in the day. By eight a.m. Kirk's time, the market had been open for two hours, so they simply checked in with each other. Kirk looked at the receiver, not wanting to pick it up. He'd been sweating this call, but especially for the last hour, since it seemed to dawdle and came in late. Maybe Ron wanted to avoid the inevitable as well.

"Kirk Dalton here."

"Kirk, how was Switzerland?"

"Hey, buddy boy, it was cold. How come you're late calling?"

"My boss had a death in his family so he held a meeting to outline projects before he left for the funeral. So, what about Switzerland?"

"There was a whole lot of snow, which we played in. We had a good time.

"Let me be more precise, how was Summer? Did she ask about me? Can I go see her?"

There was a pause as Kirk gathered his courage. "Ron, I didn't know how to tell you this before, and maybe I was hoping it wouldn't actually happen, but," he paused and took a deep breath, "Summer got married. That's why we went over there so that Darce could be her maid of honor. I hate to be the one to tell you; I tried my best to get her to change her mind, but she wouldn't listen and it happened. Summer's married."

"To whom?" Ron said in a voice of unbelief.

"A Swiss dairy farmer, an older man, heck of a nice guy, though. His cows wear those big bells that clang and echo all over the mountains. She seems very happy and he's nuts about her. I thought he ought to tone it down myself, but Summer didn't seem to mind him spouting off to every body visiting every restaurant or café bar we went to about how beautiful she is and how fortunate he is. They were married Christmas Day and the village put on a huge party."

Since no sound blipped on the other end of the line, Kirk went on, wildly making up things to add to his original lie. "They honeymooned on the island of Capri and Darce and I took care of the cows. Of course his neighbor helped out in a big way. Actually, I think we were there only to feed the dogs and cats.

They came home one day and we left the next so we didn't hear too much about the honeymoon."

He paused again, "Ron, are you there?"

"I'm here," came the soft reply. "Summer's really married?"

"I'm sorry Ron, but yes, Summer's married."

Chapter Ten
# THE PLAN UNFOLDS

Ron rested the phone on its cradle. He swiveled his chair around but not to look out the window, rather to hide the tears now sluicing down his cheeks. A dull heavy ache hung around his heart as his tears dripped onto the starched collar of his shirt. Finally, as if his battery were about to run out, he sluggishly reached for his ironed and folded handkerchief sprouting from his breast pocket, draped the cloth across his nose and pressed the corners into his eyes.

After several minutes of blotting the tears away, he took deep breaths, stood, tucked the handkerchief in his pocket and went to the executive restroom across the hall. He filled a washbasin with water and carefully splashed his face.

"Summer's married," he said sullenly to the basin. "Summer's married." His knuckles turned white as he gripped the edges. Then he looked in the mirror. "Summer's married." He gritted his teeth. "Summer's married." Picking up a white paper towel from the stack on the counter, he wiped his face, crumpled it and threw it forcefully across the room. "Summer's married!" He grabbed another, squashed it and threw it with abandon. "Summer's married!" Crushing another towel into a ball he threw it like a baseball pitcher. "Summer's married!"

After detonating a dozen miniature explosions, the door opened behind him and a senior vice president thrust his head through the door. Concerned, he surveyed the strewn bathroom floor.

"What happened here?" he demanded.

As if seeing the towels for the first time, Ron responded, "I haven't a clue."

"Are you the only one here?"

Ron looked around stoically. "I seem to be the only one in the restroom."

The VP slapped his open hand on the door frame. "Not here! I mean on the floor! Where's Harding?"

"He had to go upstate this morning. His mother died during the night."

"Is anyone else here?"

"Probably everyone went to lunch. I would have, too, except for a call I had to make."

"Then you'll have to do. The President of Entertainment Equities dropped by my office ten minutes ago. He likes to do this kind of thing. When he has something really big, he just stops in, as if to say, 'Oh, by the way, I have this little script, it's probably nothing … ' It's a parlor trick of his to keep his friends off guard.

"Anyway, he wants me to join him for lunch and since I don't like to hear these propositions without legal present, I told him I was having lunch with one of our lawyers. So I guess that's you. His name is David Raznick. Grab your coat."

"Yes, sir."

"By the way, what's your name?"

"Ron. Ron La Fave. And your name, sir? If we had lunch plans I need to know what to call you." Ron considered his question might be rude, after all as a fledging lawyer with FCA he should know the hierarchy, but at the moment he didn't care.

"Morgan Fairchild and no one calls me Morgan."

"Understood," Ron nodded.

Fairchild hesitated, "When you get back from lunch, be sure someone cleans this up. But don't bother about it now."

'Yes, sir."

Ron strolled down the sidewalk, his shoulders hunched against the wind, listening to the two men talk about their children, their golf scores, the stock market, jabbering away. Numb, walking as if remotely controlled, ice accumulating in his heart, Ron at least felt glad the moment required nothing of him except a listening ear and a recording mind.

David led them into Mardi's, a high profile gleaming wood and beveled mirrors place, fraught with ferns. The maitre'd bowed and scraped, fluttering his way to the best tables reserved for preferred customers up a few steps on a dais that looked over the other dazzling diners.

Halfway through lunch David Raznick leveled his gaze at Ron. "Mr. La Fave, you haven't said a word. Are we boring you?"

Unable even to smile inwardly at David Raznick's direct approach, Ron could not get his face to respond either. A tightly fitted rubber mask seemed to have ensconced his head. "Forgive me if I seem to be rude. My mind is tumbling over a problem. I tend to do that. My mind operates like a rotating rock polishing machine. I roll the problem around and around until I have the solution. I didn't mean to ignore you, gentlemen, but now that you've made me aware of my behavior, you have my rapt attention."

"Good." David signaled the waiter to remove his plate. "Now I'll tell you the purpose of this lunch." He pulled a manuscript from his slender briefcase and threw it on the table where his plate had been. "An agent sent this to me, writer unknown, but I like his style and I think it would make a gorgeous movie."

Morgan Fairchild tilted his head with interest. "Pitch it for us, David."

It's called 'The Clown'. It's a true story of a Clown traveling through Europe with an Italian circus. The Clown, now in his 40s, joined the circus at the age of 15. We watch him in flashbacks as the other performers take advantage of him in his youth, as he becomes more and more introverted from the humiliations he suffers, all the while flawlessly perfecting his act.

He's a favorite and as the drawing card he makes money hand over fist for the circus owners, but can't seem to acquire any himself. Flashbacks then take us into his deprived childhood and the audience grows in the knowledge that on the inside the clown is shriveled from his low self esteem. The act is all he has.

"One night, the owner of a rivaling circus, intentionally, but making it appear to be haphazard, sets fire to the tent right in the middle of the performances. The fire goes undetected until it explodes out of control bringing down the big top on the audience. Children and animals scream, parents react chaotically, some abandoning their children to rush to their own safety. But The Clown darts in and out of the fire bringing child after child out of danger. He darts in one more time and is never seen again until the fire is put out and his body is retrieved.

"I've lined up Clive for the Clown, but listen to who I've got for cameo roles: Cruise for the lion tamer, Barrymore for the bareback rider, Madonna wants the elephants and Cusack and his sister want the flying trapeze." Grinning ear to ear, David rubbed his hands together, "What do you think?"

Elongating each word, Fairchild said, "Very promising."

Both men looked at Ron. Dead-panned, Ron knew at this moment in his demolished life he didn't give a rip about this David Raznick, though he might be some prodigy steering the entire entertainment world, or what his mercurial relationship might be to FCA or how influential and far reaching his entity, Entertainment Equities. He decided his problem of the love of his life, Summer McBride, being married to someone else commanded far more magnitude than this sniveling script.

He monotoned, "I am, at the moment, the new kid on the block. My tenure with FCA as a lawyer only covers six months; but I've been around this company since junior high school and I have never known FCA to produce low brow material such as you just described. You'd be better off pitching that claptrap to Disney."

Stunned, the men sat frozen in shocked silence. Suddenly David Raznick let out a loud guffaw, "Ron! Don't hold back! Speak your mind!" He turned to Fairchild as he nodded toward Ron, "Morgan, looks like you've got a winner in your stable."

He handed the script to Ron, "Young man, I think I will leave this in your capable hands."

Fairchild visibly sighed his relief but then clutched his chest when Ron signaled the waiter, handed him the script and said, "Would you mind throwing this in the trash for me?"

"Certainly, sir." The waiter took the script and headed immediately for the kitchen.

Fairchild spent the next few moments groveling before David Raznick. He apologized profusely for the inept behavior of their recently acquired lawyer while David stared at Ron, a smile playing around his lips. Ron returned the gaze impassively.

David stood and when the other two made moves to join him he waved them back. "Stay. Stay. Order dessert, brandy, cigars, the bill is on my tab." He pointed his finger at Ron. "I like you. That's exactly what I thought of that script."

They watched him leave. Ron sat like a cold stone slab. Fairchild fairly bounced in his seat as he fiercely lectured Ron on protocol. His coffee cooled and the waiter brought another cup. Finally, he petered out. After a stretch of silence Fairchild asked, "Did you know he didn't like the script? I mean, why would he pitch it to us if he didn't like it?"

Ron shrugged. "I don't know. It was claptrap, that's all."

Ron, thinking someone else could clean up the men's restroom, took the rest of the day off and wandered the streets of New York. As he passed each place where he had previously imagined lingering with Summer, he said to himself, 'I won't be seeing her there anymore.' After hours of futilely trying to erase her from his mind, he smacked a parking meter with the flat of his hand. Vibrating on its pole the meter jingled and twanged and his hand smarted with the sting. Dismal, embarrassed by his immaturity, he headed home.

In his apartment he pulled an easy chair to the window and sat looking over the city. The light of day dwindled and the city lights sparkled scintillatingly as night deepened. He woke the next morning with the sunrise coming in his window, still dressed in yesterday's suit and still sitting in the chair.

He didn't call Kirk at 11 a.m., his usual time, as he needed some space. So when the phone rang a few minutes after 11, Ron jumped.

"Hello?"

"Is this Ron La Fave?"

"Yes."

"Well, this is David Raznick."

Ron remained silent. The memory of how he had treated this obviously influential man washed over him and he did not know what to say. Fortunately, David went ahead without noticing the missed beat of conversation.

"I was very impressed yesterday and would like to get to know you. Are you by any chance free for lunch again today?"

"I can be."

"Can you make it to Rye by 12:30?"

"Rye?"

"Yes, I'm here at my club, the Rye Country Club. I think you'll enjoy the lunch we serve."

"I believe I can arrange that. Give me your number there in case I run into complications. But sir, you must know, I haven't changed my mind about that script."

"Good. Neither have I."

Ron ordered a car and driver from the company pool and stood, arranging his desk, framing some order before leaving the office, when Morgan Fairchild strode through the door, the CEO following in tandem. "Ron, I was telling Mr. Harrington about our devastating lunch yesterday with David Raznick. David is a good friend of Mr. Harrington's and I thought you should give him your version of our conversation."

The stocky CEO glowered at Ron and did not offer his hand. "I have to tell you, it does not sit well with me to hear what Fairchild had to say. What do you have to say for yourself?"

"First of all, to have you two gentlemen appear in my office instead of summoning me to yours, indicates a justified ire. My apologies, Mr. Fairchild, for offending you and your manner of protocol."

Fairchild practically shouted, "My manner of protocol?"

Ron held up his hands. "Wait. What I was going to further say is that I had received some disturbing news moments before you summoned me and I was not in good form. But fortunately I seemed not to have offended Mr. Raznick. He called this morning and invited me to lunch at his club in Rye. In fact, I must leave now to arrive on time."

Fairchild shifted from one foot to another in pouting perplexity, but Mr. Harrington simply smirked. "I wonder what he's got up his sleeve. Forgive our barging in on you Ron; you've obviously got everything under control. David Raznick is a favorite son around here because he finances most of the best stuff on the screen. Drop by my office when you get back from this lunch and let me know what happens."

"Certainly, sir."

The driver glided to the curb under the green awning portico of the Rye Country Club and a white gloved attendant opened the limousine's door for Ron to step out. Lichen separated the flagstones forming the steps giving the club a British countryside look. The assistant manager greeted Ron by name and deftly led him to David's table in the dining room.

He pulled out a chair for Ron and said, "Mr. Raznick and Sami will be with you in a minute. They had some unexpected business in the office."

"Sammy?" Ron asked.

"Yes, Sami. Mr. Raznick's daughter."

Suddenly sweat popped up edging Ron's hairline; his stomach turned to a sopping lump of clay. Could it be this David had ulterior motives unrelated to FCA? To be set up with someone's daughter held no appeal for Ron. Not now! Not with the bitter remains of swallowing the news of Summer's unmitigated marriage still sitting in his gut. Besides, he remembered the looks of David Raznick as being akin to a mug shot of Abbot or Costello: the fat funny one, whichever one that was. Or reminding him of the flattened nose of a Pomeranian.

Trying to think of a way to escape, he looked up to see David and Sami approach the table. He did a quick two step in his mind. 'Not too bad,' he thought. 'At least her figure is fine. Her face must be like her mother's and her mother must look like a cockatoo.' Internally grimacing he shook himself by the proverbial collar. 'If I have to, I have to. I can drag myself through a date or two for the sake of FCA.' Ron stood and shook their hands.

"Ron, meet my daughter Sami. She's the third and last daughter. Throughout my dear wife's pregnancy I was certain I would have a boy. So convinced, mind you, that I chose the name Samuel. Instead we have Samuella. From day one she's been my sidekick. She's got a head like mine, all business."

Inwardly, Ron sighed his relief. 'All business. Thank goodness.'

They ordered and then David gestured to Ron. "Tell us about yourself. You piqued my interest yesterday. This business we're in is soft shoe in more ways than one. No one says anything to hurt anyone else's feelings. I distinctly remember two words you used that I hadn't heard in years yet they're some of the most descriptive words in the dramatic arena: claptrap and low-brow.

Now that indicated to me there is some depth in there I wanted to know about."

With anticipating interest they both looked at Ron. He studied them for a few minutes and then plunged into his story from the beginning with his first visit to the Gus Theatre to the present working for FCA. He conveniently left out any trace of Summer because about halfway through his monologue he felt like he had run and jumped on a circus pony. Riding the ring with aplomb he felt a euphoria he didn't think possible in his present emotional state. As he expressed some of his dreams and goals, his life plan took on a dimension it never had before and suddenly he realized there really was no place for Summer. Marrying her would have ruined everything.

When Sami called the next day and invited him out to dinner Friday night, Ron buoyantly accepted. Okay, so he silently agreed to play the gigolo, but something stirred here; something boiled inside. He didn't know what, something bigger than himself, than David, than Sami, than FCA, which he couldn't name, but he could feel it consuming him. And it felt right.

For six weeks David hosted Ron at the club, idling through Tuesday lunch. Every Tuesday, as if treading a programmed trace, a different contributing member of Entertainment Equities appeared out of nowhere to join Ron, David and Sami for lunch. Every Wednesday Ron reported to Mr. Harrington and recounted what they had discussed at yesterday's luncheon.

For six weeks Sami invited Ron to meet her for dinner on Friday night. He never asked to come in when he took her home, nor did either one make any moves toward sealing the evening with a goodnight kiss. Sami came across as flaunting aggression, the kind of woman who made Ron undergo discomfort and it took the six weeks just to feel at ease around her.

On the seventh week David met Ron for lunch, alone. David kept touching Ron's arm as he talked. He clasped his hand over Ron's so often that Ron finally put it in his lap. "My boy. All my married life I wanted a son who would be my partner. Sami's been a great replacement, but my hopes rose when my older daughters married. Both those boys wanted to go into business, but they didn't like show business. One is in shoes; the other's in computers. That doesn't interest me.

"I grew up in Hollywood. I know this industry like my pocket, as the French say. Sami is great, she's just great, but in many ways this is still a man's world. I want someone I can mentor, someone to be by my side in this wild, wonderful world of film. So what I'm proposing Ron is that you come to work for me. I've always used a law firm and I'll continue to use it, but I think a house lawyer for Entertainment Equities is our logical next step, someone to overlook the ps and qs of the legalese we use. But beyond that, I think you've got more in you than just the drawing up of contracts and I'd like to see what it is."

David stopped and looked meaningfully at Ron who, gathering it being his turn to talk, cleared his throat. "I'm enormously flattered, David. Frankly, your offer catches me off guard. To be honest, this is exactly the kind of position I would have hoped to acquire in a few years. But right now, I'm still wet behind the ears, just out of law school; there's so much I don't know."

David smiled. "Whatever it is you don't know; I do. Take a couple of days. Think about it. How about meeting Sami and me at Mardi's Friday at eight and you can give me your answer then. By the way, whatever they're paying you at FCA, I'm tripling it."

When Ron reported to Mr. Harrington the next day he repeated the dialogue almost word for word. Leaning back in his brown leather swivel chair, smiling benignly, the boss nearly lunged across his deep mahogany desk to respond, "Tripling it!"

"Yes, sir. That surprised me, too."

"Surprised you?" Mr. Harrington leaned back again. "I should think it would have stupefied you. What does he want? Does he want you to marry his daughter? If he does, then my advice to you is don't do it. David Raznick controls the breath she breathes. Marriage is hard enough without having your father-in-law be your sideline dictator."

"I don't think that's what he wants."

Mr. Harrington groused, his gesticulating arm belying the calm he was trying to imply, "Don't you two go out to dinner every Friday night?"

"Yes, but now that he has made this proposal, my reflection is that the Friday night dinners have been for Sami to interrogate me for her father's benefit. Plus, I think it gives her a little social outing she might not otherwise have."

"What about you? Don't you have any social outings, as you call them, of your own?"

Suddenly the memory of Summer sprang up in Ron's heart and with dismay he felt tears spring to the back of his eyes, but the following surge of rage dried them instantly. "No. Unfortunately, I don't. I guess I could say that I'm on the rebound and the Friday night dinners have been the same for me, social outings I wouldn't normally have."

Mr. Harrington settled back in his chair and looked sharply at Ron. "I see." Ron dropped his head to avoid the older man's eyes.

"My boy, don't make any decisions in the state you are in. If he wants you now, he'll still want you three months from now, if the offer is genuine. In the meantime, FCA will see what we can do to entice you to stay with us. You're a good man. I don't want to lose you."

The next day Ron called Kirk at eleven. "The plan is starting to unfold!" He gave him the details of David's offer and added, "I don't think I'm waiting for a counter offer from FCA. Entertainment Equities is too good to be true. I could not have designed a better company to fit my life plan."

"Does that mean you're going to marry the boss's daughter, buddy boy? As I recall, that was always part of the plan."

"I don't think so. It looks like I don't need the daughter to get to the father. He wants me to be the son he never had! Besides, the daughter scares me. She has no chin and the nose curves out like a beak. I've had dinner with her once a week for six weeks and I don't think she's ever smiled. No, I'll pass on that part of the plan."

"Are you seeing anyone who does interest you?"

Ron paused while Kirk kicked himself for opening his big fat mouth. "That's still dangerous territory, my friend. Let's not go there."

Friday night, David came to Sami's apartment in Manhattan at six o'clock before their rendezvous with Ron. He spoke softly as a manipulating father and as a straight forward negotiator. "Sweetheart, you're not getting any younger."

"You haven't called me sweetheart since my sixteenth birthday party."

Ruefully, David smiled. "Our relationship hasn't demanded it. But now I want to talk to you about matters of the heart, not business." He looked to discern her reaction, but she stared at him coolly. "Ron La Fave, it seems to me, would be a wonderful catch for you."

"David," Sami had been using his given name since graduating from UCLA as it made them more business associates than relations and David liked feeling younger. "The man is a bore."

"He's just been nervous, that's all."

"You like him, you want him in your flagship, that's your business, but leave me out of it."

"Then why have you invited him out to dinner for six Fridays in a row?" David demanded rather testily.

Sami shrugged. "Something to do. I spend the other six nights of the week reading scripts. I kind of like being escorted to a restaurant."

David screwed up his face to the edges of anger. "If you'd go see Dr. Glickman and have that chin pulled out, and the nose chopped down and the cheekbones built up, you could have any escort you wanted."

Sami stiffened her neck and gave her father a frosty look. "I'm too much like my old man. I'm not changing myself to suit anybody. That trait runs in my veins."

David snorted, "You are a chip off the old block, except that you don't seem to know how to have any fun."

They sat in stony silence until David broke it. "Look. I like this boy. I want him in the company, yes. But I'd also like him in the family. See if you can't manage to find something about him that would make you want that, too."

"I always do what I can to comply." Sami said stoically.

When Ron arrived at Mardi's, David and Sami were already seated at a table on the dais. As he took the two steps to the elevated floor, Ron tripped on the top step. Grabbing the closest table for support, the customers' stemmed drinks toppled over and Ron gave his profuse apologies while the waiter deftly removed the damage, replacing the tablecloth and snapping his fingers to the bartender to send new drinks.

Sami slowly turned her head to give David a long, I-told-you-so stare. He knit his brows. "He's just nervous."

"Excuse my staged entrance," Ron grinned as he joined them. They engaged in small talk, David leading the conversation as usual, until dinner had been consumed and cleared away.

David took a sip of coffee before offering, "Ron, I called Harrington today, I believe in being on the up and up about things, and told him I wanted to wrest you away from him. To my sheer delight, he said you had already been in to inform him. My opinion of you rose even higher."

Ron, his mouth gaping open, leaned forward intending to put his chin on his hand while his elbow rested on the table, but his elbow missed the table and he came crashing forward. Again, Sami gave her father a slow long look.

David continued mischievously, "He told me, as he told you, that he didn't want to lose you and would make a counter offer to whatever I offered. But by the end of the conversation he was only too willing to let you go. I made him an offer he couldn't refuse—a piece of my next three movies."

Ron straightened, "You did what?"

David laughed, "Don't worry about it. Even if you stay with

FCA I'll still give Harrington his prize. But I do want you with us and I hope you are inclined to join Entertainment Equities. What do you say? Have you thought about it?"

Almost huffing, Ron said, "Well, I came in here tonight convinced that your offer was exactly what I was looking for, but your conversation with Mr. Harrington leaves me a little unnerved."

This time, Sami knit her brows.

Ignoring her, David smiled and reminded him, "Aren't you the one who said you were wet behind the ears? Negotiation is an art form in this city. With Harrington one must become a horse trader. I'm poised to teach you everything I know, Ron. Just say the word."

Ron looked from one to the other. David appeared to have already won; his countenance shone with satisfaction. Sami looked bored.

"Then the word is yes."

David put out his hand to shake Ron's, as did Sami. They talked about details and timing; shortly thereafter David excused himself and asked if Ron would see his daughter home. Sami started to protest but caught her father's edifying eye. "You two go out on the town or something to celebrate while this old fogy goes home."

Ron and Sami stopped in a posh nightclub, but before they could order Sami said, "Let's go back to my place. Nightclubs have never been my style."

At her door Ron turned to go but Sami put a hand on his arm. "Oh, no. I meant for us to have a drink at my place where it's quiet. Come in. I've wanted to show you my artwork, anyway."

Ron envisioned two hours of sheer, teeth clenching boredom before he could decently say goodnight, but knew he had to endure, so he entered Sami's domain. Knowing Ron not to be much of a drinker, she offered him a Pellegrino and then said, "Do you mind? This dress chafes my skin. I'd like to change into something more comfortable. I won't be a minute."

Ron shrugged and strolled to the window to admire the

breathtaking panoramic view. He gave himself a few seconds to wonder what it would be like to stand here with Summer, but then shook himself and wondered what it would have been like to stay at the nightclub. He would have preferred to be wildly celebrating there, than trapped in this chamber of silence.

"There. This is much better." Ron turned to see Sami standing in the doorway to her bedroom, dressed only in a sheer negligee which beautifully silhouetted her exquisite body.

Dumbfounded, Ron said the first thing that came to his mind. "I thought you were going to show me your artwork."

As if she were delicately drawing a scarf from around her neck, Sami raised and lowered her hand to indicate her body. "This is the greatest piece of art I have."

Grudgingly admitting to himself that her piece of art had been nicely sculpted, even if the ghastly capital crowning the column filled him with misgivings, Ron set his glass on the coffee table and brushed past her into the bedroom. Thinking him to be swiftly coming to embrace her, Sami extended her arms and then stepped aside in bewilderment as he swept into her room. She trailed behind presuming she would catch him in the act of removing his clothes. But Ron tore the bedspread from the bed and wrapped it around her.

"Any good art should be covered when it's not in use to protect it from deterioration."

Stunned, she asked, "What kind of a man are you?"

"A businessman, Sami. One who has learned the hard way never to mix business with pleasure. You and I never have to speak of this again. Your father doesn't need to know. I don't mean to be rude, but I think the best action for me to take is to leave." He quickly took his coat and opened the door.

"Ron. Don't I interest you at all?"

"Yes, you do, Sami. Yes, you do. As a member of Entertainment Equities you interest me a great deal. Good night."

In the elevator Ron noted his sweat permeated the fibers of his suit and his heart galloped like a horse. 'Whew!' he thought to himself. 'Close shave. Close shave.' He returned to the nightclub for awhile before going home to gloat in his easy chair pulled up to the window.

Sami met her parents for lunch at Rye Country Club the next day, their weekly ritual. Her father watched her approach the table with raised eyebrows as if to say, 'Well? What happened?' His daughter advanced like an unbending piece of steel which made his heart drop until she reached the table. "Give me the number of Dr. Glickman!" she said.

David, for the first time in years was speechless. He gave her a 'What gives?' look.

"Ron La Fave thinks he can't be had."

"He can't be had?"

"In other words, he thinks I am only good for business."

David quickly scanned the dining room, "I thought I saw Alan come in. Yes, there he is over there, the one in the white suit."

"He's an odd sort of duck."

"He can afford to be."

"Didn't he invest in a couple of things we did?" Sami mused.

"Most profitably so."

"I'll be right back."

David gleefully turned to his wife, "I think our little girl is finally going after a man." To which his wife blinked and beamed but as was her custom, said not a word.

Sami returned with a confident stride, "He'll see me Monday and get me into surgery within a week."

She sat, picked up her menu and then peeked over the top. "Oh, hello mother."

"Hello, dear." Her mother said as if to a distant niece.

Chapter Eleven
# TRANSFORMATION

Ron didn't see Sami for one month. It took him two weeks to ease out of FCA and two weeks to ease into Entertainment Equities, or EE. The Tuesday lunches at the club continued and finally Ron had the nerve to ask, "Where's Sami?"

David coyly replied, "She's had some personal business to attend to; she'll be back in a few weeks. She's in good health, in case you were worried about her wellbeing, and eager to get back to work."

Puzzled, Ron wondered what could keep her away for so long, but didn't want to ask. "Good. Glad to hear it."

Working for David Raznick, Ron discovered, required more socializing than he expected. "It's all in who you know, my boy. Keep a list of who you've met, what you've learned about them, what their specialty is and how you think they might be useful for us in the future."

"Such as," Ron prompted his boss.

"Such as Lightstone over there." David indicated a man they had talked to during an all-member evening function at the club and who now lunched across the room. "He's setting his son up with his own accounting firm. Benson has been getting pricey on us. Maybe we should consider moving our account to this young man. It would set him up nicely and in gratitude he would be good to us. Know what I mean?"

"As long as Benson doesn't have anything on us." Ron added.

David guffawed and clapped Ron on the back. "Never fear. I make sure I have something on everyone I deal with so they can't pull that chicanery with me."

Ron raised his eyebrows. "Do you have something on me?" The nagging question in the back of his mind clamored to know if Sami had told her father about that fiasco of a night in her apartment.

David's placid face gave Ron the answer he wanted. "The only thing questionable in your life is that you trade your stocks through the San Francisco Exchange."

Relieved, he then wondered how David knew of his stock trades, but he simply fed his boss the information he knew David wanted. "When I was stationed at Treasure Island I did some trading myself through a stogy old broker who never questioned my requests. Finally I acknowledged I didn't know a thing about what I was doing. I found myself a broker that knew how to do what I wanted. Over time we became friends."

"I've got a good broker; why not switch to New York? The time difference alone would be to your advantage."

"One thing you will learn about me, David, if you haven't already, is that I am a determined, persevering, loyal man. I am loyal to a fault. Kirk Dalton and I are not only best friends, but I trust him implicitly. He fits right into my life plan and I will never transfer my loyalties to another broker."

"Your loyalties didn't stay with FCA." David jousted.

"FCA was always a stepping stone for me."

"And how do I fit into your life plan?"

Ron laughed, "If I had planned you and planted you in my life, I couldn't have done better."

"Ah! But am I a stepping stone?"

Ron smiled. "No. You're going to take me to the top."

David nodded approvingly and then raised an eyebrow. "I'd like to meet your best friend. Kirk you say?"

Ron nodded.

"We must get to work on this life plan. Why not invite him out here? I've tripled your salary, but I don't see you elevating your style of living, so you must be putting it into your stocks. Yes. I definitely want to meet this Kirk."

Several Tuesdays later, as Ron approached their usual table at the Club, he saw a strikingly beautiful woman sitting beside David, intently talking with him, their heads almost touching. The hair, reddish brown, bobbed at the chin line, and the exquisite figure bore a resemblance to Sami. 'Was David having an affair? So blatantly so?' he asked himself.

He stood by the table for a moment staring before they came up from their engrossed conversation. He waited for a moment for David to introduce them and then broke the silence by extending his hand to shake hers. "Hi. I'm Ron La Fave. I intended to have lunch with David today, but if I'm intruding I can make it some other time."

David and the young woman gazed at Ron as if taken aback and then both broke into gales of laughter. "Ron," David gasped, wiping tears from his eyes. "This is Sami. Don't you recognize her?"

Ron sat down heavily in the third chair at the table. "Sami? That's unbelievable. There is absolutely nothing about that face that would indicate you are Sami. What did you do ... ? Who did ... ? I don't even know what to ask? I'm floored."

David soothingly explained. "You remember Dr. Alan Glickman? I introduced you at the golf tournament. He did this miracle for my little girl. I'd been trying to get her to drop by his office for years, but one Saturday she met her mother and me for lunch and demanded his phone number. Surprised? I'll say. And now look at her. He turned her into a real beauty."

Realizing just which Saturday that would have been, Ron's face turned beet red. Sami's strikingly beautiful face smiled, but her eyes were the same shrewd Sami. "Yes. A real miracle. A real beauty." Ron attested.

"Perhaps now we'll have that celebration we missed." Sami flatly intoned.

Before he could stop the words from bursting out of his mouth, Ron blurted, "Perhaps now you'll change the personality to match the pretty face."

Sami stood, glowering at Ron, abruptly turned and headed for the ladies' room. David threw his napkin on the table, also glowering at Ron, but paused before standing. Ron rushed to apologize. "I'm sorry, David. I don't know where those words came from."

David, his elbows askew clamping his hands on the arms of his chair poised to push himself to his feet, stopped mid-movement and assessed Ron thoughtfully. "You have a way of going right to the heart of a matter, Ron. You're absolutely right. Let me talk to her."

David walked resolutely toward the ladies room while Ron sat slumped at the table; certain he had ruined the perfect setup for his life's plan. At the ladies room David tapped on the door. A dimpled woman about his own age came out and said, "Are you looking for someone?"

"Is my daughter in there?"

"Mr. Raznick, there's a raging tigress pacing the floor, but she doesn't look at all like Sami."

"Is that the only woman in there?"

"Yes. Shall I tell her you want to talk to her?"

"No thanks. But you can guard the door for me." He quickly entered the ladies room to find his daughter charging back and forth in the carpeted sitting area. "Sami ... "

Glaring, her teeth clenched, she didn't miss a step. "Is there no place you don't think you rule and reign? What are you doing in the ladies room?"

"I came to talk some sense into you."

"Sense into me! Your little protégé insults me and you want to talk sense into me?" She began muttering to herself, "I can't believe it. What have I been doing all these years?" Suddenly she swung herself in front of her father to face him two inches from his nose. Keeping her voice low so as not to entertain the dining room, she whispered fiercely.

"You're the one who brought this guy into our lives. We didn't need him. I've been your right hand man for eight years. All I want to do is produce movies. Why does he have to come along? But I accepted his arrival without a word. Then you want me to find something about him I like so maybe I can marry him. I do everything I know to do; I even get my face fixed and as you can see, he isn't buying. And you want to talk some sense into me? Here's the sense: get rid of him! Now! Walk out there and fire his smug self! Either that or I walk out of here and work for somebody else!"

Her diatribe halted and David put a hand on his daughter's arm. "Sami! You're my little girl! You'll always be my right hand man. But you have to see the bigger picture. We'll always do the best movies in the business. However, I won't always be here. Look around you. It's a man's world. Women are catching up. They're not there, yet, and I want to protect you. Ron's a smart cookie, just like you are and what better way is there to dominate the business than to have two of you at the helm?"

He turned her to look into the framed, beveled mirror. "Now here's the sense I came to talk you into. Look at that face!" She frowned at her reflection, and then couldn't help but smile. "It's a pretty face, isn't it?" She nodded. "It's a soft face, a feminine face. In business you can be as hard-nosed as you know to be, but at home a man wants softness. He wants to forget the harshness of his day, and I'd think a little softness would benefit you as well. Your business acumen won't be affected if you allow your femininity to come out once in a while. Just choose your times, that's all."

"Kind of like playing out a script, is that what you mean?"

David nodded thoughtfully, "That's a good way of looking at it."

"Then I don't have to fall in love with him?"

"Not if you don't want to. But it does make life easier."

"Well, I won't. He's not my type at all."

David frowned. "I didn't know you had a type. What is your type?"

Sami turned and headed for the door. "A tall, blond beach bum that plays volleyball."

David rushed after her, a bit anguished. When he caught her arm he asked, "You're kidding, aren't you?"

She took his arm, "Let's go, Daddy." She said in an almost kittenish fashion.

Once again Sami invited Ron to dinner on Friday, but this time for a quick bite. Remembering his fondness for the GUS Theatre, she bought tickets for the Russian ballet performance. When he took her home, he steeled himself and offered to come up.

"Ron, to tell the truth, my new face is drawing a lot of attention from other men and because of that attention I've come to a realization I've never been forced to face before. I really don't believe in sex before marriage." That last statement had been said to her by Ron's own lips on their very first evening out. Seemingly flustered, or so she thought, he kissed her on the lips with some warmth,

Ron walked home in the unusual pre-spring warmth of early April. What was happening here? He had to sort things out. Sami, now more beautiful than Summer, still did not hold a candle to her. She did take his hand during a poignant movement in the ballet and he found it surprisingly soft. Could he marry this woman and fulfill that portion of his life's plan? Should he? The thought did not bring him any peace so he put it on a shelf of his mind to be looked at later, if need be.

May came on strong, dressed up in a New York spring like only New York can put on. On a particularly balmy day, David called Ron into his office and asked him to close the door. Sitting across from him, Ron expected talk of a pending contract with delicate details, but David didn't seem to know what to say. He started and stopped several times while Ron patiently waited.

Finally David clasped his hands on his desk and leaned over them. "Ron, my boy. All things have timing. Like scripts. There's timing to when you can bring a movie out. The public is like a big body and you have to read that body to know what it's ready for. Is it ready for romance? Bring on the love stories. Is it ready for a purge? Bring on the shame and blame movies."

Ron nodded, wondering where this conversation was going.

"There's timing in each one of our lives, too. In my daughter's life, it's time for her to get married. I'll be very blunt with you; she tells me she has been wooing you for over three months now and all she has to show for it is an occasional kiss.

"Now I know my daughter. If you aren't interested, she'll move on. This new look of hers opens lots more doors than she has ever had. If I'm going to have a new son-in-law, I want it to be you, Ron. I feel very close to you and would love to hand the company over to you when I retire, but if Sami has a husband that is also interested, I won't have a choice. She's my daughter. You understand what I'm telling you, don't you?"

Ron's mouth seemed too dry to speak but he nodded his understanding. Then David said, "Why don't you take the rest of the day off and consider. In fact, take as much time as you need." Ron stood and left the office without having said a word.

He walked home and sat in his easy chair by the window, but it didn't help. That's where he still occasionally daydreamed about Summer. He stood and paced. He understood exactly what David was saying, either return with a marriage proposal, or don't return at all.

Realizing he had to get away in order to think clearly, he threw a few things in a duffel bag, pulled his car out of the garage and drove into the Catskills. That's what he had done when his professors were strongly counseling him against joining the Navy, saying it would damage his career. He wouldn't get off to a running start with the rest of his classmates.

A weekend in the Catskills had cleared the fog and he saw his dream once again. He wanted to serve his country and he was convinced it would not harm his chances. He came back on Monday and headed straight for the recruiting office. His chances were never even bruised.

Knowing he could think clearly if he went to the mountains, Ron settled into a remote cabin for the duration. This being Wednesday he wondered if he should call Sami and cancel their Friday night date, but then thought better of the idea.

He did call Kirk. After explaining the situation he asked, "What do you think? Should I marry this woman?"

"Buddy boy, I don't know what to say. When I knew I wanted Darce for the rest of my life, I couldn't wait for the wedding day to come, and I had to wait five years! Your wedding day could be just around the corner and you don't know if you want her. So it doesn't seem right to me. But Ron? You're the only one who can answer the question of whether or not you should marry this woman. I'll be praying for you."

"Praying? Since when did you start praying?"

"I've always prayed. I've just never told you about it. How do you think I know what stocks to buy? But never mind that. Go for a long walk in the woods and search your heart. You'll make the right decision."

"And you'll pray, right?"

"Right."

"I'll call you later."

Ron walked until dark crept up the mountain. He skipped dinner and lay on his bed, ruminating until he fell asleep. Sometime during the night he got up, took his clothes off and crawled under the covers, but he didn't remember when.

The next morning he woke with absolute clarity. His life plan included marrying the daughter of a wealthy movie mogul. That daughter obviously being Sami. So the mogul came first, so what? Like he thought when he created his plan, he needed the daughter to get to the father. David made it clear that the case included that action. First the daughter, then the company.

He sprang out of bed, resolved. Clarity in the mountains. He started to pack his things but thought better of it. Perhaps another day to himself wouldn't be so bad. This morning he would take another walk, after a sumptuous breakfast, and this afternoon he would saunter down to the village and buy a trinket ring.

Friday night Ron met Sami at Mardi's as prearranged. He took the waiter aside and gave him the trinket ring to plant in a chocolate mousse as the centerpiece. Ceremoniously setting the mousse before Sami, the waiter watched until certain the patron would notice the centerpiece instead of lifting the spoon unscrutinized to her lips. Sami puzzled over it until Ron could bring himself to say, "Will you marry me, Sami?"

She smiled, took the ring from the mousse, dropped it in her water glass, and then fished it out with her fork. It dangled from the tines as she gave it to Ron, cleansed by the water. "Put it on my finger and I'll say yes."

He took the ring, put it on her finger, she said "Yes" and they smiled to the applause of the appreciative customers at nearby tables.

"We can replace that tomorrow with whatever you like."

"Actually, Ron, I only want the gold wedding band. Why don't I wear this little bauble until that one comes along?"

They lingered over coffee, making plans, and then Ron took her home by cab. She invited him to come in. The thought of making love to Sami absolutely repulsed Ron. "Why don't we wait till we're married? It will be so much more meaningful then." She smiled demurely and went upstairs without another word.

The next morning David called Ron to insist he join the family at the club to celebrate at the weekly luncheon. David's wife greeted him as if he were a distant nephew. Her husband waxed ebullient! He dragged Ron and Sami to every table to announce the happy news. They planned the engagement party, they wrote the engagement announcement for the socializing New York Times, they established the date of the wedding, October 7$^{th}$, a Saturday, with the ceremony taking place at the Community Church of the Saints, with their undefined doctrine, and the reception, the happening of the decade, culminating the events, at the Rye Country Club.

By three o'clock, exhausted, they finally left the dining room. Ron stiffly held Sami's hand until they reached the door of the club. "Will I see you tonight?" he asked tentatively.

"Well, no. I have scripts to read." But when she caught her father's eye she recanted. "I'd love to see you tonight."

"Good. I want to take you on a long walk."

The three looked horrified. "A walk?" they asked in unison.

"Yes. To eat a hotdog in Central Park."

Sami's lip actually curled.

David's face brightened. "You're going to broaden the horizons of my little girl. Good for you! Have fun, you two!"

The doorman of Sami's apartment building announced Ron's presence in the lobby at 5:30. He waited till she came down and was glad to see she wore sensible walking shoes. His planned trek would take them several miles.

Every place he envisioned lingering with Summer, he took Sami. They were places that had been special to him since childhood and at each place he explained their history and significance. Sami, hardly noticing Ron's special nooks and crannies, looked at the architecture, glad to get out in New York City as it helped her envision movie sets. Bored with her guide's lectures, she asked, "Why are you showing me all this?"

"There was a time when I was in love with a girl from California. I often fantasized about taking her on this tour. Now I have you to love and I wanted to show you these places."

That piqued Sami's interest. "What happened to the girl?"

"She married someone else."

"Are you still in love with her?"

"Sami, did I put a ring on your finger?"

"Yes. But you didn't say you loved me."

Ron was not ready to be boxed in like this. "Nor did you say you loved me."

Nor was Sami. "Tell me about this girl. How did you meet her?"

Ron told her especially about Kirk and Darce, giving only scanty details about Summer.

"So the three of them are best friends?"

"Well, Darce and Summer are best friends, but Kirk and I are best friends."

"I suppose you are going to invite this Kirk and Darce to the wedding?"

"Of course. I'll ask Kirk to be my best man. Would it be alright if Darce is a bridesmaid?"

"No, it would not be alright! I'm not going to have some girl from Cape Girardeau, Missouri that I don't even know be one of my bridesmaids, especially the best friend of the groom's ex-lover."

Stung, Ron responded, "I didn't say we were lovers."

"Whatever! She's the one with whom you mixed business with pleasure, isn't she? Then she ran off and married someone else. Some lover you must have been."

Ron folded his arms across his chest and gave her a steely gaze, which she returned and then he dropped his glance to the sidewalk. "This was a mistake. Let me walk you home."

They turned and strode, each in their solitude, heading for her apartment. Ron decided, wisdom coming in a few blocks, that this marriage would only work if it were about Sami. He must leave his stinging emotions and private events out of it. "Tell me about your old boyfriends."

"I haven't had any."

"Never?"

"Not since freshman year at UCLA."

"Why not?"

"I never saw the need."

"Did the guy at UCLA break your heart?"

"He was a jerk."

"Do you mean that for, what, twelve years you haven't had a date? No social life at all?"

"I didn't say that. I've had plenty of dates. Everybody wanted to get next to David's money and connections. I just didn't have a boyfriend."

"Do you know why not?"

"Sometimes I wondered if I couldn't trust anybody to want me and not to use me to get to David. I figure it's safe to say yes to you because you've already got David. How did you do that, anyway? How did you get my father to be so interested in you?"

"Beats me. I met him at lunch one day by happenstance, told him his script was claptrap and ever since he seems to have taken me under his wing."

They walked back to her apartment, talking from a chilly distance, but revealing more and more of themselves. When she invited him up the thought of sex flashed through his mind and he shivered and declined. Back home, in his own apartment, he removed the easy chair from in front of the window. 'No more daydreaming,' he thought.

Then he noticed the flashing signal on his phone. The message from his future father-in-law rippled with excitement. "General and Mrs. Vernon have invited us for tea at four tomorrow to celebrate the wonderful announcement." And so the social frenzy began.

On Monday Ron called Kirk and told him all the news. "By the way, did you pray like you said you would?"

"Now don't mess with me, buddy boy. If I said I would, I did."

"So?"

"So what?"

"So what did the big boss say?"

"He said He would give you the desires of your heart. I read that to mean He's giving you your life plan. We're on our way, buddy boy!"

'Why didn't He give me the desires of my heart when I wanted Summer?' But Ron only thought this as he didn't mention Summer to Kirk anymore.

With high-spirited parties and organized social events springing up all over the landscape, Ron and Sami spent most of their time together and their budding relationship softened. By the first of October, when Kirk and Darce arrived to be part of the pre-wedding week, the bridal couple had developed some honest affection for each other.

Sami moved to her parent's home in Rye for the week, occupying her girlhood bedroom, and David put Ron, Kirk and Darce in the restricted Rye Lodge. The three met each morning for bagels and coffee on the veranda that circled the first floor of the building. Indian summer lingered and laced the mornings with warmth. The coved overhang secluded them, burnished with drooping ivy.

On their first meeting Darce appealed to Ron, "Listen, you've had some time to get accustomed to these wealthy people, but I don't know how to act around them. What if I make some terrible social gaff?"

Ron laughed. "You won't. Darce, you are the model of grace. And if you do, so what? I won't care and I'm the only one that counts here, aren't I?"

She laughed and reached over to pat his arm. "But what about all these parties? Your bride-to-be has scheduled three a day! What do I wear to all that? My school marm clothes won't fit in."

Ron's mouth dropped open. "Great! As soon as we finish

these bagels we'll head into the city to see my Dad. He's the best tailor in town, but they haven't utilized him for this wedding. I think they're trying to play down the fact that Sami is marrying a tailor's son. Dad can fit you two out and feel like he has really contributed to my big shindig, as he calls it."

"How much will that cost?" Darce asked, frowning.

"It will all come out of the costuming department, strictly rental and Mr. Stauffer should do that for me for free."

The week spun by with Darce not having a single moment with Sami to get to know her. On the other hand, David went out of his way to include Kirk in every business meeting and every men's social event that took place and always had him close by. But Saturday morning Darce, surprised, found herself alone with Sami isolated in the ladies room of the Country Club after surviving a breakfast for the family and close friends.

"Sami, I'm so sorry we haven't had time to get to know each other. This has been a wonderful week … "

"That's only natural, don't you think?"

Confused, Darce answered, "I don't know about that. Ron is a very special person in our lives and we want you to be special, too."

"Now Darce, have you really thought that through? You live on the West Coast, we live on the East. Your lives revolve around the stock market; ours revolve around the motion picture industry. We'll probably never see each other again. Ron has been special to you up until now, but people and times change."

"Oh no! Ron's not like that and neither are we. We'll be friends forever! My husband is his broker and he's making a lot of money for Ron."

"Do you even know what a lot of money is?"

Darce, feeling she should be wearing a jester's hat with bells, at the same time as being played for a fool, simply stared.

"I'll tell you. My father is a multi-millionaire. His estate is worth about a quarter of a billion dollars. Is your little hubby making that kind of money for Ron?"

Again she stared, frozen in her ineptitude.

Then Sami hissed like a snake in Darce's face, "Listen, we aren't even in the same league! Let me make myself clear. I don't want to associate with people like you. Ron is in my world now and, trust me, you won't be." With that she rushed from the room.

The chauffeur held the door open for Sami to join her bridesmaids in the long limousine. They would now withdraw to David's house to prepare for the late afternoon wedding. She turned to find Ron and Kirk watching her so she kissed her fingertips and waved them to her soon to be husband.

Ron smiled and waved back, and then he turned, as did Kirk, toward the direction of the ladies room, wondering what could be keeping Darce. They took up positions outside the door and Ron finally asked one of the waitresses to check the room to see if anyone were in there, specifically, Darce Dalton.

She came back in a few minutes, "The lady is crying and says to tell you when she can compose herself she will join you."

"Crying?" Kirk said, perplexed. "Darce doesn't cry. I'm the one who cries in our family."

"Maybe she's sad I've finally been hooked. Probably had a secret yen for me all this time!" Ron cuffed Kirk, but it didn't cut through his intensity.

"Seriously. Can I go in there?" Kirk looked around as if planning a heist. "I'll be quick." But just then the door swung open and as Darce emerged her red eyes drew all attention away from any other notable thing.

Immediately Ron became solicitous. "Darce! What's happened?" Kirk had his arm around her, leading her to a chair at an empty table.

She relayed the conversation she had had with Sami. Both men stood as if flash frozen. After a moment, both men simultaneously stepped back as if someone had cracked their ice with a mighty blow. Then both men drew up chairs on either side of Darce.

Kirk straightened her bangs. "Sweetheart. It doesn't matter what she says."

Ron's face turned a strained gray. "I am so sorry, Darce. Sami can be as cold and cut-throat as they come. I don't even know how to apologize for her. I just hope to God I am not making an irreparable mistake." He looked at them with dismay. "You are my best friends, and you always will be. Don't ever doubt me, please! It doesn't, however, sound like we will be having a fourth joining our little circle of friendship. We're going to the top together. David may be the Mr. Gotrocks now, but we'll see who ends up on top!"

Ron rolled his head around and clutched his stomach. "What am I saying? I can't go through with this! I'll be selling my own soul!" His face turned a mottled pink. "I think I'm going to be sick." Standing, Ron wove his way gingerly into the men's room.

Watching him go, Kirk spoke soothingly to his wife, "I've got to talk to him, hon. Will you wait for me here?" Darce wondered what else she would do as she looked into Kirk's pleading eyes. She smiled wearily and gently pushed him to go.

Ron leaned over an empty sink, unable to actually vomit, the turbulence remaining to gurgle in his gut. "Buddy boy," Kirk began as he put a hand on Ron's back. "Take it easy. Nothing has ever stood in your way and nothing will stop you now. These are bigger stakes and more intense egos than we've dealt with before, but you're the expert at diplomacy. You'll handle this just fine."

"Would you marry her?" Ron asked Kirk's reflection in the mirror.

"That's not the question. The question is, will you?"

Ron looked at his own reflection as he leaned on his hands gripping the sides of the washbasin. "I don't know if I'm up to this."

Kirk leaned back against the adjoining sink and folded his arms over his chest. "You've planned for this day since junior high school. Are you going to drop out now? Are you telling me you cannot overcome one woman's small mindedness? Have you considered that in your mind you make Sami so powerful that she can stop you? You're the husband here. Use David as your mentor in marriage. He has certainly overcome his wife.

"Besides, as I recall the plan, you needed this marriage simply to be a stepping stone? The stakes are high. The moment has come when you put all your chips on the table, or fold your cards and go home. What's at home, Ron? Can you think of anything there that's worth not taking the gamble? Remember, even if you lose everything, you've still got your secret stash and you can start all over."

Turning his gaze to Kirk, Ron asked, "What does the big boss say?"

Perplexed, Kirk asked, "Who's the big boss?"

Ron glanced upward.

Kirk blushed. Knowing the Bible's admonitions to marry for life someone you determined to love even when you didn't feel like it, Kirk also knew full well he intended to guard his own financial future in spite of biblical principle. He shrugged, "I don't know."

Ron's thoughts rummaged for something on which to pin his hopes, 'There's nothing at home. I have absolutely nothing else going for me. If I duck out of this marriage I have to start all over. What the heck! I might as well go for it and determine to come out a winner.' He stood up and smoothed his hair. Turning to Kirk he said with a half smile, "Got your cigar ready?"

"My cigar?" Kirk looked mystified.

"Yeah! For the Champs Elysees! I'm going to have my dream of you and Darce strolling down that grand avenue with me, remember?"

"You bet. But let's buy the cigars in Paris; then we can buy Cuban!"

Ron wrapped his arms around Kirk's shoulders and whispered in his ear, "Thanks!"

David Raznick strode toward the men's room when Darce called to him in order to prevent him crashing in on Ron and

Kirk. Seeing her sitting pitifully at the table with her reddened eyes, he came over and knelt in front of her. "Now what's making Ron's best friend cry?"

"I'm sorry, Mr. Raznick, I don't feel comfortable telling you about it. I'll be okay, really."

Kirk and Ron came out of the men's room and David stood up. "What's happened to our little lady here? I insist on knowing. There shouldn't be any unhappiness on a wedding day. That's not a good omen." He looked expectantly at Ron.

Piercing David directly in the eyes, Ron said, "Sami said some things to Darce that made her apprehensive about the future of our relationship. But I have assured these two that they are as close to me as family and nothing will split us up. Whatever I am involved in, Kirk will be my partner. Sami has my heart, but not my soul."

David looked at Ron thoughtfully, and then turned to Kirk. "Young man, I like you. I like the loyalty I see between you and my son-in-law. Ron has a way of expressing the heart of things. Such a friendship should never be broken because of marriage. Now, Kirk, if I appointed you to the Advisory Board of Entertainment Equities, do you think you could fit that into your schedule?

"I'd fly you and Darce out for Board meetings four times a year, at various places around the globe. You seem to have a good grasp of this industry, probably from all the research you've done for Ron. I think you'd give us stodgy old mothballs a breath of fresh air. What do you say?" He held out his hand for Kirk to shake.

"I'd say, 'awesome!'" Kirk said as he shook David's hand.

David gripped Kirk's hand as he looked over his shoulder at Darce. "Now little lady, what do you think of that?"

"I think you're a very gracious man, Mr. Raznick. Thank you."

David clapped Ron on the shoulder. "True friends are few and far between in life. Hang onto these two." Then he excused himself and headed for the men's room.

By the time of the reception, Ron, Kirk and Darce were flying high, knowing they had the world by the tail. Mr. Megabucks, David Raznick, had smiled on them and they would become filthy rich themselves. They just knew it! So they had to put up with an iron maiden. How hard could that be?

Ron experienced a momentary glitch when David announced to the approving guests his and his wife's loving gift to the deserving newly weds, a house built for them in Rye. Amid the applause, Sami demurely whispered, "Your things have been moved there today. I closed out your apartment."

"You knew about this?"

"Of course. Someone had to advise David of what we wanted."

He asked her curtly, "What did I want?" But then he smiled. After all, to become filthy rich he could put up with just about anything. He gave David a wet kiss on the cheek that practically knocked him off his feet. Then picked up the hand of David's wife, gallantly kissed it, and her cheeks turned pink.

The gift that surprised them came from the eleven other moneyed members of the Board of Entertainment Equities. David's closest friend handed Sami a small polished silver photo album with a gilt ribbon wrapped around it. She slid the ribbon off as the guests waited expectantly. With Ron looking over her shoulder she opened the album and looked at photos of a striking ski cabin. The name "Jackson Hole" had been superimposed on every other page.

Sami looked disconcerted. "I don't ski. This isn't something I wanted."

Ron saved the day. "But I do!" He grabbed the album and grinned broadly. "What a fabulous gift! Nothing could please me more!" He held up each photo to elicit the oohs and aahs of the guests, who gracefully complied. David smiled at Ron's winning ways, and then frowned at Sami.

Many followed the newlyweds caravanning to the airport where David's private jet waited to ferry them to their relaxing honeymoon, destination unknown. The next morning on the plane back to San Francisco, Darce became weepy. "If only Ron had married Summer. Why couldn't that have happened?"

Kirk raised his eyebrows and looked away.

"It was your fault. We could have all been so happy in San Francisco."

Deciding his best course stood out like a reddened line on a map which indicated take no course at all, Kirk opened his paper to read the stock news.

Chapter Twelve
# VANGUARD INTERPRETATIVE VISUAL ARTS

Sami managed to read five scripts on their two week honeymoon, starting the last one in the waiting room of the private airport where David's jet picked them up just like it had dropped them off. She finished it as they landed in the States. A chauffeur driven limousine waited for them.

"That isn't David's driver." Ron noted.

His wife gave him a disgusted look. "Of course not. It's ours."

"We have a car and driver?"

She didn't deign to give him a reply.

With the birds, Monday morning, Ron headed for the office in Rye, just a few miles from his new home. Picking up the phone on David's secretary's desk, he called David's personal line to leave a message that he would like to see him as soon as possible. However, David answered. "Ron! Welcome back! You're in early."

"As are you."

David sounded as if he were gleefully rubbing his hands together. "I could hardly wait for you to get to the office today so we could start on some plans I've had brewing. What brings you here at this hour? I should think a man just back from his honeymoon would be reluctant to get to work."

Ron paused and morosely shook his head. He needed diplomacy and he needed it now. "David, I've got things on my mind."

"Come on in; let's talk."

Ron marched to the door. Before he grasped the door knob he paused, took a deep breath and plastered a colossal smile on his face, then pushed himself into the office. "Hello, David." Ron took a seat across the desk from his grinning father-in-law.

However, David stood. "Ah! You look like a happy man!" He reached over to shake Ron's hand and then steered himself to the sideboard. He poured two steaming cups of coffee, putting sugar in Ron's and drizzling cream in his own. He set the cups on a side table situated between Ron's chair and the one he now sat down in. "Where did you spend your honeymoon? If you don't mind my asking. Sami wouldn't breathe a word before she left and my pilot said she swore him to secrecy as well."

Ron chuckled, hoping he sounded amused. "She didn't tell me where we were going until we landed. I don't know why the secrecy, but I guess it's safe for everyone to know now. We went to London."

"London? That's not very romantic. Why London?"

"Sami had theatre tickets arranged for every night we were there. She wanted to see if any of them would transform well into films."

Reacting to this statement, her father choked on the coffee. "A working honeymoon?"

"You know your daughter; Sami's a workhorse."

"What about the days?"

"We had lunch with playwrights, theatre owners, various actors and actresses. We met some fascinating people."

"I'm sure you did. But did you and Sami create any memories that will linger and hold you together when it's not so fascinating?"

Ron looked down to reinforce his composure. "Those moments will come."

David silently studied Ron and Ron did not feel inclined to fill the empty space with sound. Finally, the father-in-law put down his cup, turned his chair to more directly face Ron and said, "Why don't you tell me what's on your mind first. We can get to my news later."

Ron spoke quite evenly. "David, I don't believe it is wise for a husband and wife to work together. If they do, they only take their work home with them and there is no real home life. I'd like to keep my private life separate from the office in whatever way I can. I'm going to have to fight for this in my marriage, I can see that. So I am asking you to assign me some other place to work on some other project so that I am not working with Sami. You two have been inseparable for years and have made EE strong …"

"Stop right there! I made EE strong long before Sami came on board. I am EE." David sighed and stood up to pace. Ron sat quietly, waiting for what, he didn't know and he didn't care. Let the chips fall where they may. Trotting after his controlling wife through the wet streets of gray-skied London had built a definite mettle in him. He discovered a certain determination to change many things.

Finally David spoke. "My boy, my daughter flares up as mean and tart to me as she treats you. You've met my other two daughters; they're sweet and simple as English gardens. I don't know where Sami came from, except when I look in the mirror. I know she's a chip off the old block. But, I have the benefit of time which has softened me and taught me a little savoir-faire. Hang in there with her. She'll change. Right now she wants too much too quickly; just like I did. Be patient."

"I have every intention of doing that, David, however I'd like to separate our lives at the office."

"I understand completely. Give me a couple of weeks to work on this. Don't mention it to Sami and neither will I."

Ron visibly relaxed. "Thank you. I know I can trust you." He breathed out a lungful of air. "Now what did you want to talk to me about?"

David looked searchingly at Ron, but determining his son in law truly to be at ease, he excitedly sat down by Ron again. "There are—I don't know how to put it—there are tangible things I can feel in my bones. Like right now, the feeling I've got sends shivers all over me. It's time!" He paused, savoring his mounting enthusiasm.

That same mounting enthusiasm filled Ron with dread. The ease of only moments ago dissipated. "What's in your bones, David? Time for what? I don't know whether to be apprehensive or excited."

"All my life I've wanted to own my own motion picture studio! Opportunities have come and gone; I let them slide by because they weren't right. Oh, I've had the money to do it for some time. But everything has to be in place. Now that you've come on board with EE and the family, I think the time is right." David beamed at Ron with an expectant look on his face.

Astounded, Ron said, "You mean produce movies ourselves? Aren't you satisfied with being in on the financing of most of the countries winners? Wouldn't you unnecessarily be complicating your life?"

David grinned like a Cheshire cat.

Ron frowned. "What does my coming on board have to do with it? I don't know a thing about actual production. It seems to me you'd want somebody that knows the ins and outs, like at least how to run a camera!"

"I know all that stuff, Ron! I grew up in it; the back lots were my playground. I can run a camera, handle a shotgun mike, make it rain or the wind blow, hustle out for the catering wagon; I've done it all. My father staffed the security for several studios and they let me have the run of their places. Depending on the movie under production and the roster of actors, I chose where I would hang out. Every summer I only went home to sleep."

"Well, you've got it covered then, but how does my coming on board make any of this happen?" Ron asked anxiously.

A mischievous look covered David's face. "Give me a couple of weeks. I've got something brewing." He tapped his temple as he stood up, indicating the closure of the matter for the moment. "Don't mention a word of this to Sami."

"Okay." Ron stood, they shook hands as if they were carrying on a seditious operation and Ron stealthily left the room, covertly leaving the Rye office for the drive to Manhattan.

Sami stayed home that Monday to instruct the new household staff exactly how she wanted things done. On Tuesday she returned to her desk in Manhattan spending so much time on the telephone catching up on missed moments while in London, that she kept Ron and the driver waiting to take them to the Rye Country Club for lunch.

David rarely spent time in the Manhattan office; he worked from headquarters in Rye. Manhattan had only been opened to accommodate Sami who wanted to live in the heart of the Big Apple after graduation from UCLA. David used Tuesday lunch at the club as a time to brainstorm, to run ideas around the table, so no one was allowed to miss.

This Tuesday unfolded no differently than others. Preston Meadows from Accounting joined them as did the location manager from one of the movies currently in production, Larry Mathews. Running over budget, they needed to decide if they should cover the expenses and take a larger share of profits, or sit tight and let someone else get a percentage. Nothing in David's demeanor indicated he had something brewing in his heart that excited him more than anything else in his life had stirred him until this date.

On Friday, as Ron and Sami rode home from the office in

their chauffeur driven limo, Ron reached over and took Sami's hand. He felt her stiffen and then, with discipline, relax. She allowed her hand to be held as she looked out the window by her side.

"Seems strange not to be meeting you in a restaurant in Manhattan. We became such predictable creatures, didn't we?"

She gave him an expressionless smile.

"Why don't we do something wild tonight?"

"Like what?" she frowned.

"Oh, I don't know. Why not hike out into the woods and build a bonfire? I'll bet you've never had S'mores!"

"What are those?"

Ron smiled. "It's roasted marshmallows squashed onto a graham cracker with a slab of chocolate."

She squinted in disgust. "I don't like being in the woods at night."

"Okay, let's go strolling into old town, sit in the coffee shop and talk with the locals."

"We can have coffee at home."

"I like their coffee."

"Then have some delivered."

"Isn't that a bit extravagant?"

"You married a wealthy woman, Ron. Live up to it."

"Okay, wealthy woman, what do you suggest we do tonight?"

"I'm going to curl up on the couch with some scripts I brought home from the office. I don't know what you're going to do."

"How romantic."

"I haven't discovered marriage to be that romantic."

"You haven't given it a chance. Romance has been given; you haven't received."

"Look!" she said sharply, "I only married you because David wanted me to."

He withdrew his hand from hers and turned away. 'Ditto', he thought. They rode the rest of the way in silence. At home they ate the meal waiting for them and then retired to their respective dressing rooms to put on clothes for the evening. Ron put on slacks and a sport coat to go to old town. Sami dressed in a velour jogging suit so as to be comfortable while she perused her scripts.

As he passed her sitting on the couch, he asked, "Why don't you get Readers for those scripts and they can select only the best to give to you to read."

"Don't be stupid, of course I do that. They go through hundreds of scripts, discarding the junk and I only read the choice ones. But I have spent years developing a sensitivity to know what will work and what won't. No one else can do this job in EE. It's up to me. I'm seldom wrong anymore."

He watched her go back to her work. "Well, I leave you to it. I'm on my way down to talk to the locals. See you in the morning."

Startled, she asked, "Aren't you coming back tonight?"

"Yes. But I'll go right to bed. Goodnight."

When Ron returned he went directly to his bedroom. Almost instantly the butler knocked on his door and brought in a tray balancing two frosted champagne flutes and a chilled bottle of Dom Pérignon. "Madame asked me to deliver this and then to knock on her door to indicate your arrival. Good night, sir."

A few minutes later Sami entered Ron's bedroom without knocking, draped in a frothy, magenta negligee. "I thought it over and I'm up for trying some wild ideas. What do you think?"

He yawned. "Oh, I don't know. I've got some scripts I brought home from the office, and besides, it's too late to build a fire and have samores." He stifled his surprise as she came over and pushed him onto the bed.

Sami slept in his room, waking with a satisfied smile and stretching like a cat, until she looked around. Ron, resting on an elbow, watching her, saw the transformation and wondered what mechanism triggered it.

"Oh." She said, "I need to be in my own bed. Tell Jefferson to bring my breakfast up on a tray."

"Tell him yourself. You seem to be the boss lady around here. I'm not your lackey. I'm your husband. You should be sleeping in my bed every night."

"Don't be gauche." She tried to get the frothy piece over her head again, but couldn't seem to figure it out so she went to Ron's closet for a robe. She got halfway across the room when Ron leapt from the bed and grabbed her arm.

"I wasn't finished."

She slapped him as hard as she could with her limited arm movement, since he had crushed her to his body. "Don't you ever grab me!"

He picked her up and dumped her on the bed. "I said I wasn't finished." He poured out his passion on her receptive body. After their tryst, Sami having enjoyed herself as much as Ron, she leveled him with a steely gaze.

"Don't you ever treat me like a whore again!"

Ron's mouth dropped open. "Sami, you've been reading too many sleazy scripts." He moved to kiss her, but she pushed him away.

Tossing her parting shot over her shoulder as she slammed out of the room, Sami spat, "I don't read sleazy scripts. My staff weeds them out for me."

Two weeks later, David invited the couple for dinner on a Friday night. As they mounted the stairs to the Raznick family home, Ron pinched her bottom. After playing the roles of workaholics all week, he thought he'd liven up this sure to be dead party. She wheeled around, drawing in her breath and raising her chin. "What was that for?"

"I just wondered if the whore was still in there."

Before Sami could answer, the butler opened the door. She smoldered until halfway through dinner; then looking across the table at Ron she smiled as if she had just gotten the joke. He grinned back and turned with a frown to his father-in-law. "You know, David, we might have to be leaving pretty soon."

"You can't go yet. I have some very important news to unveil. I've been working on this night and day and chose to tell you two over an intimate, family dinner. You can't imagine how important this is to me. So no, you can't leave. After dinner we'll go into my study and I'll lay out my plans."

Finishing dessert, Sami's mother excused herself and ordered the butler to bring up a cup of tea and draw her bath. David, Sami and Ron entered the study as if playing parts in a whodunit. The butler served them coffee and then went to deliver the tea.

"I've never known you to act this way, David. Go on then, spill your big news."

"Okay. Here it is. All my adult life I've had a secret, something about me that I've told to a very, very few people. A harbored mystery. A desire I've had since I was a kid doing odd jobs on the movie lots."

"David, for heaven's sakes, tell me."

"I've always wanted to own my own motion picture studio. I've wanted my own version of Paramount Studios, my own kind of UA, and now I am going to have it. I'm going to have my own VIVA!"

"Viva?" she asked incredulously.

"Vanguard Interpretive Visual Arts!"

Ron, knowing something like this was coming, could respond with a little more enthusiasm. He applauded. "Bravo! Viva! Long live David Raznick!"

Sami's mouth hung open until she finally said, "What would you want to do that for? We're in a position to dominate the whole industry. You become a studio and all the investors will dominate you."

"I'm not going to become a studio; Entertainment Equities is going to develop one as an extension of itself. And here's the big news. Ron La Fave will be the CEO!"

The moment flip flopped into its being Ron's turn to let his mouth gape open. "Me? Why me? I don't know the first thing about making movies! No. David. It's you. You should be the CEO. It's the only natural sequence of events. You've got the knowledge; you do it."

"My boy, my boy, my boy!" David enthused. "I'll be at your side day and night. I'll mentor you, I'll position you into authority. I know you. You'll be great!"

Sami clattered her cup to her saucer. Both men looked started. "And what about me?"

Ron thought desperately to himself, 'Yeah, you could make Sami the CEO.' But he knew enough to keep his mouth shut.

"You could not fill that role, Sami. I know what I'm doing. You have another extension to create and to run. EE will develop these two simultaneously. You will ferret out and purchase the derelict movie theatres around the United States and refurbish them into movie restaurants. They'll be called VIVA Theatres."

Sami huffed, "My reaction is the same as Ron's. What do I know about finding old movie houses, and especially about remodeling? And if you don't mind my asking, what is a movie restaurant?"

"Don't get so ruffled, Sami. I got the idea while I watched you organize the building of your house. You're a natural. You'll figure out a way to find these old places. Those houses were usually beautifully built, magnificently decorated because going to a movie back then was like going to live drama now. They had velvet curtains, murals painted on the walls, sconces and dazzling chandeliers. They'll be a breeze to make over. You'll add a kitchen, get a chef, take out every other row of seats and install tables, leaving room for the patrons to sit down and room for the waiters to serve from the other side of the table."

"I must admit, David, it's a very romantic idea. Don't you think so, Sami? And I agree with your father. You could do this job with one arm tied behind your back."

"What's the date for the Board to meet to vote on this?" she asked coldly. "You know I much prefer reading and approving the scripts. I may not be able to give them a positive answer."

"Don't you worry your pretty head. I don't want to see one wrinkle come onto that expensive face because once you've got this company going, then it's a matter of maintenance and you can go back to deciding the fate of America's scriptwriters."

"David. It's a lousy idea and I don't want to do it."

"Sami. You will do this and the subject is closed. Now, about you, Ron. The studio, of course, will have to be located in the Los Angeles area. I've got a town house out there which we can use as base camp until we get the physical property established. I'll have to steal you away from New York, however, to work in LA during the week and Rye on the weekends.

"I also want you to move your office out here in Rye to be near me. Sami will need your Manhattan office for more staff anyway."

"So that's why you had me keep the Park Avenue apartment?"

"As it turns out, keeping the apartment seems to have been an inspiration. By the way, did I mention you will be the CEO of VIVA Theatres?"

"Why can't I be CEO of VIVA Studios? That seems more appropriate to me. Let Ron run the hum drum little sideline. I, at least, know something about film making. Why give him the plum job and not me?"

"Stop complaining! It's a wonderful opportunity for you both. Be happy."

David looked from one to another. Ron's eyes resembled saucers as he tried to absorb this weighty and lofty future. Sami's eyes flashed with anger as she said, "You've thought of everything."

"All except babies," David said. "I don't know what to do when you get pregnant."

"No need to worry about that. I'm not having babies."

Ron's eyes blinked as if to clear his thoughts. "You're not?"

"No."

"Don't you think you should discuss this with me?"

"No."

"Why not?"

"It's my body. I'll do with it what I want. No babies."

"You don't want children?"

"No. I have plans."

"Plans can always be worked around children."

"Not my plans."

"Am I included in your plans?"

"If you want to be."

"Kids! Kids!" David interrupted. "No fighting on the playground! We're going to have too much fun!"

Steaming, Sami did not say another word. At home, Ron put his hand on the wall to keep her from passing him into her room. "Don't be upset with me, Sami. I didn't dream this up."

She gave him a look of concentrated hatred. He felt physically attacked and backed away. She closed her door and he heard the bolt click into the lock. Shrugging his shoulders with the loathing he sensed for this fetid family, he went to bed. The next morning Ron lingered at the breakfast table waiting for Sami to come down to eat. Finally he asked the butler if he had seen Mrs. La Fave this morning.

"She left, sir. I heard someone in the garage underneath my room about three this morning. It must have been the slamming of the trunk that woke me. I felt the rumble of one of the garage doors opening. Looking out the window I saw her car drive away. I took the liberty of checking her bedroom; her door was ajar. She was gone."

"Thank you." Ron took another swallow of coffee, thinking he mustn't look too disconcerted, and then went upstairs to see her bedroom for himself. Things were awry, to say the least. She must have packed a suitcase, discarding some clothes and leaving them here and there.

Then he checked the garage. The slot reserved for her black

Mercedes stood empty. He felt like jumping into his white Volvo and getting out of there himself, but he knew he walked in a plan of his own making that, although discombobulated by David's searing ego, seemed to be working amazingly well, except for his jealous wife. Perplexed, he walked around the property as if inspecting it, while he puzzled what to do.

Going back into the house, he called David from the study. "Sami has run away. I haven't seen her since she went into her bedroom last night, locking the door to keep me out; she left around three this morning, according to the butler. If you don't know where she is, then I presume she's at the apartment."

David breathed out his agitation. "I think I presented my big plans too abruptly last night. Like I told you, I want too much too quickly and even though I have learned to pace myself over the years, this plan is too juicy for me. I should have only presented Sami's part last night, making her feel very important. But I didn't.

"She's going to love this company I'm creating for her. I've done the market research on VIVA Theatres and the public that was polled responded very positively to dinner and a movie. Sami will be heading up a market trend. All these big 20 plexes that are practically never filled, will be rushing to restructure their floors, eliminating their slope, removing a row and creating a dining base. Studios that produce short subjects will be on the rise as their films come into demand during the dinner hour.

"It's all going to be great. Don't worry about Sami; I'll take care of her. Her mother and I will have lunch at the club as usual; we'll see if Sami shows up. If she doesn't, I'll call the apartment and arrange to meet with her. If I were you, I wouldn't call her. It wouldn't be good to chase after her. Let her come home with her tail between her legs."

'Fat chance', thought Ron. "Okay, David. I'll wait to hear from you." After he hung up he wondered what he would do with an empty Saturday. What had he done in the past? 'I wandered around New York City dreaming about Summer. That's what I did.' Shaking his head in regretful disgust, he considered his other options. He didn't want to go into the office, he might run into Sami. Finally he decided to visit his father at Stauffer's. A day with the family would do him good and if he weren't home when David called back, so much the better, let them worry about him for a change.

Ron had supper with his folks, returning home a little after nine, just in time to receive David's call. "Sorry to be so late in calling you, you've probably been a nervous wreck." Ron looked at the ceiling and shook his head but said nothing as David roared ahead.

"Sami is mollified. I found her at the apartment and then we had dinner at Mardi's for old time's sake. She trusts I have her best interests at heart; but she doesn't feel the same about you. When I left she said she does not want to see you until Tuesday lunch. She wants you to clear out your office in Manhattan on Monday and she'll stay away till you're gone. Ron, go see her tomorrow. Prove to her how important she is to you."

Ron stifled a groan. "Sure thing, David. That's the ticket. I'll do just that. As for Monday, is there an office ready for me in Rye?"

"Clean as a whistle! Have your secretary hire a moving company to get your things over here right away."

"Will do. See you Monday."

After a leisurely breakfast Sunday morning, reading the New York Times practically till noon, Ron ordered the car and driver. Arriving at the elite Park Avenue apartment, the doorman opened the car door and signaled to a man leaning against the building. Before Ron could register the focused movement on the sidewalk, a flashbulb exploded in his face, momentarily blinding him.

The man operating the camera kept snapping shots while barraging him with questions. "Have you and your wife separated after one month of marriage?" Confused, Ron stood rooted on the sidewalk. "Why did she walk out on you?"

The chauffeur got out of the car and took Ron's arm. "What did you do to destroy the confidence of the movie magnate's daughter in you?" The driver tried to shove the photographer away while he guided Ron into the building. "Are you having an affair? Are you gay?"

Shoving Ron into the lobby and shutting the door, he gave a fierce look at the doorman, who pretended innocence and belatedly ran to prevent an intrusion by the photographer. With dignity the chauffeur re-entered the car and drove away.

Ron hurried to the elevator wondering why a photographer would be interested in his marital squabbles. 'Must be a slow news day.' Then he thought he'd better inform David right away.

Sami, not having received a phone call from the doorman announcing Ron's arrival, nonchalantly opened the door, but seeing Ron, pushed it closed again. However, he already had his foot in the way. Having analyzed his approach on the drive, he knew he had to use words. Words were her love language. He knew this only by mulling over the scripts she chose to finance.

He knew he had to start by making love to her. As much as she protested his 'manhandling', passion was the only thing he found that softened her. Once softened, he could use his words. Therefore, when he shoved his way into the apartment, he grabbed her arm and pulled her to him.

He covered her mouth with a kiss. When she bit him he bit her back. Swinging her over his shoulder, he carried her to the bedroom while her fists pummeled him on the back. Their lovemaking took place quickly and completely. Afterward, he looked down at her, surprised to see tears pooling in her eyes. She exhaled and turned away whispering, "I hate you."

"No, you don't. You're just afraid to love me."

She writhed in his arms. "I am not afraid of anything!"

"Yes you are. You're afraid to believe that I will love you back."

"I don't need for you to love me!" she sputtered like a spitting cat.

"Frankly, Sami, that's the only thing you do need from me."

"I don't need you for anything. All you want to do is use me to get next to my father. I can see that, now that he's made you CEO. I wanted that job. You took it from me!"

Ron shook his head ruefully. "I didn't take that job from you. I didn't know the job existed until Friday night. As for the other, I'll be perfectly honest with you. I didn't marry you because I love you. On our wedding day Entertainment Equities was a far bigger thing to me than Sami Raznick. But now I live with you. I see you in good form and in bad. And I realize that if we are going to have a relationship, then we have to make it be more important to us than anything else in the world.

"If we work at it we can have a wonderful marriage. I want that. I want to be a good husband to you and I want you to be a good wife to me. I want us to have children, to raise them with love and for us to be a tight, happy family. Family is everything on this earth. What do you win if you get the whole world, but you lose your family? Now I have you for a family and I want to love you. I don't know how. You're going to have to help me."

She whispered as if she were a lost child. "I don't want to have children."

He stroked her hair off her forehead and kissed her gently, a kiss which she weakly returned. He said haltingly, "I think you don't want children because you're afraid you won't be a good mother." The tears overflowed the corners of her eyes.

He continued, "I may be wrong, this is sheer speculation, but I wonder if David wasn't so disappointed in not having a son that you have tried to become the best boy-girl you could be in order to please him. He has a very strong personality and I think by the time you were born your mother had caved in emotionally and became a yes-man to him. He took you as his own and she's never had much input in your life.

"If you love someone else and actually try to become a womanly woman, with children, you're afraid you'll lose David's love. Right now you don't trust me to love you and you're afraid of losing your father. You think I have usurped your position with him. And you may be right. I have become his right arm. But Sami, you no longer belong there. You belong under my right arm."

She stiffened and narrowed her eyes. "You were doing great until that comment. Who are you to tell me where I belong?"

"That's what I'm trying to say. I'm your husband. And I'm determined to be the best husband you could possibly have."

Her stare pierced his eyes. "My work is of utmost importance."

"That's fine. Just leave it at the office. When we're together, we are of utmost importance. It doesn't sound like David is going to give us much time to be together, but when we are, our relationship is much more important than Entertainment Equities or any of its sidelines. Do you agree with me?"

Her eyes clouded as she considered the question. "I don't trust you. In my opinion, you're just trying to become David's heir apparent. But here we are, aren't we? I've never wanted a marriage like my parents have. I hardly know my mother."

"You're not the kind of woman your mother is. Given that you are the kind of woman you are and I am the kind of man I am, wouldn't you at least try to make our marriage work?" Ron looked at her with entreaty, but not dominance.

Quietly Sami replied, "I'll try. That's the best I can say at this point. I'll try."

Ron smiled. As he leaned to kiss her, he said, "That's a good step forward. We can start from there."

She moaned as she intensely wrapped her arms around his shoulders. Between kisses she whispered, "There are times I would like to be a feminine woman."

Surprised that those words should be such a stimulant for him, Ron proceeded to make love to her again. This time when they finished, Sami's peace was such she could hardly move. He held her gently, stroking her arm as he whispered, "You're quite a woman, Sami. Quite a woman."

She pulled her head away and said playfully. "I'm hungry. Want to go to Central Park for a hotdog?"

He grinned, "I'd love to. Think we can get through the paparazzi downstairs?"

"What are you talking about?"

When he explained she abruptly sat up in bed and dialed the phone. "Daddy! Okay, David, whatever. A photographer is downstairs asking if Ron and I have split up."

"Of course not. He's right here beside me. He's the one they attacked. What do we do?"

"Okay. So you'll take care of it?"

"Alright. We'll wait an hour before going out."

Sami spent the first part of the day trying to see New York through Ron's eyes. Then she realized his eyes saw his city through animated memories of childhood. She gasped behind a raised hand in the revelation she had never seen it through her own memories of childhood, not with David's requirements that she be an adult and skip being a child.

Tears forming as she tried childhood on for size, Sami frolicked, leap froging over fire hydrants, pouncing on park benches like Queen on the Hill, balance beaming on the fence bordering the horse trail in Central Park and licking ice cream so unabashedly that it smeared her cheeks. That day brought Sami the closest to being a girl-child that she could remember. Ron knew she lived that day for herself, he being an accessory and he willingly watched her unfold.

On Monday she helped her husband move his office to Rye. They left the building at 8 p.m. grabbed a quick bite and then packed a bag for Ron in preparation for his leaving early the next morning for California with David. Sami instructed him in the ways of Hollywood, what clothes to take and how to socialize with David.

Ron called Sami every day from the townhouse, but time took them farther apart and by the end of the week he knew he had lost her again to her work. To be fair, VIVA engrossed him.

His attempts to revitalize their relationship built in one day in the park became laborious and he settled down into building a motion picture studio instead.

Sami threw herself into VIVA Theatres with a vengeance. On the Internet she found a unique team of journeymen who called themselves Have Tools Will Travel. Their convoy of recreational vehicles traveled to any site in North America to build or rebuild whatever the customer wanted. She flew to personally inspect their work and became enraptured with the results. Her next stop landed in Portland to visit a dilapidated theater which she immediately purchased. Escrow would be finished in eight weeks and miraculously, the Have Tools Will Travel crew could start that next Monday. All of that kept her away from home when Ron came back two weeks later for a weekend visit.

He felt a mounting desire to celebrate as he and David had located an abandoned, private airstrip with two enormous hangars and an office building which contained a half dozen classrooms. Once owned by the California University system, many a pilot trained there until the Board of Directors deemed it too expensive to operate. The property lay fallow for 20 years until David hired a real estate agent to find him sufficient space to establish a motion picture studio. The deal done, Ron flew to New York to crow, but his cock-a-doodle-doo aroused no one.

He tried spending Friday night rattling around his and Sami's empty monstrosity of a house. Bored, he went to the town coffee shop to chat with the locals, but most of them had gone home and the rest poked fun at his bragging about his exploits and mocked him. By the time he got home the staff had retired for the night. He called Kirk and Darce, even though he talked to Kirk daily, but they were out for the evening.

Early the next morning he drove into Manhattan to spend the next 48 hours entrenched with his family. His younger sister, visiting from college for the weekend, gave him the most excited response, after he promised her a cameo role in one of the movies. His common sense mother treated him as if he was playing games and she wished he would get serious with his life.

Annoyingly, his father unnerved him. "Ronnie, Ronnie, what does God get from your work? That's the question. That's the only question that deserves an answer. Is it God telling you to make this studio? Then He will make the movies."

Ron pushed back from the dinner table, nonplused, "Did God tell you to become a tailor?"

"Yes. At least I believe so. All my life I have had dreams. Real dreams. I dreamed many times about sewing fabrics and so I became a tailor. I told you that story over and over when you were a boy."

"Papa, I've never had dreams like that. God doesn't speak to me. I made up my own dreams all by myself when I was a kid and this studio is way beyond every thing I ever conjured up."

"God did not tell you, 'Build Me a movie studio?'"

"No."

Ron's father looked very sad, "Then you are doomed to fail, Ronnie."

Chuckling at his father, Ron said cavalierly, "I don't think so, Papa." But as he lay in bed, awake half the night, his father's words blazoned in his brain, he waffled between incredibility and stark fear. Ron finally decided his father had simply shared his old world superstitions and he dismissed the words from his mind.

Within six months VIVA Studios shaped into operational status. The first script, a family film where the family dog finds and rescues the kidnapped kids, came from Sami's previous stack of potential winners. Ron called Kirk. "I think it's time we cashed in a few of those stocks and made a real investment."

Kirk laughed. "What do you mean a 'real investment'? Are we heading into the big time?"

Ron cautioned, "Let's not be greedy. Sell, say, twenty five percent of mine. You and Darce will have to decide how much you want to dig into. David is graciously letting us be the only individual investors. The rest will be Entertainment Equities. This one is going to be a winner, Sami and David both agree."

"Unless Darce pulls a veto, we'll do twenty five percent, too. Here we go, buddy boy!"

By the time the film "Home Dog" premiered, ten theaters under Sami's directing eye, restructured and painted, presented themselves ready to receive it. And, as she and her father predicted, it wheeled itself into being a winner. VIVA swung right into another production, again a family film selected from the same stack of potential purchases, and proving to be another sure winner. Ron and Kirk let their original investment and their earnings ride into the new film, "On Tour With Mom", a comedy disclosing the escapades of a famous singer's children as they expose the unscrupulous activities of the tour's manager and save their beleaguered Mom's career.

Sami miraculously produced twenty five theaters ready for the screening of this film, her convoy of Have Tools Will Travel having expanded from six RVs to 20. Any remaining wisps of the girl-child had been swallowed up in the consuming heat of the throbbing lights, action, camera. The utmost importance of VIVA's success consumed them all and Ron and Sami rarely found themselves roving in the same location, much less bumping into each other in their secluded house.

Again, another winner. Two moderately measured box office successes assured Entertainment Equities that VIVA, itself, stood strong. Each board member, when they met to assess their position, felt the time to be ripe to pull out all stops. The time had come to find a box office blockbuster.

Chapter Thirteen
# THE MOVIE

They met in L.A. The fifteen well heeled Board Members of Entertainment Equities sat with bated breath around the oval conference table of the Park Plaza Penthouse. David thoroughly coached and prompted every member before they flew in for the meeting, but secretly, each one not only hoped but also believed in what they planned to say.

David polled the members, spotlighting each in the presence of the others, taking turns stoically around the table. Saving Kirk to the last, David asked, "Tell us how you assess our position. From your perspective, what do you recommend for our next step, Kirk? The rest of us, except for Ron, have turned a little stale around the edges, being the old codgers that we are, but as a refreshing newcomer, will you please give us your candid opinion?"

The pencil in Kirk's hand beat violently on the sharpened crease of his new trousers; Darce insisted he buy a new suit for this promising meeting. His eyes darted around the table before fixing on David. "Sami's point is well taken. If we were prudent we would produce two more moderate hits, two more sure-fire family films and have more cash in our pockets. However, it reassures me that every one else at this table voiced an opinion in favor of finding the blockbuster. You guys know what you're doing. I'm a stockbroker. Risk is the name of my game, so naturally my vote goes for the crap shoot. Let's get the blockbuster!"

Ron smiled to himself, glad to have a down-to-earth, straight forward friend in the midst of this self-serving society surrounding him. All eyes turned to Sami who raised her eyebrows. "So, who's got the blockbuster in their back pocket?"

"Don't you?" David asked with some disbelief.

"If I had a blockbuster in the stacks of scripts I have read, don't you think I would have pulled it out before this? We've invested in several in the last couple of years, but I don't have a script we can call our own."

All heads swiveled toward David. "Can you pull aside for awhile to find us one?" They swiveled back to Sami.

Relishing the position, Sami smiled inwardly as she said with great gravity, "No. Several theatres are at critical points of completion and I am in negotiation in about five cities for other sites. I don't have a minute to spare. I can't even stay to finish this board meeting."

"What about reading on the plane? You fly around so much these days."

"That's my time for going over drawings for the remodeling."

David frowned, "Then who took over reading the scripts?"

"Nobody." Sami shrugged, "I probably have 30 of them on my desk that Readers have sent. They're sitting there clamoring to be produced because that particular script, without a niggling doubt in the Reader's mind, promises to be the next great film in movie history. This means, 99 percent of the time, the writer shows him or herself to be above average. It requires somebody with a nose for the business to screen those down to 1 or 2 scripts worthy of production."

"And you don't have time to do that?" David asked incredulously.

This time Sami gave her father an 'I told you so' look and defiantly said, "None whatsoever."

He glared back wondering whether to order her to take the time when one of the members suggested, "We have four more days to meet together. We can shift our schedule, cancel the golf tournament, maybe postpone the lunch with the mayor, and read those scripts ourselves. Could your secretary overnight them to us, Sami? We'd have them first thing in the morning and we can read and swap until we've narrowed the field down to say, five, and then you can select the best."

David quickly polled the members and everyone voted to dedicate the next four days to script selection. David's secretary called the mayor to see about switching their engagement to this evening's dinner, to which, due to an untimely cancellation, the grand public servant dutifully complied. Then David dismissed the meeting until 7:00 p.m. when they would reconvene in the Gold Rush room.

Leaving the meeting quickly, David traversed the lobby purposefully to avoid being hailed by acquaintances, keeping his eyes on the limo awaiting him at the front door. He preferred staying in his condo close by and intended to rest there until dinner. As he approached the chauffeur holding the car door open for him, a disheveled man disengaged himself from leaning against a pillar and accosted David.

"Man, you gotta read my script!" He shoved a handful of dirty pages into David's chest. "Take it! My name's on it! Call me! My phone number's there, too!"

The chauffeur stepped between David and the man, making some of the pages flutter away in the breeze. David scooted around the chauffeur, quickly climbed into the car and closed the door behind him. As the man chased after his soiled pages, the chauffeur drove away.

David watched his assailant out the window, "Someone said

that even the squirrels write scripts in Hollywood, but I didn't know the homeless people were into it too. Why would he approach me?"

"You're the head of Entertainment Equities and of VIVA Studios." The driver said a bit incredulously.

"But I keep my name out of the press. Only Ron's name is publicly known in connection with the studio."

"With all due respect, Mr. Raznick, anyone with access to the internet knows who you are and the role you've played for the last twenty five years in movie-making."

It was David's turn to be incredulous. "And you think he has access to the internet?"

"It's free in the library," the driver remarked.

David frowned. "Did you get a good look at him?"

"Yes sir."

"If you see him hanging around again, call the police, will you?"

"Certainly."

Ron stayed at the hotel with Sami. She only had the one night as tomorrow she planned to fly out to meet with certain members of Have Tools Will Travel. Returning on Thursday evening, she felt annoyed that tonight Ron chose to stay with her instead of returning to the condo.

He leaned against the dresser in the bedroom of their suite watching Sami remove her jewelry. "You really enjoyed sticking it to David, didn't you?"

She wheeled around and threw her words across the room. "Don't talk down to me from your lofty position, Mr. CEO!"

He held his hands up in surrender. "Hey! Sami. Hold on. You are doing a magnificent job with VIVA Theatres. I don't know how you did so much so quickly. You're a marvel. I just think you made your point pretty dramatically. And you're right. David took you away from what you do so well, and love to do and you're the best at it. But then, you're the best at whatever you do."

Mollified, Sami turned to the dressing table and reached to

unclasp her necklace. "Don't talk to me about my relationship with David."

Ron grimaced as he inwardly chastised himself. "You're right. I'm sorry. I broke my own rule. When you and I are together, we are more important than Entertainment Equities, VIVA Studios and VIVA Theatres." He then sauntered across the room to undo the necklace with which she grappled.

"Does that mean you're having dinner with me in the suite? I'm in for the evening."

Ron stepped back. "It's a business meeting, Sami. I have to entertain the Mayor."

"So much for being more important than VIVA Studios."

"Well, what about you? Will you work tonight?"

"If you're not here, yes."

"And if I am here?"

"Frankly, I didn't anticipate that you would be." Sami went into the walk-in closet to change her clothes, shutting the door behind her.

The next morning David ordered a different meeting venue for the Board. The hotel arranged a comfortable lounge with 14 commodious reading chairs and continuous beverage service. Beside each chair stood a small table on which the catering department served a three course sandwich lunch, plus other noshing matter upon demand so that each member could keep reading. By five they adjourned until dinner at seven.

33 scripts had to be read by 14 members until they settled on the five best to present for Sami's approval. David set the criteria that if three votes came against a script, it would be abandoned. That day the members eliminated ten scripts.

Ron remained in the hotel in order to have quality time with Kirk and Darce. David still preferred his condo. As he crossed the lobby, headed for his limo, a distinguished young man cut into his path and held out his hand. "Mr. David Raznick, I presume?"

David stopped momentarily as the man produced a binder

which had been dangling from his other hand. "I have your next hit right here. Please do me the honor of reading it."

Looking from the binder to the young man's face, he recognized him as the accosting street person from the day before. David became thoughtful, "You clean up very well. However, this is not the way things are done. Please go through the proper channels to have your script read."

The assistant manager, having noticed the interloper, appeared beside them. "Is everything all right, Mr. Raznick?"

Stepping back, David said, "I don't believe this gentleman is a guest in your hotel."

Taking the young man's arm, the assistant manager said firmly, "Come with me." He escorted him out of the hotel, and then directed the chauffeur to drive to a rear entrance where he accompanied David to make a discreet departure.

On Wednesday the Board Members eliminated thirteen more scripts, leaving ten. David instructed the hotel to make fresh copies of the remaining hopefuls so that each member would have their own to scrutinize. They dismissed at 6 p.m. but the weary members asked for a night off, each wanting to go their own way.

As David took the elevator down, he wondered if he would encounter the earnest scriptwriter again, but doubted it. Surely two humiliations were enough. As he stepped out the front door to meet his driver, an attractive young woman walking up the sidewalk hailed him. "David! David Raznick! Is that you?"

He stopped, a faint glimmer of recognition in his brain, but not enough to remember a name, he said, "Yes?"

She reached him by now and laughed. "Why, you don't remember me! We met at the premiere of 'Laughing Waters'. Angela Bassett." Holding out her hand, she smiled with pleasure.

He shook her hand, "I'm sorry. I meet so many people."

"That's quite alright. My role wasn't a major one. But as long as you're here, could I interest you in a drink?" She cocked her head back toward the hotel.

He shook his head with a smile, "I've had a grueling day. I need to go home." He turned to the limo, but she caught his arm.

"Your Board Members are meeting this week, aren't they?"

Frowning, he nodded.

"Word has it you're looking for scripts."

Disgusted, he said, "Word gets around, doesn't it?" He tried to pry her hand from his arm, but she held on tight.

"My brother has a dynamite script. Do yourself a favor and read it." David recognized the binder as she stuck it between his coat and shirt. Then she fled.

Exhaling his exasperation, he started to hand it to the doorman for disposal, but something made him take it into the limo. In his hot tub, with his head balancing an ice pack, he read the script. Over dinner he read it again, then one last time before turning the lights out.

As the members began their third day of digesting scripts, David asked them to reduce the number to three in order to save Sami's nerves. They raced through the readings, having read them before, and then tussled with each other over the pros and cons of each one. Miraculously, by three p.m. they had settled on three scripts they all felt held great potential.

In that tantalizing moment of accomplishment, David chose to pass out copies of the script he consumed three times the night before. Explaining the episodes with the scriptwriter and his sister, a character actress, having made a few phone calls and finding her to be a viable performer, David asked them to carefully consider the man's work.

During the reading several men sputtered pejoratives. David smiled, waiting for the end result.

"Disgusting!"

"Impossible!"

"No way!"

When the last member threw his script on his side table, David polled the group. "Expound. Think it through out loud. What are the possibilities here?"

"Trash! Nothing but wicked trash! Extremely well-written trash, but who could we show this to?" Member number one turned the corners of his lips down as he shook his head in disapproval."

Member number two concurred. "I agree. I must admit the vividness of the scenes hit me between the eyes. It stretched before me as if I could already see a marvelous period piece. But who wants to watch homosexual pornography? Even if all the gays in the world paid for a ticket, it would not make a blockbuster. Not for what we would have to pay to produce it."

David nodded to the next one. "We could certainly re-write the explicit sex scenes and simply insinuate them. It does make a splendid period piece. The high intellectualism of the 18$^{th}$ century as demonstrated in the Salon Society could be filmed in Paris itself. You know, I can visualize those vivid scenes in the various mansions with the corresponding costuming and I would be enthralled to watch that bit of history unfold on the screen."

The fourth member chimed in. "When you say we could subdue the raw sex blatantly written into the script, well, that kind of changes it for me. The character added a wild streak to that lofty society and made them take stock of themselves, especially at the end. This script could be a society changing tool. That's probably why he wrote it."

"The poignancy of the character's life, I mean, what tragedy. Clearly the character became the darling of the intellectual society because of his charming articulation. Really, this is one brilliant screenwriter. Yet the character must wallow in the scum pots of Paris in order to be satisfied sexually and ends up dying in the gutter from his lover's own knife. That alone might be a story worth telling, if it were heterosexual love. But that would stop the story in its tracks because he wouldn't have to go to the ghetto if he weren't gay." Member five shook his head sadly.

The sixth member stepped right in. "The way the movie ends, in silence, is powerful, with each character reading the newspaper and reacting to the column about his death without verbalization. It's going to take some fine acting to portray that. Can we afford that many heavy hitters?"

David nodded to the seventh member. "I like the title, Wild Card. In his day he may have been the wild card, but he wouldn't be that today. Maybe it's a subject whose time has come. Even so, we've got to play down the explicit sex."

Member eight asked, "Can we get this screenwriter to work with us? Or do we buy the script and hire someone else?"

Member nine said, "My thoughts were going there too. I think we do everything we can to get the original writer. I wouldn't want to diminish his writing and I can't imagine anyone else brilliant enough to add to what he has done."

The tenth member tapped his fingers together thoughtfully. "I don't like it. I don't like it at all. I don't want my grandchildren watching this kind of a movie and I think every blockbuster has to have some family appeal. Most people consider homosexuality to be an abomination. That's what it says in the Bible. However, this is a brilliantly written script. The Bible doesn't talk about the person being an abomination, only the act. If we could bring out the pathos of the main character through the desperation of his perversion, then we've got something."

"To tell the truth, the other three scripts we've chosen don't hold a candle to this one." Member eleven looked sad that that was the case.

"As much as the subject matter disturbs me, and I'm convinced it disturbs the majority of Americans, it is a hot topic and I think we are holding in our hands our blockbuster." Member twelve nodded his approval.

"Ron, what about you?" David asked.

The CEO smiled ruefully, "I'm not wild about Wild Card, but I will defer to Sami. She's the one with the nose for the business. Let her read it and tell us." Many nodded and murmured their agreement.

"And you, Kirk? Last but not least. What say you?"

"I'm not a reader; I'm a stockbroker. I think its tripe."

"Well, once again a candid opinion voiced. Thank you." David smiled. "As the last to voice an opinion, let me say I like it. I even like it with the explicit sex scenes. Let it inform the public in every way possible. Let it be the movie that every one talks about. When was the last time you saw a movie you talked about over dinner? I think we've got something solid to give the viewers. We've got plot; we've got scenery; we've got thought provocation; we've got dynamic parts for acting. We are going to be bombarded with the giants wanting to play in this. I'm sold. But I agree with Ron, let's wait on Sami."

They dismissed at six, once again to follow their own pursuits in the evening. Kirk, Darce and Ron opted for seafood overlooking the placid Pacific Ocean. As the waves lapped on shore, practically under their feet, Ron and Kirk pitched the movie to Darce. She didn't need to play devil's advocate; they were doing a fine job. They returned to the hotel in time for Ron to be waiting for Sami when she arrived.

Coming in about ten, Sami entered the suite behind the bellman pushing her luggage on a brass cart. The cell phone wedged between her shoulder and her ear did not keep her from adequately tipping the man and then rifling through her briefcase to extract a needed paper.

"Cy, I know what time it is in New York. I've got it right here; I'll take it downstairs and have the last page faxed to you immediately."

"No. You don't get to go home until you've signed off on this contract. Philadelphia is squeamish. Unless we get this deal signed, sealed and delivered ASAP, we may lose The Grand. You can call me first thing in the morning which will give you a little time to sleep in. I don't get up till seven."

By this time Sami had shut the door and headed for the elevator to fax the disputed contract with the City of Philadelphia to her tired lawyer. This would enable VIVA Theatres to buy and refurbish The Grand, a stately, unfeigned, movie house, diminished to a derelict condition, situated on the edge of the chi-chi part of town, a real plum.

Ron watched this scenario relaxing in the easy chair where he had waited for her. She had not acknowledged his presence, even though she looked his way. He neatly stacked the scripts he had reviewed over and over and went into his walk in closet and changed into pajamas,

Sami didn't return until one a.m. but when she did she came in blazing. The slamming of the door and the blaring of the overhead light woke Ron. "Have you read this?" Sami demanded, thrusting the 'Wild Card' script under his nose.

Ron nodded that he had. "Well, don't talk to me about it! I'm going to be up all night going over this thing again!" She turned on the small reading lamp by the desk and switched off the overhead chandelier. "Leave me alone!"

Ron questioned groggily, "No time for me?"

"Shut up." She scowled at him, "Go to sleep." Then she scowled at the script.

Lifting his head to look at her, Ron asked, "How about taking a few days to unwind after this and going to visit that cabin in Jackson Hole?"

"I hate the mountains. We'll wait a few years and then sell that thing, sight unseen as far as I'm concerned. Now leave me alone."

Ron turned over and obligingly went to sleep.

The meeting convened at nine a.m., as expected, around the oval table of the Penthouse Complex. These normally stoic bottom line businessmen, unruffled by any blip on the screens of life, knowing they could change things by investing money or applying intellect, seemed to demonstrate an undue amount of mopping of the brow. Any hidden nervous tic came unsolicited to the surface. However, all talk was small.

David appeared to be waiting for someone as he kept checking the door without actually opening the meeting. Finally his awaited guest slipped through the door and approached David with a bear hug, not simply a handshake. The CEO of Entertainment Equities seated his long time friend and called the meeting to order. Everyone's attention focused on Dr. Stu Huddleston. "Stu is an old friend from the neighborhood; we grew up together in the back lots of Hollywood. He went on to become Head of the Film Department at UCLA, and I landed in New York. We've kept in touch over the years and when Sami came to school out here, he took my daughter under his wing during her four years at UCLA.

"Not only does he bring his renowned expertise to our table, after all he is responsible for bringing more films to the screen than any other human being, he also brings his personal life. For years Stu has quietly maintained a home with a significant other, a certain gentleman who Stu keeps out of the limelight, preferring to keep his personal life personal. That does not mean he hides his chosen lifestyle; not at all. He lives it well. That's why he is here today.

"Night before last, when I read the script for the first time, I made a copy and called for a courier to hand deliver it to Stu. He did me the great favor of reading and critiquing the script on such short notice and now he is here to give us the benefit of his wisdom. I don't even know what he is going to say. So Stu? The floor is yours."

Stu Huddleston leaned forward, elbows on the chair arms, hands clasped in front of his well-exercised midriff. His gray hair lent him the appearance of wisdom as he smiled, his keen eyes dissecting his audience. Every man felt like a schoolboy called into the presence of the Headmaster.

"It's an honor to be included in such an auspicious moment in history, which is what I consider the production of this movie to be. Of course David will not regard my presence as a favor when he receives my bill." Mild chuckles rolled around the table.

"It will be a pleasure to pay."

Stu looked up as if seeing something far off and then paced his words. "You are astute students of the cinema. I don't need to tell you how brilliantly this script has been written. The beats cascade like those of 'Casablanca'. Tension rises and falls like a heartbeat. The writer takes two steps forward and one step backward, two steps forward, one step backward, mounting to a crescendo, keeping the audience on the edge of their seats. Regardless of the storyline, whoever wrote this script is a genius.

"But the storyline, ah, the storyline. No doubt you could replace the drama with the anguished plight of an ingénue. One can imagine a star-crossed painter, or ill-fated writer from that period in history, whose misfortunes deny him the place in society he deserves and affords him the death in the gutter. With what this writer has done you would still have a knock out screenplay.

"I think, however, you have this occasion, should you choose to accept the challenge, to forcefully bring home the dominant issue in our society today. Can homosexuals finally come in out of the rain? Making it a period piece demonstrates the issue has always been with us. Is it really up to man to decide whether it is right or wrong? The fact that homosexuality exists is enough of a case to make room for it in our society.

"Nothing to my knowledge has ever made that point more poignantly than Wild Card. I want to keep my words brief; I'm not here to sell you. But I do ask that if you decline to make the movie, please place this script in my hands and I will see to it that others will bring it to the screen. History pivots on moments like these. I won't let my generation keep plodding when I know this is available to them."

David waited, thinking Stu would continue, but he was through. Clearing his throat he asked, "Are there any questions for Stu?"

"Do you think the public is ready for this?"

"I think the public is desperate to know the truth."

"What about the explicit sex scenes?"

"It can be filmed without showing the men's private parts, even without full nudity. What is important is to show the love, the tenderness, the desire, the passion and the naturalness of it."

"What about the Bible believers? They won't buy the idea that it is natural."

Stu smiled indulgently. "One fine Christian man explained to me that God loves me but He hates what I do. I told him I believe God loves me and if He hates what I do then I would be happy for Him to change me. But He hasn't.

"We've stopped arguing about whether we were born this way or not. For most of us, it's all we can remember. I don't defy God with my homosexuality; I simply express love that way. Fortunately I live in Los Angeles and work for a University where I don't have to hide who I am, nor do I have to defend who I am. I would that the rest of the world had the freedom I enjoy. I believe this movie can break that yoke on society and let us live in peace."

The magnitude of the proposed action stilled everyone's tongue, except Sami's. "And if you're wrong? If this movie demonstrates to the populace what they already believe, that gays are self-absorbed, self-serving and twisted in their sexual preferences, who's going to do the mop-up? VIVA Studios will have a hard time fighting it's way back into the game, most of us in this room will be financially depleted, if not downright bankrupt, because we will have one of the most expensive flops in history on our hands."

No one spoke except the one who could admonish as a father, "Sami!"

She held up her hand and glared at him. "I'm not denying Dr. Huddleston the right to live his life. I am defending VIVA Studios and Entertainment Equities. For however long this earth has been populated, homosexuality has been present. One movie is not going to change the course of history."

Stu sat up straighter. "I've known you since you were a little girl, I considered you as my apprentice when you were here in

UCLA, Sami, and I have known and admire your iron will. Your desire to protect and preserve is admirable. But great film requires risk and this film requires greater risk than most. I believe in this script. I believe the time has come to proclaim this message.

"Casablanca was a great film. They rewrote history to create the script because nothing existed there. There were no refugees flooding that city. Actually, Casablanca was nothing more than a trading post for the nomads. There was no intrigue. Yet today, everyone thinks that the turning point in the war occurred by what happened in Casablanca. Think about it. You have an opportunity to forge history."

After the departure of Dr. Huddleston, heated debate took place. The members were unaccustomed to raising their voices as the force of their wills and the clout of their bank accounts usually carried the day. But the proposal on the table demanded moral acumen and that had little to do with bottom line thinking.

Finally one of them demanded loudly, "Forget all this! What matters to us is will it sell?"

There was silence. Finally David said, "Let's poll the table. " He pointed to the first one, then the second and after that the vote went automatically around the room.

"Yes."

"Yes."

"Yes." And so it went.

Only Sami remained to state her opinion. With bated breath the room waited for her wisdom. "It will sell. We should more than break even. I personally don't expect this to be our blockbuster, but it will certainly train us to operate in big budget films.

"Remember, the job I am currently undertaking will ultimately cost Entertainment Equities about fifty million dollars. Our goal is 100 theatres and so far I'm averaging the costs at about 500,000 for each completed theatre, from purchase to opening night. Before I started this monumental task, EE itself had about fifty million on reserve, half of which it loaned to VIVA Studios. The other half came as a loan to VIVA Theatres. Anything either the Studios or the Theatres do beyond the EE loans will come out of individual pockets, unless we incur commercial debt, which of course no one wants."

Heads nodded in approval around the table.

"Ron, after the final accounting for the two little films we've produced, what kind of reserves does VIVA Studios have?"

"About ten million. That's the net profit above the twenty five million we started with."

David nodded encouragingly, "Not bad for a fledgling movie studio."

"And not good for the kind of project we want to propose." Sami hurried to say. "Although I'm not proposing it. I still want to wait until we have more films in the bank."

"By then, Sami, someone else will have produced Wild Card and scripts like this come along once every ten years. I say we go for it." Coming from member number one who had initially disapproved, the others looked at each other in wonderment.

"We could take it on option," someone suggested.

"That's only a stopgap. It won't give us enough time to produce two more films." The members began to agitate in their chairs.

"Do we seek outside investors?" Sami asked.

"Absolutely not!" David roared. "We have thirty five million and if it runs higher we'll cover it in-house."

"Well none of it will come from the Theatres! You gave me a job and I intend to finish it."

Smiling at his defiant daughter he said, "I wouldn't have it any other way. One more poll. Shall we go for it?"

All fifteen voted, "Yes."

Chapter Fourteen
# FEVERED FILM MAKING

"That's a wrap!" One hundred Extras, the Talent and the Stars dropped their characters bawdy, brawling body language and sauntered toward the Wardrobe trailers, or their own. One hundred cameramen, gaffers, lighting crew, electricians and soundmen dismantled the dollies, the booms, the cranes, the lighting panels, the microphones, the sets and stored them precisely in their cases, mounting them into the awaiting trucks. Within an hour the street in the Marais resembled itself again. Nervous drivers furtively parked by the curbs; pedestrian traffic indignantly brushed past the heretofore hindering French police and the First Unit of Wild Card dissolved into the serpentine streets of Paris.

Director Garry Ginsberg sauntered the few blocks to eat dinner at Les Trois Soeurs before catching up with Unit Two. Tonight they would film Salon scenes filled with gay laughter, sexual innuendo, and brilliant repartee under feigned candlelight in the four mansions they had rented near the Trocadéro. As he awaited his meal he called Ron in Los Angeles.

"Hello Ron. Garry here. Thought you'd like to know we finally had a full day shoot. The frogs cooperated, let us use our own Talent, and brought along enough translators to communicate with the extras."

"That's good news, Garry. Now give me the bad."

"How do you know there's bad news?"

"Because we're already ten million over budget for production! There will be nothing left for promotion and that budget should be double what you spend!' Ron shouted.

Garry closed his eyes and rubbed the space on his forehead between his eyebrows as if trying to connect them. "I just didn't foresee that it would be so hard to work with the frogs."

"Maybe if you stopped calling them frogs and gave them some respect, they'd give you some!"

"Well, maybe you'd like to come over here and run things yourself!"

"Look, Garry, let me calm down for a minute. I'm sorry for popping off like that. The budget is getting to me. You're a great director and I don't mean to be disrespectful to you. As a matter of fact, I am coming over. We decided today that I would come and take the burden of negotiating off your back. I'm bringing my own translator with me and hopefully we can get some movement flowing. I'll arrive tomorrow morning. Straight away I'm meeting with the Minister of Film and Media and then I'll join you on the shoot. According to your posted schedule that will be your last day in the Marais, isn't that right?"

"Well, Ron, we may need two additional days."

A long pause emanated from Los Angeles. Ron asked. "Was that the bad news you had for me?"

"No. The bad news is about Unit Three. The mayor of La Garde Freinet put a stop to all filming. It's an important venue because it's our character's birthplace, early childhood significance and all that. The town is a grand metropolis of 500 folks. On the precise spot where his family's shanty stood, they've built City Hall. It seems the City Fathers want to meticulously determine where to place this famous house. Tourists crawl all over that village anyway, so they want to organize their future traffic. They say a scene like this can bring another 50,000 gawkers to their town every summer. And, of course, the City Fathers can't come into agreement. Not that I want to make any more derogatory remarks about the French, but I'd sure like to."

"I'll handle that when I get there. Anything else?"

"Unit Four hasn't located any vineyards that would be comparable to the standards of the 1800s. Harvesting is done by machine here and no matter what the season the vines reflect the modern methods."

"What about Switzerland?"

"Too hilly."

"Italy?"

"Another government to work with."

"Let me see what I can do tomorrow. If nothing comes up we'll send the crew to Napa."

"Why not cut it, Ron? The vineyards have nothing to do with the integrity of the film."

"I ran that by David and he vetoed the cut. He said filmgoers need to see vineyards if the work is about France."

"It's your movie."

"You say that as if you mean it's my graveyard."

"No! No! It's a beautiful film. This is one of those epics that will last forever. Be encouraged Ron. You'll see. When this is all over and you are counting the 100 million net profit, you'll forget all this stuff. This is simply your first big hair-puller."

"Well, Garry. Help me along with this. Tomorrow night show me some exquisite clips to boost my expectations, okay?"

"You got it. Sleep on the plane and hit the ground running. I'll see you in the Marais. Do you have a car and driver?"

"Taken care of. I'll see you tomorrow." Ron hung up and buried his face in his hands. What else could possibly go wrong?

Forcing himself with grueling effort he made it through and two months later Ron held the finished product in his hands.

With six weeks extra filming, negotiations with the Stars agents, the Motion Picture Guilds, paying for the adjusted schedules, the final bill came to 115 million for production costs. Now to generate the money to produce the clips for promotion and inform the public that they wanted to, no, needed to see this film, Wild Card.

Ron called a Board Meeting. The members flew to L.A. and stayed in the Park Plaza. Scrimping on their food and lodgings would not alter the disastrous price of production, besides, it mustn't look to any outside scrutinizer that there was trouble in VIVA Studios. However, both Ron and Sami stayed at the condo with David.

David sat as a member, not as controlling director of EE in charge of it all. He lolled back watching Ron. Holding the can of film in the air. Ron began, "Gentlemen, and Sami, we have accomplished our mission. Wild Card is complete and stunning. We'll have a viewing tonight in the theatre at VIVA Studios and you can see for yourselves. After dinner in the Gold Rush room, limos will be waiting to take you to the Studios.

"You know the difficulties we faced in doing a period piece on location in another country, but the trials have ended and we are on the last leg. You also know the price tag. We spent 115 million. But I think you will like the prize we purchased. However, we now have to ante-up because no one in this business tolerates late payment. The 35 million is dispensed, David personally put in another 15 million which leaves 65 million to be collected. And then we have to calculate how we finance the 65 million, minimum, for promotion. Those decisions can be saved until tomorrow after you have seen the film."

He spent the rest of the afternoon outlining in detail what happened in production. Disgruntled, they asked questions which he calmly answered. They met for dinner at six and by eight were sitting in the plush theater seats. At ten thirty when the film flickered to a close, they sat in hushed silence until one member stood in awe and applauded, shouting "Bravo!" The rest rushed to join him, even Sami. Without a doubt the film was lush, luxuriant, brilliant, emotive, and destined for greatness.

So when they met the next morning after a lengthy, celebratory breakfast, they were slaphappy in their schemes to cover the costs of the extravagant production. To wrap up the needed 65 million, each member personally pledged 4.3 million, which Ron and Kirk bravely agreed to as well. Besides David, two of the other members were also extraordinarily rich and they determined the three of them, of course acquiring a larger portion of the proceeds, would cover the promotion costs, only they didn't want to scrimp by on 65 million. They upped the ante to 30 million each.

Sami had 37 VIVA Theatres almost ready for business and it had been determined these would have simultaneous Premiere nights one week before the general release. Figuring she needed three more weeks of work, Sami doggedly spent the evening on the phone coercing Have Tools Will Travel into mind boggling schedules. Ron missed the celebration that night in the Park Plaza's glittery dining room as he hovered over the shoulder of the crew fine-tuning the final trailers for movie houses, television stations and the press releases for radio and newspapers.

On Premiere night the Board members dispersed around the U.S. to attend different VIVA theatres. Multiple Premieres were not unheard of, oftentimes happening in LA and NY, but 37 occurring at one time proved newsworthy in itself. Of course the spotlight beamed on the ground-breaking opening of the restaurant/theater concept as well as featuring a chain of refurbished movie houses, as well as the first showing of an extravagant and unrestrained film.

The Board Members planned to convene the next day at the Studios to compare notes. They hired an independent agency to present the reviews of the media and to propose further promotion after which the members anticipated they would be slapping each other on the back and smoking a few cigars. Sami attended the Premiere in Philadelphia, her most recently completed theater, David and his wife went to New York and Ron stayed in Los Angeles. All three hosted after theater dinners inviting their hundreds of most intimate friends, selected Stars and the sure-to-be congratulatory media.

Kirk and Darce attended in San Francisco, decked out in the hottest fashion, coyly smiling, masking their inward hysteria while being importantly humble. Much hoopla had been discussed prior to the evening about how to arrive. Hire a car and driver and be grandly but modestly deposited on the sidewalk in front of the theater? Drive their own car and park in the Geary Street lot? Take a cab? Darce held out for driving their own car, but Kirk ruled the day having observed the car and driver scene too many times at Board meetings.

Therefore, Darce stepped onto the curb when the driver opened her door to flashbulbs and lights popping in her face. They happened to be the only ones attending the premiere who arrived by car and driver, so they received all the attention. The big names flew to LA or NY or Philadelphia so they could have their pictures taken at the premiere with Ron La Fave, Sami Raznick La Fave and David Raznick.

Kirk and Darce faced a dilemma when they entered the theater. They hadn't decided beforehand where to sit.

"Let's stay in the back so we can see everyone's reactions," Darce whispered.

"No. We need to sit in the front so that people can see members of the Board are here."

Darce complied and they sat front and center, delicately ordering their meal from the obsequious waiter. As politely and properly as they could, they ate their meal trying not to dart glances at the audience to see if they were being watched. By the time coffee arrived, the film began.

After the opening scene a lump formed in Darce's throat. After Act One the thought trailed through her head, "Who let this film get trashy? I thought they intended to create a work of art? Would Ron do this?"

Halfway through she found the courage to glance at Kirk. His eyes glistened and his mouth hung ajar. He felt her gaze and turned to smile at her with raised eyebrows suggesting, "Isn't this wonderful?", but he turned back to the film without registering her reaction.

For the remaining half, tears rolled down Darce's cheeks which she deftly brushed away until she resigned herself to the notion that she was watching, simultaneously, a film of tainted yet understated sex, sex no family would promote in their child, and the washing away of her and Kirk's fortunes. At the end she insisted on seeing the credits to their finality before she would leave the theatre. No one was left, even on the sidewalk. Only the car and driver awaited them, which is exactly how Darce knew it would be.

A somber group gathered in the Studios theater at three the following afternoon. Most came carrying stacks of newspapers from their chosen cities for the viewing. One by one the Members gave their reports. Even when they tried to find redeeming qualities, everyone's chins remained permanently attached to the floor.

The three sparsely attended garish parties embarrassed them. Champagne and caviar sailed home concealed in the waiter's trunks because Ron, Sami and David had enough on their plates without figuring what to do with booze and fine food already paid for. The restaurants recouped most of the booty, without deducting a nickel from the tab, and the wives of the waiters, waiting for the loot, recouped the rest.

Ron, at David's cue, left Kirk to the last, as had become their tradition, giving the new kid on the block an opportunity to express his naivety. "My wife didn't like it for all the reasons you guys have already mentioned. But when she told me all that, I looked at her as if she were nuts! That was the most beautiful film I've ever seen. The words that guy used were out of this world. I'd like to be able to say things the way he did. I'd love to tell my wife I loved her like he told his lover. But I can't. I don't know how."

He looked at Sami, "I may be from Missouri, but that movie moved me. It didn't make me want to go out and promote homosexuality, but it made me want to live my life better. I couldn't identify with his love, but I could identify with his pain. He died because he loved well. The movie said to me that I will die if I don't love well. And I want to live life to its fullest."

Kirk steadied his gaze on Sami, gave her a smile and turned away, at which her eyes narrowed and her lips disappeared in a straight line. Ron looked gratefully at his friend, "Thank you, Kirk. May yours be the crowning opinion." He noticed the rest of the board eyeing Kirk with gratitude as well.

"Let's have the analysis team come in." A secretary went to the door and escorted two men and a woman into the theater. After introductions, one man signaled the technician. The lights went down and their expertly devised presentation appeared on the screen. Headlines from the Theater pages of all 37 newspapers were shown in finger snapping procession. With barely time to read them, the synopsis did not change; all were negative.

Then key paragraphs appeared which the narrator read. Many positive attributes were noted, the period piece being highly appreciated, but mostly the reporters held a dark view of the film's future. Interviews with theater goers were shown. The most common response being, "It was a beautiful film. I wish homosexuals well, but I really have no interest in watching their lifestyle."

Only the ardently gay replied with, "It's about time!"

"It was exhilarating to see on the screen what happens in my life every day!"

"Yeah! Now the world can see what we're all about!"

The analytical team followed this presentation with their conclusions, assembled in portfolios addressed personally to each Board Member. The woman, her slim figure defined by a black pantsuit with a flared mid-thigh jacket, her red hair severely slicked back into a blunt-cut two inch ponytail, took the mike. "Looking at the positives, you have made an exquisite period piece. You obviously employed the experts in film. Technically, there are so few flaws that it can be considered perfect. Your writer used words sparingly and well, in fact the dialogue offered itself as a piece of poetry.

"We commend you for convincing the rating committee to only give the film an R. In places, even though subtly done with innuendo, it should have been an X rated film. However, America is not ready for this. We are a happy ending lot. America will not tolerate the depressing ending. Homosexuality is coming to the foreground, but you have placed it too far forward.

"Our recommendations are that you send it overseas to Japan and Europe. The French should love it. In time you will be able to present it in the United States, but not yet. We do not consider this a negative report. You have produced an exceptionally fine film, but you have produced it before it's time, that's all. Be encouraged and bide your time."

Ron thanked them and the secretary escorted the team out. She also called the restaurant and cancelled the celebratory dinner asking for the meals to be delivered to the Studio instead. They argued incessantly among themselves, wondering what happened between the time they had seen it and yelled "Bravo!" and the public had seen it and turned their thumbs down. By midnight the consensus of opinion determined that Kirk had the heart of the people in his mouth when he spoke about his reaction to the film. The media, as is often the case, published a wrong verdict. The prudent course of action would be, indeed, and they all agreed, to stay the course. They approved the opening of Wild Card this coming Friday in major theaters around the US already under contract, and at least expressed confidence that it would be a success despite the miserable Premieres. But no one left that night smiling.

David, Sami and Ron reached the condo about 1 a.m. Sami headed directly for the bar where she poured herself a straight shot. Enunciating each word precisely, she demanded of Ron, "How could you do this?"

Ron looked toward David hoping for some defense, but David sat forward on a chair, holding his head in his hands. Ron tried lamely, with dark fatigue, to defend himself. "Sami, I didn't cause a poor opening. I have spent the last five and a half months putting out fires I didn't start and didn't know where to begin to salvage the damage."

With a malicious sneer she started toward him. "You're the CEO. Your word is law. The guilt and blame for all this falls on your shoulders. I told my father you weren't ready for the responsibility, but you got it, you hustler. You wormed your way right in there and took my place. I never would have let this fiasco happen. I would have said no from the beginning."

"But you voted yes with all the rest!" Ron's voice rose.

"I voted yes to get you in over your head! I wanted them all to see you didn't know squat about the industry!"

He took a menacing step toward her. "Then it must have come as quite a shock that I pulled off, single-handedly according to you, a masterpiece."

"You spent a fortune on a disaster!"

"And you were willing to lose that fortune to show me up!"

"Shut up!" David yelled.

The two went to their respective corners of the ring, heads drooping.

"This doesn't solve anything. Ron has worked valiantly and we all backed him. Wild Card is a masterpiece. Go to bed. We have to put a bright face on for the public tomorrow."

Before Friday David pulled all his strings to get positive comments printed in the columns and bantered on the talk shows. The Stars appeared on Late Night programs, the Talent even got in on the act. Extras sent letters to the editor and the Board Members had their faces plastered in every paper with lighthearted remarks. They kept this up till David felt the price too high.

Then they waited. The sad results dribbled in and by early Saturday morning they knew their masterful efforts had failed. After a week, only VIVA Theaters kept the movie on their screens, but one more week forced them to replace the showing or close their doors. Without appropriate funds to fly the Board Members to L.A. for a salvage meeting, they met by phone. Through the conference call the members determined to follow the expert advice given weeks ago: send Wild Card to Europe and Japan.

The deals were made within days. The films began showing within weeks in theaters throughout the two locations funded by marginal bids that did little for the coffers of VIVA Studios. The Members drew their collective breath and hoped for a delayed surge of public interest which would save their Studio, polish their reputations and re-build their fortunes. It didn't come. The crowds proved to be as lackluster as in the States.

Ron sent a copy of Wild Card to New York, asking his old boss Harding to watch it with the creative director of GUS Theater and to give him their assessments. After the viewing they called Ron. Harding said, "We've seen your tour de force. You've pulled off a Masterwork. The only problem is that it has no public appeal. Only a slim percentage of the population will be interested. Here, let me put Greg on the line. He can explain it better."

"Hi, Ron. I admire your work. Believe me, I am moved by the level of creativity in all domains. Great editing! It is a magnum opus! But I'll tell you what I think the problem is. The homosexual community wants to be seen as mainstream now. The flagrant, in your face, rebel, the old gay parade exhibitionist, is no longer the image they wish to present. Your main character, brilliant as he was, flaunted his lifestyle. At every turn he made his devotees uncomfortable; he was trying to force change. Nowadays, homosexuals want to be seen as the nice family next door. You've simply sent the wrong message."

"But Stu Huddleston assured us it was the right message for the right time. You know Stu, don't you?"

"Sure, I know Stu. Was he your only consultant?"

"Yes."

"Then your marketing research should have been more thorough. The script is brilliant. I imagine your Board reacted to it with absolute greed in their gullets and therefore didn't do their due diligence."

With dawning dread Ron asked, "Is there any salvation for this film?"

"Put it in the vault for five years. The public will have changed by then and you will still have a masterpiece."

"Thanks, Greg, I appreciate your time and input."

Harding got back on the phone. "I'm sorry about this turn in your career, Ron. If you remember, I am a praying man. The only one who can help you now is God. You better get on your knees, my friend, and find a way out."

Ron called a meeting, offering to make it another conference call, but the Members were so incensed they insisted on gathering at the studio. They paid their own way to L.A. for the showdown.

"So what do we do? Close the doors to VIVA Studios?"

"Where will that leave VIVA Theaters?"

"Boarded up! It turns out nobody wants to eat dinner while they watch a movie!"

"How'd we get into this mess?"

"Nepotism!"

"We ought to strangle the upstart and wrap him up like a mummy with the film."

"Frankly, David ought to pay! It was his blunder; he put a novice into power and jeopardized all of us."

"And I will pay!" David roared. "If you think I am going to allow my reputation to be smirched by this, you're all crazy. We will bury this film and start with the next one tomorrow. Any of you that want out, I will cover your losses with my personal wealth, except for the two wild cards, the interlopers who crashed into our lives. They can suffer their losses. I take over as CEO of both VIVA Studios and VIVA Theaters immediately and Sami goes back to film selection."

Only three Members remained on the Board, the ones who

could afford the loss. The rest went home to await their payouts from David. Kirk, who had not flown in for the showdown, kept in touch with Ron by cell phone and when he heard the news, broke down in sobs. Absenting herself from the meeting, Sami remained in New York, but she did not keep in touch with Ron. After the meeting David took Ron to the side.

"I want you to go back to the condo, pack up your things and clear out. When you've left, send the car back for me." His grip on Ron's arm and the growl in his voice kept the displaced CEO from doing anything but complying.

While packing, a courier arrived at the door. "A message for Mr. Ron La Fave from Mr. David Raznick." Ron took the envelope and gave the boy a tip.

He opened the envelope and read David's handwritten note. "Ron. I'll see to it that you never work in this industry again. Count on it. Consider this your severance pay and do not cross me." The envelope contained a check for $250,000.00.

At the airport Ron sent the driver back to the Studios for David and then flew to New York. Landing at La Guardia he hired another car and driver and arrived in Rye as a moving van left his driveway. The front door stood open. Hesitating, he walked inside and found the house totally empty. Following the voices he heard, he encountered a beaming couple being led around the house by a third person.

"Excuse me. I come home to find my house devoid of my personal belongings and strangers wandering around inside. Can someone enlighten me?"

"Oh, you must be Mr. La Fave," the third party gushed. "I'm Sally Saunders, the real estate agent who sold your house to these delightful newlyweds, Mr. and Mrs. Turner. I'm so glad you showed up. Your wife signed the papers, but you haven't. Would you do us the honor right now?"

"You sold the house?"

"Why yes. Your things left moments ago in that moving van which surely passed you on the road. They're headed for the apartment in Manhattan. Your wife is en route there as well. Would you like to sign these papers now?"

"What about the servants?"

"I don't know the particulars on that issue, but I do know that the Turners are interviewing them tomorrow and hopefully there will be a seamless transition. Now, about the papers ... "

"I'll sign them." Ron quickly put his signature on the appointed lines and left the house. Having not paid the driver, the car still waited so Ron had himself driven to Manhattan, where he asked the driver to wait while he saw Sami.

The door to the apartment also stood open as the moving men brought in Sami's personal items from the house. Ron entered and found her arranging things in her drawers. He stood quietly until she noticed him.

"Oh! You got back here quick."

"Yes, I followed the moving truck over, that is, right after I signed the papers for the sale of the house."

Sami looked for a reaction on his face but found none. "The furniture is going into storage until we decide how to divide it and your things will be delivered to your parents flat tomorrow. I'm glad you signed the papers for the sale of the house, that's one less thing to worry about, but don't think you'll get any money from the sale. Neither of us will keep any equity. David wants it to cover my loss."

"Your loss?"

She whipped away. "Yes. My loss. David's in his seventies, and let's face it, VIVA Studios and VIVA Theaters were his last hurrah. That's why he gambled everything. He thought I was expendable. Now that he's fallen on his face he wants me back. But I won't select scripts for him anymore. When I said no, he included me with you and Kirk. I get to pay for my portion of the loss, too. Personally, I think he should take his licks and retire, but his raging ego won't settle for that." Sami's voice softly slid to a satisfied murmur, "I'm forming my own agency. I've grown up."

"Good for you."

She turned slowly to face him. "Part of growing up is being savagely honest, and Ron, I don't want to be married to you. David accuses me of bringing you into the family. I don't want anything more to do with the family, either, but that's not why I'm divorcing you. I didn't want you in the first place. David brought you into the family; you were simply a trophy for me. That's why I had these papers drawn up. I've allocated an alimony settlement for you."

He took the papers from her hand. "Don't bother. Keep your settlement, keep the furniture." He frowned as he considered, "But there is one thing I would like. How about giving me the house in Jackson Hole?"

"Gladly. That's poetic justice, isn't it?"

Ron smiled, "I guess so." He wrote in the changes, signed the papers and handed them back. "Use the alimony to set up your agency."

She took the papers, a slight pause in her movements reflected an inward glitch of sorts, which she quickly buried and swiftly moved to the desk to enshroud the papers in a drawer. "I appreciate your efforts to be a husband, Ron, but they petered out pretty quick. I think the one thing we both got out of all this is our freedom. I'm free of my father and you're free from that compelling drive to fulfill an uninspired dream. I don't think there's any business left for us to conclude, so if you'll forgive me, I've got a lot of work to do tonight."

"Oh, oh, sure. If you need me I'll be at my folks for a few days and then I think I'll go to the mountains. I always think better in the mountains." He frowned, "But the Catskills are too small for these problems. Maybe I'll hole up in the Rockies. Thanks for the house, Sami. I wish you well." He extended his hand to grasp hers.

Looking at his hand distastefully, Sami turned and left the room. Ron watched the last vestige of his life plan disappear, then he let himself out, went downstairs and had the driver take him to his parents home before dismissing him.

Chapter Fifteen
# THE MOUNTAINS

"Ronnie." His father shook his shoulder. "Wake up. Come with me to morning prayers. It'll do you good. We'll pray for you. God knows what you should do. Ronnie."

Rolling over, he squinted at his father. "Papa, I need the sleep."

"You need the prayers more."

Groaning, Ron shuffled into his clothes and dutifully followed his father to the Salvation Army where Albert La Fave's friends had been meeting at 6 a.m. for 40 years. Emile, as customary, sat in the front row, waiting. Patience seemed to drip from his craggy eyebrows. He watched the two approach with wonder, would wonders never cease? Many a day only one or two showed up to pray, but today, ah, today there was a newcomer.

Ron and his father sat down on the bench behind the older man. "Emile, my boy Ronnie, remember him?"

"What's to remember? He's never been to morning prayers that I recall."

"He came with me a couple of times as a boy."

The craggy gentleman harrumphed and scowled.

"Hello, Emile." Ron extended his hand. Emile grasped it in his rigid grip, rough skin scrapping like a cement claw. Withdrawing his hand, almost in pain, Ron said, "Good to see you again, sir."

Emile looked him up and down, snorting, "You're in trouble."

"What makes you think that?" Ron asked pleasantly.

"Nobody's son comes to prayers except when they're scared or running."

"No. Emile. You got it all wrong. Ron, here, just completed making a movie. He's going to be famous. My boy's home for a little rest, that's all."

Emile raised one eyebrow. "I heard. You lost half your life savings. Instead of a sweet retirement, you have to work another ten years."

"It's only money, Emile. What's a little money when it's your boy?"

"Money's money."

"But I don't mind."

"You and me, we don't have the energy to make it again, Al. Your son should have taken care of you; that's all I'm saying."

Catching the criticism in the cave of his heart, Ron turned his head away. Two more men scuttled through the door, acknowledged the presence of Al's son and the prayer meeting began.

His sodden heart seemed to treble in size as he listened to the men pray. What good was this doing? Words. Lofty words that brought him no direction and certainly no peace, that's all they were. The weight in his chest hung tenuously from his rib cage. By the time the session ended Ron leaned over his knees mopping his brow and wishing he were a million miles away. But his father seemed ebullient and kept clapping him on the back as they made their way to the flat. Over breakfast Ron offered his father half of the $250,000 that David had given him, but he adamantly refused.

After his father reluctantly left for work, Ron crept from the apartment to go car shopping and bought himself a mountain ready vehicle. Returning home he found his belongings from Rye crammed into his parent's living room. Spending the rest of the day packing the minimal amount he would take, he then called collection agencies to arrange for them to pick up the rest. His mother arrived and demanded he leave the remains for her to sell. He dutifully agreed and again called the collection agencies to cancel the pick-up.

The next day, after shopping for heavy duty winter clothing, he deposited $100,000 in his Waterston and Meddling account and went home to call Kirk. The usual buoyancy could not be detected in his stockbroker's voice.

"Ron, a courier delivered a message from David. Said my share of the losses is due. If I pull out my Blue Chips, like yours, no one can find them but me, I still couldn't cover what he's demanding."

"Don't do anything, Kirk. David won't follow through. He can't afford to have anything legal trickle out, the press would be on him like a tick on an old dog. He has to forge ahead with another movie right away, that is if he doesn't have a heart attack over all this. If he contacts you again I'll do battle with him. Just forget it."

The relief in Kirk's voice fell heavily into the phone. "Thanks, Ron. What about you, buddy boy? How are you doing? Come to think of it, where are you?"

"New York, momentarily, at my folks. David ousted me from VIVA, from EE, from the condo and when I flew back here I found Sami had sold the house and drawn up divorce papers."

"Just like that?"

"Just like that."

Kirk whistled into the phone. "Those guys don't waste time. That's a blow and a half. How are you feeling about all that?"

"I feel pretty punched up inside."

"I don't blame you. What are you going to do?"

"I asked for the house we have in Jackson Hole. Sami agreed. I'm going there for awhile to walk through the mountains and think things through. I'm not going to bother with a phone, Kirk, but I'll call from time to time. Listen, David gave me some severance pay so I put $100,000 in my Waterston account. Get started on some trades and do some quick ones so that you'll have the commissions. I don't know what I'm going to do, but the mountains will know. They've never failed me yet."

"Ron?" Kirk's voice turned husky. "You're better than the whole lot of them. You're the only one of that group with class. Good riddance, if you ask me. I'll have your portfolio built back up in no time. And I'm still praying for you."

Grimacing, Ron cut the conversation short, promising to call as soon as he got settled. That night he took his parents to dinner at a neighborhood restaurant. As mistakes go, this one turned out to be the Mount Everest of mistakes. News had gotten around and most of the other diners dropped by the table to give their condolences, not to Ron but to his mother and father. He remembered as a kid how he slid underneath the restaurant table when things got unbearably boring. He wished he could do that now from shame.

Over coffee Ron said, "Papa, I'm going to make this up to you. I don't know how, just yet, but I will."

"Ronnie. It doesn't matter. Don't worry. Mama and me, we'll be fine." His mother didn't look too convinced. "My Papa sold everything he had to bring his family to the States. He started over. I've never had to do that. He worked till he died. I don't mind. My Papa was my example. I was proud of him and I'm proud of you."

His mother turned a sledgehammer face toward her son. "Settle down, Ron. Get yourself a trade. Make some money and send your Papa and me on a cruise. That's what we would have done if we could have retired."

"Mama!" Ron's father admonished. "Go easy. Ronnie's got a broken heart."

"So do I." A tear slid down his mother's face.

"I'll send you on a very nice cruise right now." Ron offered. His mother looked expectantly at her husband.

"No! Ronnie, you're a young man. You need that money to start over." Al stared his wife down. "Mama and me we'll be just fine."

Ron left early the next morning, his car packed to the roof, and began the long trek across the United States. Mile after mile after mile of mindless driving took its toll and by the time he hit Wyoming he thought he would go barking mad. This man, this being sitting in Ron's clothes, driving his new car seemed to have no identity. Outside of his life's plan, he didn't know himself. He writhed at the thought of asking, 'Who am I?' But in order to answer the question, 'What can I do now?' the first question demanded an answer. His whole life had been devoted to training for his life's plan! He didn't care about anything else!

He told himself to calm down, to wait for his meditation in the mountains, but Wyoming wouldn't quit. It kept going and going and going, monotonous plain after monotonous plain, until he crossed the Continental Divide at 9,600 feet. And then the tears came. He cried until he landed on the floor of Jackson Hole at 6,300 feet. Turning into an outlook, he pulled himself together and fished in his pocket for the directions the caretaking agency gave him when he called.

Having arrived a week after Labor Day, the traffic had thinned and Ron easily found the office. Mr. Brundage seated at his desk hesitatingly stood and extended his hand. "Mr. La Fave. Happy to make your acquaintance. Welcome to Jackson Hole."

Ron gave a limp shake, withdrawing his hand quickly. His face drooped like an expressive Bloodhound. Mr. Brundage noted Ron's mental state and hurried to give him the keys, a map to the house and to arrange further care.

"How often would you like housekeeping to come around, Mr. La Fave?"

"Once a week, no more."

"Tuesdays work for you?"

"Fine."

"And the grounds men?"

"I don't want to touch the grounds, or shovel snow, have them continue to keep it up completely."

"Yes, sir. If I can be of any other service to you, don't hesitate to call. In fact, I'll call you once a week to see whether you need anything or not."

"Don't bother." Ron turned to go.

Mr. Brundage walked him to the door. Hesitatingly, he put his hand on Ron's shoulder, "You'll find peace here, Mr. La Fave. People come from all over the world to find their peace. You'll find your peace here, too."

"Peace?" Ron's voice sounded hollow, even to him. "Why would I need peace?"

Mr. Brundage looked at him compassionately. "I read the New York Times on Sundays, and if you don't mind my saying so, it shows."

"Oh, I see. Well, thank you."

The house sat on a cul-de-sac off one of the main roads. Ron pulled into the driveway and sat for a moment after turning the motor off. He fought back tears, but they overcame him and drenched his face. 'I won't feel sorry for myself,' he thought. But the tears kept dropping down his cheeks.

Getting out of the car he noticed a shivering chill in the evening. New York, in the midst of having her Indian summer, didn't prepare him for Jackson Hole feeling like snow. The sun, setting behind the Teton Mountains, took the last fragile warmth with it. Even through his tears and the cold, he couldn't help but marvel at the beauty right outside his front door.

He pulled a few necessities out of the car, thinking to leave the rest for tomorrow's light, and headed for the front door. He entered the house directly into the kitchen, which made up a section of the Great Room. Off to the right, the main section of the Great Room rose to a Cathedral ceiling going to a two story pitch in the middle. Giant double paned windows covered the front and the back walls. In a straight line from the front door, beyond the kitchen, he could see another room.

That proved to be the Master suite, the king bed having been made with freshly ironed sheets and turned down, a flower on each pillow. The housekeeper must have just left. He dumped his things and continued his investigation. On the right side of the house three other bedrooms with two bathrooms connecting the three lined the hall. A half bath opened onto the front entry and a heated garage opened onto the kitchen.

In the center of the Great Room a majestic circular stone fireplace climbed to the peak of the Cathedral ceiling. Sliding glass panes enclosed the fire, ardently burning, so that they could be opened in the direction in which one wanted the heat. The rear Cathedral windows displayed a forest rising from the back of the grounds, about 50 feet from the house. The front Cathedral windows boasted a breathtaking frontal view of the Tetons.

The floors, wall to wall, glistened in black slate overlaid with thick, white rugs thrown everywhere. Three welcoming, black, soft, leather love seats, piled high with red and beige pillows, surrounded the fireplace on three sides. Two lounge chairs draped with red and beige throws, sat facing the windows protecting either side of the room. The far right of the Great Room contained a game table and chairs and a squared library alcove.

Ron whistled. "I had no idea! Look what they gave us." The word 'us' startled him into full-blown remembrance. "No, me. Look what they gave me! This is mine!" He felt like crying again, wondering about the possibility of a Divine Providence that would bless him in his misery. He toyed with thoughts that he should sell the house and make up his father's losses. But he canceled that thinking. 'I need this place right now. I can do that later.'

Assuming he would have to pull himself together and find a restaurant for dinner, Ron idly opened the refrigerator and found it fully stocked. Even a prepared meal awaited him. A hand-written note instructed him to pop it into the microwave and reminded him not to burn his fingers on the plastic wrap. He turned the glass doors surrounding the fireplace so they opened toward the kitchen and he ate in solitude perched on a high stool, leaning like a child on the countertop, the backdrop for the sink.

As soon as dark secured the valley, automatic lights came on in the grounds, softly lighting up the ascending forest behind the house. Ron sat in a lounger for awhile to lose himself in the beauty, but then decided to put the car in the garage and unpack before going to bed. He found the automatic garage door opener to hang in his car, pushed the button in the garage and the minute he stepped outside motion lights blazed on.

It took him a short time to settle in with his things placed here and there. Then he wandered around the house. He found no installation of stereo system or television. 'Good.' He didn't want any music, any sound or any images. He wanted quiet. 'They probably set this up as a rental. That's all I need right now.' He puttered around till midnight, moving his things around and rearranging furniture to suit his habits and then fell into bed, exhausted physically, mentally and emotionally.

Sleeping till noon, Ron lurched awake, absorbed his surroundings, remembered and pulled the covers over his head. Even at noon he did not want to get out of bed. It took him an hour to shower, shave and dress. The Great Room seemed cold and he noticed he had not closed the sliding glasses of the fireplace before going to bed. He did so and stood still. Silence. A padded wall of silence barred his exit. Tears came to his eyes. Was he so lost he couldn't find his way back?

He found some bagels in the freezer, thawed one briefly in the microwave, then popped it in the toaster. He thought of calling Brundage and apologizing for his abrupt behavior, but didn't think he could handle it and put it off for another day. After his Spartan breakfast he went out back to investigate the forest.

Tilting his head back he tried to ascertain if he could see the top of the hill, or was it a mountain? What lay beyond? What adventures of the mind would he encounter there? Going back inside, he got a sweater and locked the house. About 15 feet up the slope, a trail crossed his path coming up from the right, not an animal path, but a prepared trail like one the Park Service would maintain in the Catskills. Comforted by his find, he turned left and climbed the path as it zigzagged back and forth mounting the ascent in a sensible fashion.

The hill crested, but the path continued down a slight gorge and then up the next prominence. This configuration occurred again and at the top of the third rise Ron looked down to see if he could see his house. He could not. The crown of the hill rolled inward, preventing a straight downward vista. He felt cut off from all security and began shivering. Perhaps this was enough for one day. He glanced at his watch. He had been climbing for one and a half hours. Definitely enough for one day.

On his way down he found another path, more like an animal trail, going off to the left. It angled into the prepared path so he had not noticed it on his way up. The late afternoon glowed warmly with the sun over the Tetons bearing down on him. Curiosity led him to investigate the trail, some kind of hazy sound luring him on, until thirty minutes later he entered a clearing that opened before a waterfall. The water, maybe six feet wide, dropped from a rock shelf about twelve feet before continuing down to the valley floor.

That alone impressed all his senses, but backing up to the clearing, which measured about ten feet in diameter, stood the strong side of several close growing pines. While the surrounding growth looked to be at least a hundred years old, this clump seemed to be from an earlier forest. When Ron went around to the mountain side of the clump, he found it to have been burned out, no doubt from the fire that must have devastated the forest before the current growth. Forming a hollowed place backed by the thicker trunks and thronging bushes, Ron knew he'd found his sanctuary.

'Here!' he said to himself. 'Here is where the mountains will talk to me.' Ron nodded in acquiescence of his discovery. Walking around the little clearing again, marking his ownership with his steps, he then lugged himself back up the animal trail, scarcely buoyed by his marvelous discovery, and slowly descended to the house. By the time he arrived home, the sun had disappeared beyond the Tetons and the light trailed behind it.

Though he had done all this climbing on one bagel, he couldn't bring himself to eat. He crawled into bed at eight o'clock and didn't wake up till eight in the morning.

Chapter Sixteen
# THE MOUNTAIN MAN

Ron thawed the sausage and bagels, arranged them in the toaster oven, scrambled three eggs, threw in a fourth for good measure and sat down to a sumptuous feast. As he ate he looked at his forest, noting a definite possessive union in his heart. The trees called him. He couldn't remember, was it five that had survived the ravages of forest fire, yet still stood like stanchions of defiance?

Doing up his few dishes, relishing his independence, he formed a plan for those trees. In the garage he had seen a stack of throw rugs, presumably for the front hallway to collect snowy boots when discarded. He would take a few of those up to his simple sanctuary along with some blankets. What would happen next, after he was all moved in, he did not know.

It took him better than an hour to return to the landing by the waterfall. Hefting the rugs and blankets expended more strength than he knew he had in him. Finally, with the throw rugs creating a floor in the shelter of the hollowed out trees, and the blankets to create a modicum of comfort, Ron sat listening to the wind in the branches and the roar of water as it hit the rocks before running crazily downhill.

His thoughts lifted to the tree tops, but when he let them wander from there, they flitted back to L.A. or to New York. Worse yet, they flew to Switzerland. It necessitated him to pull them back in and keep tight rein on them. Yet concentrating on the wind or the water grew monotonous. His thoughts would not form into a simple question and answer structure. That he could deal with. That's how it had worked in the Catskills.

Suddenly Ron sat very still. An elk came ambling down the trail, followed by a doe. The wind, coming up the hill from the waterfall, kept his scent from being detected. The rack on the male indicated his verdant feeding areas. They passed so close he could have reached out and stroked their sides.

After Ron exhaled, having held his breath at their presence, he whispered. "If there is Divine Providence, thank You for sending them down my path."

Somehow the presence of the elk loosed his mind from its fevered floundering. He didn't know how long he had been sitting there, listening, not even thinking as far as he could tell. The memory of the elegant animals kept him mesmerized, so he hadn't heard any prelude. No one had come down the animal trail, which he could see to the left side of his five trunk alcove. Therefore, what he did hear shocked him and in a sense frightened him.

Just behind his trees a voice bellowed in anguish, "Great God of the Universe, Creator of all, Creator of me, my Master, my Lord, my Savior!"

Without moving Ron searched all the forest he could see. No human presence was visible.

The voice continued. "You know I love You! You know I will do anything for You. You have sent me to this place, and even though it vexes my soul, I stay. The need is great, I know. I would prefer that You send me even deeper into the mountains where I can spend my days worshipping You."

The voice caught in a sob. "Or take me home, Lord. Take me home to live with You. My heart breaks when I see the way Your people, Your Creation treats You!"

Ron couldn't hear the rest of the words as they were muffled by the man's sobbing. A word here and there indicated greed, selfishness, riches for lavish personal wallowing, a lack of appreciation for life itself, while life presented itself as such a lavish gift.

Eavesdropping intently, not knowing to what or to whom he listened, Ron waited until all sound had withdrawn, except for the splashing of the water and the blowing of the wind. Still waiting a good ten minutes more, he then quietly came out of his shelter. Creeping cautiously, he saw no one. No signs showed that anyone had been there. Reflecting on the possibility he might be going out of his mind, Ron reasoned he heard the cries of his own soul. He considered schizophrenia. An all out shock such as had been delivered to him could split a man in two. Maybe he was more punched up inside than he thought.

Noting the time, one in the afternoon, Ron thought he would return tomorrow as early as he came today and see if the phenomenon occurred again. But right now he needed civilization. He needed to leave this mountain retreat and get back to where something made sense. He left the rugs and the blankets and hurried downhill.

Occupying his mind with mundane things, Ron drove into town and opened a bank account. Not wanting any direct communication he wandered the streets, passing through several arcs of elk racks while crossing the park, and ended up in the Cowboy Grill. He asked for a back booth and ordered coffee.

It wasn't so much civilization that Ron wanted; he needed to convince himself he wasn't going crazy. He sat and watched couples coming in and sitting, ordering and talking like normal people. Others came and stood at the bar like singles do. That voice he heard out there on the mountain? It didn't sound like his; it had to come from another human, it just had to. It seemed totally out of context with what he was observing in this everyday scene.

Finally Ron went down the block and bought himself an enormous steak, which he wolfed down. Then he bought a newspaper and a few magazines to read during the evening. He really didn't want to think about the condition of the world, or even to stumble on an article about David Raznick or EE or worse yet, VIVA. However, he had to stifle the words he heard today from replaying in his mind. And they were doing just that. Over and over.

"Great God of the Universe, Creator of all, Creator of me, my Master, my Lord, my Savior! You know I love You! Send me even deeper into the mountains where I can spend my days worshipping You. Or take me home, Lord. Take me home to live with You."

The next day Ron timed himself. He got up before eight and fixed his breakfast, not quite as sumptuous as the day before. Then he headed up the mountain, taking some lawn furniture cushions with him to supplement the area rugs, and some bottles of water. Chuckling to himself, he wondered if he were building the tree house he never had as a boy in New York City.

Arriving at his simple sanctuary, Ron arranged his cushions, got settled in and once again listened to the wind and water. This time, when the elk and his doe arrived, Ron checked his watch. 11:45. The doe saw his movement and shied a few steps, but the two kept walking sedately to the waterfall.

At one in the afternoon, Ron jumped slightly when once again the voice rose dramatically in this secluded part of the forest, seemingly just behind his trees fused together by fire so long ago.

"God! You are so great! You healer of cancer, You! You are awesome! I am so full of You I feel like wall to wall Holy Spirit! You consume me! Thank You for healing Elva, Your little daughter, my sister! Forgive me for crying and complaining yesterday. You have shown Yourself strong by answering my prayers. Who am I but a grateful child of God? Who am I but a man about my Father's business? Who am I but Your servant?"

Then the voice broke into deep baritone singing. "I will follow where You lead me. You can take me where You want me to go. I will follow where You need me. I will learn the things You want me to know. Simply choose me, Lord. Simply use me, Lord. Let me say what You want me to say. Simply choose me. Lord. Simply use me. Lord. Let me be Your man of the day."

The sounds coming from behind Ron's trees sounded as if the man were jumping and leaping, crunching leaves and twigs under his his sturdy boots as he shouted. "I'm Yours! I'm Yours! You're mine! All mine! Everything about me belongs to You! Everything about You belongs to me! Your character! Your nature! Your glory! Your mercy! Your favor! Your blessings! Your plans! Your desires! All mine because I'm all Yours!"

The voice became muffled as Ron heard, "God, I think You got the short end of the stick, but I'm going to give You all I've got. My mind belongs to You. My body belongs to You. My desires belong to You. My comforts belong … " Suddenly the voice cut off.

Today Ron didn't wait. He cautiously stood and tried to peek through the separation of the trunks of his five trees, but they were about a foot higher than his head. He backed up the slope leading down to his hollow and could then see through the open slots, but not with a clear field of vision. So he came out into view.

Nothing. No sight of anyone and no sounds of movement. He listened carefully. The wind whispered in the trees and the water relentlessly fell on the unyielding rocks below. Nothing more.

Ron crawled back into his cubbyhole so undone by these strange occurrences that he began to cry. He thrashed back and forth ashamed of his tears and finally fell onto his lawn cushions and let the sobs roll forth. He'd come to the mountains for clarity, not mystery. He'd come for restoration, not intimidation. His mind lashed at the circumstances that had brought him here to this lowly place where his soul groveled in the pine needles sinking into the forest floor.

Unable to contain his own misery, Ron allowed himself to cry hard, shadow boxing with every culprit. He took his time and whacked David Raznick, Sami Raznick La Fave (but she probably wouldn't keep his name), the Board of Entertainment Equities, Vanguard Interpretive Visual Arts, Wild Card, especially Wild Card, and flattened every one.

Empty, he stood and stepped out of his hiding place. Dusk tread up the hill as the sun evaporated behind the Tetons. Spent and weary, Ron headed heavily down the path. By the time he reached home it was dark enough for the sensor lights to come on as he approached the house.

He pulled a frozen dinner out, then shoved it back in the freezer. Hungry, he couldn't eat. Instead, fully clothed, he kicked off his hiking boots and got into bed. With his fingers laced behind his head, he stared into the darkness, bland thoughts floating here and there, but none worthy of attention. After several hours of benign nothingness he drifted off to sleep. The last thought he registered in a wakeful state was the sound of the voice, "I'm going to give You all I've got."

The next morning Ron decided he could not face the mountain. Instead of cooking his own breakfast, he drove into town to sample the Donut Shoppe he noticed on his stroll. In a cramped storefront, he waited behind two men perusing the donuts in a lighted case. The first man wore a logger's jacket and jeans and seemed too large for the space.

The second man, nervous and twitchy, had the appearance of someone about to rob the place. However, when his turn came he softly ordered, paid and quickly left. Hearing the first man place his order snapped Ron's head up as if he had been struck. That same baritone voice still floated in his thoughts, "I'm going to give You all I've got."

When the two had left and Ron lingered as the sole customer in the shop, he asked the slump shouldered man behind the counter, "Who was that?"

The proprietor looked at the closing door. "I don't know. Never seen him before. Probably somebody passing through. Like you, maybe."

"I didn't mean him. I meant the man before him, the big fella."

"You mean the Preacher?"

"The one dressed like a lumberjack."

"Yeah, that was the Preacher. He's local alright. Some folks call him loco. But we're blessed to have him in this Hole. Anyone gets sick, they call him, he comes over and prays and they get well. We call him the Preacher because he preaches whether anybody listens to him or not.

"They say he preaches to the trees and the wildlife. I see him all the time down at the river preaching to the Trumpeter Swans and danged if they don't listen. They'll come right up there on the bank and settle down all around him.

"I don't know that anyone knows his name. He came into Jackson about five years ago, rented himself a little house on the northeast side of town, doesn't work that I know of, and spends his time telling people, or the wildlife, about God. At first there was talk about running him out of town, but now we depend on him. You got a need? Go find Preacher. He'll pray for you and it will turn out alright."

"Thanks. Thanks for the information. Oh, by the way, I'm not passing through. Name's Ron La Fave. I'm a newcomer."

"Welcome to Jackson."

Ron left with a sack of crullers, a large milk and hurried home. Dressing for the mountains he added a peanut butter and jelly sandwich to his bag and hurried up to his shelter. Now that the voice was no longer disembodied, he wanted to meet the Preacher.

The two elk sauntered past at their regular rendezvous, the doe meeting Ron's stare with a jaded eye but never faltering in step. And the male, if indeed he discerned Ron's presence, found it unworthy of notice. Ron quietly stood to watch what path they took. It amused him to see them walk behind the waterfall, appear on the other side and then abruptly turn left and disappear, as if being part of a scene in 'Huckleberry Finn'. 'That explains the Preacher's muffled voice and being cut off mid-sentence,' he thought.

Ever the city boy, Ron followed the path behind the waterfall, cowering by the wall as he crept along, and then rounded the corner which took him into a whole new vista of mountain cut off from his side by a towering cliff. The elk were no where to be seen, but far down the winding path leading to the spot where he was standing, Ron heard the singing voice of the giant in the Donut Shoppe this morning.

He hustled back as quickly as his wilderness timidity allowed him to scramble and stood in his sanctuary with his back against the trunks. It seemed like an eternity before the singing voice burst into earshot once more.

"You are my hiding place. You always fill my heart with songs of deliverance. Whenever I am afraid I will run to You. I will run to You. Let the weak say 'I am strong in the strength of the Lord. I will run to You."

Ron took a deep breath and came out of his hiding place to stand face to face with the Preacher. The large man clutched his chest, caught himself up and demanded of Ron, "Who are you?! And what are you doing in my private prayer place?!"

Timorously extending his hand, Ron answered, "Ron La Fave. I live an hour from here down the Park trail. I didn't realize any part of this forest could be called private. In fact, for the past two days I've been behind those trees and I've heard your voice. Frankly, I thought I might be crazy, you know, hearing voices, until I heard you order your donuts this morning and recognized your voice. You don't know what a relief your donut order was to me."

Brushing past Ron's extended hand, the Preacher stomped

around the trees to see the pathetic little hideaway full of lawn cushions and throw rugs and blankets. "Do you live here?" he asked incredulously.

"No. Of course not." Knowing he must look really foolish, Ron blurted out, "I have a house, a nice house, a really big house at the foot of this mountain. You're welcome to come visit any time."

The giant of a man eyed Ron keenly. "Why would I want to visit a man who would invade my private, personal space?"

"I just want you to know I'm not psychotic."

"I don't care if you're psychotic or not."

"I know how it must look."

"I'll tell you what it looks like. It looks like you're in the wrong place." Surveying the heaps of stuff Ron had brought up the mountain, the Preacher offered, "I'll help you cart all this back down to your really big house, if you'd like, but you're going to have to clear out of here."

"But why? You don't own this property."

"The Bible says the mountains belong to God." He thumped his chest. "I belong to God. He brings me up here in His mountains to this very spot to pray. You're going to have to go."

Stunned, Ron took a moment to form an answer while the Preacher waited, a storm brewing on his forehead. Ron spoke in a low voice. "I don't see it that way."

The Preacher bent over in the hideaway and stacked the lawn cushions. He stood and handed them to Ron who received them in robot fashion. While he folded and piled the throw rugs and blankets, Ron's explanation ran from his mouth like the accompanying waterfall. "I came to Jackson Hole because I need solitude. I need some answers. I know I'll find them if I wait long enough in this fortress of trees."

His arms fully loaded with the rest of Ron's things, the Preacher nodded at the animal trail. "Let's take this stuff back to your house. Lead the way."

Ron put his cushions down and reached to take the items

from the Preacher who pulled them decisively away. Resounding with conviction, Ron said, "I'm not leaving."

"Now, where's that house you mentioned? Down the Park trail? I'll take these things down there. If you come along I'll put them away for you, if not, you'll find them in your back yard. My guess is your house is at the end of the cul-de-sac, the big empty one." The Preacher turned and headed up the animal trail without looking to see if Ron would follow.

Which Ron did not. Fuming, he spread out his lawn cushions and sat down, muttering. 'How can I get clarity in the mountains with a bruiser harassing me!? I can see why they wanted to run him out of town!' He spent a quiet but not a peaceful afternoon on his cushions. The Preacher did not return, but he might as well have been sitting right beside Ron as he had become a permanent fixture in Ron's mind.

That night when he reached his house he found the throw rugs and blankets stacked neatly by his back door. He took them inside and put them away. The next day he drove into Jackson with savage purpose on his mind. He first stopped to buy a stereo system, CDs, a television, DVD and VCR player with DVDs and videos. He needed to divert his mind from fuming over The Preacher, and electronics, he reasoned, might do the trick.

His next stop, after a brief search, brought him to a second hand store where he bought a very heavy, used recliner and a very heavy, used side table. Ron tried lifting the chair by himself and failed to heft it off the floor. Then he arranged for two sturdy men to deliver the chair and table early the next morning and for a handsome price to carry the items to his simple sanctuary.

Realizing his perceived conquest would earn him an enemy instead of a friend intensely satisfied Ron. Right now he figured he didn't need or want friends. They'd just be in the way. Smugly coaxing the men up his mountain with his purchases, Ron paid them and saw them down the park trail toward their truck. He returned to his retreat assured of his ascendancy in the battle to be the proprietor of the forest by the waterfall.

Having seated himself in his very heavy chair Ron had just spread his ample lunch on the side table when the Preacher stepped around the tree trunk. The burly man twisted to the side as if contemplating what to do with his rage. With a sandwich clutched in his hand, hardly breathing, Ron blankly awaited the withdrawal of his opponent.

Instead, the Preacher grabbed Ron by the lapels of his jacket and yanked him from the chair, lightly tossing him into the ferns of the forest. He then hefted the chair over his head, stormed to the edge of the waterfall and threw it into the river. He returned for the table. Brushing Ron's lunch to the ground, he tossed the table into the water as well.

Ron followed, sandwich still in hand, to peer over the edge in total disbelief. There, splayed across the rocks under the waterfall, were the splintered remains of his stalwart ammunition, which should have established his reign as king of the mountain. He reassessed his opponent with wide-eyed wonder.

The Preacher, not even panting from his effort, also peered over the edge, his hands on his knees. He flashed sidelong glances at Ron and chuckled. Then he began to laugh. His laughter boisterously bounded and rebounded in the rocks, echoing back to him, making him laugh even more. Finally he grabbed Ron's shoulders; Ron flinched with fear. "Okay. We'll share the place. When do you want it, morning or afternoon?"

Ron pointed angrily with his sandwich. "What about my chair and my table?"

"A good storm will wash them down stream and the rangers will pick the debris out of the water."

"I paid good money for that set!"

The Preacher gave him a disparaging look, like a headmaster correcting a young pupil. "It got you what you were after. You won the battle. Which do you want? You take mornings, I'll take afternoons or vice versa?"

Ron sputtered, "It's not that easy. If I come in the mornings, I might not be through by afternoon. I need something. That's why I'm here. I need guidance; I need wisdom. It doesn't come that easy."

Incredulous, the Preacher stepped back. "Where do you think you're going to get this guidance? From the trees? You think some bear is going to step out and start talking? Or maybe the elk with the fine rack?"

"I just know things when I'm in the mountains; that's all."

"Like what?"

"Well, like the last time I went to the mountains for clarity I needed to know if I should get married."

"What was the answer."

"I got married."

"Where's your wife?"

"We're divorced. She's in New York."

"What kind of wisdom is that? You call that guidance? Who were you listening to?"

"Probably my own heart, but I can hear it better in the mountains."

"If I had a bum heart like that, I'd quit listening."

Perplexed, Ron noticed the sandwich in his hand. He waved it in the Preacher's direction. "You want half?"

The larger man frowned at it. "Sure."

Tearing the sandwich into two parts, Ron offered one to the Preacher. They stood staring down at the furniture fragments as they devoured their minute meal. Then they stared in silence. Finally the bear of a man cleared his throat.

"I come to this place for guidance, too, but when I come I talk to Somebody. I do my best not to listen to my own heart because it is deceitfully wicked and only gets me into trouble."

Now it was Ron's turn to look incredulous. "I would never talk that way about my heart. If a man can't plan his own path by following his own heart, then he's nothing."

"Has your heart made you into something?"

Soberly leveling the Preacher with a doleful gaze, Ron shook his head. "No. Nothing at all."

The big man sat down on the ledge lining the waterfall, his feet dangling just beyond the spray of water. He patted the stone slab next to him. "Sit down."

Ron dutifully obeyed.

"Maybe your heart is deceitfully wicked, too."

Ron didn't reply.

"Why don't you tell me what's bothering you. I'm good at giving advice."

"So I've heard."

"Oh, yeah? Who told you?"

"The donut man."

"I've never given him any advice."

"You must have given some to his customers."

"Probably. Half the town beats a path to my door. And you know? I'm glad to help. They tell me their troubles, or their dreams, or their fears, and I go to the Lord and tell Him and He always, I mean always, gives me the answer they need."

"When you say 'the Lord', are you talking about God?"

"That's right. You know anything about Him?"

"My father has friends that meet every morning at the Salvation Army in order to pray. He's taken me along on a few occasions. I never made any contact there with someone I could call God. But that's who they pray to."

"Did your father take you to his group to pray about your problem?"

"Yes."

"And?"

"The experience was worse than the problem."

"You willing to give me a crack at it?"

Ron shrugged, "I don't have any other options. But I'd like to know your name, first."

"Why? What difference does my name make? It's not me that'll be giving you the advice."

"I just like to know who I'm talking to. It's unnerving to tell my life story to a complete stranger."

"Mitchell. Mitch Henry."

Ron stuck out his hand to shake Mitch's. "I'm glad to know you. I'm Ron La Fave."

Mitch looked at the hand as if in awe. "Not too many men offer me their hand. They want my help but not my friendship. Thanks." They clasped in a firm handshake.

The two men verbally meandered through the rest of the afternoon, sitting like two boys by a waterfall, dangling and swinging their legs over the rock ledge. Ron recounted his story in detail, trekking through his life plan from junior high school ending right at the chair being thrown into the waterfall. Then he sat morosely while Mitch swung his legs in silence.

The big man heaved himself to his feet. "I'll be talking to the Lord and when I have an answer, I'll come by the house. Tomorrow I'll take morning. Okay by you?"

Ron also stood up. "Wait a minute. How about coming down to the house, I'll get my car and take you out for a steak dinner?" He clutched at Mitch's arm.

Looking disdainfully at the hand detaining him, Mitch gruffly replied, "I've got to talk to the Lord. It won't do any good to talk some more."

"Well then, thank you for listening. That talking made me feel better. Are you sure I can't keep you a little longer?"

"Naw. I'll just be itching to get to my prayer closet. Be patient. The minute I know something I'll come by the house."

He turned to go and then paused, "As for tomorrow, the Lord just told me you can have the mountain. I'll probably be in my prayer closet all day." Then he abruptly turned and passed behind the waterfall.

Chapter Seventeen
# THE EVIDENCE

Mystified, Ron watched as the big hulk rounded the mountain out of sight. What on earth could you say for an entire day inside a dark closet, talking to someone you couldn't see? He wandered behind the tree trunks to inspect the now empty space. Tomorrow he'd have to bring the cushions and blankets back. The thought of hefting all that stuff tired him as he ambled up the animal trail.

He soaked in a hot Jacuzzi when he arrived home, then, wrapped in a thick piled terry cloth robe and down slippers, he built a fire. Munching on tapas, he put a disc in the DVD, a documentary on Olympic gold medalists in snowboarding. He thought he'd try the sport this year. His mind, however, was not on the subject.

His mind imagined Mitch bunched up like a ball, sitting in the floor of a closet. Surely a prayer closet did not mean a clothing closet. It wouldn't be so bad if it were a walk in type. Ron had seen some pretty massive walk in closets where easy chairs and lamps had been part of the furnishings. However, the northeast of Jackson didn't have such houses. Maybe the narrow sliding door closets, but those homes were too small and too old for much else.

Finally he took the boring documentary out and put in a cunning movie, Dirty Rotten Scoundrels, his favorite. He identified with Michael Caine, achieving great wealth and flaunting a lavish lifestyle, colluding with a devious but playful wife like "Paula". The movie depressed him. Summer hadn't had a devious bone in her body and Sami didn't have a playful bone in hers.

What a mess he'd made. Would the day ever come when his thoughts wouldn't automatically return to the disaster of his life? Disgusted, Ron went to bed where he lay for hours staring dully into the blackness of the night. He certainly hoped the Preacher came up with some answers, because the mountains hadn't given him anything.

Nevertheless, with his undying perseverance, Ron headed out the next morning. Stacking the cushions to take them to his simple sanctuary tired him beyond belief. The reason behind his methods escaped him. Did any of this make sense? Did he think himself to be a Boy Scout, hence the adventure? Otherwise, why try to make a camp? Leaving the trimmings at home, Ron climbed the Park trail, going past the little animal path that would take him to the waterfall, hopeful of finding another area to investigate while waiting for the mountains to inspire him, he trudged higher.

Dragging himself step by step, he climbed for two hours. Nothing inspired him. He passed several animal trails, but didn't investigate a single one. Reaching a rock strewn clearing, he sat on a boulder which gave him a stunning view of Jackson Hole and the towering Tetons. His heart throbbed dully, his body ached and cramped, a hood of weariness covered his head, causing him to compare the perfection of the beauty he saw with the chaos he felt in his soul.

'I started out with such pure intentions. What went wrong?' He thought of every turn in the road where he made errors, including asking Summer for that first date. He chastised himself unmercilously. He longed for the presence of the Preacher. Something solid about the man brought peace just by being with him. Why didn't he hurry up with this talking to the Lord?

After several hours of self torment in the biting wind, he unglued himself from the boulder and plodded back to the house. No longer thrilled with his independence, he morosely assembled the elements of his evening meal. As he dumped the chopped onions in the warming oil, Ron thought he heard honking in his driveway. Wooden spoon in hand, Ron peeked out the front door. Mitch sat in a jeep, honking and gesturing with his hand for Ron to come to the car.

Shuffling to the driveway, Ron looked quizzically through the window which Mitch rolled down at his approach. "Mitch? Won't you come in?"

"No time. Get your jacket. Let's go."

"Where?"

"Just get your jacket." The look on Mitch's face left no room for argument.

"I'm fixing dinner."

"There's no time for dinner. Let's go!"

In a slow motion moment, Ron returned to the house, turned off the stove, shoved the food back in the refrigerator, put on his jacket and got into Mitch's car before realizing he had actually chosen to do so.

"What's this all about?" he asked.

Mitch backed out of the driveway and peeled out of the cul-de sac before looking at Ron. "You must be one heck of a stubborn cuss!" he bellowed. "I've been praying all day and you know what I got?" He whipped his head back and forth from the road to Ron with a demanding look on his face.

Ron shrugged his shoulders.

"Zilch! Nada! Nothing! That's not how it is with my Daddy and me. We talk all the time. But He won't talk about you! I was ready to throw in the towel and say quits when I had a stellar idea, which must have come from the Lord, because believe me, my friend, I wasn't going to give you the time of day." Mitch's eyes flashed at Ron as if he ought to feel very guilty.

Ron faltered, "I'm sorry to hear all that. I've never thought of myself as a stubborn case. What's your stellar idea?"

"I'm taking you to the Cowboy Church. The Pastor is a horse whisperer and in tonight's service he's going to break a wild mustang. The correlation he gives between us and the horse is uncanny. If you can't find yourself in his demonstration, you are truly lost."

"Great." Ron intoned disgustedly. "Really gives me something to look forward to."

"I'm perfectly serious, Ron. You'll find yourself tonight, right in that horse in the ring."

After forty minutes of hard driving they pulled into a compound with pick-up trucks parked on the grass, left awry on the gravel and stashed on the dirt. The big red barn could have held ten houses the size of Ron's. Bales of hay circled one lone, large corral plopped in the middle of the floor. Stadium seating surrounded the corral behind the bales. About 200 cowboys and locals dressed in western wear scattered across the stands.

Lights blazed into the corral as one man on horseback loped after a high-spirited herd of five horses, swinging a rope over his head. Mitch stood with a smile playing on his lips. "Good. We're in time." He swept his arm toward the small crowd. "In the summer this barn is packed, but the tourists have gone. We've got the place to ourselves."

He ambled purposefully toward the risers and found an empty section where he and Ron could talk in low voices and not disturb anybody. Ron scrambled after him almost like a crab running sideways. They sat down while various ones around the ring doffed their hats to the Preacher. The Preacher nodded this way and that, while making himself comfortable.

The man on horseback brought his horse to the center and stopped before the crowd. He turned on his wireless mike and began his monologue, "Welcome to Ruby Cross Ranch, my name is Pastor Brent and I'm a cowboy for the Lord." A smattering of applause rippled around the ring.

"We cowboys are tough people, self reliant, hardy, weather worn and sometimes that means we can be pretty tough to introduce to the Lord. We know how to take care of ourselves. We don't need His help, thank you! But once we see the truth, then we can't help but see that the Lord is everywhere and in everything we do. Remembering how I used to be, I don't think it's possible to be a good cowboy without the Lord, because He was always around me, demonstrating His presence, making Himself known. I was just resistant. That's why I use this technique of preaching in a corral, demonstrating through the breaking of a horse, the most valuable asset a cowboy uses every day.

"See the horse right there in the middle, almost as if he's trying to hide? That's the horse I'm after tonight. The other four are broke. They're helping me out. I'm going to make this horse be my best friend, just like the Holy Spirit turns us into being best friends with Him.

"A horse is the cowboy's partner, and a cowboy is the horse's partner, just like man is a partner with God and God partners with man. Each cowboy and his horse make a team. They work together like a hand in a glove. One of them can't lay down on the job, because the job can't get done without both of them doing their part. It's the same with man and God; we have to work closely with our Lord. He doesn't do anything without us and we can't do anything without Him. It takes working together as a twosome; that's why it's so important for the cowboy and his horse to trust each other and to respect each other. This is what makes a close relationship, which describes exactly what the cowboy has with his horse, a relationship, the closer the better. God builds His relationships to be close, too."

Brent clucked his horse into action, loping around the ring following the five horses. His movement made them lope as well. Brent took a lasso from the horn of his saddle and swung it overhead, then he let it fly from his hand and it landed in a neat arc around the horse's neck that he had previously pointed out. The horse obviously panicked, tightened up against another horse, but stayed in the middle of the four.

"You can see his fear. To the horse a man is a marauder. He thinks we're out to hurt him. He puts us in the same category as a mountain lion. In his mind we want to rip and tear, to bite and claw him. His only relationship to man is one of terror."

A helper on the side of the ring opened a gate and at each pass of the animals allowed one of the other horses out, leaving only the Pastor on his own horse and the horse he intended to break. "Isn't that how we are with God? Before we know Him we're afraid of Him. We think He wants to make our lives miserable. We think He's going to be mean and slap a lot of rules on us that will be like chains or a neck rope that will hurt and gag us and keep us from having any fun in life."

When the other four horses had left the ring, Brent said, "I'm going to keep the rope around this colt's neck for a bit so he can get used to wearing it." Ron watched as the colt kept up a trotting pace several times around the corral. "I'm going to put a little pressure on him now, just like God does to us. He puts a little pressure on our lives so we will turn to Him."

Brent pulls lightly on the rope, the horse stops, turns and looks warily at him. The Pastor releases the pressure of the rope and the colt continues around the ring at a faster trot. "He did the right thing there, by stopping and looking at me. That's why I released the pressure. When we look toward God, the pressure in our lives goes away as well. My goal here is for him to find out that being touched, either by the rope or by me, is okay. When he knows that, I'll get off my horse and work from the ground level. You can see right now that feeling the rope on his back frightens him." Brent flips the rope so that it lies across the colt's back. The horse bucks a bit and picks up speed.

"The feel of the rope causes him to panic like a little pressure in our lives makes us panic. Brent flips the rope so that it goes underneath the colt's tail. "To him it's like a crisis to feel the rope across his bottom. A horse's rear end is his most sensitive spot. What are your sensitive spots that the Lord touches to get your attention? Notice there's no pressure here, just the heavy presence of the rope touching him. That's quite often how the Lord works, no real crisis, just the heaviness of His Presence touches us and we panic." The horse is now racing around the ring; the rope is still across his bottom but is slack.

After several circles the horse starts slowing down. Brent has been holding the rope loosely and following from the middle at a slow walk. "The horse is discovering that the rope isn't as bad as he thought it would be. We can't be critical of him because we behave the same way. We resist God until we find out His ways aren't so bad after all. Like us, the horse has to be allowed to get into trouble so he will learn to find his way out of trouble. God allows us to get into trouble so that we will find our way back to Him."

The horse stops, turns to look at Brent who continues to come closer to him and when the horse canters off, Brent maneuvers the rope between the colt's legs. This causes the horse to careen off and Brent maneuvers the rope out from its legs. The horse comes to a standstill across the ring, digs in its feet and pulls back on the rope until he makes it tight himself.

Before releasing the rope and giving the horse relief from the difficulty he made for himself, Brent says, "He has to learn I am trying to help him. In his mind I am still no good." He flips the rope and it goes slack. The horse begins licking its lips and chewing on them. "See what he's doing with his mouth there? That's a sign he is learning. The lesson he is learning is that when he does the right thing, the pressure is released."

The horse starts pulling back again, but not to the point of pressure on his neck. "He's waiting. Waiting to see what I will do. We do the same with God. We wait suspiciously to see if he's going to zap us; but He never does. Like I would never choke this horse down. I don't want to hurt him; I want him to be my friend. God wants us to be His friends, too."

Then the horse aggressively backs up, shaking his head trying to get rid of the rope. Brent tightens the rope to put pressure on the colt again. The horse abruptly stops and stands, looking at Brent who immediately releases the pressure. "When the colt makes the right decision I give him relief from the rope. When we turn and look at God, waiting to see what He wants, He releases the pressure."

The colt starts to walk docilely around the ring. Brent follows him on his horse with the rope swinging languidly between them. "The panic is gone. When there's panic, there's fear and where there's fear there can be no logic. Now the horse is ready to learn. It's easy to see this operation in a horse because he is easily trained; unlike man who can sometimes take a lifetime to learn that God loves him and means him no harm whatsoever. In fact, everything God does and has planned for man, is good."

The colt stops rather near to Brent and looks him over without pulling on the rope. "Now you can see by his actions that he's thinking and not just reacting."

The horse pulls on the rope, thinks better of it and releases the tension himself by moving closer to Brent. But when Brent moves closer to the colt he turns his rear to him and aims a kick which Brent avoids. The horse returns to docile walking and shaking his head up and down. Then he jerks and backs up to the fence, pulling on the rope, his neck stretched out.

"He's taking a stubborn attitude which he has the right to try until he figures out something else. Don't worry, I'll let him go if he chokes himself down because if I hurt him then I lose. Just like God is patient with us, I must be patient with him. God doesn't hurt us to teach us something. We hurt ourselves, like this horse is doing right now."

The horse's sides are heaving; he is gridlocked with all four hooves resisting the pull of the rope. "Can any of you remember behaving this way with God?" Brent chuckles into the microphone.

"I could force him off this stubborn resistance, but he wouldn't learn anything. I want him to figure out that he must come off that pressure by himself, by being compliant to what I want, by choosing right behavior. Wild nature wants to run away. Horses, like man, are flight animals. When we can't get away, a horse or a man, our tendency is then to resist. A horse resists man's friendship; a man resists God's friendship. For both the horse and the man it comes down to a matter of choice. We can choose to resist or we can choose friendship."

The horse pushes himself out of the resistant attitude and ambles toward Brent, who curls the rope as he comes. He reaches into his pocket for a white, soft glove which he puts on his right hand. They are about five feet apart when Brent moves toward the colt. For a brief moment the horse turns to resist but when the rope gets taunt he instantly stops, turns and looks at Brent, who releases the pressure while continuing his slow gait toward the colt. He comes right alongside him and starts rubbing his neck and saddle area with the gloved hand.

"The first touch must be very gentle and must mimic what his mother did when he was born. She licked him all over. This is like a moment of rebirth for him. When man stops resisting God and believes in Him and His Son Jesus, that's when a man experiences a new birth. God treats us like a new baby, tenderly welcoming us into His family. As that moment is the most precious one of our lives, this moment for my horse must be the same. From this moment on he will trust me like he trusted his mother."

Brent rubs the colt with long, sweeping strokes which the horse obviously enjoys as it even closes its eyes and heaves a sigh. Still caressing, Brent slides to the ground and a helper leads the saddled horse out of the corral. Backing away from the horse he takes his rope and swings it in loops down by his feet, while he walks around and around the horse about ten feet away from him.

"He's learned a few things about me, but not everything. He already knows my voice and my touch; he's gotten used to my smell and now I want him to know I am not a threat on the ground either. I'm not a hazard to his life, in fact I am a blessing, the teammate he's been longing for. I want him to learn to get caught. The method for teaching him to want to get caught is to show him that the alternative is a lot of work." Brent runs at the horse, clucks and waves his arms trying to get him to run away, which he does momentarily, but then he slows to a walk, blinking his eyes and licking his lips.

"That's the change of attitude I want to see. It shows me he understands. He's like us; without understanding how can we know what God wants? When the horse makes the right decision, we give him rest. When we make the right decision, God gives us rest. When a horse is wild he won't eat grain out of our hands, we can't pat him, so right now our relationship is all about pressure. As spiritual babies we are considered wild because we're still full of the world. God can't give us His promises or flood us with His Presence so He deals with us in simple ways that babies understand; pressure."

The horse walks in a circle at this point with Brent following him, still twirling his rope. He stops and looks at Brent. "One thing about a horse is that they don't like to be followed. They can take it for awhile, but sooner or later they will turn around to take a good look at what's following them. Because I want him looking to me for leadership, I release pressure when he does this." Brent backs up a few steps.

"The hind end is a horse's defense. Their kick is their weapon." Brent tries to get the horse to present his hind end, but the colt constantly turns and looks at Brent. After backing off for awhile, Brent waves at the horse to get him to run.

"I'm going to rope a foot, not for the purpose of jerking him down, which I couldn't possibly do because he's stronger than me, but to teach him to be calm if his feet get in trouble, like, say, being caught in a wire fence."

Brent lassos one foot and puts some pressure on the rope. As when the rope had been around his neck, the horse stops and looks at Brent. Putting the rope on the ground, the Pastor walks on it until he is right by the horse. He puts his hand out to be smelled. The horse extends his muzzle and his nostrils flare as he smells Brent's hand. Then Brent offers his arm, which the horse inquiringly smells and finally Brent turns his back to the horse who nuzzles up to him.

"I am teaching him, by doing this, to submit to me. Not in the sense that he is a slave and I am the master, but that I am the leader and he is the follower. That doesn't make the horse less than me, it simply creates partnership. God is our leader and we are His followers. We have a partnership with Him. God wants us to reach out to Him, to touch Him. If I can get the horse to touch me of his own free will, like this colt is doing now, I will have won. If God can get us to reach out to Him and take hold of Him, He has won. I want God to be the winner. How about you?"

The cowboys murmured a "Yes" all around the crowd.

"Think of a horse racing out on the prairie; he's a free spirit. He doesn't want to be roped and subdued. He doesn't want to be forced. He likes his free will. Does that sound like anybody you know? They're like cowboys, aren't they? Free-spirited individuals who love wide open spaces and independence. We have to learn to want to be captured by God and to give Him our lives of our own free will. If we don't, we'll never make a difference in this life, we'll never accomplish anything, we'll just be puffs of air chasing around the prairie."

Brent walks to the rail and gets a bridle. He comes back and rubbing the horses head, especially over his eyes, he slips the bridle in place with no resistance from the horse. "My touch shows him that I like him." Then he rubs the saddle area. He gets down on his knees in front of the colt. "I want him to know that when he is with me he can be comfortable." The horse nuzzles Brent while Brent rubs the horse's chest and legs.

He stands to walk to the corral fence to pick up the saddle blanket. "I believe he trusts me now." He holds the blanket to the horse's nose. The horse pulls back so Brent pulls the blanket back. "I won't force him to do anything. I'll keep letting him smell this until he is comfortable." He presents the blanket until the horse stops pulling back. Then he rubs him all over with the blanket. Finally he puts the blanket on the horses' back and leaves it there.

Brent goes back to the fence and gets the saddle. "I think he's ready." He swings the saddle onto the colt's back; the ears flatten and the horse takes a few strong steps forward as if to flee, but Brent has a grip on the bridle. He moves the saddle around a bit and then returns to rubbing the colt, especially the face. The ears come forward.

"This is where the rubber meets the road. Is there trust or is there not? God brings us to these moments, too. He has a plan for our lives and in relationship with Him we will accomplish it, but if we don't trust Him, there is no relationship. So God puts that relationship to the test quite often. He also has His moments of rubber meeting the road with us, not so much to determine if we trust Him, He already knows where our faith level is, but it's to show us where we are in our relationship with Him.

"This kind of horse is not flighty. He's the kind that will stick in his feet, like we dig in our heels, and then the colt will blow up and bust." Brent tightens the cinch.

"This kind can be tough because they're easy to saddle, but hard to ride. They don't want to move so they stick out their feet in resistance."

Brent swings into the saddle; the horse stands still. "I weigh a little more but I'm the same thing as a saddle, just something he is carrying on his back." The helper comes in the ring behind the horse to help get him to move. Brent rubs him down on both sides of his neck. He clucks and the horse moves forward. The helper lightly touches his flank with a rope and the colt moves into a trot.

"Now a canter," Brent says. The helper chases faster and the horse breaks into a canter.

"Okay, now let's go the other way." The helper gets in front of them and the colt makes a natural turn and canters in the other direction.

"Nice move. Nice move. A horse has to move in a way that comes naturally for him. If you force him to move in unnatural ways he won't be any good. God created us to have individual ways of doing things; He doesn't want any cookie-cutter Christians. He wants us to be authentic, individual, like He created us."

Still cantering, Brent takes his coiled rope and rubs it on the horses shoulders, loops it over his head and back and the horse doesn't flinch. Then he acts like he is roping a cow and the rope flies out over their heads and lands in front of them to the side. Still no reaction. He brings the colt to a standstill in the middle of the corral.

"My horse and I have now become partners. It will be easy to teach him other things because he respects me and he trusts me. God wants to make a partner out of you. He wants to bring you to the point of believing in His Son, Jesus Christ, and accepting Him as your Lord.

"Jesus said, 'I am the way, the truth and the life. No man comes to the Father except through me.' The Bible says if we seek with our whole hearts, we will find the One we're looking for. It's a simple quest, really. We only have to say in our hearts, 'Jesus, will You make Yourself known to me?' You can be brutally honest with Jesus. You can say, 'If You're real, cause I'm not sure You are, then make Yourself known to me. Show up. I'd like to believe in you.'

"The same relationship a trainer has with a horse is the relationship God has with His man. He doesn't force us; he loves us. He wants to train us up to be the beautiful thing He created us to be. Isn't a well trained horse a thing of beauty? Think of a horse that doesn't even need a bridle, but responds to his master's little pressures. Isn't that a thing of beauty? That's what God is developing in us.

"We run here and there, trying one belief system and then another one, really believing that what we think is what's important, or that our own plans are the best, or surely there is something out there other than God that's going to make us happy, and we work hard at it. But such a path pretty soon gets us into trouble. We learn from our experiences that God's plan is the best for us. When you find God and let Him lead you, that's when peace comes, when you're willing to submit.

"An attitude of submission brings obedience and the atmosphere of obedience is trust and that's what we want to do with God. Trust Him. The finished work of a horse is when he becomes one with his rider and has a relationship of absolute trust. When we become one with God, we let Him lead and we follow so closely behind we can't tell where God ends and we begin.

"It's your turn to choose. There are cowboys sitting on these bales of hay who have given their lives to Jesus. If you're ready, come on down to them and let them lead you in a prayer to tell Jesus you believe in Him and you want Him to be your Lord." Brent swung a leg over the saddle horn as the horse stood placidly under him and allowed his rider to rest as he watched about ten people make their way down the steps to let the cowboys pray for them.

Mitch looked at Ron, "Are you ready to go down?"

Ron gaped at him. "You mean go down and have a cowboy pray for me?"

Mitch nodded vigorously, "Yes. That was the invitation."

"Mitch." Ron floundered, gesturing helplessly with his hands. "I've never been on a horse in my life. I didn't come here for cowboys. I came here for the mountains."

"It's not the cowboy that counts. It's the decision."

"Look. This is the first time I've ever encountered such a

thing as a decision to be made for God or against God. Ease up on the rope, will ya?" Ron stood. "Maybe you could take me home now?"

With barely disguised disgust, Mitch got to his feet and fished in his pocket for the keys as they made their way to the door. After a quiet ride home, Mitch said, as he dropped Ron at his house, "You can have the mountain tomorrow; I'll be in my prayer closet all day."

Oddly enough, the next day Ron couldn't bring himself to hike, or to go into town, or to read. Instead he spent the day plastered to a lounge in front of the television watching old movie after old movie. By dinner he felt wasted, out of sorts, pathetic, disjointed almost, after junking an entire day.

He opened the refrigerator door, his head practically buried in the shelves looking for what would satisfy him while acknowledging that food was not the answer, when he again heard honking in his driveway. He opened the door to see Mitch waving to him frantically to get into the car and hollering unintelligible reasons.

Ron sighed, collected his jacket, locked the door and got in the car. He didn't even say hello. He moaned inwardly at the inevitable evangelizing of the stalwart Preacher that he knew was coming. But some spark down in his gut breathed excitement into his chest.

Mitch busied himself with backing out of Ron's driveway. "Don't ask questions. I don't want to grieve the Holy Spirit."

"Can't I ask where we're going?"

"You'll see soon enough. God requires trust. Just trust me enough to know that if He sent me to get you for this visit, then He must have something for you."

"Who are we visiting?"

Mitch slammed the heel of his hand on the steering wheel. "Didn't I say no questions?"

"You mean you want me to sit here in silence?"

Mitch looked as if he were speaking to an imbecile. "Yes!

The Holy Spirit is speaking to me and your questions interrupt Him!"

Ron looked as if he were listening to a mental patient. "Ah, maybe I should just go back to the house."

As he jerked his head toward Ron, Mitch also jerked the wheel. After they careened a few yards, he said, "I do whatever God says to do. He said to pick you up. Now be quiet."

They drove for almost an hour in total silence making their way into the darkened woods off the main roads. Finally Mitch pulled into the yard of a minuscule wooden cabin. The windows glowed ruby yellow and smoke curled from its chimney. Obscurity closed around the cabin making it the only source of light and life in the vicinity, yet the looks of the place made Ron feel like he had stopped on the road to hell.

Mitch turned off the motor. Ron croaked, "Where are we?"

"No talking!" Mitch pointed his meaty finger in Ron's face. "Follow me. And remember, no talking."

Ron got out of the car and followed Mitch to the cabin. Mitch pounded harshly on the front door, then the two of them waited, their hands stuffed into their pockets. After some time the door swung open. An emaciated man half hid behind the entrance. His body had the appearance of a corpse; his face, deeply creased and sallow, leered at them. He nodded, "Preacher."

Mitch stepped into the house and also nodded, "Leroy." He indicated Ron. "This is Ron." Leroy nodded and Ron followed suit.

Leroy closed the door, glaring at Ron. "She's in the back."

Mitch immediately headed down a dark hall and Ron followed right on his heels, not wanting to be left alone with Leroy. But Leroy followed Ron as closely as he followed Mitch. The three men, almost in march-step, entered a bedroom where an equally emaciated woman lay in bed.

She did not open her eyes. Her body barely made a mound under the bedclothes. Blood soaked the bedding around her head and down the front of her as if she had projectile vomited. Mitch went to one side of the bed, Leroy commandeered the other and Ron stayed discreetly at the foot.

"What did you do to her this time?" Mitch asked as he gently took her hand in his.

Horrified, Ron's eyes widened at the sight and he didn't realize he was holding his breath until he wanted to gasp at what happened next. Leroy slapped Mitch's hand away and leaned over the woman's body, resting on his knuckles on Mitch's side of the bed. He reminded Ron of a gorilla, in fact, it seemed like hair sprouted on the man's arms and the back of his hands.

"She's mine." Leroy growled at Mitch.

Mitch took his time to respond. He put his knuckles in front of Leroy's and swung his head in position, his nose inches from the nose of the fiendish man. Leroy's eyes darted, avoiding locking eyes with Mitch who stared deliberately at him. Both men breathed heavily, not from exertion but from anticipation. Smoke seemed to dribble from Leroy's nostrils.

Ron thought how ludicrous this would sound in a court of law, "Yes, your Honor, smoke actually emitted from the man's nose." But there it was. How could he explain this? Ron gripped the iron railing of the footboard.

"Leroy. Call off your demons and back away. I am here to get your woman healed. You want her better, don't you?" Mitch sounded threatening and placating at the same time.

A snarling voice gave the reply. Ron was sure that was not Leroy's voice, at least not his regular voice. "Don't touch her."

Mitch snorted in disgust and stood up. "So tonight is finally the showdown, is it? Alright, I'm ready for you. You've brutalized this woman long enough."

The sound of ripping air seemed to precede the jump, as Leroy leaped across the bed and like an ape, his knees up at his sides, his feet planted on Mitch's hips, he encircled the big man's neck with his scrawny fingers like an iron clamp. Mitch peeled the little man from his body and threw him back across the bed as if he were a mere ant.

Landing on his backside, Leroy rebounded with what Ron ascertained could only be superhuman strength, his legs thrashing in the air as if making the long broad jump at a high school track meet. One foot came down in the woman's stomach causing her to vomit more blood and lifting Leroy to a height from which he crashed onto Mitch's head and shoulders.

As if flipping a grasshopper from his body, Mitch pitched the man to the floor and put his foot on him. "In the name of Jesus, be still!" he roared. Splatting flat on the floor, Leroy became limp as if spent from his efforts. "Who are you?" Mitch demanded.

"I'm Leroy," the cringing man whimpered.

"No! I want to speak to the demon that drives Leroy!"

Suddenly Leroy's body swelled again as if filled with boundless energy. "Who wants to know?" he bellowed.

"Mitch! A son of the living God and a little brother of Jesus Christ!"

"You have no authority over me," the emaciated face sneered. "Leroy wants me to be here. And if he wants me here, you can't throw me out! Leroy's got free will, you know."

"Not if you're blinding his mind, he doesn't. With you in there, Leroy is a slave. Now in Jesus name, who are you?" Mitch demanded again.

Hysterically Leroy shouted, "Rage! My name is Rage!"

Mitch pulled himself up tall and shouted back, "Rage, in the name of Jesus Christ, come out of Leroy now!"

The hairs on the back of Ron's neck stood up. He wasn't sure if he actually saw it or if he felt something come out of Leroy and stand, facing Mitch in abject fear. The air seemed to crackle with electricity. Continuing to sleep, the woman looked to be impervious to the noise around her.

"I loose you from him, and I bind you in the name of Jesus! I cast Rage out of Leroy!" Mitch shouted again. Ron watched incredulously as whatever it was that came out of the man formed into the shape of Leroy and completely detached itself from his body.

"I command you to flee as far as the east is from the west and do not return and do not retaliate on anyone we love or even know." The smoky image fled through the closed window and a strange calm settled in the room.

Leroy's feeble voice could be heard from the floor, "Please, Preacher, help my wife."

With stunning compassion, Mitch took Leroy's hand and helped him to his feet. "She isn't your wife," he said quietly.

Whimpering his great sadness, Leroy said, "Yes she is. We've been together ten years. That makes her my common law wife."

"Only in the eyes of the law. You know yourself she isn't your wife. Not in the eyes of God. He wants His daughters to have husbands who love them, protect them and provide for them. He wants them married to men of God. All I've ever known you to do is beat her, use her and live off her income. That's not even being a man, much less a husband."

"I don't know how to be anybody else. My paw treated my maw like that. I hated him for it, but it's the only thing I know."

"God can train you otherwise."

"Pray for me, Preacher. Please, pray for me."

"Pray for you to receive Jesus? Pray for you to get born again? Pray for you to die to yourself and let Jesus fill you up with His life?"

"Yes. I know I need Him."

"You surely do." Mitch put his hands on Leroy's shoulders. "Repeat these words after me."

Leroy nodded his assent.

"Jesus, be my Lord."

With quavering lips Leroy repeated the words in a voice so low it could not be heard.

"Speak up, man!" the Preacher shouted. "God wants a bold declaration. Cannonball yourself into the Kingdom!"

"Jesus, be my Lord!" Leroy croaked.

"Good. Now say, 'I've been a terrible sinner.'"

Leroy said the words with even more strength.

"Please forgive me and wash my sins away with the blood of Jesus."

"Make me Your son."

"I give You my life."

"Live Your life through me."

"Amen."

When Leroy finished repeating the words he burst into tears. "Thank you, Preacher, now, help my Aggie."

Mitch closed his eyes while Leroy retreated to the corner to whimper. "Lord," the Preacher pleaded. "Teach us how to pray for Aggie's healing."

Suddenly he opened his eyes and grabbed Leroy, pulling him to the side of the bed. "Lay hands on her head and pray for her your own self."

Leroy recoiled. "I can't do that. I don't know nuthin' about prayin' for healing."

Mitch pushed him back in place. "You're a Christian now. Every Christian can pray for healing. It's just your first time, that's all. Pray."

"Jesus," Leroy said timidly, "please heal my Aggie. She don't deserve to be so messed up. I done it. I beat her good. Don't let her suffer because of me. Fix her, Lord."

Ron watched incredulously. The woman's face actually filled out and she looked ten years younger. Her breathing deepened and she began to moan. Leroy cried into his upper left arm as he moved his hands to lay them gently on her stomach. "Don't let her bleed inside, Lord. Fix everything. Make her better than she was before."

Leroy pushed Mitch aside and climbed up on the bed. Gently he lowered his body across her so that his abdomen covered her abdomen. "Heal her, Lord. Heal her. Please."

Suddenly Aggie's eyes fluttered open and she smiled. Then seeing the men in the room, she pushed on Leroy's arm. "Get off me," she said playfully. "We've got company. What're you doin' lying across me anyway?"

"The Lord done told me to do it."

She pushed on his side, "Well get off me. Let me get up and fix them some coffee." Leroy lifted up to his hands and knees and climbed down to the floor.

"Hi Preacher." Aggie sat up and swung her legs over the side of the bed. She reached for her robe and said, "I've made some fresh chocolate chip cookies. How about settin' fer a spell?"

Full of polite manners totally unassociated with the last 15 minutes of craziness, Mitch bowed slightly, "I'm afraid we haven't time, ma'am. Thank you anyway."

"Who's your handsome friend?"

"Forgive my manners, Aggie, this is Ron La Fave."

"How do you do." Ron offered.

"Mighty pleased to meet you."

Mitch pushed Ron ahead of him out of the room. "We'll stop by another time, Aggie. You'd best be teaching your man the Bible now. He's finally been born again."

As they left the house Ron could hear the reconciled couple cooing to each other indistinguishable words.

Chapter Seventeen
# RON RUNS HOME

After Mitch pulled the car onto the forest road, Ron startled him by bellowing, "Just what was that in there?" Mitch looked at him as if seeing a strange being.

Ron's voice mounted. "You owe me an explanation! You badger me into coming out here with you. You force me into some lunatic's house. We see a cadaver on a bed. The husband, or paramour, or whatever he is, of said cadaver for a split second turns into a gorilla! A gorilla! At least he appeared that way." Ron mimicked the man leaning on his knuckles.

"With superhuman strength he leaps over the bed and attacks you, and you, with even more superhuman strength, toss him off like he's a gnat. Then the cadaver fills out like somebody slapped meat on her bones, gets up as if nothing had ever been wrong with her and offers us freshly made chocolate chip cookies!

"Don't look at me as if I'm out of my head. If the Donut man hadn't given you such a glowing report, I'd jump out of the car right now and walk home because I would be certain I am riding in a car in the presence of a stark raving maniac–and he's the one driving!"

With rising indignation, which could not match that of Ron's, Mitch blasted his reply. "The only reason you were invited to see what you saw tonight, and trust me, normally such a deliverance is pretty private, not for public eyes, is because what you saw tonight answers the riddle of your life! Thank God He let you see it. It's not often that He answers in such a flamboyant, unforgettable fashion. Face it; you'll never forget tonight, will you!"

"Forget it? I don't even understand it. I just want an explanation!"

Furious with his dullard of a student, Mitch roared, "Your life has been controlled by demonic power since you first hatched that ridiculous life plan as a kid."

Ron wanted to strike this unwelcome mentor. "What are you talking about? My plan has nothing to do with what I saw tonight! I've never beaten a woman in my life. I could never, ever, bring myself to beat anyone until she is bleeding internally and close to death. What kind of a man are you accusing me of being?"

"And what if the woman on the bed represented you?"

"Me?" Ron slapped his hand to his chest in confused wonder.

"Yes, you!"

"How in God's name could she represent me?"

"Satan beat you to a bloody pulp. You're the 'cadaver' on the bed, as you call it. That's why you're in Jackson Hole. You need healing."

"Healing!"

"Yes, healing. It's your life that needs healing."

"Satan beat me to a bloody pulp?"

""Yes!" Mitch looked up, "Lord, help me! I forgot how clueless a non-believer can be!"

"Why would Satan single me out for such special attention?"

"Because God has always had big plans for you, He's had them from the foundations of the earth, from the day He designed you and Satan wants to destroy you and prevent the plans of God from being fulfilled."

"You're nuts!" Ron turned back to sit straight in his seat. Both men breathed heavily as they calmed down. In a lowered voice Ron said, "I don't even know if God exists."

Mitch softened his voice as well. "After tonight would you say that Satan exists?"

"Before tonight, I never gave it a thought. But I have to say, I certainly saw something evil in that cabin, something hell bent on destroying that woman."

"So you admit there could be a hell, huh?"

"Because I used the words 'hell bent'?"

"Yeah."

"I don't know what to think."

"Analyze this, Ron. If there is the possibility of a hell and an evil being called Satan, then it's also possible there's a heaven and a good being called God."

"So you're saying that an evil being, called Satan, punched me up on the inside until I am bleeding internally, so to speak. He did this because a good being, called God, has good plans for me and Satan doesn't want me to know what they are, nor to do them."

"You're a quick learner. That's exactly right."

They drove in silence a bit more. Then Ron broke it. "What happened to that guy tonight, anyway?"

"Leroy? It's quite a story. To hear the townsfolk tell it, Leroy's been a demon possessed man since he was a teenager. Those are the kind who usually prey on innocent Christian women. Since I came to Jackson five years ago, I've been mopping up his messes with Aggie. She wouldn't leave him. Said it was her cross to bear; she'd made her bed and she'd lie in it."

"You mean he's beaten her up like this before?"

"She's been worse off than tonight, but God always has mercy on her. The Lord kept sending me back out there to talk to him and pray for her. She, herself, is a mighty woman of prayer and faith. Sometimes they're the ones who get in the worst trouble because they know with the Lord's help they'll get through it."

"I never have understood why a woman lets a man treat her like that. All she's got to do is get up in the middle of the night and crack his skull open with one of her iron skillets."

Mitch rolled his eyes. "Yeah. Prisons are full of women like that."

"So what did you do about it? Did you make a citizens arrest?"

"Look, Ron, I don't understand these women either. Every time Aggie would beg me not to put him in jail. So, I didn't. That demon wouldn't show itself when I was around, either, but tonight it reared it's ugly head."

"Is that why you called it a showdown?"

"Yup. Every chance I got for the last five years, I've talked to Leroy about the Lord and the terrible choices he was making. I knew the day would come when Leroy would have to choose between God and Satan. I think Leroy must have finally been coming to his senses and tonight that demon had to make a last stand to try and keep him, but it failed."

"Wait a minute, if the evil one had him, why would Leroy be coming to his senses?"

"Because God never gives up on anybody. The whole time Satan had him, God was wooing him. Leroy gave his life to the Lord Jesus when we prayed and God filled him with His Holy Spirit. That's why he was able to pray for Aggie's healing, himself. This may be a little much for you, but I think he had to put his abdomen on hers because that's where the Holy Spirit lives and Leroy, being a spiritual baby, hasn't been filled with much power yet."

"You're right, that makes no sense to me, so let's not even go there. I don't even want to know about power."

"You're going to have to learn sooner or later because power exists."

"Then let it be later." They recoiled from each other into silence, then Ron hesitatingly asked, "So this God, this good being you're talking about, He healed Aggie? He somehow, without the help of medicine or a doctor, made her body return to normal?"

"That's the pow ... "

"Mitch! Just answer the question."

The Preacher nodded. "Yes. He made her body return to normal." They drove in silence for awhile; Mitch looked at Ron's set face in the darkened car. "You mean the lawyer has no more questions? Impossible."

Ron snorted a little smile. "I don't know how to assimilate all this information. If I hadn't seen it with my own two eyes, if you'd simply told me about such an experience, I wouldn't have believed you. Now I've got to make some sense out of it for myself."

"The Lord's on your case, Ron. He'll make sure you make sense out of it."

At home, Ron surveyed all the doors and windows to make sure they were locked and, where possible, double locked. He turned the heat up a notch above normal and built a fire in the fireplace. Still he couldn't seem to shake the chill he felt. He draped a throw from a lounge over his shoulders and paced the floor, going from room to room, checking closets, looking under beds.

Pausing in the living room, annoyed with his juvenile fear, he shouted into the ethers of his two story space, "I'm not afraid!" Something dark near the ceiling seemed to snicker at him. Wanting to lock himself in his bedroom, he closed the circular glass around the fireplace in order to suffocate the fire. Instead it flamed into a roaring inferno, or at least that's the impression it gave.

He opened the glass and threw several tumblers of water on the flame, which stilled it into smoldering embers. Then he closed the glass and retreated to his bedroom where he locked the door and propped a chair under the doorknob. He thought about calling his father in New York but resisted the idea of rousing him from bed. Finally Ron fell into a fitful sleep and awoke with a start at the crack of dawn.

Shaking off last night's phantasms, and realizing he had missed dinner altogether, Ron drove into town for breakfast. Noting a Christian book store a few doors down from the diner, he quickly entered the restaurant as if eyes were boring into him. After attacking the Blue Plate Special of eggs, bacon, hash browns, toast and pancakes, he strolled outside, trying to appear to be without purpose. Glancing around, he sauntered to the bookstore and ducked inside.

No one seemed to acknowledge his entrance. Finding a saleswoman straightening shelves, he asked, "What would you recommend I read if I'm interested in researching the existence of God?"

She appeared to be startled at his request, then brightened. "I always recommend three books. *The Late Great Planet Earth, The Cross and The Switchblade* and *Surprised by Joy*. One of them should answer your question. If not, come back. I've got plenty more."

She found the three, he paid for them and left. Not willing to acknowledge his reluctance to go home, he took the books to the City Square and found a bench in the sun. By one in the afternoon he had sailed through *The Cross and The Switchblade*. Needing a restroom and a cup of coffee, in that order, he found a coffee shop and ensconced himself.

By six he had finished *The Late Great Planet Earth*. Finding it almost dark, he rushed home so he could enter the house with some daylight remaining. He was rummaging in the refrigerator for something to eat for dinner, when a forceful pounding beat on his front door. With his eyes a bit widened, he looked through the peephole. The Preacher stood with his back to him watching the tail end of daylight slip over the Tetons.

Ron opened the door. "Mitch? I hope you don't think you're taking me out again tonight."

"Actually, yes. But I believe it was your idea. You offered me a steak dinner. Come on. There's a great place just outside of town toward the airport. My treat."

Ron looked back over his shoulder into his living room. "I don't mean to sound like a scared Boy Scout standing with his back to the bonfire looking into the forest at eerie sounds, but Mitch, something weird is in my house."

Mitch peeked around the doorjamb. "Yup, there sure is. Let's go to dinner, and then we'll come back and sanctify this place."

"What does that mean?"

"It means we will establish this place as a house of God. We will order the darkness out and forbid any other evil spiritual beings from congregating here. We'll anoint your doors with oil and that will be the end of weird things being in your house."

"What the heck does 'anoint my doors with oil' mean?"

"It means I'll take a little olive oil, you do have olive oil, don't you?"

Ron nodded yes.

"I'll put some on my finger and rub it on your doors and windows. It's a sign to the devil that the people in the house are invoking the name of Jesus. The devil runs away from that name."

"That's spooky."

"The devil's spooky. But nothing to be afraid of. Come on. I'm famished."

After they ordered, Mitch leaned back and smiled at Ron. "I've been thinking. You really need to hear my testimony. Hear the love side. You've been exposed to the 'spooky' side, as you put it. So now let me tell you the other side."

Ron settled in, enjoying the ambiance of the dark wood gleaming in candlelight and the high backed booth giving them such privacy. "Go for it."

"I grew up in Chicago. My father, apparently playing a one

night stand, never reappeared. My mother couldn't figure out which one night stand he was. She kept me until I was five, bringing different men into the house, that's how she earned her living. Then one day I came home from kindergarten and she told me to sit on the front steps while she backed out of the driveway. I watched as my mother waved and drove off.

"I stayed on the steps until it turned dark and then I went next door and told the neighbors what had happened. The lady called the police and for the next 13 years I lived in 15 foster homes. I hated my mother. The older I got the more enraged I became. That's why I could handle Leroy's demon of Rage so well; I'd already handled one as big as his.

"All anybody had to do was look at me a little funny and I beat the tar out of them. The police would bring me to the door after a bloody fight, and my foster parents would head right for the phone to call Social Services to come get me.

"I stayed away from those homes as much as possible and I learned that a warm place to hang out was the public library. I loved to read. One day I dug a book out of the used book bin called The Late Great Planet Earth."

Ron interrupted, "Wait a minute. I just read that today."

"Good for you! Read it again. And again. I read that book till it fell apart in my hands. Then one night I couldn't sleep; it seemed like there was someone in the room with me, someone calling me. It was Jesus and we talked all night. At 5 a.m. I knelt on the floor and asked Jesus to be my Lord. I gave Him 100 percent of me. I hated me. I didn't think He was getting much. But He was thrilled and the Holy Spirit moved right in and took over the direction of my life.

"Not long after that I ran into a hardy, but I thought foolish, evangelist on the street, out by himself, preaching the good news of Jesus Christ and passing out tracts. An older guy by my standards, so I hung around because I thought he needed some protection. As he preached, I asked questions. Then he preached just to me for a couple of hours. Others stopped, listened a bit, took a tract and went on. But I couldn't get enough.

"He took me home that night, called my foster parents, and asked if I could stay. They didn't care. The next day he went to Social Services to see if he could get custody of me and since I was already 17, they let me go. He mentored me into a deep understanding of Jesus and of the Kingdom of God.

"When I understood that God is love, He is made of love, everything He does is love based, and I understood that I am made in His image, I realized I needed to become a man of love. The first person I had to love was my mother. I worked really hard to forgive her. When that was complete, I could hardly wait to find her.

"I did my research and found she was living right there in Chicago. I practically ran to her house and pounded on the door. I thought she'd be as glad to see me as I was to see her. When she opened the door I thrust some flowers at her, smiled real big and told her I was her son. She actually snarled at me and slammed the door in my face. I couldn't believe it.

"It was my first test to see just how real my love was. It took another four years. My mentor had gotten me into Wheaton College on a scholarship; I spent every weekend with him, evangelizing on the streets of Chicago, and every weekend I pounded on my mother's door, handed her some flowers and every weekend she slammed the door in my face.

"Every time, I shouted through the door, 'I forgive you, Mom. I love you.' After two years I stopped saying, 'I forgive you.' She didn't need to hear that anymore. I didn't want to remind her of her faults. I wanted her to know I loved her. I sent her gifts whenever I could afford them. I prayed for her every day. Her salvation became more important to me than life itself.

"Before my graduation from Wheaton, my mentor went to her house. He was a real sweet talker and she invited him in. He led her to the Lord and brought her to the ceremonies. I cried like a baby when I saw her in the audience. Then I understood how much God loves us and to what extent He'll go to prove His love just to get us back.

"He gave His Son, Jesus, to die for us, to pay for our sins, and why? Because He wants us to be with Him for eternity. To live in heaven our sins must be washed away. We can never be good enough for heaven. It's a perfect place. If you let one imperfect person into heaven, then heaven is no longer a perfect place. So Jesus died and His blood became the payment for all sin, for all those who receive Him as Lord."

Mitch sat back, apparently finished with his testimony, and dug into his steak. Ron had finished his and stirred his coffee as he contemplated Mitch's testimony.

"Wow. Some story," he finally sighed. "Mitch, like you said, I'm the lawyer and I've got to ask questions to fill in the holes. Where's your mother now?"

"Still in Chicago. She became a steadfast member in a church back there and ended up marrying the Pastor after his wife died. Talk about a woman of love, my mother is it! Their church runs half way houses for kids from broken homes, runaways, any kid in distress. She's awesome and so is her husband. They're past retirement age, but they'll never quit!"

"How did you get to Wyoming? Why aren't you still in Chicago?"

"I went on to graduate school and when I was ordained, I asked to be placed in a difficult environment that was lacking love. By that time my mother was married and I had hard evidence that love works.

"This little church in the southeastern corner of Wyoming had had eight Pastors in eight years. It was out in the boonies, the only church in a 50 mile radius. They had asked for their ninth Pastor a week before I filled in my request at the Placement Office at Wheaton.

"You know me a little by now. I'm a gruff, no-nonsense type who tolerates no foolishness. I'm ardent, fiercely pointed, direct and humorless." Mitch gave Ron a sideways grin. "But I sing like a lark."

Ron chuckled. "Maybe more like a bald eagle. I gather the members of the church didn't take to you too well."

"To the contrary, they likened me in character to John the Baptist. They were rough and ready plainsmen and they appreciated my commitment to Christ. They liked the way I prayed and especially the way the Lord answered my prayers. But ... "

"I've been waiting for the 'but'."

"So you think I would have had a problem there?"

"You're just a hard guy to know, that's all. They probably wanted you to be friendlier, more, more normal. Like them."

"I bet you're a good lawyer. You hit the nail on the head. I lasted ten years, had the Deacon board cowed and the Missionary board awed. But they rallied together and demanded a new Pastor. I wouldn't leave, I refused. So my mentor came for a visit. He lived with me for awhile. We spent hours in the fields, walking and talking with the Lord, because that's what I always did. I didn't care who stumbled across my path, I didn't stop for one minute to consider their presence. If I was having a conversation with the Lord, that took precedence over any other thing.

"We visited with and ministered to every single person within that 50 mile radius of the church, because that's what I always did. I exhorted them about the Lord and prayed with them, but never once did I socialize. My mentor called a church meeting and told them they were the most blessed congregation he had ever seen because they had a true man of God at the helm.

"I stayed another ten years and they called another church meeting. This time they were very humble and appreciative of all I had done over time. But, they said I had encouraged and prepared their children for ministry or the mission field and now they had no one left to work the fields. Would I please leave?

"The morning of that meeting I received a phone call saying my mentor had died and I was requested at his funeral and the reading of his will. I very quietly resigned and went back to Chicago."

Mitch sat back and glanced around the restaurant. Ron was dumbfounded. "Come on! No witness on the witness stand leaves a jury hanging. Finish the story. We're not quitting till all the facts are in."

"Who's the judge?"

"I guess we all are. I know I am. I want to hear the whole thing."

"Why?"

"Because I want to know how you happened to be on my mountain and what prompts you to rummage in my life. How did you get from there to here?"

"Maybe God sent me."

"I don't reject that idea. Please continue."

Mitch grimaced and rubbed his eyes. "In Chicago I received the shock of my life. My mom and her husband, they were in their early sixties then, operated ten halfway houses for teenagers, all of them supported by my mentor. It turns out that sweet, little, old, street evangelist who adopted me and mentored me was the only child of a railroad tycoon, a billionaire. When the lawyer read the will I found out I was the sole beneficiary. All that money became mine with the one stipulation that I would always finance the halfway houses and Wheaton."

Ron shook his head as if to clear his mind. "You? The Preacher man on the mountain? You're a billionaire?"

Mitch nodded. A little smile played on his lips. "You're the first person I've told, outside of my mother. If the folks around here found out, I'd be under siege all the time; people wanting handouts."

Incredulously Ron demanded, "You have been sitting on a billion dollars in that dinky little house in Jackson for five years? Why?"

Mitch gave Ron an 'oh, you poor sap' kind of look. "The Lord told me to come here and He'd tell me why after I got here. I've been waiting on the Lord for five years. And as for the money, the dang stuff keeps growing while I wait. The Lord must have something wonderful to do with all that money and I'm waiting for Him to tell me. I have a feeling you're part of it."

"Me?" Ron's astonishment mounted.

They sat in the restaurant for several hours. Ron asked questions about the investments the lawyers made with the money, thinking his role might be advisory. Mitch kept bringing the subject back to his new birth, hoping to explain more to Ron, but Ron single mindedly fixated on the money. Finally Mitch shoved his chair back, threw a hundred on the table and said, "Shall we go get your house cleaned out?"

Ron indicated the bill and asked, "Don't you want to wait for change?"

"No. Our waitress is a single Mom."

Looking dubiously at the $100, he stood up with Mitch. "Okay. Let's go."

Although Ron had left lights on, the house seemed to shine with an eerie brilliance when they drove into the driveway. Mitch turned the car off and sat looking at it. Ron certainly had no intention of opening his door before Mitch opened his. "Well, they know we're here."

"Who knows we're here?" Ron nervously interpolated.

"They do." Mitch seemed to be in no hurry to leave the car.

"Who's 'they'?" Ron knew he was in no hurry to leave without Mitch.

"The demons you've got congregated in there. They must have followed us from Leroy's house. They were probably hanging out in the yard when we had our deliverance, so they came with us to your house hoping to find a place to live and now they're waiting for you to be so scared you'll invite them to stay."

"That doesn't make sense. If I'm scared then I definitely won't invite them to stay."

"Demons ride on lies. Satan is the father of lies. If you'll start believing a lie, like the thought that you'll never get rid of them, or that they're not so bad, or maybe if you let these little ones stay they'll keep the bigger demons away, or any such nonsense, that is like opening the door to them and inviting them to stay."

"So, how are you going to get them to leave?"

"I'm going to talk to them."

"Talk to them?"

"Of course. They are simply disembodied spirits." He grimaced at the house and then resolutely opened the door, "Let's get this over with."

Inside, Ron asked, "Shall I find the olive oil?"

"I'll get them out first."

"Be my guest." Ron looked apprehensively at the ceiling. "Strange how I know they're there without seeing a thing."

"Anybody can feel an evil presence. The hair stands up on your skin, it can feel cold and there's the sense of danger. Everyone was made in God's image. We know when His enemy is around."

Ron looked at Mitch in disdain, "This is no time for a philosophical dialogue, just get it, or them, or whatever it is, out of here."

Mitch half smiled, "This might be a good time to dicker with you about the mountain. You'd probably let me have the whole thing back if … "

"It's yours. I'll find someplace else to walk."

"Just kidding. I'll find someplace else to walk."

Mitch turned and paced the living room floor underneath the unholy grouping at the peak of the ceiling. Suddenly he shouted upwards, "He has delivered us from the power of darkness and conveyed us into the kingdom of the Son of His love."

He paced some more, a sense of righteous indignation seeming to gather on his shoulders; he shouted again. "For we do not wrestle against flesh and blood, but against principalities, against powers, against the rulers of the darkness of this age, against spiritual hosts of wickedness in the heavenly places."

Trembling in his intensity, Mitch shouted, "Therefore, let us cast off the works of darkness, and let us put on the armor of light."

Pointing toward the ceiling, he bombarded the darkness, "In the name of Jesus, get out of this house! I call this a house of God! I claim this man, Ron La Fave, for the kingdom of God. You can not have him. You cannot stay here. You and your minions cannot be within a mile of him wherever he goes. I command it in the name of Jesus! Now go!"

With that he swept his arm toward the door, pointing at it, his face sternly fixed and his stance squarely planted. Ron, standing halfway between Mitch and the front door, felt a rush of air, as if a window suddenly opened into a storm. The purge took only seconds and then all was still.

"It's gone!" Ron's mouth hung open in amazement.

Mitch nodded and put his finger to his lips to indicate silence. "Now, in the name of Jesus, I proclaim this house to be a house of God. Only the Lord Almighty and his servants are allowed inside this house. I invite the angels of God to camp out in this place. And Lord, please bring the owner of this house into the kingdom of God, I ask in the name of Jesus."

He smiled at Ron, "Now I'm ready for that olive oil."

"Having angels in your house is a good thing, isn't it?"

"Best protection you can have."

Ron returned with the oil and Mitch stalwartly went from window to window, door to door in every room of the house, rubbing a little olive oil on the frames of each one. As he did so, he said, "This oil is a symbol of the Holy Spirit. I do this to honor His presence and to commit this property to Him. This oil is a seal in the name of the Father, of Jesus and of the Holy Spirit that this house is now the property of God and as such will not be trespassed by His enemy, Satan, or by any of the demons of hell. I declare this in the name of Jesus."

He handed the bottle of olive oil back to Ron. "It's done. You can put that away."

Ron's face had screwed into incredibility. "Not one bit of that made sense. What's a little olive oil and some words going to do?"

"Do you have any coffee?"

"Yeah," Ron said with hesitation.

"Why don't you make some. I think we're in for a long night."

As Ron made the coffee, Mitch highlighted what happened. "You don't think words will do anything because number one you don't know the power of the name of Jesus and number two you don't realize that the supernatural realm operates only on words. Angels and Demons are waiting around to hear what you say so they can go ahead and enforce it. You say something evil those demons are rubbing their hands together in glee. They get to do something evil against you. You say something in line with God's Word, which is always good, the angels rub their hands in glee and do it immediately."

Ron looked at Mitch in shock. "I consider most words to be superfluous, just air fillers. People occupy time and space with words that mean nothing."

"Yeah, but have you ever noticed that people get what they say? It's a simple rule. The ones who talk about how sick they are, they're always sick. The ones who talk about how poor they are, they're always poor."

"Maybe, but I know people who talk down about their money and yet they're rich."

"God created us with a safeguard. The heart and the mouth must agree and when they do, you will have what you say. Aren't those people who downplay their money actually bragging? Isn't their heart rejoicing in the fact that they are rich?"

"Hmmm, I see your point. But give me some kind of principle that would prove what you're saying is true."

"If you read the Bible, you'll find it all in there. The principle comes from the fact that God created the earth by speaking words. The world is held together by those words and will stay in the form that it is until all God spoke from His mouth has been accomplished."

"What did He say?"

"There's too much to convey in one night. Read the Bible for yourself. The important thing for you to know is that He said you must be born again."

"I must be born again? My name, Ron La Fave, is in the Bible? Ron La Fave must be born again?" Ron gave Mitch a smile as if he'd caught him.

Mitch smiled back, knowing he could out step any trap this lawyer tried to lay. "In John 3:3 it says, 'Most assuredly, I say to you, unless one is born again, or born from above, he cannot see the kingdom of God.' No, your name isn't in the Bible, but it is included with the rest of humanity in that single word 'one'. You must be born again, Ron, that is if you want to accomplish the great plan God made for your life from the foundations of the earth."

"What great plan? I don't see anyone living out any great plans. I know some pretty wealthy people and I don't see that their lives or their accomplishments, when it comes right down to what they produce, is anything great. It's more like greedy."

"Then they aren't living out the great plan of God, they are living out their own greedy plan. Just like you tried to do. But somehow God managed to keep your heart soft. If you'd become hard hearted, God would have had to take His hands off you and let you have your own way. Instead, He arranged for you to be right here right now with me."

Ron hung his head. "If there's anything soft in my heart, I think it's that I still love Summer. As much as I try, I can't forget her completely."

"Maybe she's the wife God had planned for you."

Shrugging his shoulders Ron sighed. "I wouldn't doubt it, but she's married now."

They sat in silence for a minute. "Well, you don't have to be married to accomplish the great plan God has for your life. But you do have to be born again."

Again Ron sighed, deeply. "Whether I'm ready or not, I have a feeling you are going to tell me how to do that."

Mitch cast him a reproving glance. "You're ready."

"Well, then, go ahead."

"Remember, your heart and your mouth must agree. You have to be at the end of yourself. In other words you have to know you are incapable of directing your own life, that you really need a Savior and you truly need a Lord to take charge of you."

Mitch looked steadily at Ron who looked steadily at the floor. "And then?"

"Then you talk to Him. He's omnipresent, which means He is everywhere all at once. He's waiting for the words from your mouth that will bring Him into your heart. Right now He is all around you, but He isn't inside you. When you confess your belief in Him, you invite Him in. Then He will flood your spirit, your soul and your body with His Presence and you will never be the same again."

"What do I say?"

"It's best if you make up your own words, but you say something like, 'Jesus, I need you. I believe in You. I know You are the Son of God and Your blood has saved me. You and Your Father and Your Holy Spirit created me and I want to give myself back to You. Please take me, make me one of Your disciples, live in me and lead me in the way You want me to go. Thank You for paying for my sins and giving me everlasting life. Amen.'" As an afterthought, Mitch added, "It's also nice to tell Him you love Him."

"Thanks."

"Thanks? You don't want to say that prayer right now?"

"Oh, is that a prayer?"

"Prayer is only a word that means talking with God."

"I thought its meaning was a bit more religious than that."

"People have made it religious, but the truth is God is a person in three distinct personalities. You talk to the Father, or to

Jesus, or to the Holy Spirit as if you were talking over a cup of coffee."

"But He doesn't talk back, does He?"

"Sure He does. You have to learn to hear His voice, that's all. There's all kinds of voices that talk to us without coming through a body. Our emotions talk to us; our wills talk to us; our minds talk to us; our bodies talk to us. Then there are all the demons and angels around. And our consciences. Memories can talk. Sometimes other people's thoughts talk to us. Thoughts have a trajectory of a couple of feet from a person because they have an electrical charge. But they have to be really strong thoughts.

"God's voice, in the midst of all these, is usually very soft. The Father, the Son and the Holy Spirit all have the same voice because they are in constant agreement. Their voice is the only one that always, and I mean always, affirms us. Even when they are upset, they always speak in love. No other voice has that much love, that much care for us."

"Can I hear Him, or them, now?"

"Only from the outside. You have to invite them in."

Ron looked at the Preacher with evident gratitude. "Thanks, Mitch. I really mean that. And thank you for cleaning out my house. And thank you for dinner. I don't know … Where can I get a Bible? I'd like to read some of this for myself."

"I have dozens of them at the house. Want to come over and pick one out?"

"No. I'd rather have one of my own."

Mitch paused as he tried to analyze Ron's state of mind. He knew he should get up and leave, but he was reluctant to drop this fish back in the water. "Would you like … "

Ron held up his hand to stop the flow of words. "I've heard all I can hold for right now. Give me a couple of days. I'll drop by and visit."

After Mitch left Ron walked up and down the floor in the great room, occasionally glancing up at the ceiling to reassure himself the evil presence had, indeed, left. His thoughts flipped about, none of them making sense; after an hour or so he decided to talk out loud to see if there wasn't a stream in his consciousness that he could grab onto.

He found himself speaking about Summer and agonizing over the way he had treated her. Then other dreadful things came to his mind and he spoke about those. His behavior reminded him of movies he had seen where Catholics went into a little box and confessed their sins to a priest. "If I'm confessing my sins, who am I speaking to?"

A warmth whipped around him as if he were being wrapped in a heated blanket. He began to cry. He cried throughout the rest of his midnight confession. Finally at four a.m. he felt empty and tired and dragged himself to bed.

Arising in time for lunch, Ron had one thought only: to buy a Bible. Stopping in the Christian book store before going to the diner for lunch, he was nonplussed by the number of different versions he found on the shelves. He backed up to find the saleswoman. "How do I know what Bible to buy?"

"That all depends on what you're looking for?"

"I don't know what I'm looking for. I had no idea there would be versions of the Bible. I thought there was just one Bible."

"There's only one Bible. Don't be concerned with the variety because they are not versions, they are translations. They all say exactly the same thing, just in different words. Greek words can have different variations of meanings, so different translators express the same thoughts of the Bible with varying words. Is this your very first Bible?"

He nodded yes, overwhelmed by the choice before him.

"Then I would suggest you buy two. Buy the Living Word Bible because it is written in every day language and you should read that one first. Just read it right through, cover to cover, because the Bible is written in progressive revelation, meaning you will learn more and learn it more deeply as you progress through to the end.

"After you finish that buy the New King James Bible for the

beauty of the language and for its accuracy. And because of its accuracy, I suggest you keep the New King James as your daily Bible. But when you finish reading it cover to cover you will want to start some research.

"You should then buy yourself an Amplified Bible as that Bible includes all the words that define the Greek text. A Thompson's Chain Reference Old King James Bible will be useful so that you can research the Scriptures by reading other similar verses. The Thompson's Chain puts a list of other Scriptures next to a verse that either say the same thing, or expound on the meaning. Lastly, I would suggest a Spirit Life Bible with commentaries in the margins from today's ministers of God."

Ron bought all five, writing down the order in which he should read them. He took the heavy package to the car, extracting the Living Word to take into the diner. As he sat eating lunch he was unaware of any glances in his direction as people wondered why he would read his Bible in the diner. Which they did.

He read until dinner time, then ordered a sandwich to go. He took it home and ate it while he read some more; in fact, he was up till early morning reading. Waking early, he found himself full of energy, wanting to read more.

He walked and read, sat and read, laid and read, lapping up 15 hours, in between which he did eat and stretch. By early evening of the third day he found himself at the end of Job and he laid the Bible on his chest.

'That's me! Mitch was wrong; I am in the Bible." He mused. "It may not be my name, but that's my life. I had everything and I lost it all. I wasn't making sacrifices like Job did, but perhaps my father's prayers were the sacrifices. And then Job came face to face with God. Does what God say to Job also apply to me?'

Ron read the first four verses of chapter 38 again only this time he heard them in his mind as if they were directed at him. "Who are you, small man with no wisdom, to question Me? Now it's My turn. Be brave and answer my questions, if you can. Were you there when I spoke and all matter came into being? Were you standing by Me listening to My words? Can you tell Me how My words create? Describe it for Me, if you understand it. Who, as the architect of the Universe, determined its size and shape? Where are the four corners of the earth? Surely you jest if you think you know! Who laid out the blueprints of everything that would ever be created? How did I get it to all hang together? What keeps it in place now? Shouldn't those suns, balls of gas you call them, without replenishment have burned out? Who sent Jesus, the very cornerstone of all creation, which made all the stars sing like a choir and all humanity waiting in Paradise shout for joy?"

Silence. The Bible seemed to be waiting for an answer. "I don't know. I don't know anything. If this is God talking to me, then I have to say You probably know everything. I've certainly acted like I knew everything in the past. But I didn't."

Dinnertime came and went. Ron mulled over his thoughts about God knowing everything and him knowing hardly anything at all, then with trepidation he continued into the Psalms and stopped at 118:8. "It is better to trust in the Lord than to put confidence in man." He remembered Mitch saying he must know that he needs a Savior and a Lord. Certainly no man could be that.

It was 11 p.m. Surely it would not be too late for Mitch. Ron put on his parka, the nights were preparing for winter, and drove to the north end of Jackson. He knocked quietly on the door. Mitch opened it swiftly as if he had been standing on the other side waiting for his tremulous visitor.

"Mitch. I need a Savior and I need a Lord."

"Come in."

Ron shrugged off his parka, hung it on a hook by the door and sat on the couch without being invited. Mitch, immobilized by the small whirlwind, refound the motion in his legs and sat in the Lazy Boy across from the couch.

"I got to Psalm 118 ... "

"Verse 8, right?"

Ron nodded.

"The middle of the Bible. It doesn't take long for God's Word to work. So, what's the problem; what do you want?"

"I want you to lead me in that prayer."

"Have you tried saying it yourself?"

"No. I didn't want to leave out any points."

"A warm heart that spills the words out of itself is far better than the cold repetition of someone else's words."

"But I don't know ... "

"Just do it!"

"Do I close my eyes?"

"It doesn't matter; I find it's easier that way. I can be closed in with God and not distracted by the physical world."

Ron closed his eyes. His shoulders, seemingly of their own will, hunched up under his ears. His hands monotonously rubbed his jeans on the top of his thighs. "Jesus, I know You are the Savior and I know You are the Lord. I know these things because Mitch told me, but I also know them because You wrapped me up the other night and You put the story of Job in the Bible for me and You questioned me today.

"I don't know how to do this so I will just say that I give You my entire life. You gave me life, now I give it back to You. I've made a mess of it so now will You please use my life for Your plan instead of mine? I want to contribute something to this fabulous world You've made.

"But most of all, come live in my heart and be so close to me that we share a heartbeat. Let us breathe the same breath and think the same thoughts. Let me be like David; let me pant after You like a deer pants for water.

"Thank You for paying for my sins. I cannot comprehend what that took on Your part; I just know I am grateful. I could never have paid for them myself, but You Lord, carried my whole burden and the burdens of everyone else who ever lived. There is no God like You. You are the One I want. You are the One who died for me. Now help me die for You. Help me to die to myself and what I want and to live for You and what You want.

"I love You, Lord. I've never loved like this before. Not even Summer. Please forgive me for hurting her and thank You for making her happy in spite of my sins. Please forgive me for having used Sami. Please make her happy in spite of my sins. Please restore all the money everyone lost in VIVA and bring somebody like Mitch to every member so they will have an opportunity to know You. Thank You. I love You."

Ron opened his eyes. Mitch dried his. "Say 'amen' after every prayer. It means 'so be it'."

Ron quickly closed his eyes and said, "Amen."

A mild winter settled on Jackson that year, which meant the snow level in town hovered at two feet in depth and the air didn't freeze the lungs as one inhaled. The elk still gathered in the field across from the Christian bookstore where they would be fed all winter by the Park Rangers. Ron saw them daily as he devoured the books from the store, and returned with his questions for the saleswoman.

He and Mitch strapped on snow shoes and trudged through the lower hills and fields. Together daily, they talked and prayed, the mentor and the attending votary. Mitch emptied himself into Ron and the Lord built Mitch up more. Ron, in searching the Scriptures under Mitch's direction, praying with him and through his gruff encouragement, grew into a giant in the faith.

At night they wrote the revelations the Lord gave them that day until finally Mitch held up a sheaf of papers and roared, "Do you realize what we've got here?"

Puzzled, Ron answered, "A bunch of papers with some words written on them?"

"We've written out a vision. God has given us a plan. I was right! You're part of my plan. I've been waiting five years for this vision!"

They continued to journal what they received each day until they arrived at the point where they knew God had given them everything He wanted them to know about His plan at this time. Ron took the pages and wrote an affidavit, an oath. They both signed it as if it were a legal document in pledge to one another and to God.

When spring came, which it did abruptly in a one day melt, Ron remembered his sanctuary up the mountain, mainly because when he wondered where his patio cushions were, he remembered where he had left them. Taking the trek up the hill, he found his secluded spot covered over with branches that had been deliberately dragged there. Looking inside, he found his cushions were a wreck, obviously having been bedding for a large, restless animal.

He didn't touch a thing and left them. They had a new proprietor and Ron didn't need the sanctuary anymore. He'd found his answers, but this time the mountains didn't give him the solutions he sought. The Maker of the mountains hand delivered the resolutions. The One whose arms Ron ran into when he ran home delivered him into the kingdom of the Son of His love.

Chapter Eighteen
# THE GLORY TRAIN ROLLS

School let out. Ron knew because when he visited Mitch he saw the kids outdoing themselves at all times of the day on the dirt bike track they devised and manicured in the empty lot next door. Sturdy houses stood in this quarter. That's about all that could be said for them. He knew their waitress at the Steak House, Tori, lived in one with her two boys, who no doubt free-wheeled their bikes up into the air as he approached Mitch's door.

Ron waved his bill of sale in Mitch's face as he passed him on the way to the kitchen to pour some coffee. "I'm ready to roll! Signed the papers today, the money's being put in the bank as we speak and the President, himself, will wire Dad's losses to him. Now my mom can take that cruise; thank heaven that weight's off my mind! The Salvation Army comes to pick up the odds and ends tomorrow and the next day The Glory Train will be packed and we're outta here!"

A big smile graced Mitch's face, unaccustomed as that expression felt on his mug, he stroked his beard with glee. "Tori moves in the day we leave. I pack my things and she takes care of the rest, selling what she doesn't want, like her old jalopy. She'll keep my four wheel drive. All she has to do is move across the street."

Ron looked at his mentor with doe-eyed awe. "In a way, you're doing this for your Mom, aren't you?"

Mitch blushed, "Maybe in a way. If somebody would have given her a hand she might have been able to stay with me. I'd help all single Moms if I could."

"It must feel good."

"It does."

"By the way, look out the window."

The instant gruffness came back, "Why should I look out the window?"

"Just look out the window! Aren't you ever compliant?"

Mitch scowled and went to the window to comply. It took a minute to locate Ron's surprise, but then he whooped. "The Glory Train! When did you have that done?"

"Yesterday. While you and I roamed the mountains saying our goodbyes to waterfalls and lichen, Stan from Artistic Expressions had the keys to my garage and he did it. Pretty fancy, isn't it?"

"I love it! We'll use it! Letterheads, company name hanging over the door, credits, everything. Buy some master copies from Stan. The Glory Train!" He looked at the curlicue letters painted on Ron's new car parked by the curb. Since the Lexus, traded up from the mountain jeep, belonged to God, the name God had given them for their enterprise seemed appropriate painted on God's car.

Several days later, headed for San Francisco, Mitch abruptly interrupted their quiet ride. "I've got something on my mind, and until I get it off my chest, I'll feel like an overblown balloon ready to pop. Now don't think I haven't given this a lot of prayer, because I have. I know it sounds a little carnal, but I'm convinced I have the mind of God on this. The thing of it is, I'd really like to live on the water. Maybe buy an old barge for cheap and fix it up; moor it someplace and roll around on the waves that lap into shore."

Ron frowned. "Sounds pretty time consuming to me. Won't that interfere with our affidavit?"

Mitch looked out the window as Ron drove. "Humpf. I don't know. I thought it was God that gave me the idea. Well, maybe you're right. First things first. Someday I'd like that, though. I guess I better leave it for later."

They thought they'd take their time getting to San Francisco, meandering for at least four days, but by the middle of the second day, their intensity having overpowered their roving, they parked in front of Kirk and Darce's door angling the tires to the curb to keep from skidding down Twin Peaks. When no one answered their knock, they put on their hiking boots and climbed to the top of the Peak. There, surrounded by communication towers, they could see the whole bay area, even sighting the Farrallon Islands.

"Doesn't the significance of this hit you upside the head? Our first day in San Francisco and we see the world encircled by communication towers? We couldn't have planned this if we tried! I think God's showing us that we're on the right track."

"Yup," Mitch agreed. "He likes to punctuate His leading with little signs like this."

They sat watching the sparkling bay. Not a cloud threatened any corner of the vast expanse, not a wisp of fog lay on its stomach over the water, nor did it rush up from the ocean and tumble down the hills. Presenting itself as perfect a day as San Francisco can get, which happens only in June before the tourists bring the dismal weather. It's almost as if The City By The Bay loves its own and frowns when vacationers come to town.

Down below they could see Darce pull into the driveway. They both stood. No amount of waving caught her attention. They glanced around, reluctant to leave, but when they saw her haul bag after bag of groceries into the house, they yelled with all their gusto for her to wait and they would step and fetch it. But the wind carried their voices up, not down. They arrived when half the bags were unpacked and shelved.

Darce gave Ron a major hug and delivered a minor one to Mitch. Ron could see she took to the Preacher instantly and he had to admit, as he watched them get to know each other, he felt a certain pride in presenting the man. With his short, cropped white beard, an added aspect for their new venture, his ramrod straight stature, and his piercing crystal blue eyes, Mitch looked like he should be in the movies. Throwing in his direct response to life mixed with humility which made him a pleasant companion, despite his gruff ways, Ron knew he'd introduced a major player to their threesome.

Darce picked up the phone, "Kirk said to call the minute you got here. He'll be one unhappy boy if he misses a single word of what you two have to say." Mitch and Ron exchanged a look and a raised eyebrow.

While they waited for Kirk to arrive, Darce settled them in their rooms. The house, being new, gave the allure of shining like a freshly peeled egg. With two guest bedrooms, each man had his own and they shared a bath down the hall. Kirk and Darce occupied the master suite and an office otherwise known as the fourth bedroom.

They heard Kirk unlock the front door, but before they could move toward him, he bounded up the stairs and grabbed Ron in a bear hug. "Buddy boy! Glad you're back!"

Shaking Mitch's hand vigorously, he said, "I could hardly stand it till you got here. I've been calling Darce every five minutes to ask, 'Are they here yet?'"

"He's been worse than a child."

He tugged on Ron's sleeve, "Come on, let's get to the coffee and the big talk. Forget the small talk." With his other arm he grabbed Darce around the waist and pulled her with them down the stairs. "This is it, babe. I told you Ron's the one to take us to the top. We thought we were there once, but we were on the wrong water slide. Now we're gonna make a big splash!"

Mitch followed amiably, praying under his breath. In the kitchen they found small talk difficult to avoid. For one thing it fills the void. For another, when certain ones don't know the subject at hand and the ones who do are reluctant to divulge what they know, bantering occupies time until a successful launch can be made.

"Come on, come on, spill the beans." Kirk drummed his fingers on the table.

"Well, Mitch here, he wants to live on the water. Do you have any suggestions?" Mitch developed a surprised furrowing to his brow.

"Maybe. But first, why did you guys decide to come here? What are you, or we, going to do in San Francisco?"

Ron leaned back, "Slow down. First we have to get established, set some parameters. We need a place to live, he'll need a car pretty soon, office space, draw up papers."

"What kind of office space?"

Ron put his hand on Kirk's arm. "There you go again, bucking ahead. Nobody's leaving you out of anything; it's just that first things come first."

"What Ron's leading up to, in his diplomatic way, is that we want to know if you and your missus are born again?"

Ron smiled at his friend's BB gun approach. He wondered what part of Kirk's anatomy Mitch hit.

"What's that mean? Some kind of business club we're going to have to join?"

Mitch guffawed; Ron smiled. Darce blushed, "Kirk, that's the same question Summer asked, remember?"

"So did that Tommy Tyson." Kirk looked apprehensively at his inquisitor and the couple both looked embarrassed as they furtively glanced at Ron and cleared their throats. "I guess you'd better explain because we didn't get it when either of them tried. Why is this coming into the conversation now?"

"Like I said, first things first." Ron solemnly replied.

"To put it simply, your friend, Ron here, got born again last fall and we've spent the winter and spring studying the Bible and praying out the business plan we want to set before you."

"That's it! That's what I'm waiting to see! The business plan!"

"But it's a plan, Kirk, that can only be produced by people who are born again."

"Sheesh! That's such a dumb expression. Car lots talk about having 'born again cars', beauty shops talk about having 'born again hair', it's a publicity gimmick, what are you using it for?" the exasperation in Kirk's voice barely contained itself.

"We're using it to talk about Jesus."

"Darce and I know all about Jesus. We grew up in church. We know all the stories of the Bible."

"Do you call yourselves Christian?" Mitch carried the ball of this conversation while Ron observed.

"Of course."

"Are you really?"

"As far as I know we are. What am I missing here?"

"What you might be missing is the new birth."

"New birth? Born again? Come on, turn the lights on for me."

"Nicodemus pretty much asked the same question of Jesus. He came to Him at night so that no one would see him. He held a pretty high position in the leadership of the Sanhedrin, the ruling party of the Jews and didn't want to be recognized at the door of this renegade preacher. He told Jesus he knew He came from God because of the way He taught and what He taught. You could say the same, couldn't you? You know Jesus came from God."

"Sure. Everyone knows Jesus was the Son of God."

"Nicodemus wanted to know what he, himself, was missing. Jesus said he had to be born again. Nicodemus asked all kinds of questions about how that could happen as it was impossible to reenter his mother's womb and Jesus basically said he had to be born from above. Are you with me so far?"

"Yeah. I think I remember this story. Jesus talked to him about the wind in the trees, didn't He?"

"Exactly. The Spirit of God is likened to a wind because He cannot be seen, but He can be felt and He can be heard. He talks to us. To be born again is to get the Holy Spirit living inside of us so we can feel His urgings and hear His voice. That's how Ron and I received this business plan."

"You heard it on the inside of you."

"That's right.

Ron interjected, "You pray all the time, don't you Kirk?"

"Yeah, I do."

"Do you hear God's voice when He answers your prayers? For example, how do you know what stocks to buy after you pray?"

"Well, I don't hear any voices, I'll tell you that. What happens is that I look at a computer screen and the name of a company will jump out at me. I can't explain it any better than that. All other names become faint but the one I end up buying is like screaming at me."

Mitch stepped back in. "That's God talking to you from the outside. He will help anybody who prays. If you have Him on the inside, He talks to you in one form or another, it may be a voice or an intuition or a desire. The difference is like that of being an affiliate or being a member. Have you ever told Him you believe in Him, that you believe He is the Son of God. Have you invited Him to live on the inside of you?"

Kirk looked at Darce. They both shrugged their shoulders. "Maybe at Confirmation," she offered.

"It's a blessing to grow up in church. Because you hear the Word of God and learn about His ways, you can follow them pretty closely and be blessed. But the biggest blessing comes from total obedience, inviting Him to give you the new birth, to give you a new spirit and to settle down on the inside of you to direct your life."

Darce put her hands on her hips, "I'm pretty sure neither one of us has ever done that. I'd know if we had."

"Ron did it last fall. That's what we've come to see if you are willing to do. I'll tell you what, do you have a Bible?"

Darce nodded yes.

"Why don't you get it and let me show you the Scriptures that talk about this."

From mid-afternoon to midnight they talked and read the Bible. "Look in Romans 10 verses 9 and 10." Mitch instructed.

Darce looked it up and read, "If you confess with your mouth the Lord Jesus and believe in your heart that God has raised Him from the dead, you will be saved. For with the heart one believes unto righteousness, and with the mouth confession is made unto salvation."

Through the hours they continued their discussion and Bible study; they ate dinner, did dishes, took care of needs. Best of all, they finished the evening in prayer where Kirk and Darce told Jesus they believed in Him and wanted Him for their Lord. Then all four faces dissolved in tears. The four of them happily embraced Jesus and hugged each other.

As they climbed the stairs for bed, Kirk asked, "Mitch, as far as I know you're a man of the mountains. Why is this voice inside me saying I'm going to work for you? What can I do for a trekker?"

"Both Ron and I have known that you would work for me some day. But that subject has to wait till tomorrow. I'm beat. Oh, by the way, can you take the day off?"

"It's done. I'm yours."

The following day they started with prayer and a Bible study. All of them were amazed at how much Kirk and Darce knew. They realized all those years of hearing the Word of God and reading it in Sunday School and youth group had made deposits in them and now that they wanted to know it, they could remember. Delighted, Mitch knew he wouldn't have to spend nine months to bring them up to speed, like he did with Ron.

By eleven they were ready to get down to the business plan, but no one seemed eager to talk about it. Conversation wandered aimlessly around the table until Mitch spoke with a bewildered tone, "I keep hearing something in my spirit that sounds weird."

"What is it?" asked Ron. The two men had learned to help each other puzzle things out in the spirit.

"Something like 'Sauce Little Toe'. No, no, its more like 'Salsa Lee Toe'."

The other three hooted with laughter. "That's Sausalito." Kirk slapped Mitch on the back, barely able to catch his breath from glee. "Salsa Lee Toe!" he snorted with pleasure. "Who's Lee? And why does he want Salsa on his Toe?"

Mitch grinned, "What's Sausalito? I thought maybe it was a place to have lunch."

Ron suddenly sobered and his eyes grew big. "You're right. It's a good place to have lunch. It's also a good place to look for a barge to live in."

"I thought you said my idea would take away from our plan, and yet you're the one who brings it up all the time?"

"Don't ask me. In my spirit I can see that barge plain as day."

"Why don't you guys live with us? We've got plenty of room. That door we put between our bedroom and office makes it easy, Kirky and I pretty much hang out there all the time. You could have the run of the whole house."

"Darce, when I said we'd be friends forever, I didn't mean that close." Ron grinned at her.

"I'm serious. Kirk, what do you think?"

"Well, I'm not against the idea. But let me ask this, how would I chase you around the house."

She grinned her infamous half-smile, "You never chase me around the house. I'm always the one chasing you."

Kirk abruptly turned serious, "That way we could have prayer and Bible study every day. Yeah, I'm for it."

"Let's pray about it and see what the Lord has to say. Maybe for the summer." Mitch, as unappointed father of the group, had the last word. "Christians always want to live together. There's something very comforting about a community of believers."

Ron drove them to Sausalito, cruising down to Jack's for lunch and then they coasted along to the flotilla of houseboats floating at the end of the town. Mitch walked along the piers gaping in disbelief. "I had no idea a water village like this existed. The idea of the barge … "

"There it is." Ron suddenly interrupted, stretching out his arm and pointing,

"What?" Darce asked.

"The barge I've been seeing in my spirit. The exact one. That's it! I knew it was big, but that's a whopper!" The four of them walked to it like bears smelling honey.

Kirk looked at the name molded decoratively in tin and nailed to the piling beside the barge. "I know this guy, or at least I know his stockbroker." He said in astonishment. "He lost a bundle in the market. I mean a bundle! His wife died a few months ago and in a fit of depression he invested wildly and lost it all. His broker made out fine, in fact like a bandit. We've black-balled him at work. Nobody even talks to him at the water cooler. That's no way to treat a client. We're supposed to be watching out for our investors.

"The guy and his wife were hippies back in the 60s; they bought this barge and according to the broker, turned it into a little palace over the years. Raised their kids here and everything."

A man in his mid thirties surprised them by speaking from behind their little group. "Excuse me. I'd like to get on board. Do you mind if I step through?"

Flustered, Darce moved aside to allow the tall, lanky figure to pass. "I'm sorry."

Mitch looked into the young man's soft brown eyes. "I'm looking for a barge to buy and we were admiring this one. Are you the owner?"

"No, my father is. But I can help you. It is for sale." He turned to look at Kirk. "I'm glad to know you're blackballing that …

Since I'm in polite company I won't use the term. Any stockbroker that allows a client to jump off the deep end like that doesn't deserve his license, to say the least."

"I'm very sorry." Kirk intoned.

The young man shrugged, "What's done is done." He extended his hand. I'm Jason Widman." He smiled wryly, "My parents were hippies. You heard right. They named me Wildcard Widman. Fortunately, they threw in the Jason at the last minute. My cards read W. Jason Widman and some of my friends call me W.J."

Kirk and Darce exchanged shocked looks. As the rest of the party followed Jason up the gangplank, Ron stood rooted on the pier while they went on board, his mouth hanging ajar. Mitch returned to call to him, "Ron, it's not coincidence. Let's get to the root of it. Come on." Almost shaking himself to get himself to move, Ron walked up the ramp to enter the most posh boat he had ever seen, even in the movies.

Counting the hull, three decks configured the ship. Stored supplies filled the bottom. The second deck contained commodious bedrooms, three built along each side and the seventh, the Master. took up the bow. Each included a bath. The main deck started with the kitchen at the stern connected to the dock by a separate gangplank for bringing groceries and catering supplies on board.

The dining room traversed the width with a stunning view of San Francisco off the port side. One long highly polished wood table stretched from starboard to port which easily sat 30 people on each side. "What if you only have 15 guests?" Darce asked as she followed Jason who led them through the barge.

"Then you bunch them at one end. It can be quite cozy because the table is narrow as you can see."

"And how about normal dinner parties, anywhere from 4 to 12 people?"

Jason removed a painting from a section of the bulkhead. Built in china cabinets covered the entire wall and every ten feet, the cabinets stopped to give space for a painting to hang on the wall itself. However, Jason pulled a brass latch and swung a table down which extended to hold up to eight people. "For more we can seat them in the living room."

Between the dining room and the living room sat two little rooms, little in the sense of comparing them to the others. One held an impressive library. The other, offering a full view of San Francisco, had a custom built cast iron pot bellied stove with an open-faced fire. Its chimney rose like a stove pipe hat up through the ceiling. Three couches surrounded the fire; one could easily imagine this being the coziest place on the barge during inclement weather.

It's there that they found Steve Widman and his daughter in law, Jason's wife, Samantha. The old man trembled as he shook hands around. Samantha, in her early twenties, came and took Jason's arm. She smiled but did not extend her hand. "I'm showing them the house, Dad. The gentleman expressed interest in buying a barge."

Steve looked at Mitch dubiously, "You came at the right time. It's a fire sale." He took out a handkerchief and wiped his eyes.

Jason patted his wife's hand. "I thought you were going to cheer him up, sweetie?"

"I tried. But he's had me in tears all morning."

He extracted her hand. "Let me finish the tour. I'll be right back." Jason took the party of four into the living room which spanned half the barge. Furnishings for eight conversation groupings splayed around the room. In the center, circling a support pillar, stood a specially made table which obviously provided the serving spot for hors d'oeuvres or a buffet, or sit-down for that more intimate dinner party of 12.

A spiral staircase rose from the corner starboard leading to the roof. "The top deck is flat and fenced. We've had dinner parties for 125 people up there. As a teenager I had dances for 250. Those are fire marshal limits.

"What do you do if it rains?" Darce asked, ever the practical teacher.

"We tent it. We rent heaters and we go on dancing, or eating, or whatever." He smiled at them. "Would you like to go up?"

While the three politely shook their heads no, Mitch delightedly said, "Yes, most definitely."

Jason looked wistfully toward the fireplace room, but turned with grace and headed for the staircase. "Follow me."

The deck stretched flat and sturdily fenced with a glossy wooden rail on which people could lean to watch the view or chat. Except for the aperture where the fireplace chimney protruded with its protective fencing, the expanse resembled an aircraft carrier.

"How many people do you think could sit up here in rows of chairs?" ask Mitch. The others looked at him, perplexed.

"That I don't know. We've never had that kind of an event. My parents weren't political or anything. But at a couple of my parties the wait staff counted at least four hundred."

"Four hundred!" Kirk exploded. "Where did you find that many kids to invite to your parties?"

Jason shook his head in memory. "When word got out that W.J. was having a party, kids came from all over, even from the East Bay. Takes a lot of guts to crash a party, but no one ever got turned away, and only decent kids seemed to find the house. We never had any trouble."

Jason looked at Mitch curiously. "Why did you ask about seating people up here?"

"Because it looks to me to be about the size of a 500 seat church."

"You want to put a church on a barge?"

"It's not what I want that counts. It's the Lord."

"Oh, are you a minister or something?"

"Yes."

Jason looked like he wanted to bolt. "I see. Well, folks, I better get back to my Dad and my wife. Let me take you to the gangplank." He turned to lead the way.

Mitch took his arm to stop him. "Not so fast. I'm very interested in this barge. What are you asking for it?"

"Well, sir, I spent the morning with a realtor who handles exclusive properties. She wants to put a price tag of ten million dollars on it, but she thinks it may take up to five years to sell, since it's such a one of a kind item. Not every one is lining up to buy luxury barges. That's why I need to talk to my Dad. We want a quick sale; I think one million is more likely to make it move fast. So, if you don't mind."

"Son, I know you don't think we have the means to buy such a property, but I think I can swing it. Tell me about the parking lot? Could there ever be a possibility it would be sold? With your barge moored right at the end of the main pier, people can park there, and it looks like hundreds of cars would fit, and it's maybe a hundred yards from here to there. This barge has more possibility for me than I can figure! But only if the parking lot stays connected to the pier."

"The Houseboat Owners Association owns the parking lot and it will never be sold. From time to time a houseboat has to be pulled on shore to be worked on, and that's where they do it. Membership in that organization is mandatory and they have to approve of you before the sale can be complete. With your projects you might be a difficult person to earn their vote. Most of them are rebels from society."

Mitch clapped his hand on Jason's shoulder. "If God's behind it, nothing can stop it. Why don't we go talk to your father together?"

Jason resisted Mitch's pull toward the stairway, "I don't want to waste your time or his; he's obviously quite upset today. He's probably been reminiscing and gotten his emotions all riled up."

"Trust me, I can help."

"Sir, we're experiencing a very difficult time for our family. First we lost my Mom and now we've lost our fortune."

"If you don't mind my asking, how did your father make his money?"

"In tin. See those warehouses over there? He bought and sold tin as well as fabricating various objects from it. They're all sitting fallow. After Mom's death he let the employees go and left the tin stacked up in there. We can't get him to do anything, much less make sensible decisions."

"Can't you rehire the employees and get the business moving again?"

"One would think that would be the case, but I have my own company and this comes at a time when I am putting in 12 to 14 hour workdays."

Mitch scrutinized the entire row of seven 100 foot warehouses lining an apparent street running down to the water. "Would he be willing to sell those as well?"

"I don't mean to be disrespectful, but offering well-meaning gestures to a man in his straights would almost seem inhumane."

With compassion Mitch turned to the young man. "What kind of company do you have?"

"Film editing. Have you seen 'Shadow Catcher'?"

The four agreed, none of them had seen the film. "It's the current blockbuster and it's my best work so far. I opened my doors two years ago and haven't had time for a vacation yet."

Ron and Mitch exchanged looks. "What do you call your company? I hope it's not Wildcard." Ron shuddered.

"No, I wanted to use that name, but at the time a film had gone into production called 'Wildcard', so I chose 'Pie in the Sky' instead."

Darce asked, "Why did you choose that?"

"My mother played the constant hostess. She had a continual stream of guests staying at the house and one time, about five years ago, this preacher pointed at me with his fork and said, 'You're going to have pie in the sky in the sweet by and by, but steak on your plate while you wait.' I've never forgotten that. I figured this might as well be the sweet by and by."

Ron said softly, "Wildcard was my film."

Jason said, "I'm sorry," not quite comprehending.

"I'm responsible for Wildcard."

"What does that mean, did you write it?"

"I produced it."

Jason looked perplexed. "I thought David Rasnick ... "

"I was the son in law."

With recognition, "Oh, then you're Ron something. I'm sorry, I never noted your last name. You were known in the industry as Ron Raznick."

"That's good. Maybe no one will associate me with that film."

Jason stuck out his hand to shake Ron's. "No. No. That was a masterful work! It was just bad timing. Knowing the public appetite is a tricky thing."

Ron accepted Jason's handshake, "I used to think that too. Now I've learned to wait on God's timing."

Freezing for a moment, Jason smiled and then turned, "Let's get you folks back to the pier."

Mitch grabbed his shoulder. "Jason, please listen to me. I'm a Christian, son, a born again Christian. I know how to bring your father peace. Please let me talk to him. I am not making a well-meaning gesture; I'm telling you the truth. Give me fifteen minutes and if you don't like what you hear, then stand up and that will be the signal for us to leave."

Jason's face clouded with sorrow and he caved, "Okay." He led the way retracing their steps down the circular staircase and entering the fireplace room. Darce sat in the middle on one couch, Ron and Kirk perched on either side of her. Samantha sat in the middle of the center couch, Steve and Jason positioned on either side of her. Mitch commandeered the remaining couch.

Jason explained to his grieving father and his distraught wife that Mitch wanted to have a talk with them, and then turned the floor over to the Preacher. Mitch wasted no time. "Has anyone in your family ever known Jesus Christ personally, having taken Him as their own Lord and Savior?"

"Oh, yes, Wilma did. That was my wife. Five years ago, before she got sick, she invited some evangelist to dinner. We could count on Wilma to go out and meet people. Me? I could stay home and read and watch my beloved bay, but Wilma loved people. She brought this guy home for dinner and all he did was talk about the Lord. I could hardly wait for him to leave, but Wilma hung on every word." Steve started to cry.

"She gave her heart to the Lord that night. I'll never forget it. She was so happy. I tried to do it too, but it didn't come out the same. After that every traveling evangelist coming through San Francisco wound up at our dinner table and usually stayed in one of our bedrooms.

"When she got sick you should have seen her! Bright, cheery, happy, you'd never know the doctor had given her such dismal news. Terminal cancer. You can't imagine how those words hit you when they are applied to your wonderful wife. Wilma read the Bible every day and kept pointing out the verses that talked about her healing. I tell you that woman believed she was healed. The doctor called it a state of denial, but I couldn't see she was denying she was sick. She knew she was bad sick. But she believed in the power of Jesus to heal her. Even in the last moments before she died she clasped my hand and said, "Honey, please believe in Jesus. I want to spend eternity with you. I'm going to a place where I will be healed. I want you there with me." Steve couldn't go on because of his sobs.

At length, he whimpered, "I don't know how to get there."

"Steve, I know how you can get there." Mitch said softly. When he had Steve's attention, he told them the whole story and ended by saying, "It's a matter of believing. If you believe in your heart that Jesus is the Lord of all and you say with your mouth that He is your Lord, the Bible says you will be saved. Do you believe in your heart that Jesus is the Son of God and that He paid for your sins with His body and blood on the cross?"

Babbling through his tears, Steve said, "I've believed that all along."

Mitch looked at Jason, who responded, "I listened to those preachers, too and yes, I came to a place where I believe that."

"And Samantha?" Mitch asked.

She barely whispered, "Yes, I believe."

"Then the next step is to confess it with your mouths. Say these words after me and believe them in your hearts." They all nodded their compliance.

"Heavenly Father," Mitch intoned.

"Heavenly Father," the three repeated the words and then followed him in every sentence down through the 'Amen'.

Steve absolutely looked like he could fly; a sheen or a glow seemed to emanate from his face, "I made it, Wilma! I'll be with you forever, honey, because of our wonderful Jesus! And wait till you meet our new friend, Mitch. You'll love him, Wil! Oh, thank You, Jesus!"

Samantha and Jason nuzzled and kissed, so happy they had taken this important step together. Darce wiped away a few tears and Kirk blew his nose. Ron looked a little sad but he kept it to himself.

It was past supper when they finished. However Mitch asked if they would all give him just a few more minutes and pray about the sale of the barge before thinking about dinner. All seven put themselves immediately to the task. They earnestly sought the voice of the Lord to see what He wanted in this situation. Should Mitch buy it?

After the "amen" Mitch asked what they heard. Kirk said, "I could only see this big blue word, 'Yes!'"

Darce responded, "One word kept whispering in my heart, 'yes, yes, yes, yes, yes, yes, yes'."

Ron saw the tin plate nailed to the piling with Mitch's name on it and underneath it said, "The Glory Train".

Jason saw the Lord hand him an envelope. "It was like one of those envelopes at the Academy Awards and when I opened it and pulled out the card, it read 'Yes'."

Samantha said, "I just have the feeling you're the one who's supposed to buy it."

To end with Steve said, "You're the only one that I want to have my beloved home on the bay."

Mitch pulled out his check book and wrote a down payment check for $250,000, then he invited them out to dinner so they could celebrate. This time they dined in Tiburon.

Finally, in the car headed for San Francisco, Kirk exhaled sharply. "Okay, Mitch. Enlighten me. Who the heck are you? I watched you pull out your checkbook and write a check for a quarter of a million dollars like you were buying a tube of toothpaste. Then you talk coolly about buying a street of warehouses–in Sausalito, for crying out loud. I can't even imagine what they will cost you. Who are you?"

Mitch filled the ride home with his testimony and Kirk and Darce became the third and fourth persons he told about his legacy from his mentor. When they got inside the house, Mitch said solemnly. "I think it's time you started doing the investing of my money, Kirk. Can I put you on my payroll as my personal stockbroker?"

"I don't have that kind of status."

"Can I buy it for you?"

Kirk grinned. "Anything is possible."

Chapter Nineteen
# LAYING THE PLAN ON THE TABLE

By August first Steve Widman accepted the offer made by Mitch Henry to buy his seven warehouses totaling $3,500,000 and they waited for the City Council to approve their application to use them for film production. Steve would then have six months to remove the tin, during which he would pay a modest rent of $35,000 a month until the warehouses were swept clean and ready to present to their new owner.

By September fifteenth the purchased barge would be vacated and the keys handed to its new owner, Mitch Henry. Ron thought he could live there too, without feeling crowded, so the two of them waited out the transition occupying Darce and Kirk's guest bedrooms.

Kirk was right. They had daily prayer and Bible study. Since Kirk worked from home, his on the job religious activities presented no conflict as his boss led the study. But after a month of steady meetings with inspectors for the buildings, and individual City Council members, Kirk, isolated by staying home to do investments, had enough of the mystery.

"Okay. Things have to come to an abrupt halt until you guys tell me the vision. What's our plan? Apparently we're going back into the business of making movies, but I'm at a loss as to what our goal is. Mitch, you don't need to make money. Ron, isn't this more of the dog that bit you?"

Mitch looked at Ron and nodded. "Show him the affidavit." Ron went to his briefcase and pulled out two pieces of paper. He gave them to Kirk and both he and Darce read them silently.

"We, the undersigned, Mitchell Henry and Ronald La Fave, do hereby decree and declare on this 17th day of April in the year of our Lord, 2008 that we will proceed with and perform the following for our Lord Jesus Christ.

"In view of the fact that the general populace of the entire world has a thirst for the knowledge of God and a desire to be reconciled with Him, and because our Lord Jesus Christ created the only available avenue for the people of this world to know God by giving His life and paying for ours with His blood, we will present to the entire world the means of actuating that reconciliation.

"In view of the fact that this generation populating the earth at this time, has turned, or has been turned into a visually receptive people, a population that learns by seeing images in still pictures and in moving pictures, all people groups being drawn by television and most especially movies, we will present the message of Jesus Christ to the entire world through motion pictures at the beginning and with television series to follow and whatever else the Lord lays on our hearts to produce as we go along.

"In view of the fact that no one can go to heaven to live with God for eternity without accepting Jesus Christ as their personal Lord and their personal Savior, we make it our utmost goal to reach every human being on the planet through the medium of film with the profoundly simple story of Jesus Christ the Son of God and with instructions on how to receive Him as their personal Lord and Savior.

"In view of the fact that personal testimony is a biblically sound method of winning people's souls, we will create our plots from true life testimonies of how Jesus actually enters a person's life and changes it. Our first endeavor will be the story of Mitchell Henry. By proposing examples of actual events we will inspire others to follow the same path to and through the new birth that has been trodden by other seekers since Christ sent the Holy Spirit back to earth to lead all people into all truth.

"In view of the fact that fine filming is the standard set by the world and that expectations exist in the minds of the viewers for a standard of excellence, and because the Bible calls for us to have a spirit of excellence, we will do everything humanly possible and expect divine help to produce the very best movies, television series and other film projects available on the planet.

"In view of the fact that we have access to an inordinate amount of money to accomplish this task, we will seek to first find ways to make the money grow, and second to conserve the money by pledging to be good stewards, to never hold back from spending for excellence and to always hold back from spending for self gratification.

"In view of the fact that Christian enterprises are notorious for being 'cheapskates', we pledge to bring honor to the name of 'Christian' by being at least competitive in our salaries, if not superior to those of the world.

"In view of the fact that distribution of films and the movie theaters themselves have historically presented difficulties for Christian producers, we will strive to create a new method of distribution that will by-pass the existing structures.

"In view of the fact that we have no idea how we will accomplish these goals we pledge to begin each day with whomever is under contract at the time in a session of prayer and Bible study. No contract will be signed with any person or company that does not stipulate that the person or persons indicated in the contract will attend daily prayer and Bible study meetings.

"In view of the fact that we are servants of God, we will accept no glory for any thing we accomplish. All the glory is to be given to God. He is the engine that makes this train roll. We are the cars that roll along in The Glory Train!"

Kirk pushed the papers aside and stood up. "Whew!" he looked around the room at the others. Shoving his hands in his pockets he paced a bit, stopped to regard Ron with baffled amazement and then paced some more. Everyone waited for him to respond, especially Darce.

The words burst from his lips. "Ron! This is ridiculous! What do you expect me to think of this, this testament?" He continued to pace, his arms ramrod ending in fists in his pockets.

Ron waited.

"With VIVA you wanted a blockbuster. Okay, I thought maybe we could do that. I went along. In fact it was exciting, more like a jet plane, then a rolling train. However, we got ruined! Ruined! Don't you remember that?"

His face reddened as he spoke. No one moved except Kirk who jerkily paced. "But with this you want the world! Now it's not okay. I don't think you can do that. I don't think a billion dollars is enough to reach the whole world. Christians have had this goal since Christ. And there's been megabucks spent on stuff like this. Look at the money the Catholic Church has spent sending missionaries and building churches for what, two thousand years? With all their resources they've never reached the entire planet. This is sheer fantasy!"

Darce intently bit her lower lip. Ron waited; Mitch took his cue from Ron and kept his silence. Kirk stopped in front of his client whose job was to take him to the top.

"Besides, there's no mention in here of making money." Kirk bent toward Ron pointing his finger at his own chest. "I'm not going to make a fortune doing this. Mitch has given me a very nice salary, but you haven't written about any shares or profit taking. You're not taking me to the top! Are you? Admit it! This is all benevolence work. Charity. At the end of the day we'll all have shining reputations and Darce will have to keep teaching school till she retires at 65, because her promising young husband spent his time spreading goodwill."

Ron remained silent. Kirk straightened and ran his fingers through his hair. "This affidavit changes everything. I've gotta have some time by myself." He picked up the affidavit. "Can I take it?"

"It's your copy."

"I've never been on the top of the mountain. I think I'll go up there and study this."

As he started out of the kitchen, Darce stood and asked, "Kirk, shall I ... ?"

He put his hand up to stop her and seeing his crumpled face she sat back down. He went out the back door and they watched him through the window as he started up the slope. She looked imploringly at Ron.

"I had to go through the same thing, Darce. It's very difficult for a man to give up his life. We're programmed to think and plan for what we're going to do, what we're going to accomplish. Changing that thinking is called 'dying to self'. We can't even go to God and say 'What can I do for You?' because He doesn't need us to do anything for Him. He wants us to ask, 'What can I do with You?'

"The last thing I personally want is to get back into the movie business, but I have to admit, I'm pretty well trained. The joy in it for me is the obedience. Once I wrote up that affidavit, peace and satisfaction flooded me. Now it's day to day, minute to minute, asking the Lord what to do, talking things over with Him and having Him point me in the direction He wants me to go. All the pressure is off my life. He'll talk to Kirk, too."

Normally effervescent, Darce looked morosely at the table.

Ron asked softly, "What about you, how did that affidavit affect you?"

She twisted her wedding ring back and forth as she talked. "I have never been interested in the money, like Kirk. Being a multi-millionaire doesn't hold much glamour for me; it's just more stuff to be responsible for. I want kids but Kirk wants the money before the kids. We bought the house so we could at least start getting ready for a family."

"You must want two." Mitch interjected.

"That's what Kirk wants. He says he doesn't want any more kids than there are laps to sit in. He's so adamant about controlling when we have kids and how many kids we'll have that he threatens from time to time to have his sperm frozen and then get himself fixed. I don't know what your affidavit will do to him."

Ron sat down beside her. "I want to know what it does to you."

"Me? I don't know. I mean, well, when I was reading it my heart beat so fast I could barely breathe. I kept thinking how awesome to be involved in something that will turn the world upside down, like the twelve disciples did after Jesus died. Then I wondered what kind of part I could play. Am I supposed to continue to teach school and be a sideline cheerleader? I mean, those are the thoughts I had."

She looked at Ron with awe. "I think that affidavit is the most exciting thing I have ever read, outside of the Bible, of course."

Ron leaned toward her almost conspiratorially, "What kind of a part would you like to play?"

"Me? I don't think I'm qualified to play any part."

"Well, would you consider something?"

"Sure. But I won't get in over my head."

"That's exactly why I'm asking you to consider this, because you are sensible, detail-oriented, efficient, you have a spirit of excellence and you display wisdom in your dealings with people. I think you are extraordinarily qualified. Would you consider being my administrative assistant? You see, Mitch holds the purse strings; he has ultimate control. But he has named me the CEO. I need someone exactly like you to help me run this thing. Pray about it."

"Run the Glory Train?"

"Well, run behind Jesus of course."

"But I've never run anything."

"I think running a classroom of kids just about qualifies you to run anything. I wouldn't hesitate to turn General Motors over to you."

She grinned in embarrassment. "When would I start?"

"Tomorrow."

"You mean quit school?"

"You're on summer break, right?"

"Yes, but I still have to submit my resignation."

"Then if the answer is yes, do that tomorrow and start work for me right away. There's much to do."

"I'll have to talk to Kirk."

"Of course."

Kirk didn't come home till after dark. The two men were in Sausalito having dinner with Jason and Samantha. Darce had a candlelight dinner laid out in the dining room with a meal ready to heat at a moment's notice. Kirk quietly came in the back door, his clothes disheveled and mud on his face. Having intermittently wiped away tears with hands that threw dirt clods made his cheeks dirty like a little boy coming in from play. However, the throwing of the dirt clods did not even resemble play. The stained and folded affidavit jutted out of his shirt pocket.

He took it out and spread it on the table. His words barely escaped through a tightened throat. "Darce, this is one of the finest documents ... " He couldn't finish the sentence.

Now he outright cried. "I know I promised you the moon and the stars. I feel like I'm failing you when I say this, but I want to reach the world with Ron. No, I don't want to reach the world with Ron; I want to reach the world with Jesus. I want to do this, Darce. I want to throw all caution to the wind and give my whole being to God. It makes no sense and it makes all sense."

He took her hand and pulled her into his lap. "Is that too much? Will I lose you?"

Her tears blended with his tears as she put her cheek to his cheek. "It's what I want, too, Kirky."

The next morning after prayer and Bible study, Darce intended to hurry down to the main office of the San Francisco school system to turn in her resignation. But her trip was stalled.

After they closed their Bibles, all four of them still seated at the table, Ron said, "I'd like for us to start praying about finding Christian writers. I've never heard of a Christian script writer, but they must exist. I just don't know where to find them."

Darce looked at Ron in amazement. Then she looked at Kirk in even more amazement. With an assertive thrust to her chin she said, "Well, I thought the ones Summer wrote were pretty good. Not that I read a lot of screenplays, but hers were captivating."

Kirk blushed heavily. Fascinated, Mitch looked from one to the other of the three.

"What did you think of them, Ron?" Darce asked with a trace of defiance in her voice.

He stuttered, "I ... I don't know what you're talking about."

"The screenplays Summer sent over from Switzerland."

"I still don't know what you're talking about."

"Summer wanted to raise money for that place where she works, so she wrote three screenplays and sent them to us asking us to send them to you. Didn't you read them?"

Ron spread his fingers on his chest. "Honestly, Darce, I have never received any screenplays that Summer wrote, or believe me, I would have read them."

All eyes turned to Kirk. He sucked in a deep breath. "You didn't receive them because I didn't send them."

"Kirk!" Darce hit him on the upper arm.

"Ow!" he rubbed his arm and scowled at her. "Look, we were in the middle of 'Wildcard' and I thought it would be best if Ron weren't bothered with any silly scripts."

"What do you mean, silly scripts? Did you read them?" Darce huffed.

"No. I didn't want to. Let bygones be bygones."

"You didn't even have the kindness to read them?"

Kirk avoided his wife's eyes.

"Where are they?" she demanded.

"In the garage under the tool chest."

"She's still my best friend, Kirk. You could have read them for that fact alone!"

There was silence as Darce glared at Kirk and Kirk studied his fingernails.

"Darce, do you think I should read them? Frankly, I don't know if I could do business with her if I had to meet her husband."

Kirk groaned and turned away in his chair.

"What husband?" Darce asked with ice in her voice.

Ron grinned, "Well, she can't have more than one, can she?"

"She doesn't have any. What makes you think she has a husband?"

"Well, Kirk ... You were her bridesmaid ... He's a dairy farmer in the Alps ... Darce, didn't Summer get married?"

With elevated voice, Darce answered, "She never married. You broke her heart and she's been working at that mission over there ever since. She's happy enough, but she refuses to think about falling in love. She's dedicated her whole life to that mission and I think we should be supporting her. Kirk! How could you? Why would you tell Ron she's married?"

Baffled, Ron chimed in, "Yeah. Why would you do that?"

Kirk reared back in his chair. "To save you from yourself. I mean, you were ambivalent. On one hand it was yes! You wanted her. But on the other hand, no you didn't. You being so wishy washy was getting in the way. I thought her being married might get her out of the way altogether."

Ron mulled this over for a few moments, "You mean out of your way, don't you?"

Kirk floundered. The three watched as he wrestled internally. "Okay, okay. The truth is, I've wanted to keep you two apart from the very beginning. I told Darce it was a big mistake to have invited her to that little dinner party. And since then I've done ever kind of conniving, evil, dirty little deal to separate you and I don't even know why I did it. No, I do too know. You thought you needed a high society wife and I was hell-bent on making your life plan come to pass because it would make my life plan come to pass. And look where it got us."

A long moment passed as all eyes looked at Ron's reaction. He stood up and circled the table rubbing his eyes. Then he stopped behind Kirk's chair and clapped his hand on Kirk's shoulder. "Buddy boy, it got us right into the heart of Jesus. I wouldn't change a thing that happened. If I had succeeded anywhere along the line I wouldn't have run into Mitch and he wouldn't have led me to the new birth and we wouldn't be launching into the greatest adventure I could possibly imagine."

"But what if Summer is supposed to be the screenwriter for this great adventure?" Darce clamored.

Ron frowned in bewilderment, "Summer's not married?"

"No. And her screenplays are good."

"There's no dairy farmer? No cows with big bells clanging around their necks up in the mountains?"

"No!" Kirk expelled. "Forgive me. What I did was reprehensible. Summer never married."

Darce twisted in her chair. "Ron, I've got to admit, I'm as guilty as Kirk. I didn't think you wanted her because you never lifted a finger to find her. I could have given you her address, but I made sure you never got it."

Mitch stood and went for more coffee. "It sounds to me like you all played into the devil's hands, but retribution won't serve any good purpose. Let's look to the future. We've got a lot at stake here."

"He's right, Ron, and if I'm your administrative assistant you have to listen to me, you know. And I think you ought to read Summer's screenplays as soon as possible."

Ron shook his head slowly back and forth. "Summer's not married?"

"Would we all agree that a trip to Switzerland is in order?" Mitch offered.

"Not so fast. I doubt she'll even talk to me after what I did to her." But they could all see a new light in Ron's eyes. "One step at a time. Let me read the scripts. Then we'll go from there."

Chapter Twenty
# THE CHRISTIAN SCREENWRITER

Ron landed in Geneva so early he thought for sure it must be time for bed. He missed a night somewhere and he couldn't focus well enough to remember where he left it. Nor did he take into account the night before that when he couldn't sleep because of the two soldiers standing guard at the end of his bed: Fear and Trepidation. His body laid like a slab of cardboard on a bed of concrete while his mind slipped and slid like dishwater sloshing over every surface surrounding Summer.

Today he had to get a better grip on himself. Planning sensibly in his mind, he took a cab to the little village, Stade des Etoiles. No one, however, in their right mind could call the price of that cab sensible. He presumed he would clear his head by sleeping for awhile in his room, which he could hardly wait to get to, and then plan his next move.

He had not called or written to Summer; he just wanted to show up. One look at her eyes would tell him all he needed to know; was he welcome or should he turn on his heel and go. Summer expressed everything with her eyes. But he ought to look into them when he wasn't so tired. Yawning wide, he watched the countryside from the back of the cab. Beautiful. Absolutely stunning. That's as far as his sensibilities could speak from his sleep deprived mind.

By the time he unpacked his suitcase in the charming Pension, his two bodyguards with folded arms had popped up as if part of his baggage. Following him wherever he went, in reaction he suddenly jarred alert and couldn't think of going to sleep. He went downstairs for the petite dejeuner. Gulping very hot, very strong coffee, he pushed the food aside and asked the man at the desk for directions to La Centre de la Paix Divine. He tried to write them on a notepad but his shaking hands wouldn't allow it. Could the caffeine really be that strong he wondered?

Lying directly uphill and on the road curving left, the Center could be seen from the Pension, in fact it could be seen from every aspect of town. In its heyday the Centre had been the primary reason Stade des Etoiles existed. Ron trudged slowly uphill as he talked things out sotto voce. "If the look in her eyes has any interest at all, I'll invite her out to dinner tonight. We'll go someplace romantic. I wonder if the Swiss are ever romantic, or are they only practical?"

He brought himself to think the unthinkable. "But if her eyes are flat and her gaze bores right through me, I'll just ask permission to produce her screenplays. I want them even if she doesn't want me. She'll like the check Mitch authorized me to write. Then I'll tell her I needed a vacation and that this seemed as good a place as any to take one. I'll still invite her out to dinner. You never know. She might have a change of heart."

Kicking a rock so hard it hurt his toe, he chided himself, "What am I talking about! I can't lie! I can't pretend my heart isn't why I'm here! I've got to tell her the truth. I'll say it right out. I'll tell her I know I broke her heart, I was a cad, I was a fool, but that I never stopped loving her and I hope she will forgive me." He breathed his resolve in hard and then smiled with confidence and straightened his shoulders.

Then he slumped, his confident grin turning to a frown. "Well, that isn't the truth either! I'm hoping she'll marry me!"

Fuming at not having the right approach, he thought, "Maybe I should just start off telling her I'm born again. That should answer all the questions by itself. She'll know I'm repentant. She'll know I want to make things right."

Feeling worse with that approach than any of the others, he thought, "That doesn't solve the problem at all! Any bozo can say he's born again if he knows the girl is born again and he wants to take some advantage of her! Wise up, Ron! You're almost there! Hurry up! Come up with something!"

Rounding a forested corner, he stopped breathless, not suffering from the climb but impacted by the beauty of the Center of Divine Peace. The towering wooden structure climbed high above the flawlessly arranged gardens. A mountain streamlet babbled through the heart of the grounds. Pines created forest clusters. Lawns constructed patches of intricate design, punctuated by paths of varying surfaces for the gentlefolk to take their daily promenade. But the flowers took his breath away. Cascades, stands of brilliantly colored flowers encircled buildings, trees and shrubs.

The world surrounding this magnificent masterpiece seemed still. Yet a movement caught his eye. Someone was cutting flowers. Someone garbed in a lovely summer dress covered with an apron, someone whose lithe form he remembered so well. He stood stock still in the road, unable to move, barely able to breathe. Not one solid thought came to him of what to do or what to say.

She straightened, arranging and rearranging the flowers in her hand when she glanced at the road. Looking back at the flowers, she suddenly jerked her head to look again. Then she stared squarely at him. Her blond hair swirled as she looked behind her, probably thinking of flight, but then she turned her body and started for him with a slow, long gait. The cutting shears dropped from her hand. The flowers traipsed to the ground one by one, forming a crazy little path on the cut grass. She fixed her eyes on him as if he were a target on a sonar screen. Her trajectory seemed to take forever. Then she leapt across the ditch separating the property from the road.

Ron watched her come. Someone had mercilessly nailed his shoes to the asphalt and tied weights to his fingers so that he could not move his arms. He had envisioned a million receptions, all of them involving his arms. She had run into them. He had reached out for her. These arms that now hung stupidly by his side had played the major role, his hands caressing her hair, his arms crushing her to him, picking her up in his arms. And now they betrayed him and went AWOL.

Her delicate slow motion steps performed ballet with the caressing grass while her slender legs played hide and seek with the layers of cloth swinging in her skirt and apron. Having good common sense her arms swung by her side until they reached for him as she bound across the rivulet to the road. She came to him, pulled his head down and gave him a long kiss on the mouth. When she finished she retreated three giant steps and put her hands behind her back.

"I told myself that if I ever saw you again I would simply go up to you and kiss you because I never got to kiss you goodbye. I waved, but I never got to kiss you."

Still rooted to the road, a permanent fixture with which all future traffic would now have to grapple, Ron's mouth moved but no sound came out. Finally he cleared his throat and hoarsely replied, "I'd rather you kissed me hello."

Squinting her eyes as if to protect them from a sudden mushroom cloud, she whispered "I couldn't do that." She turned to retrace her leap across the little stream, but she spoke over her shoulder. "You're a married man."

"No. Wait. Please. No, I'm not. That's not right." At least his mouth was responding. Now to crank up the motor on the rest. "I'm divorced. Didn't Darce tell you?"

She stopped her foot from extending to the other side and withdrew the motion. "No." she answered carefully.

Taking in a deep breath which broke off the squeeze of the iron lung, Ron laughed a phony hearty laugh which rang out over the hillside. "That little minx! Summer, we've both been living in a valley of lies. Years ago Kirk told me you were married. Even before I met my ex-wife. Darce nearly tanned his hide when she found that out. It was just a few weeks ago that he told us both what he had done. I couldn't believe my best friend would do that to me. But Darce did the same thing to you by not telling you I was divorced! Wait till I tell Kirk!"

"Hold it. I'm supposed to be married and you're not married?"

He looked deeply in her eyes to see her reaction. "That's right. I'm not married." An air of puzzlement and wounding seemed to pour from her being.

"Why not?"

"My wife and my father in law kicked me out. I am nothing and I have nothing."

Gazing back with a flood of compassion she said, "Nobody can say that about themselves, Ron."

"I don't mind. Remember my life plan?"

Summer nodded numbly and the wounded air settled on her again.

"It turned out to be a fiasco." Incongruously, he smiled big. "Because of that, I found Jesus. He's everything to me and my nothingness is what He asks for. Because He's my Lord I have everything in Him and He owns it all. Does that make sense? Do you know what I mean?"

Summer nodded slowly, "Yes, I do. Do you call yourself 'born again' then?" she asked suspiciously.

"In every sense of the word."

"You really did find Him, didn't you?"

Ron nodded.

"I'm happy for you."

A moment of silence passed as the mountain breezes played around them. "You don't seem happy."

"It's too bad this couldn't have happened before, you know, before the sub went under the Golden Gate."

"I can't turn back time, Summer, but I ... "

She turned away. "My parents used to play a cassette for me, a stageplay called 'The Fantastiks', about a boy who had to be 'burned a bit and burnished by the sun' before he could find true love. You make me think of that when you talk about your fiasco."

"I was burned more than a bit. That sun fried me to a crisp. I returned to San Francisco with one thought in mind: to find you and to marry you."

She gave him a withering look. "I doubt that, Ron. If you'd wanted to find me you would have."

Ron, his body still behaving like a weathervane on a perfectly still day contemplated a dozen approaches. "I won't lie about it, Summer, or try to softsoap you. The truth is, I was a fool. I jumped off the deep end thinking I was going to make myself into something spectacular, and I found myself in a pot of boiling oil which burned me alive. But Jesus is making it all turn around for the good. I'd like to have the opportunity to tell you the whole story. Will you have dinner with me tonight?"

She looked toward the Center. "I don't know. I do wonder why you're here, though, why you came all this way. Maybe we should let the past stay buried; we're both going on with our lives so what's the point?"

Summer fingered her skirt as she gazed wistfully at the Center, then dropped her head to ponder the road. "I guess ... " She paused. "I guess I could be free for dinner." She turned toward him. "Would you like to eat in our dining room?"

"No. I'd rather we went someplace where we can really talk. That seems to be the only thing I can do right now since my hands and feet won't move. They feel like they're filled with lead."

Regarding his stationary stature she laughed. "Am I that frightening? Remember, I didn't go see you; this time you came to see me." Then she frowned and shook her head. "Why would

Kirk tell you I was married when I've never been married, at least not to anyone but you?"

With that his arms and legs came to life and he reached out to grab her and hold her close, but she stepped back looking regretfully at his gesture. "Don't." she said.

Ron retreated, "Kirk wanted to keep us apart. I think he was protecting both of us, at least I believe that was his motive. But he's finally given up. He received Jesus as Lord just a couple of weeks ago and now he's thrown all that control he thought he needed to the winds. He's hoping you'll come home with me."

"Why would I go home with you?"

"We all want you back."

She plucked a flower from the edge of the rivulet while he watched her. "You've changed, Ron."

"I hope you find that to be a good thing."

With her chin thrust forward she asked, "What is the one thing you want to say to me now? I know you came here to say something. What is it? Unless I know what that is, I want to walk back into that Center, shut the door behind me and never see you again."

For some reason the horse at Ruby Cross Ranch came into his mind. He could see him plant his feet and pull back on the rope, tightening the noose around his neck. Ron took a step back to relieve the pressure. "I was wrong. So wrong! I ruined our love. I've never loved anybody like I loved you and I've never been loved like you loved me.

"And I ruined our life together before it even got started. I was a cad. I was egotistical and self-centered. I thought my life plan was so grand, so glorious. I was like the guy who got to the top of the ladder and found out his ladder was leaning against the wrong building. I stupidly let you slip through my fingers as if you were something I could toy with. No, worse than that, I left you.

"God brought you to me; I am convinced of that. You are the woman He intended for me to spend my life with. Together we make an awesome force. I have never stopped loving you. I simply denied myself the pleasure of you. I'm desperate for you to forgive me. I'll just get down here on my knees ... "

Summer took a step toward him, looking over her shoulder at the Center. "Don't do that. Do you know how many eyes are watching us right now?"

"Then will you forgive me?"

Summer shrugged her shoulders. "I already have."

"Good. I'd hate to think of that lovely head of yours carrying around any bitterness or regrets."

She smiled and turned away a few steps. "No. I don't have either one of those."

He followed after her, "I've grown up."

She gazed at the fine building. "It sounds like you have, but I can't leave my post here. They depend on me."

Ron pulled a brown leather envelope from his breast pocket. "I've come with a very comforting offer to your boss, Tommy Tyson. There's a check in here in US dollars for the Center of Divine Peace to buy up your remaining contract."

"My contract?" She laughed as she turned to look. "That's a euphemistic way of speaking about my job. How much is the check?"

"$200,000."

"$200,000! They pay me $8,000 a year, plus room and board!"

"This ought to make them very happy then."

"Why do you and Kirk want me back in the States?"

"First, we want you back because we both love you." He grinned, "Maybe I love you a little more than he does, but we need you back so you can write screenplays."

"Screenplays?"

"Yes. It turns out you are a very fine writer, but I can tell you all about that at dinner."

"I can write screenplays from here."

Ron's heart sank. "But I can't live here, Summer, I need to be in the States."

"Then go back to the States."

"I can't go back if you're here. I'm not going to spend one more moment of my life without you. I'm not leaving you ever again. I want to love, honor and cherish you till death do us part and then through eternity to be by your side. I want you to be my wife. I long for you to be my wife. I will be miserable until you say you will be mine. Will you marry me, Summer?"

A long moment passed. "That's a lot to absorb."

"Then maybe we should start with hello. Will you give me that kiss hello I asked for and then we can go from there?"

She smiled as she leaned toward him. "Hello." She closed her eyes as his mouth descended on hers and this time his arms worked as well as his lips.